Untie the Winds

Untie the Winds

JEAN CLARK

Macmillan Publishing Co., Inc.

NEW YORK

Macmillan Publishing Co., Inc.
866 Third Avenue, New York, N.Y. 10022
Collier Macmillan Canada, Ltd.

Library of Congress Cataloging in Publication Data
Clark, Jean.
Untie the winds.
I. Eaton, Ann—Fiction. I. Title.
PZ4.C5929Un [PS3553.L2855] 813'.5'4 75-31595
ISBN 0-02-525780-3

First Printing 1976

Printed in the United States of America

To Jason
and *to*
Dorothy Olding

EXPLANATORY NOTE

Untie the Winds is the story of some of the people in the New Haven Colony from its beginnings in 1638 to its reluctant merger with the Connecticut Colony in 1664. The main characters are based on actual people in the colony and the main events are derived from church and town records, but the loves and hates and conflicting human relationships that lay behind what went on in public are the province of the novelist's imagination.

Two of the characters, Lurinda Collings and Timothy Evans, did not exist *per se*. They are composites based on recorded incidents related to people of their particular class.

It should also be noted that the last mention of Ann Eaton in the New Haven town records occurred in 1657, when the court granted her an escort to Boston. Although writers of most accounts assume she went directly to England from Boston at that time, I have chosen to keep both her and her son David and his family in America until 1662.

All dates have been adjusted to conform to the modern calendar.

. . . untie the winds and let
them fight against the churches. . . .
—*Macbeth* IV.1.52

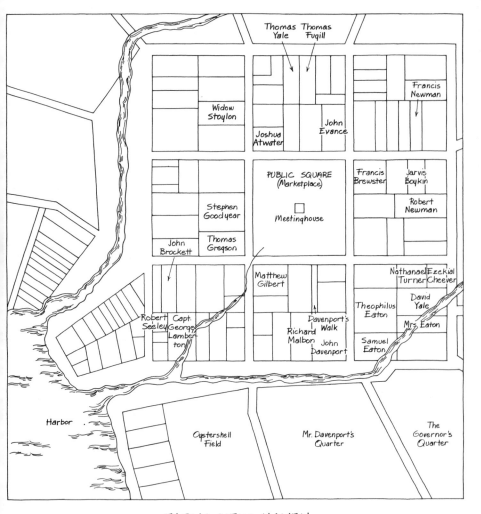

EARLY NEW HAVEN
showing land assigned to or occupied by people in this book

ANN EATON / APRIL 1638

Ann Eaton went up onto the forecastle to be as far forward as possible as the small, high-pooped ship left the open waters of Long Island Sound to tack into harbor. The journey down the coast from Massachusetts, though less than three hundred miles, had been rough and had taken nearly two weeks. The winds had been so strong and the seas so high that they had been forced to hull for two and three days at a time. Few of the other women had ventured from their cabins, but she had been on deck whenever weather permitted, eager for the first glimpse of the land that would be her new home.

Yesterday, leaning against the rail with the salt spray sharp in her face, she had seen the Thames River that led up to the settlement at New London. Early this morning she had been on deck to see the rip tide at the mouth of the Connecticut River, and now, thirty or so miles to the west, with April's late afternoon sunlight slanting across the water ahead of them, she saw for the first time the land of the Quinnipiacs.

The coast to the left of the harbor was lined with evergreens. Growing to the water's edge on the right were massive oaks, their limbs bare now at the end of a bitter New England winter. But Ann's eyes were fixed on the land beyond: a broad plain covered with open forest. To the west and east of the plain, hills of reddish rock rose steeply. It was on that plain, guarded by the red rocks, that they would settle. Theophilus had described it to her after his trip down here last summer. Even now, homes were being prepared for them by Joshua Atwater and the six men in the company who had remained for the winter. Her heart lifted. A new home in a new land. A new way of life.

Here, after more than a year of living without privacy, either in a crowded ship's cabin or in the homes of hospitable Bay Colony settlers, she and Theophilus would once again be able to live as husband and wife. The thought of being alone with him once more—perhaps even tonight—made her pulse quicken.

The gulls which had been following the ship wheeled in large circles, crying. She wanted to lift her arms and join in their exuberance, but of course it would not have been seemly, especially for a woman whose children—some of them, anyway—were nearly grown.

Quickly she looked around. The older ones—the three whom she had brought to the marriage eight years ago and the two Theophilus had brought—could take care of themselves. But Hannah was only five and young Theophilus only seven. She saw them finally, playing with some corks in the shelter of the poop deck. Let it be a Christian game, she prayed, for they do seem to be enjoying it.

Inside the harbor the waves had become whitecaps and the ship rolled less. The men shouted to each other as they slackened the sails, slowing the speed of the ship. Soon the more delicate women would begin appearing.

"It's a fine harbor," someone beside her said. "Your husband has chosen well."

Recognizing the special resonance and preciseness of Ezekial Cheever's voice, she turned and gave him a warm smile. She had not known him in London, but on board ship and during their year in the Massachusetts Bay Colony she had become well acquainted with this tall, broad-shouldered young man with the darkly intense eyes, the man who would be the plantation's schoolmaster.

"Theophilus always does choose well," she said. "He plans carefully, he considers every possibility, and then he makes an irreversible decision."

His eyebrows lifted. "He's a fine leader. As is our pastor, Mr. Davenport. Leaders who vacillated wouldn't inspire confidence."

"Yes, of course. They are both good men." Then, to make it clear she had not been criticizing her husband, she repeated the words. "They are both good men. Very good." She lifted her head, breathing in the freshness of the westerly wind that blew out from the new land. "Are you excited, Ezekial? You're young. You have a whole lifetime ahead of you in this new land."

He looked amused. "One would think you were old and gray. But, yes, I am excited."

Squinting a little, she said, "I wonder where the houses are."

"Farther back, perhaps."

"No, they were supposed to have been built on the plain, within sight of the harbor." Both knew that it had been more than three months since a runner had come up through Hartford and over to Boston with news. From Ezekial's frown she was sure he was remembering, as she was, Sir Walter Raleigh's little settlement, far to the south at Roanoke, that had so mysteriously disappeared forty-eight years before.

"Oh, wait," she said. "Look. A canoe is coming out of the creek." She held her breath a moment. Indians? But if they were Quinnipiacs, it was no problem. Theophilus had told her the Quinnipiacs were friendly, and willing to sell land in return for protection against the Mohawks.

As if he knew what she had been thinking, Ezekial said, "No, not Indians. Our own men."

Her breath came out slowly, but the excitement remained as the ship drew closer to the canoe and the land beyond. She wanted to share this moment with her husband. Turning, she searched among the people who were now crowding the deck. Theophilus, standing with his back as straight as the ship's mast, was absorbed in conversation with the godly Mr. Davenport. Talk, talk, talk. Didn't they ever run out of things to say to each other?

Her daughter Ann emerged hesitantly from the forecastle cabin helped by her brothers, Thomas and David Yale. As she looked at her, Ann felt her chest constrict with a puzzled sadness. The girl's moods swung from careless joy to deep withdrawal. At times Ann felt she saw her own impulsive nature reflected in her daughter's face; at other times she wondered how she and her first husband Thomas Yale could have produced such a changeling.

Young Ann's moods had intensified since her marriage to Edward Hopkins, a man twenty years her senior, now awaiting her at the newly established Connecticut Colony in Hartford. I was married as young as she, Ann thought. Was I like that? Lighthearted, yes. A young woman who had brightened Thomas Yale's manor in Denbighshire as no Yale wife had done before. But never had she

3

shut herself up in her room to write long, strange poems, never had she lain on her bed for days, staring at the ceiling, refusing to talk to anyone.

The young girl stepped reluctantly into the sunlight. Glancing up at her mother, she smiled vaguely. Thomas and David led her close to where Theophilus and Mr. Davenport were talking. She stood still, looking back at the wake of the ship.

Ann came down from the forecastle and waited a moment near the little group. When she saw Theophilus turn, she spoke his name softly. Like an echo, it was immediately repeated in a thinner, higher voice as old Mrs. Eaton, her head partially covered by a gray wool hood, emerged from another cabin. She was followed by Mary, Ann's thirteen-year-old stepdaughter.

Theophilus helped his old mother to a bench. With one hand lovingly on her shoulder and the other pointing to the plain beyond, he said, "There it is, Mother. There is the land where our home will be, God willing, for the rest of our lives. Mary"—he gestured toward his daughter—"come look."

"A fine place. Well chosen," the old woman said. "We'll build a fine home there. How good it will be to be in my own home again, surrounded by my own family." Her sharp glance found Ann. "Hello, my daughter. You seem to be excited. Your color is very high." She made the high color sound like some kind of shameful papal trapping.

"It's the wind that gives me color," Ann said easily. "But I suppose I am excited. Surely everyone is, now that we are so soon to set foot on the land that will be our home."

Her mother-in-law smiled complacently. "You'll have to contain your excitement until another dawn, I'm afraid. It is not good to start a new enterprise on a Friday. Isn't that true, son?"

Mary nodded her approval, her nose sharpening at the scent of disagreement.

Theophilus hesitated. Although his expression did not change, Ann was sure he wanted to leave the ship as badly as she did. He exchanged glances with Mr. Davenport and with his brother Samuel, who was also a churchman. Both nodded.

"You are right, Mother," he said. Not looking at his wife, he lifted his hands for silence. It was not easy to achieve, for some of the men were dropping the anchor and others were calling out to the three men in the canoe as they approached the ship.

When the crowd had quieted, he said, "We will not disembark

4

until tomorrow." A murmur rose. It diminished as both he and Mr. Davenport looked around frowning.

"For most of us," he continued, "the establishment of this plantation is the most important undertaking of all our lives. Friday, as you all know, is not an auspicious day for beginning a new enterprise. We have all waited a long time with great patience. I am sure God will reward us if we wait with patience for one more day." He paused. No dissenting voice was heard. His face lost its sternness. "In a few moments, our pastor will lead us in worship."

Mr. Davenport waited to pray until the men from the canoe were helped on board. They told of a winter of hardship and illness, of the death of one among them. They had built only one dwelling, but they had, they said, been able to dig habitable cellars out of the sand banks along the creek.

When their story was finished, Mr. Davenport stepped forward. His round face quivering with holiness and thanksgiving, he prayed at length, thanking God for delivering them to this fair haven. He followed the prayer with a sermon.

Ezekial had come down behind Ann from the forecastle. During the sermon he stood by her side. The deck was so crowded that he was forced to stand very close to her in an intimacy that would have been unthinkable on any other occasion.

Once, when he heard her sigh, he whispered, "Patience. It's only twenty-four hours—twenty-four hours out of a whole lifetime."

She nodded. Long practice made it possible for her, as she listened to Mr. Davenport's sermon, to compose her face so that it was properly reverent. She had few doubts about her adopted Puritan faith, but this seemed to her more a time for action than a time for praying and waiting. She almost wished she could be like her daughter, letting time slide by, hardly aware of its passing.

No one else seemed to feel as she did. Everyone in this company was a rebel. Otherwise they'd all still be in England, docilely reading the Book of Common Prayer. Yet now they stood like cattle, waiting with dumb patience for the shepherd to decide when to take them to the common.

What was wrong with her? Did she lack grace? She clasped her hands, her fingers so tightly twined that they began to ache. Looking up to heaven, she saw the gulls still wheeling and diving. The voice of the Reverend Mr. Davenport droned on, but now she heard nothing but the gulls screaming their independence.

JOHN DAVENPORT
APRIL 1638

The April air sparkled with new-world freshness. Beneath the Reverend John Davenport's muddied boots, the first green shoots of spring formed a resilient carpet. Leaf buds on the massive sheltering oak formed a golden hazelike halo over him and his company of more than two hundred souls.

With a feeling of satisfaction he surveyed the people now assembling for their first Sunday service. It was a fine group, with more well-to-do, well-educated, and devout people than in any other plantation in this new land. Despite the wretched cellars that were all they'd found when they disembarked the day before, all had managed to set up temporary abodes and to find suitable Sabbath dress.

With a soft, satisfied sigh, Davenport clasped his hands over his rounded waist. He knew now how Moses had felt when he had led his people to the promised land, for here the Elect would be free to worship God in the one true way. Here he could give guidance without fear of royal disapproval, without fear that the corruption of theater, dance, song, and pagan festivals would undermine his influence. Had ever a man been so smiled on by God? His throat was so full of emotion he was not sure he would be able to speak.

It was almost time to begin. All were here; all were waiting. Even the two Quinnipiacs sitting on the ground looked at him attentively.

He was clearing his throat, preparing to sanctify the moment with the Word of God, when anger suddenly struck him. Where was *she?* Had she decided to stay away from this first formal call to worship? Did she dare to flout his authority?

Quickly he went over to Theophilus Eaton, who was standing not far from the two savages.

"Is your wife unwell?"

"Ann?" Theophilus seemed surprised. "No, she is quite well."

"She is not here."

"Oh? Well, she'll be along shortly. The light is not very good in our cellar. She was looking for something when I left—a special petticoat or a flower or something."

The indulgence in his voice would have angered Davenport even more had he not so pitied his friend. Eaton was a man who knew Roman law and the classics, who had learned the languages of the Low Countries, who had been Deputy Governor of the East Land Company, who had amassed a fortune trading in the Balkans, and who had been the King's agent in Denmark. Yet despite his education and intelligence, he was apparently unable to see what was so obvious to others.

Nor had Davenport ever found the right moment or the right words to point out Ann's faults and inadequacies. It was the one area in which their confidences never went deep enough for real understanding, even though they had been close friends since they had attended the Free Grammar School in Coventry together. On all other issues they had always confided in each other. When Theophilus had lost his first wife, he had come to his friend for comfort and advice. But when he had thought of marrying the beautiful young widow Ann Yale, he had not sought advice. He had merely announced his intention.

"You are sure?" Davenport had asked him.

"Very sure."

"Is she a Puritan?"

"She has seen the light in a quick and miraculous conversion."

Davenport had little faith in quick and miraculous conversions. They were too often visited upon people of unsteady temperaments, but his friend's face had been so full of joy that he had been hesitant to speak his thoughts. Nor did he want to mention that it was rumored that her first husband, Thomas Yale, had sometimes attended the theater in London, even those dramas by the notorious and godless Will Shakespeare. Who could be sure his wife, well masked, had not been with him?

7

Instead he had said, "I know very little of her first husband. But nothing I've heard indicates he sympathized with us. As for her father, I understand he was a great admirer of Queen Elizabeth, despite all the popery she let creep back into the church."

Eaton had not seemed disturbed and Davenport had said no more, but as he had grown to know Ann Eaton better, his feelings had become increasingly uneasy.

Fleetingly his thoughts went back to their journey across the ocean on the *Hector*. Many times when most of the women were confined below with seasickness, she had appeared on the narrow, crowded deck, stepping briskly back and forth, the color high in her cheeks, her dark hair streaming out behind her, her ankles occasionally revealed as the wind whipped her colorful petticoats around her legs.

It was hardly proper for a woman to be so vigorous. Women were ordained by God to have children, to serve their husbands with meekness. The death of so many in childbed showed that this was the function for which they had been given life. When they were young, God gave them a bloom so that men would seek them out for the purpose of bringing forth children in His image. It was part of God's plan that the bloom should fade with the performance of wifely duties. And surely it was not in keeping with God's plan for a woman who had had children by two husbands to still retain her youthful bloom and vigor.

One warm day on board ship while they were watching a small group of women sewing and talking in a sheltered spot on the deck, he had said to Theophilus, "Listen—that ring of laughter. Your wife laughs more than any of the others."

"Yes, a happy woman." Theophilus had spoken with a grave pride, as if her happiness reflected favorably on the role he played as her husband.

Another time Davenport had remarked on her dress. "The colors—the red especially—are so very intense," he said. "More so than those worn by any of the other women."

"That is true," replied Theophilus. "Only in the East Indies can they produce colors with such vibrancy."

Unless love had blinded him, how could such an intelligent, cultured, and experienced man time and time again look directly at his wife and be so unaware of the lack of restraint in her dress and manner?

Yet Davenport's love for his friend was so great that he could bear him no malice. He realized that he would not even be standing here at this moment if it were not for Eaton: his wealth and influence, his marvelous ability to plan and organize. For it was Eaton who, after gaining experience in outfitting ships for some of the earlier New England colonies, had done the major planning for this emigration and had completely outfitted the two ships that had brought them from England to Massachusetts a year ago.

It was on account of Eaton that the people in the Massachusetts Bay Colony had been anxious to have the group remain there. It was better, though, that they had left. Dissension had risen in the church in Massachusetts. Had they stayed, they might have become involved. Here all were of the same mind.

Or almost all. Standing on the other side of the group, a little apart as always, was Samuel Eaton, brother of Theophilus. At first glance he looked enough like Theophilus to be his twin: tall, spare, with the same dignified bearing and narrow, intelligent face. But a more careful look revealed that his lips were thinner, his nose sharper, his eyes paler. He was a man of the cloth and an accused and convicted Nonconformist, yet despite all they had in common, Davenport could never summon a feeling of warmth for him. And he wondered, as he did every time he looked at the unrevealing face, what Samuel Eaton's expectations were. Did he hope to become the spiritual leader of the plantation? And if he did make a move in that direction, would his brother support it? How distressing it was that the only two people in the plantation who were likely to create difficulties were so close to the man whom Davenport loved and trusted most.

"Here comes my wife now," Theophilus said.

Automatically, the people drew back and made a path for her. Head held high, her dark hair glossy beneath a scarlet-lined hood, Ann Eaton swept down to the front and took her place between her mother-in-law and her stepdaughter.

Davenport had a quick impression of a lacy furbelow, a huge scarlet rose at the waist, a scarlet petticoat trimmed with black lace peeping out from beneath her loose cloak. He had grown used to seeing his well-to-do parishioners stream into St. Stephen's on Coleman Street in London so richly attired—but here? In a wilderness? Had she no sense of propriety?

Behind her was his own wife Elizabeth. Ann turned to her and made a remark followed by a rich laugh. Many times he had heard her laugh like that at dinners at the Theophilus Eaton home in

London. Even on such secular occasions the laughter had, as it did now, rung out in an unseemly way.

Next to Ann Eaton her mother-in-law disdainfully drew her somber cloak closer to her fragile body, thus increasing the distance between her and the offender. His own wife had responded with a polite but properly cool smile. Elizabeth was a good woman. Perhaps with her help and that of old Mrs. Eaton he would be able to bring Ann Eaton closer to the God she so badly needed, to imbue her with a sense of what it meant to be a Puritan. The task would be easier now. They were all housed in a small community where he could keep her under close surveillance. She was one of the burdens God had placed upon him, perhaps as a test of his spiritual strength, a burden he must assume with cheerfulness, tact, and patience.

With a nod to his friend, Davenport moved back to his position under the oak tree. Closing his eyes, he sent a silent prayer upward, asking for help in conducting the first Sunday worship in this greening wilderness they would tame and make their own.

When he opened his eyes, refreshed and strengthened, he found himself again looking at Ann Eaton. He saw her glance upward at the golden haze of leaf buds, then at the savages, then down at her ringed fingers, and then off in the distance toward the red rocks. He could almost see the frivolous thoughts bouncing off the surface of her mind. Clearly she was not spiritually prepared for the service.

Seeing him frown benevolently at her, she folded her hands, lowered her eyes modestly, and inclined her head forward in a meditative position. Ah, that was better. Much better. The muscles in his stomach loosened beneath his clasped hands.

The crowd was silent, waiting. The measured beating of his heart increased. The presence of God surrounded him. Lifting his hands, he said, "My text for today is: 'Then was Jesus led aside of the spirit into the wilderness, to be tempted of the Devil.' Matthew 4:1."

He began to preach. He said that they had at last reached the wilderness and that the Devil was everywhere. He said that because they had reached their goal, they must not become complacent and self-satisfied. The Devil would try to create dissension; he would encourage greed and lust; he would do all he could to set obstacles in their way.

His voice deepened, became more resonant. "The Devil knows why we came here. He knows we came to set up a plantation whose design is religion. The Devil does not want a state that worships God with one mind. It frightens him. It undermines his power. He will do anything to weaken us and make us lose our courage. We must always be on guard.

"Already he has taken the life of one of the men who spent the winter here. By means of cold, illness, and hunger he made it difficult for the others to prepare proper homes for us. Some of you are living in cellars, some in tents or tepees. The Devil hopes you'll be uncomfortable. He hopes you'll complain, fall ill, grow tired of this experiment.

"Our journey from Boston should have taken only a few days, but the Devil sent storms to delay us and seasickness to plague us. He will continue in every possible way to hinder us. We must always be alert."

On and on he spoke, his voice rising as he outlined the Devil's fearful plans, lowering as he spoke reverently of the God who would help them overcome.

Almost everyone listened attentively. A few, needing and wanting his warnings and reassurances, were taking notes. Mrs. Eaton's gaze never left his face, but it was like the stare of someone lost in thought. Once he saw a faint smile lift the corners of her mouth, and he was sure her mind was again taken up with frivolity.

Yet at the end she was the first to come forward and hold out her hand. For a moment they were strangely joined as the vitality and warmth of her handclasp communicated itself to him, becoming briefly so much a part of him that his own blood pulsed warmly at his temples.

"That was an excellent sermon, Mr. Davenport."

"Thank you." He looked seriously at her, acutely aware that she was two inches taller than he. "When I heard your laughter earlier, I wondered whether you were spiritually prepared for it."

Her dark eyes glinted. Was it with mockery? "I was prepared, sir. My heart was full of joy and thanksgiving. For the kingdom of God is not meat nor drink but righteousness, and peace, and joy in the Holy Ghost."

He recognized her quotation from the fourteenth chapter of Romans but noted the special emphasis she had given to the word *joy*. "Even during the service I saw you smile. At a solemn moment, too. Surely you must remember what was said in Ecclesiastes: 'To all things there is an appointed time . . . a time to weep, and a time to laugh.' "

"You are right. To everything there is an appointed time." She tipped her head to one side. "I'm trying to remember when it was that I smiled. Oh, yes. Now I remember. It was when you spoke of forbearance and the way our faith would help us. 'Thy word was unto me the joy and rejoicing of mine heart. . . .' "

"You know your Bible well."

"Should I not? I learned to read from it. I have heard discussions about every verse in it. That's what comes of being the daughter of a bishop."

Davenport thought of George Lloyd, the Bishop of Chester, without pleasure. No doubt Mrs. Eaton had learned much from him. And along with her facile biblical interpretations she probably harbored other dangerous knowledge. His nerves tightened. How much better it would be if women were never taught anything at all. Born meddlers, they always used their limited knowledge to cause trouble in the affairs of men.

"One should rejoice, of course," he said judiciously. "But you'll notice that Jeremiah spoke only of rejoicing in his *heart*. Too much visible evidence of joy betokens irreverence."

"You are probably right," she said. "In the future I shall try to govern my facial expressions with more care."

She turned quickly and walked away from him toward the cellars in the banks along the creek, lifting her skirts a little to keep them out of the mud. He saw a flash of pink-stockinged ankle and looked quickly around to see whether any of the younger men were watching. For was it not Ecclesiasticus in the Apocrypha who had said, "Turn away thine eyes from a beautiful woman, and look not upon other's beauty; for many have perished by the beauty of women, for through it love is kindled as a fire."

He was relieved to see that no one was watching, for young men of full vigor were likely to be doubly tempted by such sights, twice as easily corrupted as those who were more settled. Yet still he stared, his mind reviewing her behavior, until she was well out of sight. Had there not been mockery in her last words? Had there not been a challenge in her tardiness and failure to apologize for it? Did she think he was still the hunted, powerless man he had been in England?

3

THEOPHILUS EATON
APRIL 1638

As the predawn light filtered into their cellar, Theophilus awakened. Full of energy, he slipped quietly into his breeches, boots, and waistcoat, and went to the doorway. There he knelt and prayed, the thanksgiving in his heart taking precedence for a few moments over the ideas that filled his mind. As he stood up, he decided he would immediately lay a town plan before the company. People must not be allowed to build helter-skelter, to make the town a hodgepodge of crooked streets with no provision for the future.

Outside the air was fresh but damp. A mist hanging over the plain obscured the harbor. Quickly he walked to the flowing spring nearby to refresh himself.

On board ship and again on Saturday he had talked to John Brockett, an experienced surveyor. Brockett was to meet him here an hour after sunup to begin work on his plan.

Looking back, he saw Ann emerge from their cellar. Smiling, combing her hair with her fingers, she came to him.

"Are we alone, Theophilus? If so, it is one of the few times in more than a year that we have been really alone." Standing on tiptoe, she put her arms around his neck and kissed him. Her lips had a morning softness.

"Oh, my dear," he said. "Out here? Where anyone can see us?" He was as much upset by her public gesture as he was by his reaction to it. Even though he was in his late forties, his healthy, disciplined body never failed to quicken at his wife's closeness. During their unsettled year in the Bay Colony, their opportunities for being alone had been rare. He had felt the deprivation in ways she would never understand, for good women did not, of course, experience the same feelings as men.

"Who can see?" she asked. "There are no windows."

"I would not want to be surprised by anyone." Taking her two hands, he stood a moment looking at her, feeling both pride and pleasure in this wife of his choosing. "There is much work to be done, my dear. Right now we cannot think of ourselves as man and wife, but rather as members of a group. We have a town to plan, houses to build—"

"I know where I'd like our house." She pointed to a rise to the north. "From the front I could see the harbor and from the side windows the red hills, and from the back—" Seeing him shake his head, she broke off. "What is it?"

"I'm afraid not. John Brockett and I have a tentative plan for laying out the town in nine squares. The central square will be the marketplace, the common. I think the spot you mentioned would fall within that area."

Her face grew quiet. "When did you make these plans?"

"On board ship. And on Saturday he and I paced out an area. We're planning to lay out a half-mile-long line on the north side of the west creek. Then we'll inscribe a square on it."

"Inscribe a square? I don't quite understand."

"Of course you don't. That's why I felt it foolish to take you into my confidence. You shouldn't even try to understand—any more than I try to understand how you make bread."

"If you'd take a moment or two to explain it to me, I'm sure I'd understand."

"Perhaps so. But what would be gained?" He smiled patiently. She had never been a truly docile wife. Back in London she had complained because he'd had to travel so much, and at times she had flared up angrily at his mother, but beneath the occasional irritations had been an acceptance of his authority as a husband.

Ever since they had begun making plans to come to America, however, he had noticed a change in her. It was as if she had translated the idea of independence of worship and defiance of royal authority into independence and defiance in her private life.

He understood something of what she felt. He, too, had a sense of entering on a new life. It was like being given a second chance, and it made him feel young again. Yet he must make her understand that her basic role would not change in this new land.

Firmly, and with a note of dismissal in his voice, he said, "I think I hear voices coming from our cellar. I am sure you are needed. I'll be in shortly."

Alone, he took a deep breath and exhaled slowly. His mind was divided into compartments: business, religion, plantation, family, each with problems requiring different kinds of wisdom. Too many women lived in his family establishment, each making different demands on him, but, with God's help, he was sure they could live together in amity in this new world.

While he had been talking with his wife, the mist had lifted. The horizon beyond the harbor turned the color of rich cream. As he watched, the color brightened and overspread the sky and the water below until the whole harbor was a great bowl of liquid gold. He felt a sudden joy. It was as if God were allowing him a secret glimpse of riches and glory and giving him evidence of His favor.

Truly, finding this place had been providential. The previous summer, shortly after the end of the Pequot War, he had spoken with Captain Stoughton and Captain Underhill who had pursued the Indians far down the coast. They had stayed with their troops on this very plain and had described the land and harbor in glowing terms.

Theophilus looked around now, his mind busy. He did not see only swamp and forest and a broad plain where generations of Indians had opened their oysters and left the shells behind. He saw a neatly laid out city with commercial establishments and well-built houses. Where some might have seen only the huge, sheltered, empty harbor, he saw busy wharves and seagoing vessels in abundance. And where some might have seen nothing more than the beginnings of a tiny, struggling farming community, he saw a thriving city that someday would be the heart of an even larger colony extending farther than his mind could measure. But it would be, he thought reverently, a colony pious in its prosperity, a colony aware that such prosperity was granted only to those whom God had found worthy.

Forcing himself away from the view, he walked back toward their dugout. Although the sun had risen, little light penetrated the cellar. Theophilus lighted a candle, opened his Geneva Bible, and leafed through it, looking for the place where he had last stopped. It had been a long time since they had worshiped as a family unit.

Coming back in after shaking a blanket outside, Ann hesitated near the entrance. "How it smells in here. Surely, Theophilus, you're not going to have worship right now?"

"Why not?"

"Because it smells. Because we're too crowded. Because we have too much to do."

Old Mrs. Eaton cleared her throat.

Theophilus said, "Should we only worship when we are comfortably situated and have nothing else to do? If that were the case, few prayers would ever rise to His throne."

Ann looked chagrined. "I just thought that this first weekday with so much to do—"

"Exactly. How many of you think it might be better to forget family worship until we are better situated?"

David Yale, Ann's oldest son by her first marriage, said, "Truly sir, there *is* a great deal to do. Before next winter everyone must have better shelter than this."

"And if we forego family worship, who will be happier, God or the Devil?"

"The Devil," Mary said promptly.

"Yes," said Theophilus, proud of his thirteen-year-old daughter's quickness. "And these are the temptations of the wilderness. 'Forget worship, the Devil whispers, so you will have more time to build Zion.' For the Devil knows that if we forget worship, we will never build Zion."

"But we would still have public worship," Ann said.

Theophilus smiled. "Do you see how the Devil works? His suggestions are always full of logic. Might not his next suggestion be that we forego public worship until we have a meeting house?"

Mary, all eagerness and zeal, said, "And next he might suggest we build fine houses before we build a meetinghouse."

Old Mrs. Eaton cleared her throat again. "Why not proceed with the Scripture, son. Scorn what the Devil suggests as he speaks through your wife."

The line of Ann's jaw grew rigid. Seeing it, Theophilus said gently, "The Devil speaks through all of us. Even I, this morning, found myself questioning the need for family worship at this time. Then I realized that my very questioning indicated how great the need was. These, as our pastor said yesterday, are the temptations of the wilderness. We must ever be alert to them."

He waited a moment to see whether his brother Samuel wished to add anything to the discussion. When Samuel did no more than nod, Theophilus turned the pages of his Bible to the twenty-seventh chapter of Isaiah, finishing with the verse, "In that day also shall the great trumpet be blown, and they shall come which perished in the land of Assyria: and they that were chased into the land of Egypt, and they shall worship the Lord in the holy mount at Jerusalem."

He looked up. "And why did I choose this chapter ending with this particular verse?" he asked. Without waiting for an answer, he drew parallels between the beleaguered children of Israel and the beleaguered Puritans of England, and the need to worship after being delivered to a new land.

Finally, he motioned for everyone to stand. "Let us now sing Psalm Ninety-two," he said.

Their voices rose, filling the dank cellar with gladness. "It is a good thing to praise the Lord and to sing unto Thy name, O Most High, to declare Thy loving kindness in the morning and Thy truth in the night. . . ."

When it was quiet again, Theophilus bowed his head. "Dear Lord," he prayed, "we thank Thee for this bright new morning in this bright new land. We ask Thee to make Thy presence felt, to guide and help us in all our decisions and in all our relationships with others throughout this day. For Jesus' sake. Amen."

Afterward he went outside, strengthened by the conviction that the Lord would work through him on that day and would shed His blessed light on his family. This time his brother Samuel accompanied him.

John Brockett was waiting near the spring. As they hurried toward him, Theophilus heard Ann calling out to him. He stopped. Catching up with him, she said, "When will we be building our home, Theophilus?"

"Soon."

"Yes, but how soon? That cellar is very unhealthy. Already your mother has catarrh. She clears her throat constantly."

"I told you—first we must lay out the town and the streets. I want this town to be well planned with plenty of room for growth."

"I understand that. But once the town is laid out, can we not begin immediately on our own house? I know just what I want. I've even made sketches." She gave him a wistfully appealing look. "Would you like to see them?"

He was glad no one but his brother was present to see her trying to use her feminine wiles to gain her way. Or to note how difficult it was for him to refuse her. Shaking his head, he said, "No, I do not need to see them. Our house will be built when the time is right. Plans I brought with me from England will be used." Noticing that she was about to interrupt, he added, "It would be best, Ann, if you went about your woman's work and left me in peace at this time." He hated speaking so abruptly to her, but she seemed bent on hindering his efforts this morning. Gently he added, "When the house is built, you will be free to place the furniture and hangings and carpets where you wish."

"Or where your mother wishes." She was angry now.

Samuel discreetly moved away, pretending to examine a new plant.

"Remember," Theophilus said, "that with our marriage she became your mother also. And one other thing, Ann. If you have any doubts about when, whether, or how God should be worshiped, it might be better if you voiced them for my ears alone. Or discussed them with Mr. Davenport. What you say has a strong influence on the young people."

"I talked too much this morning?"

"It would have been better if you had said less." He put his hand under her chin, lifting her face so that she had to look directly into his eyes. Couldn't she see that his concern for her behavior was a part of his love for her?

Perhaps she sensed it, for she said almost humbly, "I only say, in all honesty, exactly what I think."

"Your honesty is commendable. But you have surely lived long enough to know that it is not necessary to say everything you think. Not on all occasions."

"Especially if you're a woman." She turned. "I'll leave you in peace now. To do your *man's* work."

As she walked away with rapid, angry steps, he felt regretful. It was unpleasant to have to be stern with her; he knew he had hurt her. Had he loved her less, it would have been easier to deal with her feminine vagaries. As it was, he constantly had to fight his desire to give in to her every whim. He must, especially here in this new world where they were making a new beginning, treat her with the special firmness that her mercurial temperament seemed to require.

EZEKIAL CHEEVER
JUNE 1639

Ezekial planned to dismiss the boys early so he could go to the meeting in Newman's barn. Apparently they had guessed it, for they were whispering and shuffling their boots on the rough board floor. Ezekial stroked his beard and, as they noticed this sign of his displeasure, the boys gradually became quiet.

At the request of the town, and for the sum of twenty pounds a year, he had begun the school within two months after the landing. In the year it had been in session he had acquired a reputation for sternness as well as for the thoroughness of his teaching in English, Latin, and writing.

"Eaton?"

"Yes, Mr. Cheever?"

"Eaton, what is an adjective of three terminations?"

Immediately Samuel's face—so unlike that of the austere uncle for whom he had been named—began to shine. "It means that it has—uh—three terminations."

An explosive laugh came from the end of the table where Lamberton and Goodyear sat. Ezekial frowned and the laughter broke off sharply.

"And what are those three terminations, Eaton?"

The boy perspired some more, wriggled, and then blurted out, "The letters *us, a,* and *um.*"

"Excellent," Ezekial said. "You may all rise now. School is dismissed."

So far, his one-room house served as both schoolhouse and home. That he lived alone was a tribute to his respectability, for it was felt that a bachelor should live with a family where his morals could be guarded by a responsible married man. Perhaps, he reflected, it was because he had been one of the dozen men who had formed the nucleus of the company in London.

He liked teaching. When he was not teaching, he enjoyed working on a textbook which he planned to call *The Accidence.* It presented the Latin language in progressive steps, exactly as he taught it in the classroom. When people asked him if he minded living alone, he replied that he didn't have time to be lonely.

The June day was so warm that he had not put on a waistcoat and he could smell the spicy gillyflowers blossoming in sheltered places near the house. The accomplishments in the town during the first year had been tremendous, he reflected. The first summer the air had been filled with the fragrance of freshly cut wood. Everyone had been busy chopping, sawing, digging cellars, framing houses, shingling roofs, building roads, fencing land, and planting, or with caring for the cattle that had been driven down from Massachusetts. The town's original half-mile square, laid out on the north side of West Creek, had been divided into nine smaller squares. Two suburbs had been added close to the harbor for new arrivals.

The central square was commonly owned. Land for residences had been apportioned according to the number of shares owned in the original company. Everything had been carried out without dissension, even though the plantation had operated for fifteen months on nothing more than a simple covenant. Today, however, formal government was to begin.

Ezekial decided to walk the long way around the square that had come to be known as Newman's quarter. His own house was in Mr. Eaton's quarter, in the northeast. At the corner he glanced down the street to the left, impressed as always by the magnificence of Theophilus Eaton's home—a home so large it could accommodate nineteen fireplaces. Quinnipiac had more two-story structures than any other New England settlement, but even here most of them were two stories in the front only, with roofs slanted steeply at the back. Mr. Eaton's, however, was a full two stories with two large wings on either side and a smaller wing at the center so that it looked like a huge printed *E* lying on its side. Ezekial remembered houses in England like this, most of them built during Elizabeth's reign.

The Eatons always entertained any distinguished visitors who came to the plantation; they also entertained friends on Sunday evenings when the Sabbath ended. The only times Ezekial felt lonely were when he went back to his silent little house after an evening with the Eatons. Then even *The Accidence* was not enough to keep him from realizing how cheerless a house can be when it lacks the warmth that can only be brought to it by a woman.

He was about to cross the street when he saw Mrs. Eaton emerge from her house. She waved, and he waited for her to fasten her gate to keep out the cattle grazing on the common.

"Have your boys deserted you?"

"No. I dismissed them early so I could go to the meeting at Newman's."

She gave him a quizzical look. "Aren't you going the wrong way?"

"I've been confined all morning. I wanted to walk a little, to enjoy some of this beautiful day."

"I understand. You could as well ask me the same kind of question. Why am I going to the Widow Stolyon's for needles when I could as easily send a servant? My answer would be that I wanted—needed—to be away from the house."

"Really? I didn't know women ever felt that way."

"Didn't you?" She seemed amused. "Well, they do. You'd be surprised, Mr. Cheever, to learn that although we differ from men in our ability to bear children, we often have the same kinds of thoughts. We cherish the same longings and are often interested in the same things. For instance, I, today—I cannot think of anything I'd rather do than go to the meeting in Newman's barn. Surely the women in this plantation are as involved in its operation as the men."

At times when they had argued on Sunday nights about doctrinal points in one of the day's sermons, he had been impressed by her intellect. Now, though, she seemed incredibly naive. Reassuringly he said, "You're wrong if you think women aren't involved in this plantation. Why the whole enterprise would collapse without them."

In an edgy voice she said, "It would also collapse without horses and cows." Then suddenly she smiled. "How foolish of me to rail against this. In England I did not even think about such things, but here where everything is starting new—oh, well, it doesn't really matter. I've said enough. You'll be sorry you stopped to talk with me."

"No, oh no. I'd rather talk with you than—" He checked himself. *Than anyone I know?* Whatever had made him prone to express himself in such an extravagant way?

"You're always kind," she said. "Somehow I trust you not to betray my foolish thoughts." Her high cheekbones caught the sunlight as she smiled again. "But then you're a schoolmaster. You probably hear much foolishness."

"And forget it as quickly." Feeling oddly awkward and uneasy, he looked beyond her, his gaze caught by the waters of the harbor glowing in motionless submission to the noonday sun. He shivered a little. So it had been on that June day a year ago, the day of the great and terrible earthquake when the earth had rumbled and trembled, and the water in the harbor had seemed to turn over. It was as if the Lord had roared from Zion as in the days of Amos. Mr. Davenport had said that it was God's way of reminding them of His might. "He does not want us to forget that the only purpose of this settlement is His proper worship and glorification."

Though the memory was awesome, Ezekial reminded himself that earthquakes were rare and that people who lived in goodness need not fear God's wrath.

He heard Mrs. Eaton say, "You'll be late for your meeting."

"And you'll never get your needles."

She shrugged. Her eyes were very clear and dark.

"I wish you *were* going to the meeting," he said.

"It doesn't matter. Perhaps all I needed was to talk about it." Moving away from him, she began picking her way through the muddy ruts in the street. She looked back once. "Be sure to come Sunday night. We're having strawberries on biscuits."

When she lifted her petticoat to step over the last and deepest rut, he was struck by the delicacy of her pink-stockinged ankle. His throat swelled curiously. Stop looking at her, he told himself. "Thou shalt not covet thy neighbor's wife." But he did not covet her, of course. He merely felt a sympathy for her, an understanding.

He walked rapidly up the side of Newman's quarter that paralleled the common. At Francis Brewster's place on the corner, an Indian lounged against the fence. A beaver pelt was slung over his shoulder, and bone pendants carved in the shape of birds hung from his ears. It was said that when an Indian was attracted to a woman, he gave her bracelets, belts, and chains of wampum. If she accepted them, they lived together for a while to see whether they pleased each other. It was a shameful practice. Shameful and immoral.

The Quinnipiacs had, however, been honest and friendly in their dealings with the English. Because their tribe had been reduced by the fierce Pequots to the east and impoverished by the even fiercer Mohawks from the north, they had welcomed the settlers and had willingly sold them land for coats and knives. The English, in return, were to defend the Indians and to allow them to continue hunting and fishing in the area.

The Quinnipiac plantation was fortunate, Ezekial thought as he rounded the next corner and entered Newman's barn, to have friendly Indians nearby. Other settlements had not fared so well. Not long before their plantation had been established, several members of the Abraham Finch family in Wethersfield had been murdered in a surprise attack.

In the barn Mr. Davenport was standing in front of the crowd, his round pink face shining above his immaculate white bands. After asking God's blessing, he said, "We are gathered here today because our town is growing. Already we have purchased land from the sachem of Wepowaug for a new settlement to the west. It is fitting now that we should lay the groundwork for a formal government, and that all males over sixteen in the plantation should vote on what it will be. I have five questions to ask you. You will signify your assent by raising your hands."

The first four questions quickly received an affirmative vote. Everyone agreed that, as stated in the original covenant made after the landing, the Scriptures held forth perfect rules for doctrine and duty, and that all things pertaining to the gathering of a church and the choice of magistrates and civil officers should be ordered by the Scriptures. They also signified their desire to seek membership in the church and to establish a civil government designed to secure the peace and security of the church.

Mr. Davenport nodded approvingly. "Last of all," he said, "shall none but church members have the power to choose magistrates and officers, make and repeal laws, and handle all civil affairs?"

Silence spread through the barn. Many of the men there realized that God might never fit them to become church members. They knew, then, that they would have little or no say in town affairs in the future. Ezekial, however, saw no reason not to raise his hand. He was already a church member. Gradually, the more hesitant raised their hands, probably, Ezekial thought, because their livelihoods depended on the favor of the wealthy merchants who were sure to be church members.

"There is, then," Mr. Davenport said complacently, "no dissent." He added, as if it were a necessary formality, "If anyone opposes any of these questions, let him speak now."

A hand went up and a calm, cultured voice said, "Reverend sir, I am in opposition to the fifth question."

Davenport's head jerked upward. A murmur rose as it became clear that it had been the voice of Samuel Eaton, the quiet, austere brother of Theophilus Eaton.

Lifting his hands for quiet, Mr. Davenport said coldly, "Mr. Eaton, when I asked for a vote of assent on the fifth question, you raised your hand."

"Yes, I did."

"But you did not agree?"

"No."

"Then why did you raise your hand?"

"Because I do agree that all magistrates should be God-fearing men—members of the church. I feel, however, that *all* free planters should be allowed to choose these magistrates. Surely you are aware that though many men desire to become church members, few will be chosen."

Mr. Davenport's face was white now. "I am surprised, sir. You, a man of the cloth, a man once imprisoned for nonconformity—it is especially surprising that you should now side against the Nonconformists."

"I am not against them. But I do not think they should have all the power. And it is precisely because of my imprisonment that I feel this way. I have been tried by the Star Chamber. I have been imprisoned with men whose ears have been cut off, whose tongues have been cut out, whose nostrils have been split, and with men who have suffered even more barbarous cruelties. All this was done by a civil government allied with an established church, a government that persecuted those who did not conform."

Mr. Davenport sighed with strained patience. "Perhaps we

should put the question to another vote. Will all who feel that church members only shall have the power to choose magistrates and officers from among themselves, please raise your hands."

This time Ezekial's hand did not go up quite so readily. Samuel Eaton's argument did not seem unreasonable. Other men frowned, glanced at each other. But slowly hands were raised.

"You are assenting, Mr. Eaton?" Mr. Davenport asked.

"Yes. It is apparently what the people want. But I did not wish to assent without registering a protest."

After that, Mr. Davenport guided them to the decision that twelve men should be nominated. Later, these twelve men would choose seven of their number to organize the First Church of Christ in Quinnipiac. Ezekial was one of the twelve nominated, an honor he was not sure he deserved. If those voting had been able to look into his mind earlier in the afternoon, would their choice have been the same? But surely one vagrant moment of fancy was not enough to impair his ability to choose those seven who would organize the church?

As Ezekial went down the street after the meeting, a light-haired girl carrying a spinning wheel came out of one of the houses. Evidently she had been working in the company of a neighbor. Ezekial stopped.

"May I carry your wheel for you?"

She was too shy to meet his eyes. All he could see were her finely veined eyelids with the dark-gold lashes fanned out beneath them.

"It isn't far. I can manage."

He picked up her wheel and walked to the next quarter with her. She did not speak. Finally he said, "We men had a meeting today to plan the government."

She nodded.

"Only church members will be allowed to vote."

She nodded again.

He could think of nothing else to say until they had reached her house. "Do you wish you had been at the meeting?" he asked.

"Me?" Lifting her head, she showed him surprised gray eyes. "But I was spinning."

He touched his hat. "Good day, Miss—Miss—?"

"Mary."

"Good day, Miss Mary."

"Good day, Mr. Cheever. And thank you."

Her transparent skin, delicate as a baby's, let a pinkness show through from beneath. But she was not a baby, nor even a child. Her curves were womanly, made to the shape of a man's touch. A tremor passed lightly over his body. Oh, Ezekial Cheever! Twice in one day? It was enough to make the Lord roar down from Zion.

One day soon he would ask her father's permission to call.

5

THEOPHILUS EATON
OCTOBER 1639

For Theophilus Eaton the day marked by the meeting in New-man's barn had been a good one. Though disturbed by his brother's need to express his dissent, he felt that the unanimous vote for the fifth question had demonstrated the strength of the whole company's belief in the colony's godly purpose.

It had been a good day and it had been a good omen for what was to follow. In August the twelve who had been nominated met and selected seven in the group to be the pillars of the church. All were men of substance who could be counted on to act with wisdom and discretion.

Late in the summer the Reverend Henry Whitfield arrived from England with a new group of settlers. It was an exciting arrival— the first time a transatlantic ship had sailed into the harbor. It was, Theophilus was sure, the first of many, the beginning of the direct trade with Europe he had planned from the first.

In the fall Whitfield and his company bought land and moved to Menunkatuck, about a dozen miles east on the coast. They planned to call the settlement Guilford.

In the fall, also, Peter Prudden and his company, who had originally come from Herefordshire in England and who had come to Quinnipiac with the settlers the previous spring, removed to land bought in February about nine miles west along the coast. The Indians called it Wepowaug, but the settlers spoke of changing the name to Milford.

Theophilus thought of these moves as a broadening of the outlines of Quinnipiac rather than as desertions. Though each of the new settlements was independent, all looked to Quinnipiac as the Greek colonies along the Mediterranean had looked to Athens. It was their mother city, and he felt that given time and tact he could bring them, and any others that might be founded, into one political entity.

In October the seven pillars of the church organized the government and set up a civil court. Theophilus was elected magistrate, and Robert Newman, Matthew Gilbert, Nathanael Turner, and Thomas Fugill were elected deputies. The court was to be the only governing body. It would make, interpret, and enforce the laws. Though the magistrate would welcome and respect the advice of his deputies, he would make all final decisions himself. No body of law was needed, the court felt: no English statutes, no common law, no canon law. They would draw all wisdom from the Word of God as stated in the Bible.

Word of his election had reached his home before Theophilus did, and the family was ready with a celebration. Madeira was served in pewter cans and His Excellency was toasted. Ann kissed him without shame in front of the others and for once he did not admonish her.

While he was in the midst of enjoying a stew of sweet, plump oysters, Ann suddenly said, "I wonder if here in this new land a woman will ever be allowed to serve on a jury. The law says 'a jury of his peers.' Wouldn't that entitle a woman, if she were being tried, to have women judging her?"

"I don't know," Theophilus said absently. He was feeling comfortable and satisfied, and the prattle of the women and children slid around the edges of his mind, hardly requiring thought for an answer. "We won't be using the jury system here."

"But you must. The Magna Carta has guaranteed that to Englishmen for—"

Theophilus put down his spoon with a sharp little crack, cutting off her words. "We are no longer subject to English law. We are independent people living on land we have bought. Our law is the Word of God and such regulations as the court finds it necessary to set forth from time to time, all to be based on the Scriptures."

"And don't forget, Mother," said Mary, "there are the deputies. They'll be acting something like a jury. Isn't that right, Father?"

Theophilus hesitated. Finally he said, "In a way, yes. But not exactly. You see, they only advise. The decision is up to me. I saw this work very well in the Balkans," he said to Ann.

"I'm sure it works very well for the judge," she replied. "And if a judge should happen to be corrupt—"

"Are you implying that my son is corrupt?" old Mrs. Eaton said.

"Your son? Of course not."

"Ladies, please," Theophilus said crisply. His appetite and all his pleasure in his new office left him. "It may be that my wife has a point. It is true that total power in the hands of one man can sometimes wreak great harm. But I do not think anyone has need to worry. My term is only one year. A new magistrate can be elected at the end of that time, which limits the harm that could be done."

He was grateful when the meal ended. As he left the table and started up the stairs, he could hear the women's voices rise. It was a relief to close the door to his closet and be alone with his books and papers. And from his window he could look across the street and see his friend John Davenport when he entered his own closet after supper. He had told him he would be over for a visit around eight.

It was a good friendship. Theophilus sometimes felt he knew John Davenport as well as he knew himself. Whenever the women in his family proved too overpowering in their petty rivalries and bickerings, he could always escape to his warm friendship and cool rationality. The only other man for whom he had a similar feeling was Edward Hopkins, husband to Ann's daughter. Although Edward was ten years younger, he felt closer to him than to any of his own children. Their minds worked in the same ways, each combining a keen business sense with strong religious feelings.

Tonight Theophilus didn't feel like working. He got out Fox's *Book of Martyrs*. As he read the familiar accounts of the bravery of those who had challenged Reginald Poole, who had gone to the stakes singing God's praise, who had continued to pray and sing even on damp days when the fire burned slowly and the torture was prolonged, his family troubles seemed no more than the tickle of a feather that had worked its way out of the bed at night.

The light began to fade and a silvery dusk filled the room. It always seemed to him that even the darkness had more light in it here in the new world. He was about to light a candle when he glanced across the street and saw John Davenport closing his study window against the night air. He put his book away and went downstairs.

Ann was alone in the great hall, hanging a pan on the wainscoting next to the fireplace. He loved watching her go about her household chores. If only she were content to be what she seemed to be: a woman to grace his hearth and warm him with her love. But her mind was like a cauldron boiling over a fire, with new substances constantly bubbling to the surface.

"I'm going over to talk with John," he said.

"Oh? I had hoped perhaps you and I could talk for a while."

"Did you really wish to talk? Or were you hoping to fling more criticism at me?"

"I'm sorry, Theophilus. My intent was the very opposite. I want only to be close to you, to your mind as well as your heart, to share everything with you."

At the moment she looked pathetic, yet he knew that in a flash a new argument would develop if he allowed the conversation to continue.

"You are overly tired," he said. "Would it not be best if you retired immediately?"

"Perhaps. Will you light a candle and carry it for me? I'd like to get some warm water."

He lighted a candle and waited while she went to the kitchen for water. She preceded him up the stairway and down the hall to their room. It was a lovely, large room with a green Turkey carpet and wall hangings.

After putting the candle down, he placed his hands on her shoulders and kissed her smooth white forehead. "You must try to get more rest, my dear. It will help to keep your nerves calm. After all, you have stopped breeding. Obviously you are approaching that time in life when a woman—"

"Rubbish. No woman in my family ever had an early change. We stay young forever. Look." She bent her head in front of him. "You don't see any gray hair—do you?"

"Well, no." He had to be honest. "But the light here is not good. Only one candle."

She lifted her head. "But even in sunlight you've never seen any. Have you?"

"No. But I haven't been looking. And of course much of the time you wear a hood or a cap."

Laughing, she put her arms around his neck. "You would have

noticed. Or your mother would have. And *she* would not have hesitated to mention it." Moving back, but keeping her hands clasped behind his neck, she turned her head so he could see her profile. It was still well defined, following the strong bones of her face. "See? No double chin."

"Vanity," he said.

"I am not vain." She rubbed the bridge of her nose where there was just the faintest suggestion of a bump. "I have not said that I was pretty, only that I am not yet old." Her expression softened. "Theophilus? Even though we have our own house now, we are seldom alone. I do not mean to get angry or excited, but when I try to talk with you about things that matter to me, the others seem bent on trying to create friction between us."

Her hands at the back of his neck were soft and imploring, but the words sounded like the beginning of a discussion he was too weary to tackle. He took her hands by the wrists, kissed the back of each one. Releasing them, he went over to the window and drew the curtains. "It might help you, my dear, to pray—pray for patience, for guidance, for forbearance."

"Theophilus, please stay with me a while."

Her voice had softened almost to a whisper. It was hard to resist its soft insistence. Outside, he heard the eight o'clock watch being called.

"We will talk later," he said.

"Please don't go."

Quietly he repeated the words. "We will talk later."

He went outside and closed the door. As he walked down the hall, he heard something hit the door. It sounded like a woman's slipper.

JOHN DAVENPORT
OCTOBER 1639

Nearly half an hour before, John Davenport had closed his study window against the night air. Now a few late-season moths hurled themselves against the glass like sinners who had not yet found the true way to the Light. It was after eight. The watch had already been called. Where was Theophilus?

He stood looking out the window, his hands clasped behind him, his chest rising and falling in shallow, contented breaths. How well everything had gone today; in fact, how well everything had gone in the year and a half the company had been in New England. Surely this was due to the quality of the leadership and the influence of the church. A plantation could not fail to succeed when its leaders were so patently instruments of God.

He knew that some people claimed he had dissembled when, as a young curate, he had denied accusations of being a Nonconformist. But he had not been officially a Puritan then, despite his leanings in that direction. Why should he not have denied it?

Others had accused him of deception when he had returned disguised from Holland, to avoid arrest and torture. A shudder passed over his body. What gain for the Puritans would there have been in that? Would this plantation ever have become a reality, this true church-state ever have been formed? The Christian Church already had its share of martyrs. How much better it was for him to have remained in hiding until it was time to cross to the new world. And God's approval of all he had done was revealed today when the formal church-state had been established.

Elizabeth came downstairs after hearing their young son's prayers. She came in and tucked her right hand under John's arm. In her left hand she carried a candle.

"I'm going to bed now. Will you be coming soon?"

He felt the softness of her familiar body close to his. Even, as now, when he was so preoccupied with plantation affairs that his body remained quiescent, his sense of comfort in her presence constantly increased. Theirs was, he reflected, a true Christian love.

He kissed her gently on the cheek. "Not right away. Theophilus is coming over. We have much to discuss." He gave her a searching look. "Do you mind?"

"No. Oh, no. You need to talk with him. I don't understand affairs of government. You know that. He is good for you, and you, of course, are very good for him. He has too many women in his household."

He looked out the window. "There, he'll be along soon. He's drawing the curtain in the front bedroom." He managed to conceal his irritation. Only the machinations of Ann Eaton could cause her husband to be so late.

A few minutes later Theophilus came in. Davenport brought out the Madeira.

"Ah," said Theophilus, "the second time today. Soon they'll be haling me before the court for drunkenness."

Both laughed, both aware that only in each other's presence and only out of long friendship and understanding could such jokes be made and as quickly forgotten.

"Well," Davenport said, raising his cup, "you have been elected chief magistrate. You are, then, the head of the plantation. Its ruler. As one of your loyal subjects, I hereby offer you the proper homage."

Theophilus was properly humble. "You're forgetting, my friend, that this is a church-state. You are the head of the church. That means that you are the head of the plantation."

"Let us not argue. Let us just say that each of us will play a leading role." Davenport hesitated, swirling the wine in the cup, realizing that he must speak now with great care. "One thing nags at me. But perhaps it would be better if I did not speak of it. No such thing may ever happen, and you may think less well of me for allowing such a thought to enter my mind."

"John, there is nothing we cannot speak of to each other. I can think of nothing that could lessen my feeling of friendship for you."

"What if a question about colony affairs should come up, one on which we do not agree, or one which might involve one or the other of us in a personal way?"

"Whatever it is, we will discuss it and come to an amicable settlement."

"And if it should prove difficult for us to discuss?"

"Then each will trust the other. Has it not always been so?"

"Yes, but we have never before been responsible for so many. Things could happen here which might be a strain on our friendship."

Theophilus crossed his legs. An easy smile came to his lips. "I cannot think of anything which would strain a friendship of such long standing and of such close bond."

"Well, supposing Goody Baldwin steals a trinket and you sentence her to stand two hours in the stocks. Then supposing a week later my wife is found guilty of the same crime. What would you do?"

"Elizabeth would never—"

"That is beside the point. Women are unpredictable. New circumstances sometimes enhance qualities hitherto unnoticed." He could see his point was making itself felt as Eaton's expression tightened. "Never mind whether or not it is likely to happen. What would you do if it *did* happen?"

"I'm afraid I would have to sentence her to two hours in the stocks also. I could not do otherwise. It is the rule of law. But how would you feel if I did so?"

"Angry. Humiliated." He paused, then added firmly, "Glad. Angry because a crime had been committed, humiliated because it had been committed by my wife, and glad that justice was being done. I might even be glad that it was my wife in the stocks, for it would prove to all how diligently we seek justice."

"It would take great strength."

"God would give you the strength to convict, me the strength to bear it." Davenport placed his fingertips together with great care. "Now, let us go a step in a different direction. Let us suppose your mother suddenly began to flout the teachings of the church."

"My mother!"

"A remote possibility. Yet"—he leaned forward, picked up his

35

cup, and took another sip of wine—"yet was not the possibility equally remote last June that another member of your family would object to the limited franchise that is the very basis of our government?"

"Ah—Samuel. My own brother. Yes. John, I can only say this: his behavior on that day was as great a surprise to me as it was to you."

"Did my handling of the situation offend you?"

"It was exactly as I would have done were I as quick-witted."

His muscles tense, Davenport watched his friend closely now. "You do agree, then, that the good of the plantation comes first, that we cannot allow our feelings for those close to us to interfere with our decisions?"

Theophilus answered as soberly as if he were taking an oath. "My personal feelings will never interfere with any of the decisions I must make as a magistrate. Nor will I interfere with any of the pastoral decisions you must make as head of the church."

Davenport felt the tension slip away. He felt filled with the power of God, the God who had shown him the way. "Nor will I interfere with your prerogatives as head of the civil government."

Theophilus moved his cup to his left hand and stretched out his right hand. "Agreed," he said.

The spontaneous gesture, with its implications of full and perfect trust, made Davenport feel faintly guilty. He had to remind himself that in order to carry out God's work, it was sometimes necessary to manipulate even those whom one loved best.

They were silent a moment as the warm handclasp forged an even closer bond between them. "We have come a long way together, my friend," Davenport said.

"Yes, John, and we will go further still. I looked today at our little settlement and in my mind I saw the huge state it will someday become, prosperous and important, perhaps even so important that England herself will be glad to bargain with us."

Davenport loosened his doublet and leaned back, clasping his hands over his rounded belly. He smiled warmly at his best and dearest friend.

"May the Lord God Jehovah continue to shed His grace on us."

THEOPHILUS EATON
OCTOBER 1639

The court began to meet that same week in the great hall of the Eaton home. The magistrate and his deputies sat at the dining table with their backs to the stone fireplace.

One of the court's first acts was to establish a military order. Two men who had distinguished themselves in the Pequot War became the town's chief military officers: Nathanael Turner was made captain and Robert Seeley, marshal. They were to handle all military affairs as well as security within the town.

It was a wise move, for on the first day the court was held an arrest was necessary. An Indian, who said his name was Nepaupuck, came to the Eaton house with a deerskin slung over his shoulder. He made it known through the uneasy Quinnipiac who accompanied him that he had come to make a trade.

To Theophilus, the name Nepaupuck had a familiar sound, an elusive but unpleasant connotation.

"Where are you from?" Theophilus asked.

"From the land along the Great River."

"Near the Great Water?"

"No. Farther up."

"Near Hartford?"

"Downriver from Hartford."

Probably around Wethersfield, Theophilus thought. And suddenly he realized why the name Nepaupuck had seemed unpleasantly familiar. An Indian of that name had been involved in some brutal murders there. A tribe of Indians had been driven from their reservation following a quarrel with the English. They had incited some Pequots into surprising the inhabitants at Wethersfield. Three women and six men had been killed.

The people at Hartford had wanted to send troops to retaliate. They had asked Theophilus for help, but he had felt it unwise to begin a war. They had no military force to send so soon after their arrival. It was important also to be friendly with the tribes close to the plantation. The tribe just north of the plantation was headed by a son of the sachem of the Wethersfield Indians. If the English had attacked, they would only invite further retaliations.

Perhaps the Indians knew it was he who had vetoed the attack. Perhaps they thought he would be lenient toward Indian behavior, no matter how savage. Otherwise, he thought, how could Nepaupuck so boldly enter his house, expecting to be treated like any honest trader?

How did Nepaupuck dare to come to this house with the blood of innocent Englishmen on his hands? Theophilus thought of the women and children in his own home. How would he feel if he found them killed and mutilated?

To Robert Seeley he said sternly, "Take this man into custody, charged with the murder of Abraham Finch and others at Wethersfield."

Nepaupuck was put in the stocks. Two days later he was tried. Theophilus was careful to give him a fair trial. First he carefully questioned a number of Quinnipiacs whom he trusted. They all admitted that the arrested man was Nepaupuck, and that he had bragged of killing Englishmen and cutting off their hands.

Only Mewhetabo, a Quinnipiac who was Nepaupuck's kinsman, said he was not guilty. But after Theophilus had questioned him in great detail, he became entrapped in his own statements and began to tremble; then he, too, admitted Nepaupuck's guilt.

After that Nepaupuck was called in. As he heard them recount the exploits of Nepaupuck, he smiled proudly. The court grew silent and sober and the proud smile vanished. Nepaupuck turned as if to run. He saw the armed men behind him. Hitching his shoulder uneasily, he said, "Nepaupuck is great man, but I am not Nepaupuck."

Again Theophilus called Mewhetabo to the front. Pointing to Nepaupuck, he said, "Is this man your kinsman, Nepaupuck?"

Mewhetabo bent his head in sadness. "Yes."

Nepaupuck looked at his kinsman without malice. He listened while other Quinnipiacs came forward and pointed their fingers at him. One even said that he had witnessed the killing.

At this point, Nepaupuck drew himself up proudly. "I am a great captain," he said, folding his arms. "I have murdered Finch and others. If I must die, I am not afraid. It is *weregin.*"

At first the interpreter did not translate *weregin.* He said the English had no word that meant the same thing. Finally he said it meant something like *well* or *fitting.*

Theophilus consulted with his deputies. "What advice do you offer?" He looked first at Robert Newman.

Newman turned his hand over, palm upward. "He expects death, I think."

Matthew Gilbert said, "Death it should be or the savages will feel that they can kill unpunished."

"We must remember," Nathanael Turner said thoughtfully, "that this crime was committed outside our jurisdiction before we even had a government. Is it our duty or even our right to try and sentence in this case?"

"It was Englishmen he killed," Thomas Fugill said. "We must act as one to protect each other."

And Gilbert added, "Let the savages see that we mete out justice, that we all stand together. Let them know that we all stand ready to act for each other should even the smallest settlement be attacked."

After they had all spoken, Theophilus sat quiet for almost ten minutes while the Indians waited stoically and the deputies busied themselves with papers. Why was he so hesitant to pronounce a death sentence? It seemed all at once too great a decision for one man to make.

He passed his hand over his forehead and found that it was damp. Whence had come this sudden squeamishness? Perhaps it was because the murders had taken place in the past, and he had not known those who had been murdered. If someone in the Quinnipiac plantation had been brutally killed, if he himself had seen the mutilated bodies and severed hands, perhaps these feelings would not have come to him.

He thought of the members of his family, of the planters whose interests he had been elected to protect. Even now plans were underway to distribute land outside the town plot for farming purposes. Some of the settlers were planning to move out there, to live in isolation. Was it fair to make a decision that might endanger them?

Thomas Fugill placed an open Geneva Bible in front of him, his finger marking the sixth verse of the ninth chapter of Genesis: "Whoso sheddeth man's blood, by man shall his blood be shed."

Theophilus nodded and rose.

In a deep, steady voice he said, "I sentence the Indian Nepaupuck to death on the morrow for the crime of killing Abraham Finch and other Englishmen from Wethersfield. He shall be beheaded and his head placed on a pole in the marketplace so that all may heed the lesson therein. 'Whoso sheddeth man's blood, by man shall his blood be shed.' "

At that moment Theophilus noticed his wife standing at the back of the room. Her face expressionless, she watched Nepaupuck receive the sentence. Theophilus waited for her eyes to turn to him. When they did, he raised his eyebrows a little, half questioningly, half imploringly. At this moment, more than ever before, he wanted both her understanding and her approval. Her eyes met his for a long moment; then, her face still expressionless, she turned her back and walked out the door.

That night Theophilus did not join his family for supper or for evening worship. Instead, he went directly to his closet and fasted and prayed. No visions came, no indications that God had disapproved of his decision. He was tempted, late in the evening when he saw John Davenport's candle still burning, to go over and ask his advice. But he knew he should not. He was magistrate; this was his responsibility alone.

But was there any reason he could not go over merely to talk? His position had made him feel remote from all men who had no greater decision to make tonight than which nightcap to wear. He had a strong need for casual conversation and the warmth of friendship.

He went quietly out and across the street. John must have seen his light and suspected he might come, for he answered the door at the first light tap.

They settled themselves before the fire with a warming cup of wine. They talked of the meetinghouse which would be built shortly. They talked of the two new settlements. Already it looked as though in Prudden's settlement as Milford a dangerous amount of freedom was to be granted. Word had filtered back to them that Prudden favored giving the franchise to all free males.

When Theophilus felt that all his tension had been dissipated in the glow of good talk, friendship, and wine, he rose to leave. It was then that John said, "Today it was that you sentenced the murderer Nepaupuck to death."

"Yes." Did he compress his lips? Did an expression of self-loathing or pain cross his face?

"A man in power," Davenport said, "must often make painful decisions. Yet he must always remember that the power he has is a responsibility to the people. He can consider neither himself nor the feelings of the guilty party. He must consider only the welfare of those for whom he speaks. 'Whoso sheddeth man's blood, by man shall his blood be shed.' You made a wise decision."

"It is *weregin,*" Theophilus said with a faint smile.

He felt much better when he left and was able to sleep well and to eat a hearty breakfast. He conducted family worship with no discussion—merely a prayer and a reading from the Scriptures—before leaving for the marketplace.

Most of the settlers gathered to watch the execution. Theophilus saw his own family there, including his wife. He had not expected her. She had been silent at breakfast. He had asked her if she were well and she had shaken her head. But when he had suggested that Mr. Augur come to look at her, she had again shaken her head. "I am not sick enough for a surgeon. I merely do not feel very well. It will pass."

It occurred to him that she might be feeling out of sorts because of the argument two days before about the powers of the court. If she disapproved of Nepaupuck's sentence, she did not indicate it. Her presence here now showed that she felt he had done the proper thing. He was pleased; oddly, he wanted her approval in this.

His feeling of well-being increased when he saw his brother Samuel. Samuel had been in Menunkatuck during the past week, checking a place where another settlement might be made. Theophilus had mixed feelings about Samuel's plan to start a new plantation with himself as leader. It might be good for Quinnipiac if Samuel, who had a tendency to be critical, left. On the other hand, he might set up a plantation similar to Prudden's. This would disrupt the plan Theophilus had for uniting all new settlements, for unless they all agreed on the kind of suffrage permitted, real unity would not be possible.

Yet he was pleased to see his brother. His presence at the execution was a sanction of it. Though they sometimes disagreed, he had great respect for his brother's opinions and for his sincerity.

A drum rolled; the prisoner was released from the stocks and led over to a log. Theophilus read out the crime and the sentence. John Davenport prayed, then asked Nepaupuck if he had any last words. Nepaupuck murmured something. Theophilus caught only the word *weregin*.

The Indian knelt and placed his forehead upon the log with infinite grace and nobility and with no trace of fear. Robert Seeley, his face grim and colorless, stepped forward. He lifted his axe and it came down on the Indian's neck. The crowd gasped. The blow had only cut a gash on one side of the neck. The Indian remained kneeling without moving or uttering any cry. Once again Robert Seeley lifted the axe and, with his lips compressed, came down hard and accurately. The head rolled off onto the straw, staining it red.

Theophilus slowly let out his breath, but his chest felt tight and hard. Surely he had never seen a man die more bravely. It was the way all men, he thought, would like to face death, the way most men feared they would not.

Seeley looked at him and Theophilus nodded. Seeley picked up the head by the twisted lock of wiry black hair and stuck a spiked pole up into it. He placed the bottom of the pole in a hole that had been especially dug and put a few stones around it for support.

The Quinnipiacs, who had watched the whole procedure stoically, asked if they might take away the body. Permission was given.

From the top of the pole, the severed head looked down on all the living. No one had bothered to close the eyes.

ANN EATON / OCTOBER 1639

Before she left the house, Ann had given the servants instructions about dinner. She knew she should go straight home to oversee their work. Yet she found herself walking slowly. She felt a need to think her own thoughts, to decide which thoughts she must take care never to express in words. In Denbighshire where she had lived with her first husband, and in London, she had had close women friends. With them she had not been afraid to say what she thought. Here, she realized, she missed a sympathetic friend with whom she could talk over her doubts and worries.

A few times she had taken her spinning wheel across the street to work with Elizabeth Davenport. But Elizabeth talked of nothing but her young son, and besides, Ann felt that anything she said might well be later retold to Mr. Davenport. Elizabeth would feel it was her duty. She was unquestionably a perfect wife and mother. Ann admired her and felt she should be like her. She knew she never could be.

Instead of turning in at her gate, Ann found herself walking by. Just a few minutes, she thought, just a few more minutes before I go in. Walking rapidly, she went down to the point where she could look far out across the harbor; then she turned and started walking around the quarter in the opposite direction from her home. If only, like Elizabeth Davenport, she were the kind of wife who could accept every pronouncement of her husband's, who could completely submerge every thought and feeling in deference to his. Why did she always question? Why did she doubt the rightness of men who were surely better Christians than she?

The Reverend Mr. Davenport would say that it was the Devil within her, twisting her thoughts, making her think right was wrong. Yet if this was the Devil's work, then the very foundations of her intelligence were laid by the Devil, for it seemed to her that all she had ever learned in life had been a result of this same kind of doubt and wondering.

It was a damp, gray day. A chilling wind tugged at her hood and whipped her petticoats sharply against her ankles. Her hearth at home glowed warmly, she knew, but she could not at this moment make herself return to it. When she came to the creek that crossed the corner of the lot that had been assigned to Samuel Eaton, she hesitated, then sat down on a shelving rock at the water's edge.

She was glad her daughter Ann had not been there to see the execution. Nowadays she was spending most of her time in Hartford, where her husband had recently been elected magistrate. Nor had the two youngest children, Hannah and Theophilus, been there, but young Samuel had been at the front of the group, never taking his eyes off the prisoner for a moment. He was too young to have developed real sensitivity, and she was fearful that such a spectacle might coarsen him.

A snapping of twigs startled her. Quickly she looked around and saw it was Brigid Brewster, a woman who lived up in the next quarter, the one that bordered on the common.

What Ann saw on Brigid's plain, freckled face was a mirror of her own feelings: doubt, sorrow, uneasiness.

Ann moved closer to the end of the rock, leaving a space, in unspoken invitation. After a moment, Mrs. Brewster came over, lifted her skirts, and sat down.

Mrs. Brewster passed her hand over her eyes. "I could not go right home. That girl who works for me—"

"Will want to talk about the execution."

"Yes."

"And you do not want to talk about it."

Mrs. Brewster gave her a hard look. "Do you know everything I am thinking? Perhaps you are a witch."

Ann smiled. "Perhaps I am only voicing my own thoughts." She waited a moment. "Even though you do not want to discuss it with your servant, perhaps you'd like to talk with me about it."

44

"With the wife of the chief magistrate?" She laughed a little unpleasantly. "I should think not. I am probably already in trouble for suggesting she might be a witch."

"I knew you were joking. And jokes are all too rare here, it seems. I miss an occasional laugh with a friend."

Mrs. Brewster gave her a long look, as if trying to tell what she was thinking. Her eyes were light blue and set well apart. After a moment she turned away and said, "Look at that funny little upside-down bird on the oak tree. I wonder what it is."

"I don't know. All the birds here are different. No finches like ours—"

"No nightingales."

"No weavers."

"Yes, so much is different."

"No juries," Ann said softly, tentatively.

"No Magna Carta," Mrs. Brewster replied.

For a long time neither one spoke. Then Mrs. Brewster said, "You could have me put in the stocks for this, but I'll say it anyway. No matter how savage his crime, we here in Quinnipiac did not have the right to take his life."

Ann could feel her heart expand with warmth. "That is true," she said. She stood up. Shivering a little, she said, "Winter seems to be beginning early. If it is as long and as cold as it was last year, there will be time for seeing friends now and then. Why don't you bring your work over to my house some afternoon so we can talk some more?"

Mrs. Brewster lifted her freckled face. When she smiled, she was less plain. "I'd like that. But why don't you come to my house? There are fewer people there."

"Yes, that would be better."

They walked up through the woods together, stopping where they could see the imposing Davenport residence through the trees.

"Our pastor has a fine home," Mrs. Brewster said.

"Yes."

"I hear it has fifteen fireplaces. Is that true?"

"I think so."

"The Lord has surely smiled on him."

"Yes."

"Well, don't forget. Some afternoon soon. And bring your

wheel." She lifted her hand in a jaunty wave. "I'll go out to the street from here."

Ann liked her lively step and erect posture. Sluggish, slouching women irritated her. Smiling to herself, she continued through the woods behind her home. This area, going through to the opposite side of the quarter, had been assigned in two lots: one for Ann's son David and the other for old Mrs. Eaton. The far end of David Yale's property bordered the rear of Ezekial Cheever's lot. Both David's and Mrs. Eaton's lots were still empty. David was restless. Ann sensed that he would not remain long in the town. In a way it was good that he had not built yet, for the empty area behind Ezekial Cheever's home and school gave his students a place to roam during the brief recesses he allowed them.

And old Mrs. Eaton, of course, enjoyed living at the home of the most important man in the plantation. She enjoyed meeting their guests and coming forward with outstretched hand the moment they entered as if she, and not her daughter-in-law, were mistress of the house.

The trees had not yet been cut here and the ground now was covered with leaves. A few of them were blood red. Ann stared down at them, her mood changing. A pressure started at the back of her eyes. For a moment she thought she was going to cry. She must not. She must not let her emotions take possession of her.

Lifting her head, striving for control, she walked rapidly, her eyes avoiding the ground as she circled the far end of their garden area. This way, she saw Ezekial Cheever just as he was about to step into his house with a turnip he had pulled from his garden.

"What brings you out at this time of day?" he asked.

"I went for a walk"—she paused delicately—"after the execution."

He nodded noncommittally.

"Were you there?" she asked. "I didn't see you."

"Yes. Some distance behind you."

She was annoyed by his seeming neutrality, by his failure to express distaste. "Many seemed to enjoy it. Perhaps you were one of them?"

"No. But I recognized the necessity for it."

"Which was?"

"To keep law and order—both inside and outside our community."

46

"I think it was wrong, Ezekial. Illegal, even."

He smiled. "And where did you get your legal training—at the Inns of Court?"

"You're making fun of me."

"I'm sorry. I didn't mean to. But I do feel that decisions about such things should be made by those who have had legal training or governing experience."

"I suppose you're right." She felt sad, ineffectual. And her head had begun to ache. "It's true that I've had no legal training. I live mostly by instinct. But I like to think that I, too, have an intellect."

"You have. Perhaps that is a problem."

"But if God gave me a mind, shouldn't I use it?"

His expression was kind, but more remote than usual. "Use it, yes. But use it in your own sphere, always remembering that God made you a woman for a special reason."

"I'll try."

He glanced toward his house, then down at the turnip he held in his hand.

"I'm keeping you from your dinner," she said. "It's time I went home, too."

He nodded. She had the feeling that he wanted to get away from her. Reluctantly, she moved through the garden and into her house. As she entered through the kitchen, she heard her servants talking about the execution. It had been a good show, they were saying, and the first inaccurate blow of the axe had increased the suspense and excitement.

Ann made no comment. She told them to set an extra place at the table for Mr. Samuel Eaton. They replied that old Mrs. Eaton had already told them to do so. When she suggested it was time to make the Indian pudding, they told her that old Mrs. Eaton had already instructed them to do so and that it was, in fact, being cooked.

When she came into the great hall a little later, she found Samuel Eaton standing by the fire.

"Did you have a good trip?" she asked.

"Yes."

"How is the land—adequate for a settlement?"

"Perhaps."

He was not being rude. He simply was not a conversationalist.

He was a man who seemed to care more for ideas than for people.

The kettle of Indian pudding bubbled over on the fire. Ann checked it, moved the trammel upward, and watched the bubbling settle down to a gentle simmer. She went to the kitchen behind the great hall where the remainder of the food was being prepared. When she returned, the rest of the family had gathered. The dinner was brought in and all stood while Theophilus said the blessing. With a timbre peculiar to his voice when his emotions were stirred, he asked for guidance and an open mind to receive God's wishes.

Theophilus sat at one end of the long refectory table with his mother on his right and his daughter Mary on his left. Ann sat at the other end with Samuel Eaton on her right and her son David Yale on her left. The other children faced each other from either side.

"It has been a good morning," old Mrs. Eaton said. "Did you see the expressions on the faces of the Quinnipiac savages? Clearly they realized that, though we are kind and considerate, we are also capable of meting out punishment should they transgress. It was a good lesson for them to learn. Do you not agree, Samuel?"

"Possibly. Then again, it is possible that they would simply infer from our kind and considerate treatment that we believe in justice."

Young Samuel, his eyes unnaturally bright, said, "His head looked *so* funny when it went rolling off."

"I'm sure I saw his eyes blink afterward," her second son Thomas Yale added.

The younger children listened carefully, their glances darting from speaker to speaker.

"That's quite impossible," his older brother David contradicted him. "Once the head has been severed from the body—"

"Please," said Mary, making a little face, "we're eating. That is, we're all eating except our mother." She looked at Ann who was trying to swallow a mouthful of food through her tight, almost closed throat.

"What is wrong, daughter?" old Mrs. Eaton asked.

Ann managed to swallow the food. "I am not hungry. You will remember that I was unwell this morning."

"That is true," Theophilus said.

Old Mrs. Eaton looked hard at her. "Perhaps it is the execution that has made you squeamish."

"She's squeamish anyway," Thomas said. "She won't even go out in the yard when Anthony kills a chicken."

Thomas was not very intuitive. He heard only surface conversations. He would lead a happy life, Ann was sure, unaware of undercurrents, uninterested in philosophical questions. Already he had asked permission from Captain Turner to visit his daughter on Sunday nights. Like his father, Thomas Yale, he would be a kind husband, hard working and appreciative of any attentions his wife gave him. He would accept his wife as she was, without trying to understand her or make her over.

"Is it squeamishness," old Mrs. Eaton said, "or does it have something to do with the way the sentence was passed? I seem to remember a great deal of criticism leveled at our judicial methods only a few days ago."

Here Theophilus broke in. "Ann is unwell and that is all there is to it. I see no need to probe for reasons. Do you wish to leave the table, my dear?"

She gave him a grateful smile. At such times her love for him was very strong. "No. I'll stay."

"Perhaps some beer will help," David said, pouring her a glass.

Theophilus turned to his brother. "Did you have a good journey?"

"Very."

"Have you come to a decision about a new settlement?"

"Not yet."

"Naturally, it takes much thought. At any rate, you have returned to find some changes here. We now have a formal government with—"

"With Theophilus at the head of it," old Mrs. Eaton said.

Theophilus put his hand lightly on his mother's arm. "With a court to make laws, try cases, and take care of all civic affairs. And you arrived in time to see our first sentence carried out."

"Yes."

"Did anyone tell you the nature of the crime?"

"I talked with Captain Turner."

Theophilus nodded. "In that case, you understand all about it."

"Not quite." Samuel put down the piece of meat he had been holding, lifted his napkin, and touched it to his thin-lipped mouth. "I do not understand how a government which had been in effect for only three days could undertake to execute a person for an act committed nearly two years before in another jurisdiction."

"Because all we Englishmen have more or less agreed to protect one another's interests."

"*More or less agreed,*" said Samuel. "That hardly constitutes a treaty or even a formal plan of action."

"Already," Theophilus said stiffly, "Governor Winthrop has suggested a union for purposes of defense."

"But such a union has not yet been consummated."

Ann listened to Samuel with rising interest. He was saying exactly what she would have liked to have said. The difference was that when Samuel spoke, people listened.

"It was a particularly heinous crime," Theophilus said. "A surprise attack and very savage."

"They even cut off their hands," Mary said.

"You are calling it a crime," Samuel said. "But cruel as it was, is it not true that Wethersfield and the Indians who had been driven from their land could be construed to have been in a state of war?"

"Certainly they were."

"Thank you, Mother. Now tell me, do civilized nations hold individual soldiers responsible for homicides committed in battle?"

Theophilus moistened his lips. "You are quite right, Samuel. *Civilized* nations do not. But you are forgetting that we are dealing with uncivilized savages. They know nothing of the progress made in law and order among nations. They do not fight like civilized people, sending an army out onto a battlefield to stand up and fight fairly like gentlemen. Instead, they come stealthily by night or when least expected; they attack women and children and kill without mercy. It is exigencies such as these that have forced us to change our tactics."

Ann looked quickly at Samuel to see what answer he would have for this, but instead she heard her son Thomas speaking earnestly.

"The Indians themselves believe in taking a life for a life, whether or not the first life was taken in legitimate battle. Even Nepaupuck seemed to feel that we were justified in giving him the death penalty. He even had a word to describe it. What was the word, Father?"

"*Weregin.*"

Again Ann turned to Samuel, but now he was nodding. "The principle of natural justice," he said. "I suppose the Indian is not aware of territorial limits or jurisdictions. To him all white men are brothers and belong, so to speak, to the same tribe."

Ann listened to his words with growing anger. This was as the meeting in Newman's barn had been reported. Samuel voiced his objections; he seemed compelled to do so by his conscience. But once he had done so, he evidently felt relieved of further responsibility. He never took a firm stand and never did he act. He did not care as she did. Suddenly she felt helplessly, hopelessly alone.

THEOPHILUS EATON
OCTOBER 1639

Theophilus spent the afternoon in his study. The execution remained vivid in his mind, as did his brother's critical remarks. Surely this had been one of the most difficult days of his life.

Although executions had been common in England, he had always avoided them—not because he disapproved but because he felt a truly righteous man, who was unlikely to commit a crime, had no need for such a spectacle. But now he wondered if he had been completely honest with himself. Was there within him, as in his wife, a certain squeamishness, a reluctance to face the unpleasant necessities of life?

He must be strong. Kneeling, he begged God to increase his strength. He could not lead his people unless he was willing to look at their wrongs dispassionately and see to it that they were punished with all the severity they deserved.

After he had finished praying, he remained on his knees, as he often did, in an attitude of silent reverence. At such times he could almost feel the spirit of God settling on him, purifying his soul. When he rose from his knees, it was with a new feeling of courage and dedication.

He studied Governor Winthrop's plan for confederation. Then he made a map of Indian encampments and possible danger spots and laid out a plan for discussion with Captain Turner about organizing the watch.

Late in the afternoon Captain Lamberton came to see him. He

was a sea captain with a reputation for bravery and navigational skill who had already made one trip to the West Indies. They talked about a regular trade along the coast. Were there, Theophilus asked, any likely locations farther down the coast where trading posts could be set up? Lamberton said he had heard the Delaware Indians were willing to sell some land, but that there might be trouble with the Dutch if trading posts were set up south of New Amsterdam. Theophilus asked him to find out more about it on his next trip south.

By suppertime all the various strands of his work had been woven into a net that nearly obscured the image of Nepaupuck in his mind.

The smoky smell of salt pork being tried out in a kettle came up the stairs. Following this came the even more enticing smell of clams. Fresh chowder. As he rose from his desk, his mouth began to water. Although he had dined in some of the most famous inns in Europe, the clam chowder here in the new world was the finest dish he had ever eaten. He followed the appealing odor down the stairs.

The group at the table was smaller than it had been at noon. Thomas was courting at Captain Turner's, and his brother Samuel was at John Davenport's. At least, with Samuel gone, the chances for dissension were diminished. All too often Samuel stirred up a fire and then backed off, leaving others to put it out.

Though he had sat down with a feeling of well-being, he realized, as soon as he saw the faces of the women, that the meal was not going to be a pleasant one. In an attempt to divert them he began to speak of the West Indian trade and of the possibility of buying land near Virginia. Only his mother and David Yale seemed interested.

Soon his mother turned to Ann. "You're not eating any more than you did this noon."

Theophilus said to his wife, "You rested this afternoon. Didn't it help?"

"A little." She did not look directly at him. "But I'm still not very hungry."

"She's still upset about that Indian," Mary said. "She doesn't like to see anything killed—hens or Indians."

"Killing a hen and executing a murderer are two very different things," his mother said. "Surely my daughter does not feel qualified to question her husband's decision in condemning a savage heathen for killing innocent settlers."

Ann's bosom rose and fell rapidly but her voice remained controlled. "He may have been a heathen savage, but he broke no law here. Samuel Eaton pointed this out."

Trying to remain calm, Theophilus said, "He broke the Sixth Commandment: *Thou shalt not kill.* I'm afraid you do not fully understand Mosaic law."

"No? Are you forgetting that I am the daughter of a bishop?"

"How could we forget?" Mary said sweetly. "You remind us nearly every day."

Ann's face flooded with color. "That will be enough of your insolence, young lady."

His mother said, "The child was only stating a fact."

Theophilus lifted his hands. "Ladies. Ladies. Did I flee England to escape dissension, only to find it at my own table?"

Mary gave him a winsome smile. "We do not like it, Father, when she speaks harshly of you."

"I was not referring to you personally," Ann said. "I was only speaking of principles of justice."

Theophilus said in a kindly voice, "It might be better, my dear, if you confined your thoughts to principles of housewifery. In fact, if all of you did this, our table would be a happier place."

David Yale had not spoken during this exchange, but a nerve at his temple twitched. Theophilus could hardly blame him for wanting to leave this house.

"Housewifery does not inspire thought," Ann said. "The work is there to be done. Once it has been done, it begins to undo itself until it has to be done again. The butter must be churned, the beer made, the food prepared, the yarn spun, the cloth woven, the house cleaned. One does not have to weigh the merits of each job or ask for Divine guidance on it. Instead of occupying the mind, it leaves it free for all kinds of wanderings."

"This would not happen," said his mother, "if you directed your thoughts toward the welfare of your family, or the state of your immortal soul."

"My immortal soul? If you would just—"

David put his hand on her arm. She put her other hand over his, smiled vaguely at him. "If you would just—" But now she seemed to have lost the thought. "Will you excuse me, please. Actually, I do not feel well. I think I have done overmuch today."

"Certainly," Theophilus said, rising. "You do seem over-tired."

She passed by him, her skirts rustling to the particular rhythm of her moving body. They made a whispering sound that sounded like *follow me*. Was he, Theophilus wondered, the only one who heard the sound?

As he sat down, his mother said, "Done overmuch? So far as I know, she's done nothing at all today."

He finished his supper quickly, hardly aware of the conversation that flowed so much more easily with his wife absent from the table. Yet the food tasted less appetizing now: the chowder required more salt, and the beer seemed flat.

After family prayers, he went back upstairs. He stood at the top, longing to go immediately to their room. *Follow me.* He took several deep breaths. A stack of work remained on his desk. Work came first. Only after a man's work was completely done should he allow himself the luxury of dalliance with his wife.

He worked in his closet until the fire on the hearth died down and a chill began to settle on his skin. Then he went down the hall and stopped at the doorway of their bedroom, speaking his wife's name and quietly lifting the wooden latch to open the door before he heard her answer.

Almost immediately the soft green colors of the room had a gentling effect on him. Tension, exhaustion, and heavy responsi-bility always fell away from him in this room.

Ann was lying on the couch by the fire, reading. She had un-dressed and was wearing a blue rail, ruffled at the throat. Her un-bound dark hair fell around her shoulders and against the hollow of her cheek. The bones of her face were intermittently defined by the flickering candle. When she saw him, she quickly pushed her book down between the cushions and stood up.

He wanted to enfold her in his arms. Every event of the day seemed now to have been only a preliminary to this moment. Wisely, however, he recognized the Devil's promptings. The Devil wanted him to forget that as head of the house, his duty was to see to it that all behavior was pleasing to God.

"What were you reading, my dear?"

"A book."

"I was quite aware of that. What book is it that you feel you must hide from me?"

She lifted her chin defiantly. "It is a book that my husband—

my husband Thomas—gave to me. I am reading *The Tragedy of Hamlet, Prince of Denmark.*"

"It is a play and it is immoral. I would prefer that you not be subjected to its corrupting influence."

"But I have already read it many times. If it is a book that corrupts, then I have long since been corrupted. Or is that what you're thinking—that I am already corrupt?"

"Not corrupt, certainly, or I would not have taken you for my wife. But it does seem to me that your first husband gave little attention to your immortal soul. Or to your training as a wife and mother who should always set an example for the younger members of the household."

"I am a poor wife. I try your patience." Her words were humble, but the lift of her chin was not.

"Yes, often you do. But I tell myself that it is because you still have much to learn about what it means to be a Puritan."

"But what if, as I learn, I find myself even more at odds with your beliefs?"

"Then you must question me more. But only when we are alone. It is best not to communicate your doubts to others, especially the young." He moved closer to her. "But let us not talk about that for a while. It has been a long and difficult day and I wish now to forget it."

As he approached her, warm with desire, it seemed to him that she backed off a little. He put his arms around her and immediately felt her resistance. When he tried to counter it, she pressed both hands against his chest and wrenched herself away. She stood with her back to him.

"Ann, my dearest. What is wrong?"

"I do not like being touched by a man with . . . blood on his hands."

"I have no blood on my hands."

"Nepaupuck would still be alive if it were not for you."

All the energy that had been channeled toward love abruptly flamed into anger. How could she be so stubborn? Why couldn't she ever see things from his viewpoint?

Taking her by the shoulders he turned her around. "How do you think *I* felt when I said Nepaupuck must die? How do you think *I* felt when I knew that I and I alone was responsible for taking another man's life? Don't you suppose *I* have suffered? Don't you realize that it took every ounce of strength God gave me to keep my eyes on him when the axe fell?" He gave her shoulders a little shake. "Do you think that simply because you are a woman and can give vent to tears and sighs that you alone are capable of feeling?"

For a moment she studied him silently. "But then why did you do it?"

"Because it had to be done. Because I knew I must put aside my personal feelings and act in a way that would be best for the plantation. This is what a leader must do, Ann. He must forfeit his personal feelings for the good and the safety of the people he rules."

"Why did you not tell me this before?"

"Because these are things a man should not have to say."

"If you talked to me more often—"

He began to feel weary. "We talk a great deal."

"But not about things that really matter. When you are really concerned about something, you do not come to me. You go across the street."

Dropping his hands from her shoulders, he stepped back. "Are you jealous of John Davenport?"

"Perhaps. Oh yes, probably. But only because he enjoys so many more of your confidences than I do."

"We talk of government, of colonial growth, of synodical affairs. You would not understand."

"How you do know when you never try me out? I want to be your partner, Theophilus. I want to share everything with you."

Weariness had now invaded every bone and muscle. The price one paid for a beautiful and spirited wife was a high one.

"You haven't been very willing to be my partner tonight," he said. "It makes me wonder if your love for me is equal to mine for you."

Smiling faintly, she moved close to him. "No, Theophilus, our two loves are not equal. Mine is much greater, my husband, for I love you all day, wherever I am. But often I think you love me only in the bedroom."

She was very near to him and he was aware of her scent, the familiar woman-scent that rarely failed to stir him. But it was failing at this moment. His desire had slipped away into weariness and frustration.

"Then I will not be guilty of that tonight," he said. "I think I shall retire." Kissing her quickly on the forehead, he turned and started out of the room.

"But Theophilus, do you not wish . . . ? I mean, now I no longer feel—" Modestly, she hesitated.

"I realize that, my dear. But suddenly *I* feel very tired. I fear that I, too, have done overmuch today."

He smiled at her, trying not to take pleasure in returning her earlier rebuff. Yet he could not help enjoying a perverse, though mild, satisfaction. Did women think they were the only ones who could turn away from importunate mates with pleas of weariness?

ANN EATON / JUNE 1640

Even before the house had been completely finished with wooden latches on every interior door, small, diamond-paned casement windows, Turkey carpets in the parlors that flanked the great hall, and, out on display, the gold-chased silver ewer and basin— gift of the East Land Company when Theophilus had retired—Ann had begun entertaining on Sunday evenings just after the Sabbath ended at sundown.

Sunday night, it always seemed to Ann, was the best night of the week. But for the last few weeks, it had been dull. As she carried some bedclothes downstairs and out to the washhouse on a warm June Monday, she tried to decide why her gathering the night before had left her feeling bored and frustrated. The answer came to her as she stepped outside the kitchen door and looked past the garden and uncut trees to the far corner of the square where she could see the back of Ezekial Cheever's house. He had not been present last night; he had not, she suddenly realized, been present for three weeks.

The washhouse was warm and steamy and smelled of strong soap. "Oh?" said Ann to the two women servants there. "You've already begun?"

"Mrs. Eaton told us to, ma'am. She said the clothes would never dry if we didn't get them out early."

It was true, Ann realized. Sometimes she did not get the women started on the washing early enough. A sigh climbed up out of her chest. She suppressed it just as she suppressed the flash of annoyance that had struck her when they had referred to her mother-in-law as Mrs. Eaton—as if she were the *only* Mrs. Eaton.

Briskly, pleasantly, she said, "Yes, it's a good idea to get started as early as possible. You really shouldn't need instructions either from me or from the elder Mrs. Eaton. As soon as you get up Monday morning, you should have Anthony start the fire out here."

Neither one of them answered. Handing them the clothes, she turned away. At the door she said, "I think we'll have fish for dinner today. Where's Anthony? I'll send him out for a large—"

"Today's a flesh day, ma'am. Mrs. Eaton said so. She said we should have pork."

"Yes, of course. And some new peas would go well with it."

"Yes, ma'am. That's what she said."

It would not be this way forever, she told herself. She was sure that Theophilus still planned to build a house for his mother. But the men in the town had been busy with the really necessary buildings.

The exterior of the meetinghouse in the center of the marketplace had gone up early in December, right after the court had passed an ordinance saying it should be built. People had brought their own chairs until the benches had been completed later in the winter.

Now all men were busy with gardens and farming, hoping enough grain could be raised this summer for the settlement as well as for trade with the West Indies and Boston.

Certainly no one could begrudge the time spent on all these activities. But soon, perhaps after the harvest, work ought to begin on old Mrs. Eaton's house. Surely, her mother-in-law wanted to be mistress of her own home. Or did she? Was she not already mistress of Ann's home? Ann tried to put the thought aside. On such a day, all green and gold and freshly new, she could not help feeling that all would work out happily.

Before she went back into the house, she glanced once more through the grove of trees. And again she wondered about Ezekial's absence.

She always took a notebook to church and jotted down points from the sermon that seemed controversial. Sometimes she tried to discuss these with Theophilus. The results, however, were never satisfactory. He always explained things to her as if he were talking to a child. But Ezekial took her opinions seriously, and he had seemed to enjoy their discussions as much as she did. What had made him stop coming? Had she tactlessly said something to hurt his pride? Or had some member of her household made him feel less than welcome? Mary? Old Mrs. Eaton?

If she or anyone in her household had been discourteous to him, she wanted to know. She could still remember vividly the day the ship had come into the harbor and the way Ezekial had stood by her side. He was the only person on board who had understood her eagerness, her impatience, her great joy in arriving at this place of new hope, and her great disappointment at not being allowed to disembark that same day.

It was good to have him for a friend she thought, as she went back into the house and up to the wing where her room was. Directly across from it was the room that her daughter and Edward Hopkins occupied when they were in Quinnipiac. All was quiet inside.

Edward had brought young Ann down from Hartford three weeks before to stay while he went on a trip to the Bay Colony. He was very busy these days with both politics and business. In April he had been elected Governor of Connecticut Colony, and already he had an apparent monopoly on the fur trade on the Connecticut River.

Ann could not have asked for a more worthy son-in-law than Edward, yet she worried a great deal about young Ann's continuing moods of despondency. Theophilus had suggested they call in Mr. Augur with his leeches, but this had thrown the girl into such a hysteria of fear that the matter had been quickly dropped.

Despite the quiet in the room, Ann had a feeling her daughter was awake. She knocked lightly and heard a soft response. Lifting the wooden latch, she opened the door.

Young Ann was sitting in a rocker by the window, her hands idle in her lap. She wore a pale pink rail with dainty pink morocco slippers with silver buckles on her feet. The unmade bed gave the room an air of disorder. Brisk and efficient herself, Ann was irritated by lethargy in others. The shadow on the noon marker in the back garden had shown the morning was almost half over. If nothing else, a woman should be dressed and have her bedroom neatly straightened by then.

Her irritation vanished when she saw her daughter's face. Two tears were poised just over the curve of her cheekbones.

"What is wrong, my child?"

"Nothing."

"You are crying."

"Am I?" She touched her cheeks. "It's nothing. I can't really—" She lifted her slender hands, palms up, as if about to explain something, and then dropped them. "Perhaps it is just that I am homesick."

Homesick. Oh, Ann knew the feeling—the emptiness, the ache, the memory of pleasant times that could never be repeated. Her thoughts spun back, not to London where she had lived with Theophilus, nor to Chester where she had grown up, but to Denbighshire where she had gone as the happy sixteen-year-old bride of Thomas Yale.

Some quarrels and unhappy times must have marred those years before his sudden death, but she could not remember them. She remembered only the joy in loving and in beginning a family. She remembered sitting in front of a mirror with Maud Porter dressing her hair and flattering her about the sensation she was creating in the neighborhood with her beauty and hospitality. Foolishness, yes, and Maud often exaggerated, but those times she had spent with Maud were as vivid and pleasurable in her memory as the parties themselves had been.

She knew now that such frivolity was wrong. Often she was glad she had not known then, for guilt can erase the shine from any moment. And these moments still shone sweetly in her memory and tugged nostalgically at her heart.

To her daughter she said, "You *are* home, child. You must always consider this your home."

"Yes, but—"

"You'll feel better when Edward returns."

The girl nodded, but Ann had noticed that often these moods persisted even when Edward was there. Could it be that such a vigorous man was too much for so delicate and sensitive a girl? But Ann could not bring herself to ask so intimate a question. Perhaps, she told herself, it was simply the great change—the ocean crossing, the completely new way of life.

Swiftly, Ann made up the bed, plumping the feather mattress and spreading the covers smoothly over it. While she worked, she tried to distract her daughter with talk about the guests the previous evening.

"Ezekial wasn't here. Did you notice? This makes three times in a row."

"You mean Mr. Cheever?"

"Yes. What do you think of him?"

"Mr. Cheever? I don't know. I've never really talked with him. The only thing I can tell from watching him is that he admires you."

Ann felt pleased. This reminded her of the conversations she used to have with Maud Porter at Denbighshire. Then with sudden sternness, as she realized who and what she was now, she said, "Surely, you're not hinting at any impropriety."

"Of course not," young Ann said gravely. "I only meant that he seems to like to talk with you. And I have seen his gaze follow you sometimes when you cross a room. I think he likes you because you do not talk like other women. I mean you do not talk about the household or gossip about other people. You talk about things that are going on in your mind."

"What a nice compliment you have given me."

"Why not? I have always admired you and been proud to have you for my mother." She rubbed her forehead with the back of her hand. "If only I could be like you—full of life, able to talk with anyone, unafraid of the world." Abruptly she stopped speaking, and the little animation that had brightened her face melted away.

Ann made a quick attempt to keep her thinking of things outside herself. "I thought I might walk over to the schoolhouse this morning to find out if anything is wrong. Would you like to go with me?"

The girl shook her head.

"Please. It would be good for you. You have no idea what a beautiful day it is outside."

"No. I'm too tired. And I really don't feel like talking with anyone." Her hands moved with a wringing motion. "And my head aches so."

"Come. Lie down. Perhaps it's rest you need. All this traveling back and forth to Hartford may be too much for you." She settled her daughter on the bed and gently laid a quilt over her. Puzzled and heavy-hearted, she stood looking down at the pale, delicate features. For a moment, until the face turned restlessly away from her, she stroked the girl's damp forehead.

Still feeling disturbed, Ann went downstairs and out onto the street. The velvety air and the smell of damp ground and green growing things lifted her spirits. Across the street Edmund, Mr. Davenport's houseman, was sweeping the stoop. He gave her a respectful bow. Everything seemed so normal that the scene in the bedroom diminished in importance. Surely young Ann would be all right. She just needed time to adjust to a new life, a new country, a new husband, a new womanly role.

At the corner, Ann looked across to the marketplace. A few cows grazed peacefully among the stumps. At the far side, where it was low and damp, a profusion of wild iris made a haze of blue. In the center of the marketplace stood the new meetinghouse: square, with a pyramidal roof. The door was open and Sister Preston emerged with her broom. She had been assigned to sweep once a week for a shilling.

Below the meetinghouse, near the corner of the square, was the watchhouse. Here the guards reported when they finished each night patrol of the town. These patrols, and the militia set up by Captain Turner, gave the townspeople a feeling of security.

As she turned the corner and walked down the street toward the schoolhouse, she noticed that the morning light and wind were different. Being out in the morning gave her an odd sense of freedom. It cheered her and lent vigor to her step as she approached Ezekial's house.

The spring term was over, for the boys were needed in the fields. Ezekial was at the front of his house putting clapboards on a new addition. He was dressed like a common workman in muddied boots and leather breeches and doublet, rather than in the garb of a gentleman. The bulky clothes gave him a look of workmanlike solidity, of outdoor masculinity. Accustomed as she was to thinking of him only as a scholar, she was almost embarrassed by this glimpse of a different side of him. He, too, seemed a little shy.

Not quite looking at him, she gestured toward the house. "I didn't realize your addition was to have been so sizable. Are you expecting more pupils in the fall?"

"No, but it seemed wise to enlarge the house now, now while I have the time, rather than later when I . . ." He left the unfinished sentence dangling in the air between them. His face was redder than a few hours of exposure to the sun would warrant.

Something definitely was wrong. She could see no point in pretending otherwise. "You have not been at our house for three Sunday evenings now, Ezekial. Is something wrong? Have I or has anyone in my household offended you? If so—"

"Oh, no," he said quickly. "Your hospitality has always been warm. I have enjoyed every moment I have spent in your presence." His gaze rested on her with warmth and admiration and an answering warmth rose within her. "But," he went on, his discomfort still evident, "recently I have—have—" He looked away. "It is not good for man to live alone, you know. And here it is frowned upon."

"But, Ezekial, you're a schoolmaster and an elder in the church. Surely no suspicion has fallen on you."

"No. But still—" He paused again, frowning.

Ezekial was a man who never had any difficulty expressing himself. His vocabulary was as extensive as Mr. Davenport's. It was not lack of vocabulary that was holding him back now, she realized. It was an excess of emotion. Her heartbeat hastened, anticipating his next words even before her mind had apprehended them.

Suddenly she remembered having twice seen him talking with a young woman, Mary somebody-or-other. "Is it Mary?"

"Yes. I have been calling on her these past Sunday evenings. And at other times. We are betrothed. In two weeks you will hear the first of the announcements at Sunday meeting."

A picture came into her mind of the pale, light-haired young girl with enormous gray eyes. Very young, soft-spoken, no vivacity. What had they possibly found to say to each other through those long evenings of courtship?

"Well," she said. "Little Mary. A sweet child, though shy." Her tone seemed to lack enthusiasm and she tried to compensate for it by giving him an especially bright look. "I do not know her very well," she added, "but she, too, will be most welcome at our house whenever you wish to bring her." She held out her hand.

He was holding some nails in his right hand. Awkwardly he dropped them into a box, spilling two onto the ground. He took her hand. "Thank you. I'll tell her."

"Bring her soon," she said.

Leaving, she walked beyond his house, turned the corner and continued until she came to the creek. She walked along its banks, stopping now and then to examine some of the delicate white flowers that grew there, until she came to Samuel Eaton's lot.

It was probable that Theophilus's brother would never build on this lot. He had decided to found a new settlement and was getting ready to return to England to try to interest others. Sometimes she wondered whether he would ever return. He was not so determined a person as his brother, not so much a man of action. And surely he must have guessed that John Davenport would expect to have a strong voice in the organization of the church in any new settlement. Perhaps this place would always remain her private refuge.

It was here, she remembered as she settled herself on the rock by the water's edge, that she and Brigid Brewster had first known they could be friends. The new friendship had brightened her winter even more than she had hoped.

She drew up her knees and hugged them, staring at the water, feeling vaguely depressed. Why had Ezekial been so embarrassed, so reluctant to speak of his coming marriage? Why had she not been more pleased to learn of his decision? It was only, she told herself, because she did not see it as a suitable match. It did mean, of course, the end of her friendship with Ezekial, the end, at least, of their stimulating discussions. Her daughter had said that Ezekial admired her. She had known it, or sensed it, and, perhaps without thinking much about it, had actually enjoyed it.

It was wrong, of course, for a man to admire another man's wife or for a woman to enjoy being admired. Early in their marriage Theophilus had discussed this with her. "To admire a woman is to covet her," he had said. "And to covet her is to wish to lie with her."

Ann sighed, thinking back to some of the social gatherings in Denbighshire. In those days she had not thought it wrong to attract men's admiration. Was it not part of God's plan for pairing people off? And if a woman belonged to someone else, could a man automatically shut off his admiration? Her husband Thomas had not objected; he had even been pleased by it. "They're all envious of me," he used to say. "Who among them would not change places with me?"

A shallop in the harbor approached the pier, reminding her of the day she had sailed into the harbor. How full of bright dreams she had been then, dreams of a new way of life, a new kind of partnership with her husband. And what had come of her dreams? She shook her head quickly. It was pointless to brood. She could not complain of her husband's treatment. He was kind and trustworthy and, when they were alone, affectionate. But how rare it was that he ever looked at her with real approval and admiration. What she really wanted, she realized, was not attention from other men: it was simply the approval and admiration of her own husband.

The sun was almost directly overhead now. Hastily, she got up and shook out her skirts. Dinner would probably be on the table by the time she got home and old Mrs. Eaton would be complaining of her absence.

Everyone would want to know where she had been. If she told the truth, much would be said about the virtues of being industrious and the evils of whiling away time in dreaming. If she lied, she would have to spend much time on her knees seeking forgiveness. Mr. Davenport had said at Sunday meeting that there were no circumstances under which a lie was acceptable to God.

Reluctantly she made her way through the heavy undergrowth near the street. She had nearly reached her doorway when she heard someone call out to her. It was Edward Hopkins, back from Massachusetts, well dressed and looking as fit as if he had been on no more than a few hours' journey. Evidently he had been on the shallop she had seen.

"How is my wife?" he asked right away.

"Quite despondent. I think she has missed you."

He looked worried. "Often she is like that even when I'm with her. I wish I knew what to do."

She put her hand on his arm. "I'm sure she'll be all right in time. How was your trip?"

"A good one. I sent some fine skins off to London." The hardships of travel never concerned him; only his accomplishments were important. "Oh, I have something for you. A letter."

She looked at it. It was from Denbighshire and the sight of that name sent a wave of nostalgia over her. "Thank you." Opening it, she glanced quickly at the signature. It was from Maud Collings— no one she knew.

"Dear Mrs. Eaton," the letter read. "Do you remember Maud Porter who used to be your maid at the Yale manor house? If you had not taught me to write, I would not have been able to send you this letter. It always seemed to me that you were somewhat fond of me. I am writing to you now because I am worried about my daughter Lurinda. . . ."

Ann looked up to see that Edward was holding the door open for her. She put the letter back in the envelope to finish later.

JOHN DAVENPORT
SUMMER 1642

In the fall of 1640 the name Quinnipiac had been changed to the more English-sounding New Haven. Ever since then, Theophilus had spent a great deal of time on horseback. He visited the new settlements, helped them to set up their governments, advised them on civil and mercantile affairs, and conferred with their leaders on possible combination with New Haven.

Returning from a walk one warm evening in the summer of 1642, Davenport saw him ride down the street.

"Come in for a few minutes," Theophilus said. "I have a great deal to tell you."

Davenport followed his friend inside, seated himself in a rocker, and watched Theophilus shake out his long dust-covered riding cloak. One candle burned on the long refectory table to light the room. In the air was the lingering smell of boiled turnip.

"You looked tired, my friend," Davenport said.

"Yes. It's been a long day. Even my horse grew weary. He stumbled so many times during the last hour that I feared I'd be thrown."

"Perhaps it would be best if we talked at another time."

"No. It rests me to talk with you. Just let me refresh myself first." He went out to the kitchen and Davenport could hear the splash of water in a basin.

Theophilus returned with his face freshly damp. He had brought more candles from the kitchen and he lighted them and set them on the table. "How quiet it is."

John smiled. "Hardly a cause for complaint."

Theophilus responded with an answering smile. "True. At this hour of the night, and especially after a day rife with problems, one does not miss the prattle of women and children. I can be grateful that my reception committee has retired."

He removed some papers from his leather traveling bag, placed them on the table and sat down. For some time the two men had been working on plans for ways of combining new settlements with New Haven. They were agreed that the main criterion for entry should be that the new settlement would set up a government similar to New Haven's. Only members of approved churches should be allowed to vote or hold office.

In 1640 land had been bought from the Indians about forty miles west of New Haven. It had been settled by the Reverend Richard Denton and about thirty families from Wethersfield, where there had been dissension in the church. This settlement, called Rippowams, but renamed Stamford, had accepted New Haven's jurisdiction.

In 1640 land had also been bought on the eastern end of Long Island from an agent of the Earl of Stirling. This had been settled by a band from Salem led by the Reverend John Young. More independent than the people at Stamford, Southold had not yet joined with New Haven.

Milford was the big problem at the moment. There a government with an unrestricted franchise had been set up. Because of this, New Haven had rejected Milford's first application for admission.

Davenport was especially irritated by Milford's behavior. Milford was led by young Peter Prudden from Herefordshire. When Quinnipiac had first been settled, Prudden and his flock had been given the southwest quarter, one of the best areas in the plantation. Prudden was a fine preacher. Davenport told himself he certainly was not jealous of him. It did seem to him, however, that the young man might have shown more gratitude. Much assistance had been given him, first to build temporary shelters in Quinnipiac, and later to move to the new location. Now Prudden wanted the advantage of being part of New Haven, but the prerogative of running his new plantation in his own way.

As if he had read his friend's mind, Theophilus began talking about the stubbornness of the leaders at Milford.

"Good men, I know," he said, "but misguided. We simply cannot combine with them if we have dissimilar governments. We cannot have all freemen voters in one plantation and none but church members in another."

"It would make for restlessness here."

"Of course."

"Since Prudden is proving so difficult," Davenport said, "it's probably just as well he and his group left here. If they had remained, they surely would have stirred up all kinds of dissension."

"You're right. At least now, if no compromise can be worked out, we won't have to deal with them."

"Compromise? Why should we compromise?"

Theophilus laughed. "You're a good churchman, my friend. But perhaps I am a better politician. The church was founded by God, but civil governments are established by the agreements and compromises of men. If agreement is to occur, then each side has to give a little."

"Why can't we just ignore them? Why even try to bring them into the fold?"

"Because one day they, too, may wish to expand. Then we might find ourselves with far more difficult problems on our hands. They're quite close, you know, and in an ideal spot for further expansion along the coast. We have one thing in our favor, however. If we join a confederacy with the three other important New England colonies, we'll have a lot more protection to offer the new settlements. We'll be in a far better position to bargain."

While Theophilus was talking, Davenport suddenly looked past him and saw Ann Eaton standing in the doorway that led to the stairway. He could not be sure how long she had been standing there.

"Then you think," Davenport said, "that we should join the confederacy?" Surely now that she realized they were speaking of government affairs, she would turn around and go upstairs.

"Oh, yes. Between the Dutch and the Swedes—or for that matter, the Indians—any kind of trouble may develop. If we were members of a confederation, we could bargain with our enemies from a strong position. If necessary, we could retaliate with armed forces from four colonies."

They were already aware of the kinds of trouble the Dutch and the Swedes could make. As a result of Eaton's efforts, a thriving trade had early been established with Virginia, Barbados, Bermuda, and the Azores. But Theophilus had wanted established trading centers that might grow into plantations of importance. In 1641 money had been raised to buy land from the Delaware Indians. A settlement had been built there with a church and some trading posts. Both the Swedes and the Dutch had opposed the settlement and the Swedes, early in 1642, had arrested Captain Lamberton as he had brought his shallop into the port at Delaware. He had been released but not without a severe warning.

The men at New Haven had judged that the Dutch and Swedes were making idle threats. The new settlers bravely remained in their homes. But a little later in the year the Governor of New Amsterdam had sent an armed force to Delaware, had burned the trading houses, plundered the stored goods, and seized some of the men.

The Dutch had made trouble for the Connecticut Colony from the first, especially at Hartford, and when Edward Hopkins had made a business trip to England in the fall of 1641, he had been asked to try to persuade the government to arbitrate with the Dutch. But England was beset with internal troubles, and Edward had returned unsuccessful in the spring of 1642.

New Haven even now had a population of less than eight hundred. It needed, Davenport realized, the strength that an alliance with Massachusetts, Plymouth, and Connecticut would give it.

Davenport looked up from the papers Theophilus had pushed over to him to see that Mrs. Eaton still stood in the doorway. He grew more and more uneasy as his friend continued talking.

"It's also high time," Theophilus said, "that some boundaries were settled. Look at all the trouble Connecticut and Massachusetts are having over that land upriver from Hartford. As we move to the north and the east, we, too, might have disputes with Connecticut. It would be wise to settle these problems before either of us makes any more new plantings."

Davenport half rose from his chair.

"Where are you going?"

"It's best I leave. Your wife awaits."

"She—" Theophilus turned. "Please sit down, John." He went to Ann and kissed her cheek. "How long have you been standing there, my dear? Why did you not speak?"

"If I had spoken, you would have stopped talking. Perhaps I might never have found out all the interesting things that are going on."

"Why had you come down?"

"I couldn't sleep. I've missed you. Then I heard you come in, and I was anxious to greet you and talk with you. I didn't know you had a caller until I got to the bottom of the stairs and heard voices."

"Well, now that you do see I am busy, it would be best for you to return to your room. I'll be up soon."

His hand was on her shoulder. John saw his fingers bend as he attempted to make her turn around. "You will leave us alone now, my dear."

Clearly she was resisting. Her lips were pressed tightly together, her mouth like that of a child who refuses to accept his parents' authority. As their pastor, Davenport could not maintain silence. Straightening his band to ensure proper ministerial dignity, he said in a deep voice, "The first duty of a virtuous woman is obedience to her husband."

"Yes, that is true," she said, and now she smiled as her husband dropped his hand from her shoulder. "But should not a virtuous woman be so totally interested in her husband that she cannot help being interested in all that he thinks and does?"

"Interested, yes—if he chooses to take her into his confidence or ask her advice. But these are not personal business affairs of your husband's that we have been discussing; they are colony affairs that concern everyone in the area."

One of her dark eyebrows lifted. "Then am I not one of those who should be concerned?"

She had a way of twisting everything, Davenport thought angrily. And though she was being completely illogical, he found it difficult to shatter her argument. Accustomed to straightforward thinking, he was poorly equipped to deal with the deviousness of women.

"You should be concerned," he said finally, "with those colony affairs that concern women: with the home and the bringing up of children and with teaching them their letters, fear of God, and obedience to their parents. If you have time left over, you should spend it in meditation and prayer. You would best spend your time learning humility and practicing obedience to your husband and your God."

72

She looked at Theophilus as if she expected he might come to her defense. When he did not, she said coldly, "I am sorry for having interrupted you. Good night." Slipping through the doorway, she pulled the door shut hard behind her.

Theophilus sat down. Not looking at his friend, he leafed through some papers. When the sound of her footsteps in the hallway above had died away, he said, "My wife has a very active mind—for a woman. Like a child's, however, it needs guidance. She questions many things."

Still irritated, Davenport said, "I see nothing to question in our way of life."

"Nor do I. That is why I do not like to be away for long. Then I can resolve these little problems as they come up." He scratched at a mosquito bite on his neck. "Well, let us go on with our talk. Where were we? Was it the confederacy we were speaking of?"

Now that Theophilus himself had changed the subject, Davenport hated to return to the problem of Ann Eaton and to his feeling that Theophilus should be much firmer with her. Perhaps he would get a chance later on to mention all those aspects of her behavior that concerned him. One Sunday in the spring, when Theophilus had been away, she had failed to attend church. Late in the day, however, he had seen her leave her house looking perfectly healthy. Probably, if accused of impropriety, she would have excused herself by saying her unfortunate daughter, who had spent the winter with the Eatons while Edward Hopkins was in London, had required her attention.

Also, several times lately at Sunday meeting he had been sure her thoughts were far away. At one of the most serious moments in one of his sermons, when he was proving an oft-disputed point about the Elect, he had seen a dreaming smile light up her face. It was so out of keeping with his words that he had paused, looking at her. Lifting her chin, she had stared back without a trace of humility.

Worst of all, she spent far too much time away from her home, and spent it in the company of women like Brigid Brewster, who were hardly of her class. Theophilus had spoken of getting a personal maid for her—a young girl who was the daughter of the woman who had served her in Denbighshire. If she had so little to do that she could spend a large part of her time away from home, it hardly seemed that she needed someone to make her duties even lighter.

One day he would talk to his friend about some of these things, but now Theophilus seemed too tired; besides, his mind was on the colony and the confederacy.

"Yes," Davenport said, "we were speaking of the confederacy. You do feel, then, that we should join?"

"Yes, depending, of course, on how willing the other commissioners would be to work amicably together. My feeling is that Thomas Gregson and I should go to the meeting next May as Governor Winthrop has suggested, empowered to vote for union if it seems the best thing for us to do."

"Then I give my approval. Bring it up at the next session of the court and present your idea to the other magistrates." He hesitated, clearing his throat. "It might be best not to mention my approval of the plan. Governor Winthrop has already accused Connecticut of being ruled by clerics. You can come and tell me about it when all is settled." He rose and held out his hand.

Theophilus held it a few seconds in his firm grasp. "How well we work together, my friend," Theophilus said. "How glad I am that we decided long ago to embark on this enterprise together."

Davenport nodded. He was moved, so much so that he made a sudden resolution not to say anything about Ann Eaton's behavior—unless or until it became so flamboyant and unbearable that he could not ethically remain silent.

THEOPHILUS EATON
JUNE 1643

When gentlemen like New Haven's chief magistrate and Thomas Gregson traveled with him on his pinnace, Captain Lamberton always gave them his cabin. Thomas had gone there a few minutes after they had left the Boston wharf, but Theophilus had remained near the stern, his gaze intent on the foaming wake so quickly swallowed in the fog.

Later in the morning a warm June sun would probably break through, but now the wind that came off the land was cold and penetrating. Theophilus drew his cloak closer at the throat as a raw blast rocked the small vessel near the harbor mouth.

Still, he did not seek shelter. As the wind blew against his face, a rare feeling of freedom lightened his heart. He had left the problems of the United Colonies behind in Massachusetts and did not need to take up the duties of New Haven until the journey was over. While he was at sea, he need make no decisions, utter no verdicts. No matter how rough the waves, a man could sleep well at night if he had not that day condemned a man to death. And at sea he was free of all the soft, tender, passionate, querulous voices of women constantly trying to turn him this way or that.

The sea was a man's world. Well . . . not quite. He turned as he heard the familiar rustle of petticoats.

Lurinda had risen from her sheltered place near some huge casks and was tying her hood firmly beneath her pointed chin. Her mother, Ann's servant during her first marriage, had sent the child over as an indentured servant. She had written to beg Ann to take her because the family's pub was no place for a young girl.

75

Looking at her pale, drawn face, Theophilus felt disturbed. She had come to work as his wife's maid, but she looked delicate enough to require care herself. When he had mentioned how thin she was, she had insisted that it was only the long voyage and seasickness that had weakened her.

She stood quite still now, gazing eastward. Was she homesick? Guilt tweaked at his Christian heart. She had arrived in Boston from England a week ago, but he had been too busy for more than a brief conversation with her. After finding her a lodging, he had not seen her again until this morning. It was time they became better acquainted.

"Lurinda," he called out. "Come over here. I want to talk with you. Are you homesick, my child?" he asked as she approached him.

She looked up at him, her sea-green eyes as impenetrable as the fog the changing wind was now chasing back toward the land. "*Home*sick? Actually, sir, we didn't have a home. It was just a pub, you know. We were all together in the kitchen sometimes, but it wasn't a real home."

"*Homesick* is just a word, Lurinda. It isn't usually a place we long for, but people. Surely you miss your family? Your mother especially? I have heard from my wife that she is a very fine woman."

The green of Lurinda's eyes deepened; the black centers were so large he could see his reflection in them. She looked away. "She works very hard."

"I'm glad to hear that. We Puritans believe in hard work. I'm glad to hear she has set you a good example."

Lurinda did not reply.

Finally he said, "You're not a Puritan—are you?"

"No, sir."

"Did your family belong to any church?"

"They might have been members of the Church of England, but we never had a chance to go. Sunday mornings we had all the beds to take care of, and, of course, there was always the cooking."

"I see. I think you should understand that things will be different in New Haven."

"That's what my mother said."

"In New Haven we do no work on the Sabbath, except for the few chores that are absolutely necessary."

"Really?" For the first time since she had come over to him, a faint smile curved her lips.

"The household work is twice as hard on Saturday—cleaning the house and preparing food. Then on Sundays we go to church in the morning and again in the afternoon."

"While the servants rest?"

"Oh, no. The servants go to church too."

"Even if they are not members?"

"That makes no difference. All townspeople go to meeting whether or not they are members—unless they are very sick. They are punished if they do not attend."

"I'm not sure I'd know what to do, how to act. But I suppose if I sit next to Mrs. Eaton and do everything she does—"

It was amazing how little the girl knew. One would think she had never been in church at all.

"Mrs. Eaton, as the wife of the chief magistrate, sits in the first row of the church. You, as a young girl, will sit upstairs in the balcony."

"Oh."

"Let me tell you a little about my household, Lurinda. You have already heard about my wife from your mother. Living with me also are my mother, as well as my daughter by my first marriage. You will be required to obey both of them. Especially my mother. Because of her years, she must be shown every respect. Then my wife's daughter, Mrs. Hopkins, is quite often there. She is . . . rather moody. She has a nervous temperament and sometimes requires delicate handling. Do you understand what I'm saying?"

"I think so, sir."

After a moment she asked, "And do you have only women in your household?"

"No. We have three children: my eldest son Samuel, named after my brother, a younger boy named after me, and a small daughter, Hannah."

"How old are the little boys?"

"They're not so little. Samuel is fifteen, like yourself. He'll be going off to Harvard soon, if his health is good enough. He's had many illnesses, though of a mild nature, since we settled at New Haven. Young Theophilus is twelve and Hannah is ten. We had two other young men in the house: Mrs. Eaton's sons by her first marriage. One of them, David, recently left to settle in Boston. The other, Thomas, is married now and lives outside town on one of the farms."

Her shoulders rose and fell as if she were sighing. She was a strange child. It was impossible to tell what, if anything, was going on in her mind.

"And your brother, Mr. Samuel Eaton," she asked, "is he with you?"

Now Theophilus found himself sighing as he thought of the letter that had crossed with Lurinda from England, the letter from Samuel saying he did not plan to return to America. Samuel had said John Davenport would probably be relieved, yet Theophilus was sure that his friend, like himself, would be saddened by the news.

To Lurinda he merely said, "No. My brother Samuel is in England."

After filing this away in her mind, she said casually, "Who are the other servants?"

"We have a married couple who live with us, and servants we hire by the day. We also occasionally have young girls living with us, just to learn how to run a large household." Reaching out to give her a fatherly pat on the shoulder, he saw her recoil as if fearful of his touch. He was pleased rather than disturbed. Maidenly modesty was a desirable trait. "Don't worry, child. Your duties will not be overly heavy. Although you are a servant, you will be kindly treated."

"Thank you, sir."

Looking beyond her he saw that the sandy-haired boy who had come over from England on the same ship with her had emerged from the hold.

"That lad—what is his name?"

"Tim. Timothy Evans. He was very kind to me on the way over. He felt sorry for me, I guess."

"Timothy," Theophilus called out.

The boy, immediately alert, came toward them. He, too, looked as though he had had a bad voyage. His skin was mottled and his eyes were rimmed with red from exposure to wind and sun. Light-haired people were often affected that way at sea. But despite his poor appearance, he did not appear to be shy. He had good shoulders and he carried himself well.

"Where do you come from, lad?"

"London, sir."

"And your parents—what did they do?"

"They—well, sir, my father died when I was two or three, I

guess. My mother married again and had more children. Her new husband put me out as an apprentice to a leather worker when I was ten."

"You have a trade then."

"Well, yes and no. I was badly treated and I ran away."

"You went back home?"

"No, sir. They'd have treated me rough there, too. No, I found work. Mostly around the docks. That's where I heard so much about America. I didn't think I'd ever be able to get over here until I heard about how some people were willing to pay the passage in return for a few years of work."

"America is a hard country, lad. Your few years of work may be hard ones."

"I won't mind that, sir. I've always worked hard and it hasn't done me any harm."

A good boy, Theophilus thought. If his physical stamina matched his spirit, he'd do well in America. "Who will be your master here?"

"Mr. Robert Newman."

"You'll be doing farm work then. He has such a large barn that we held our public meetings in it before we built our meeting-house. Do you like farm work?"

"I've never been on a farm. But I hope to learn quickly. I'd like someday to have my own farm. Or perhaps deal in furs. The time I spent in the leather trade in London taught me how to know a good pelt."

Theophilus smiled at the boy. He couldn't help wishing his own son Samuel had some of this enterprising commercial spirit. "America holds much opportunity for young men who are willing to work hard, to learn, and to lead godly lives. Are you a church member?"

"No, sir. But I am hopeful that someday I may be."

"I wish you much luck. And the Lord's blessing."

Theophilus glanced toward Lurinda, who had been listening quietly. "And when the time is right, I hope you will marry and have a fine family."

The blotches on the boy's cheeks darkened with embarrassment. Smiling vaguely at each of them, Lurinda walked away. She knelt down by her leather trunk and began unfastening the straps.

The boy recovered his composure quickly. "While I was in Boston, sir, I heard talk about the United Colonies of New England. Does that mean the four colonies will become one?"

Theophilus shook his head. "No. It's just a kind of friendly alliance." He was pleased at the boy's intelligent interest and went on. "We've all been expanding. We had to develop some method for handling boundary disputes. We also needed to plan for mutual defense. With civil war in England, we probably couldn't expect any help from home in case of attack."

His gaze swung out to sea again. When he looked back, he saw that Timothy had his eyes fixed on Lurinda. She had taken a small hand mirror from her trunk and was smiling into it as, with pointed chin lifted, she tucked some stray wisps of red-gold hair under her hood. Her look was rapt and self-communicating, shutting out the rest of the world.

And Timothy looked as all young men in love do—full of misery and longing.

Theophilus said to him, "She mentioned that you were kind to her on the voyage from England. If at some time you should wish to speak for her, do not hesitate to come to me."

Timothy was silent a moment. Then he said, "Thank you, sir. But I rather think that she expects to do better than I."

LURINDA COLLINGS
JULY 1643

It was unusually cool for July. All day a cold rain had fallen, and now in the evening a heavy fog hung over the valley between the red-rock hills. The fog had a soothing effect on Lurinda. It reminded her of England and made the new land seem less strange.

The routine of the Eaton household had gradually become familiar to her. Of all her duties, she was happiest when serving Mrs. Eaton. Her most pleasant duty of the day was taking a small can of Madeira to her mistress before she retired.

She could, on this misty July evening, have taken the Madeira up one of the back stairways. Instead, she chose to go through the great hall.

Young Samuel was there, reading a book by the firelight, with the fire-shine playing on his smoothly combed hair. She hesitated. He was everything her mother had said a young gentleman should be. As she looked at him, she was grateful that her mother had insisted she cross the ocean to come to this household. Samuel frowned as he bent over his book, his lips moving to the sound of words she had come to know were Latin. Latin was something that gentlemen studied.

And Samuel was surely a gentleman. Never in her presence had he made a suggestive remark; never had he tried to pinch her or even touch her; never had he even looked at her the way the men in her father's pub had.

Would he look up now? Would he speak? Did he know she was there? Her heart paused . . . thumped . . . paused again.

"Good night, Master Samuel."

"Good night—uh—Lurinda."

Unlike young Theophilus and Hannah, who loved to talk to her and who sometimes even came to her room at night for the stories of shipwrecks and ghosts she'd heard many a night in the pub, Samuel had little to say to her. He never called her anything but *uh Lurinda.* Even though she had been a part of the household for more than a month, he seemed to have difficulty remembering who she was.

She could hardly blame him. The clothes she and her mother had so carefully sewn, the clothes that had looked so fine before she had left, now looked drab and flimsy compared to the heavy-textured, richly dyed gowns of the Eaton women. Compared to them, she was like one of those dowdy little birds that nested under the eaves of the washhouse and cried "Phoebe" all day long.

Lifting her skirts a little, she went up the stairs. The door to Mr. Eaton's closet was open. He looked up as she went by.

"Good night, my child."

"Good night, sir." Her heart thumped. Whenever she was near Mr. Eaton, she was filled with awe.

He was like God, caring for his children, loving them, but expecting duty and obedience. She had learned a great deal about God since she had come here. The Bible was read and explained and discussed more often, it seemed, than food was served.

The wrath of God, she had concluded, was not an explosive shouting like her father's, but a quiet controlled anger like that which Mr. Eaton displayed on rare occasions. Her father's rages had made a person want to shout back; the chief magistrate's anger made a person hang his head in shame and beg for forgiveness.

Mrs. Eaton was different. She often gave way to a fit of anger or pique. But if the anger had been unprovoked, she always did or said something later to show she was sorry. Although Mrs. Eaton's behavior made Lurinda faintly uneasy, her anger was the familiar kind she'd grown up with.

Still, she approached Mrs. Eaton's door with a certain caution and knocked very lightly.

"It's Lurinda, ma'am."

"Come along in," Mrs. Eaton said pleasantly.

Evidently this was an evening when she was content. It was hard, though, for Lurinda to understand how someone like Mrs.

Eaton could ever be unhappy. She had everything a woman could want: beauty, wealth, a lovely home, healthy children, and a fine husband

She lay now on a couch near the fireplace so that the firelight added to the brightness of the candle. The rosy brightness was reflected on her face, making her look younger than she did in daylight.

"Ah, my Madeira." She smiled and the tightness in Lurinda's stomach went away.

Putting down the book she had been reading, Mrs. Eaton sat up. She did a great deal of reading. More even than sewing. And she read as if she actually enjoyed it. Possibly it was all the reading she did that made her so moody.

Apparently she felt like talking. As she took the wine from Lurinda, she said, "Let's see now. How long have you been here? Sit down, child." She motioned to a chair.

Lurinda sat down. She did it awkwardly and knew it. Embarrassment prickled her skin. At home you only sat down when you were exhausted, and then you collapsed into a chair. But she had noticed recently that when a real lady sat down, she did so with grace, prettily spreading her skirts so they did not wrinkle beneath her. If a lady crossed her legs, she did so at the ankles, allowing her shoes and a bit of colored stocking to show.

"Something over a month, ma'am," Lurinda said, carefully crossing her ankles.

"And do you like it here?"

"Yes, ma'am."

"Does everyone treat you well—the other servants, the other members of the family?"

"Oh, yes. I think perhaps some of the servants—well, they may envy me a little." She saw Mrs. Eaton smile. "The children—they remind me of my own little brothers and sisters. Miss Mary and Mr. Eaton's mother—they're nice to me—but they wouldn't ever treat me like this."

"Like what, Lurinda?"

"Like . . . almost like a lady. Asking me to sit down, talking to me as if I were a friend."

Mrs. Eaton rose. She walked around behind Lurinda, and rested her hand briefly on Lurinda's head.

At first it made Lurinda feel strange to be sitting while Mrs.

Eaton was standing. She uncrossed and then crossed her ankles again the other way, her toe pointing daintily at the green Turkey rug. After all, why should she feel awkward? Perhaps someday her name would be Eaton too. She might even be mistress of this very household. Her chin lifted and she could almost feel her backbone growing more firm.

"Your mother was my friend," Mrs. Eaton said. "I was always very fond of her. She was such a gay creature. It was too bad that—" She stopped. "Is her life very hard, child?"

Lurinda could feel her eyes widening. Did Mrs. Eaton know about her mother's marriage date and the date of her own birth that had taken place far too soon afterward? Just thinking of it, and remembering the night her mother had told her about it, made a hot shame rise inside her.

"Yes, very hard," she said.

"And is your father good to her?"

"Well, he—" She could not bring herself to mention the quarrels, the bitterness between her parents. Her father did not treat her mother well. It was the kind of treatment, her mother had explained, a woman could expect from a man who had been allowed to have his way with her before they were married. "But if you marry someone from the gentry," her mother had said, "and if you have kept yourself pure for him, then you can be sure of respectful, kindly treatment. You'll have a good life, fine clothes, and jewelry. This is the kind of man you can have if you'll do as I say and go to America."

"She wanted something better for me," Lurinda said to Mrs. Eaton. She could still remember how her mother's face had looked—work-hardened and lined and wet with tears, her eyes averted because she could not speak of her past and look at her young daughter at the same time. It had cost her a great deal to talk about her past as she had. She had done it only because Lurinda had so long resisted the idea of coming to America.

"I'm sure you will have a better life here," Mrs. Eaton said. "Tell me, have you seen that young man again—the one who was so kind to you on the boat?"

Lurinda felt a flash of anger. Why did everyone want to pair her with Tim simply because they had arrived on the same boat?

"Only in church."

"If he wants to call on you, he has only to ask my husband."

Lurinda's lips set stubbornly. "I'm not ready to think about marriage, ma'am. And when I am, it may be that I'll want some-one who isn't—who hasn't always been a servant."

Mrs. Eaton lifted her eyebrows, but gradually, as she looked at Lurinda, her expression changed. Lurinda knew that her features were too sharp, but this was mostly because she was still too thin. Her skin was clearer now, however, and some of her roundness had begun to return. Mrs. Eaton looked at her ankles, at the way she was sitting, and something like respect came into her face.

"You may succeed, Lurinda. This is a new land. Anything can happen here. I wish you luck. I'll even help you, if the situation is right. But be careful, child. People who want too much sometimes end up with nothing at all."

And who was to decide that what she wanted was too much, Lurinda asked herself. Not even Mrs. Eaton had the power or knowledge to decide that.

A knock sounded at the door. Lurinda jumped hastily to her feet as Mr. Eaton came in.

"That will be all, Lurinda," Mrs. Eaton said briskly.

Picking up her candle Lurinda went out quickly, not liking her abrupt dismissal. In her little room at the back of the house she undressed quickly, blew out her candle, and lay face down on her bed. Why had she told Mrs. Eaton so much? She never should have said a word. Probably Mrs. Eaton would tell her husband. Perhaps they'd even laugh over her foolish ambition, though it was unlikely they would ever guess exactly whose wife she aspired to be.

Back home when her mother had spoken of her marrying some-one of quality, she had been unable to visualize the kind of man her mother had meant. She had never known men like the Eatons and the Gregsons and the Malbons—the dignified and intelligent men she had met here. On the way over, distressed by the discom-fort of the voyage and frightened by the storms, she had often been bitter about her mother's decision to send her across the ocean.

But her few weeks in the Eaton household had changed her mind. She knew now what her mother meant when she had spoken of a fine home and of gentlemen and ladies. She knew now what she wanted. She wanted a home with many chimneys, with Turkey carpets, with heavy silverplate on display, with a brewhouse that was separate from the main house so that the smell of beer did not linger in every corner and hanging.

Most of all she wanted a husband like young Samuel—someone

good-looking and confident, sure of himself and his place in the world. She clenched her fists and hunched up her shoulders. Someday he'll notice me. He'll see me, really look at me, and realize I'm not just a servant but a girl with all the makings of a lady, a girl who would be a suitable wife for a future leader. The thought of Samuel looking at her with warmth and love and appreciation became so real it was almost like a memory of something that had already happened.

Why had Mrs. Eaton brought up the subject of Timothy? It made Lurinda feel guilty; in fact, she felt that way whenever she saw or even thought of Timothy. Timothy was clearly prepared to love her. Perhaps he already did. But why should he expect her to return the feeling? It was true that she had leaned on him and accepted his favors and protection on board ship, but did that mean she owed him something? She had a right to a new life here in America. Why did he always make her feel as if there were some bond between them?

Uneasy now, she got up from the bed, crossed the room, and opened the window. The fog lingered here and there in the hollows. The wind had blown away enough of the clouds so that a few stars glimmered through the darkness. From the moist ground of the garden below a fragrance arose. Lurinda closed her eyes and breathed deeply.

Was it anise she smelled? Her mother had once told her the seeds were used to provoke lust. She tried to imagine Mr. Eaton with lust shining in his eyes, but it was impossible. Surely all Puritan children were conceived in coolness, in dignity. Surely none of them had been shamefully conceived in a wine-soaked, dance-exhausted May Day moment of sweetness.

Her throat ached. "Oh Mama. Poor Mama," she breathed softly.

ANN EATON/JULY 1643

Old Mrs. Eaton pulled her mouth together like the top of a drawstring bag when she saw Ann getting ready to go out. "Leaving the house again?" she said. "You're away so much that sometimes I wonder who's the mistress of this house—you or I."

A quick response came to Ann's lips. She clamped her teeth hard and let the anger churn inside her. Who was it who gave most of the orders to the servants? Who was it who hastened forward when guests came? Who was it, all too often, who managed to have the first conversation with Theophilus on his return from a journey?

Give her a soft answer, Ann told herself. A soft answer putteth away wrath. Besides, the church said that a woman must consider her mother-in-law her mother. *Honor thy father and thy mother.* It was not easy.

Drawing on her gloves, picking up her basket of knitting, she said in an even voice, "You must remember that many of my visits are not social. I spent yesterday and the day before, as you must know, at the Cheevers' helping with the birthing of the new baby."

"Is that where you're going now?"

"For a few minutes. Just to see how Mary is. Then I may go on to the Brewsters'." She was annoyed with herself because the old woman had succeeded in making her feel guilty. She shouldn't go out so much. She knew that. But she sometimes felt that if she stayed at home all day directing the recalcitrant servants, listening to the hypercritical conversation of her mother-in-law and stepdaughter, finding herself caught in the crossfire of their barbed comments, soothing her daughter who was again visiting them because of the excessive summer heat in Hartford, her reason would surely escape her.

"What about Mrs. Hopkins?" old Mrs. Eaton asked as Ann reached the door.

"What do you mean?" Ann replied, knowing perfectly well what her mother-in-law was implying.

"Am I to be responsible for her?"

"Of course not. She's in her room working on the book she's writing. Lurinda is with her, doing some mending for me. Ann is perfectly all right—she is merely sensitive and easily depressed." God forgive me, she thought. For the girl was not all right.

"You feel Lurinda is capable of handling an emergency?"

"Perfectly."

She *was* very pleased with Lurinda, she thought as she went out. She was a quiet, intelligent girl who had already unconsciously flattered her mistress by imitating her mannerisms and inflections of speech.

It was pleasant, too, to be able to talk about the old Yale manor house and the people she'd known so well when she'd lived there.

As she walked down the street toward the Cheever house, she felt in her bag to see whether she had the book with her. Yes, it was there. Its presence made her feel like someone planning treason. And in a way she was. The book had made her realize how little she had exercised independence of thought in the past. Her husband, John Davenport, and all the elders of the church had so impressed her with their rightness that it had never before occurred to her to question any of the tenets of their faith.

Ezekial came to the door when she knocked, holding the new baby. Their second child, just barely able to walk, was sitting in a damp circle on the floor. Their first baby, Ezekial, had died in infancy. Neither Ezekial nor his wife had taken this easily.

"How good of you to come again," Ezekial said, speaking almost in a whisper. "Mary is asleep. She'll be sorry she wasn't awake to talk with you."

More likely she'll be relieved, Ann thought, for she had long felt that Mary did not like her. After his marriage Ezekial had brought his wife to a few of the Eatons' Sunday night gatherings. Gradually they had come less often. Although Ann had gone out of her way to make them feel welcome, they had not come at all during the past two winters.

But perhaps she was only imagining the dislike. Mary was young and not much of a talker—the kind who probably felt most secure in her own home. When she had visited the Eatons, she always sat quietly, a tense look on her face, her soft gray eyes following Ezekial as he moved easily among the other guests. She had never expressed an opinion. Her silence could have been caused by shyness, Ann conceded, but it could also have been that she had no opinions. How boring for Ezekial, who so loved discussion and argument, to spend his days with such a woman.

Ann swept the kitchen and changed the older child. By that time, the low voices had awakened Mary. When she called out, both Ezekial and Ann went into the next room to see how she was. Smiling faintly, Mary said to Ann, "Oh, I didn't expect to see you here again."

Ann said warmly, "You're not very strong yet. You can still use a neighborly hand. Do you want the baby now?"

Mary nodded and Ann placed it close to her. She put her hand on Mary's forehead. It was dry and very warm. The girl was delicate; the birth had been long and painful. Her face now was the gray-white of the oyster shells in the field below the town. She would not survive the birth of very many children, Ann felt, and in her sturdiness and vitality, she felt a surge of pity for the younger woman.

After Mary had nursed the baby and her eyelids had begun to droop, Ann slipped away and went out to the kitchen. Ezekial was busily shelling some beans. The little girl was just taking the brown book out of Ann's bag, which she had left on the floor near the table.

Ann bent down and snatched the book away. She held it guiltily against her, aware of Ezekial's curious gaze. "Excuse me for being so abrupt with the child," she said, "but this is rather personal, rather private."

"She must learn not to touch things that do not belong to her." He slapped the child lightly and made her sit facing the corner.

"I don't like to be the cause of a child's being punished," Ann said.

"She must learn," he said sternly. And then, still rather sternly, he said to Ann, "May I see the book?"

It would have been easy to shake her head and put the book back, but something perverse—a desire for argument, or perhaps even a wish to provoke him to an outburst—made her hand it to him.

"It isn't some new book from England, if that's what you're thinking," she said. "In fact, as an elder of the church, you'll probably disapprove."

He opened it, looked a long time at the title page, looked back at her with thoughtful, unsmiling eyes, and then opened the book here and there and read. Her nerves tightened in the long, uneasy silence. He did not seem pleased. Obviously no one in this household found her pleasing today. She felt as guilty as the child quietly sniffling in the corner.

Closing the book, he handed it back to her. "Where did you get this?"

"A woman in the Bay Colony gave it to me. Lady Moody."

"Are you in sympathy with its teachings?"

She drew in her breath. "Yes. I think so."

"Have you discussed this with your husband?"

Almost angrily she thrust the book down into the bag inside her knitting. "When could I? He's never home. Off to Massachusetts, off to Southold, off to Milford or Stamford. When he comes back, he's busy with town problems. Or has to confer with Mr. Davenport."

"Then have you talked with Mr. Davenport?"

"I do not wish to. Not just yet. When I have fully made up my mind, then perhaps—"

"It might be better if you talked with him now, while the questions are forming in your mind. Surely as you read this, you must have some doubts about the statements it makes."

"I have few doubts. After reading this, I cannot believe that babies should be baptized. How can anyone believe it? The babies have not experienced a desire for baptism. Baptism should be limited to believers. Nor can I believe that Christ's death was atonement for only a few elected people."

He stroked his beard thoughtfully. "These are the beliefs expressed by people who are sometimes now called Baptists. They are contrary to our own Puritan beliefs. Are you aware of that?"

"Yes." She smiled tentatively. "And I realize that as an elder of the church you could report me."

"You have put me in a difficult position."

"But you will not report me—will you?"

His face remained stern. "How do you know?"

Was it bravado or was it some sense that went beyond the others? "You will not," she said.

"For the moment I will pray about it. Please think it over very carefully. If you, the wife of the leading man in the settlement, should show signs of a weakening Puritan faith, it could have an adverse effect on everyone in the town." His sternness melted a little. "Remember, the worst crime is to try to turn others from the faith."

She picked up her bag, preparing to leave. "Perhaps we can talk about it again some time." When he nodded, she added, "Don't make her stay in the corner."

Picking up the child, he held her close to him. Ann now saw a gentleness in him. It had been there all the time beneath his sternness. If he was overly strict with his pupils, she thought as she went out again into the summer heat, it was because he felt they needed discipline in order to learn.

Brigid Brewster was waiting for her, her freckled face full of cheer. After sending the servant girl out to the summer kitchen, they sat down at the table and began to talk eagerly. Mr. Brewster was at his farm. "How I love the warm weather when he goes off for the whole day," Brigid said. "When he's around, it's hardly safe to think."

The two women had long exchanged confidences without fear. Ann had lent Brigid her book and they had discussed it at length. They enjoyed feeling different, being more perceptive and knowledgeable than the others in the plantation.

Ann told her about showing the book to Ezekial.

"Why did you do that?" Brigid asked, frowning.

"I don't know. It was just an impulse. But he won't report me."

"How do you know he won't?"

"I don't know. I just feel that he won't."

Brigid poured beer for both of them. Picking up some mending, she moved to the rocker by the fireplace. "It would almost seem," she said thoughtfully, "as if you wanted to be caught."

Ann was startled. But after a moment she said, "Perhaps I do. Or maybe, at least, this is a sign that I am about ready to make some public gesture. Last Sunday at meeting, when those two babies were being baptized, I could hardly stay in my seat. I felt like getting up and walking out."

"You wouldn't!"

Ann sipped her beer thoughtfully. "I would. At least I think I would."

"What if they punished you in some special way? What if they banished you?"

"Then I'd leave."

"I'll tell you what we'll do," Brigid said. "If they banish you, I'll get up and tell them that you made a Baptist out of me, too, and then we'll go off somewhere and start a new plantation together."

Outside the kitchen door, the floor creaked. Putting her finger to her mouth, Brigid got up and tiptoed to the door and opened it quickly. Her maid stood there, her mouth open with dull surprise.

"Well, my girl, what do you want?" Brigid said briskly. "Did we fill your head with a lot of nonsense to take directly to Mr. Davenport? That was why we spoke as we did. It was to test you. We knew you were there. Here now, go to the town well and get some water. While you're gone we can talk about things that really interest us instead of putting on a show just for you."

After she was sure the girl was gone, Ann said uneasily, "Do you think she believed you?"

"Probably not. But it was worth trying. Let's have some more beer. All the way to the top?"

"Yes, indeed."

"So . . . we really can talk now," Brigid said. "What did you think of our pastor's sermon last Sunday?"

"Young Theophilus often speaks with more wisdom—and the boy as yet has little wisdom in him."

Ann sipped some more beer, feeling relaxed and happy. She still had not yet begun knitting. Must a person never be idle? Must the fingers always be in motion? At last she said, "Did you go to the whipping last week?"

"The one for unnatural filthiness? No. I cannot bear those whippings." She looked up. "Did you?"

"No. I, too, cannot bear them."

"My son went," Brigid said. "He told me they were cruelly whipped. He said he'd rather fall into the hands of the Turks than into the hands of those who render justice in New Haven."

"Poor fellows," Ann said. "Had they been good-looking enough to have attracted women of their own, they might never have engaged in such practices."

"But those who make the laws do not consider such things. They are concerned only with punishing, with constantly setting examples. I can only say I hope they never choose to make an example of me."

"Or me."

Brigid looked at her with concern. "Then use care in your behavior. Talk freely with me, but forget about making a public gesture."

Thoughtfully Ann lifted the cup of beer to her lips. "If I ever do make one," she said at last, "it won't be because I have planned to do so. It will be because a voice within me tells me that it is the right and only thing to do."

THEOPHILUS EATON
AUGUST 1643

On a simmering August afternoon Theophilus came riding in from Milford. The mosquitoes in the low wet places had been dreadful. His shirt stuck to his perspiring body and the insect bites itched and throbbed. Tying his horse to the post in front of the house, he called out to his manservant Anthony before going inside.

Lurinda was dusting the great hall as he entered. She had changed a great deal in the three months she had been in his household. The contours of her face were now softly fleshed and tinted and her body seemed to move with more grace.

"Where is my wife?" he asked.

"She is out calling on a friend, sir."

"Yes, she's out again," said his mother, coming into the room behind Lurinda. "You may leave, Lurinda. I'd like to speak alone with my son."

Lurinda made a brief half-curtsy before starting for the kitchen. She really was quite charming. And very polite and respectful. He asked her to take some warm water to his room.

"I don't trust that girl," his mother said. "She'll try to hear as much of our conversation as possible so she can report back to your wife."

Theophilus held back a sigh. He must try to be as patient with his household problems as he was with town problems. If only they would give him a chance to refresh himself before they assailed him. He was tired. Perhaps it was to be expected at fifty-three, but he told himself it was the endless travel that drained his strength.

Once the new settlements were operating under one government, he would not have to be away so much. His tiredness was satisfying, at least, for his work had begun to bear fruit.

Since the United Colonies had been formed, the towns around New Haven had seen it would be to their advantage to join with New Haven. Stamford, Guilford, and Southold, Long Island, had qualified by setting up governments like New Haven's. But in Milford the six men who had been admitted as burgesses without church membership refused to give up their voice in the government. It was discouraging. Theophilus had spent most of the summer making trips back and forth trying to settle the matter.

"Can we talk later, Mother?" he said.

"*She* may return. Though perhaps I don't have to worry. When you're not here, she often stays out until suppertime."

"She's lonely, Mother. Remember, in England she had many friends. She needs to have women to talk to."

"Am I not a woman? Is your daughter not a woman? Why cannot she stay here and talk with us?" When she saw Theophilus was about to interrupt, she added quickly, "But that is not why I wanted to see you. It is not only her being away so much. But when she goes out she associates with women who are not of her class."

"Like whom?"

"Brigid Brewster for one. She has a reputation for speaking out against things, for making fun of those in authority."

"Of me?"

"I can't prove anything. But she doesn't have the quality I'd like to see in a friend of your wife's. And two other women visit there also—a Mrs. Leach and her daughter Mrs. Moore. They're not ladies by any definition of the word. Mrs. Moore isn't even a church member." She touched Theophilus on the chest, irritating a swollen insect bite. "If your wife must be out so much, she should be associating with women like Mrs. Goodyear and Mrs. Davenport."

Theophilus agreed with his mother about Ann's associating with women of a lower class. If he became governor, such socializing would be even more unsuitable. "I'll speak to her," he said.

"Wait, don't leave yet. That's not all. When she's here she's always flying into a temper. She disputes everything Mary and I say. She does not treat me with the respect due a mother. She has even accused Mary of unseemly conduct."

"I'll speak to her about that, too, Mother."

"You always say that, son, but her behavior does not improve. In fact, it grows worse. I cannot help wondering if you really *do* speak to her." With eyes modestly downcast, she added, "A wife can sometimes use her feminine wiles to turn away a husband's criticism and soften his righteous anger." She looked up again. From the expression on her face he sensed she was about to brandish a really important charge. "Perhaps you do not think it significant, my son, that she keeps this household in a turmoil, but what would you think if you learned she was about to stir up the towns-people?"

"In what way?"

"Supposing she began to differ from the tenets of our faith? Supposing she began to spread her ideas and created dissension in the church?"

He felt a prickling inside his collar that was caused by more than perspiration and heat. "What are you implying?"

"I cannot prove anything. But from little things I've seen and overheard, I think she may hold Baptist views."

He was quiet for a long moment as he absorbed this new and discomfiting news. Finally he said, "Thank you, Mother, for telling me all this. I think I'll wash and change my clothing now."

After he had changed, he went to his study to go over accumulated papers. He was hardly settled at his desk, however, before a messenger appeared with a letter from Edward Hopkins, now Deputy Governor of the Connecticut Colony at Hartford. It dealt with a situation already worryingly familiar to Theophilus.

Miantonomo, Chief of the Narragansetts, a trusted friend of the English during the Pequot War, was entangled in an endless saga of Indian revenge with Uncas, Chief of the Mohegans. Earlier in the year a Mohegan had been murdered by a relative of Miantonomo's. Uncas had taken revenge, killing several warriors and plundering and burning.

When Miantonomo had begun to plan his revenge, he had presented his case to the authorities at Hartford and Boston, in accordance with treaty pledges. He asked permission to attack Uncas. Governor Haynes of Connecticut had refused permission. Governor Winthrop of Massachusetts had replied that the English would leave him free to choose his own course.

Miantonomo had attacked and had been captured by the Mohegans. Fearful of reprisals from the English if he killed his prisoner, Uncas had taken Miantonomo to Hartford for judgment. Hopkins said in his letter that they had told Uncas they would have the commissioners decide Miantonomo's fate at the first formal meeting of the United Colonies in September.

They were holding Miantonomo, Hopkins went on, because there were rumors that he had been planning to attack not only the Mohegans, but also the English. A united Indian attack against the British had been rumored all summer, and settlers had gone from house to field each day wearing arms. Now the evidence seemed to be stronger.

Theophilus called a servant and sent a message to John Davenport to ask when he could see him. The answer came that Mr. Davenport would be free to see him at seven and Theophilus went down to the great hall where the table was being set for supper.

Young Samuel sauntered in, jaunty and well-clad, looking as if he had not done an hour's work all day. Theophilus was tempted to ask him what he had done, but he feared the answer might necessitate a lecture, and at the moment he preferred to avoid a confrontation.

Besides, the boy seemed to want to talk of town affairs and was curious about what had gone on in Milford. It was a pleasure to talk to him and to look at his handsome, attentive face.

Theophilus had just finished recounting the Milford affair when Ann came in.

"Oh, Theophilus." She dropped her knitting bag and rushed to him, impetuously throwing her arms around his neck, as abandoned as if Samuel were not there observing them. Though stirred by her greeting, Theophilus took her hands and kissed her chastely.

"How good it is to see you," she said. She frowned, studying his face. "But you do look tired, my poor dear Theophilus." Tracing the deep line from his nose to the corner of his mouth with her forefinger, she said, "When can we talk? I have so much to ask you, to tell you. Can we be alone, perhaps right after supper?"

"I . . . wish I could be with you then. Unfortunately, I have an appointment with—"

"John Davenport, of course."

"On town business."

"Of course."

"I'll try to discuss it quickly and return to see you before you retire."

"Oh, I almost forgot," Samuel said. "Did you know that Uncas has taken Miantonomo prisoner? Instead of killing him, he took him to Hartford to let the English decide what to do with him?"

"Where did you hear that?" Theophilus asked in a sharp voice.

"Over at the square. Some of the men at the watchhouse were talking about it."

Theophilus could feel annoyance prickling his skin, further irritating the insect bites. How often it was that news was known to all before any announcement was made. He was also annoyed at the idea of Samuel's loitering near the watchhouse where men of lower class were likely to gather.

"What will they do to him?" Ann asked. "Will they let him go?"

"Kill him, probably," Samuel said.

"They'll do neither one," Theophilus said. "They're turning the matter over to the commissioners of the United Colonies. It will be decided in September."

"Surely the English don't want the blood of Miantonomo on their hands?" Ann said. "A man who has always been their friend?"

Theophilus shrugged, trying not to show his own uneasiness. "If it is true that he was planning to attack the English after defeating Uncas, then we certainly would be within our rights."

"What will be your proof—the testimony of the Mohegans?"

"We will have to have proof. That is all I can say."

Ann gave him a look that seemed to be indicting him for decisions not yet even reached. After she had left the room, Theophilus placed his hand on his son's shoulder. "Women," he said, "are notably unrealistic. They judge only with their hearts, and often, feeling pity, they carelessly overlook conspiracy and evil."

Samuel nodded, his lips thrust forward as if silently forming words of agreement.

It was true, though, Theophilus thought: women did sacrifice reason to emotion. Even his mother, though far more reasonable than most women, was turned this way and that by the vagaries of emotion. It was hard to deal rationally with them. He looked forward to seeing John Davenport after supper, to quiet, reasonable talk, to decisions judiciously reached.

And their meeting turned out to be as pleasurable as he had anticipated. Although they went over weighty problems, and although his day had been long and tiring, he left the Davenport home after two hours feeling unburdened and refreshed.

His wife had more candles burning in the bedroom than most families used in a week. When he entered, she rose and came to him. He put his arms around her, and she put her cheek against his.

"I really did miss you, Theophilus. I wish you didn't have to be away so much."

He led her back to the couch. Sitting down, taking her hand, he said, "Perhaps after all the towns have been united I'll be able to spend more time here with you."

She shook her head. "No. You'll be buying more land, founding or sponsoring more settlements, then bringing them into the fold. As your dreams begin to come true, you always build bigger dreams."

He knew she was right, and because she had been so perceptive he felt uncomfortable, as if she had exposed him in his nakedness. Changing the subject, he said, "What did you do while I was gone?"

"What does a woman do all day? Housekeeping is a never-ending task."

"Then you did not go out at all?"

"I did not say that. Of course I went out. Occasionally in the afternoon I made calls."

"On whom, may I ask?"

"You are not usually so interested in such details." Her look was amused, yet it was an amusement edged with anger. "I suppose you were talking with *her*. Honestly, Theophilus, I don't know why she should resent my leaving the house now and then in the afternoon when my work is done."

Theophilus smiled to himself. A moment ago she had said housekeeping was a never-ending task; now she was saying her work was done by afternoon.

"She does not resent your leaving the house. I'm sure she realizes that you miss the social life you had in England. She is only concerned because the name Eaton stands for something in this town; she feels, and I do also, that when you go out it should be to associate with people of your own social standing."

"Brigid Brewster is a good woman."

"How about Mrs. Leach and Mrs. Moore?"

"I know them less well. But I have no reason to think that they, too, are not good women."

"It is said that they—all three of them—are sometimes critical of those who order the affairs of our town and church."

She stared at him.

"It is also said," he continued, "that you and they hold views which say that infant baptism is sinful and that, worse still, atonement is for all. Is that true?"

Her eyes were very large and dark. "Which statement—all of them, or the last one?"

"All of them," he said sharply.

"I don't like your tone of voice. We're not in court. You're not the magistrate in our bedroom." She stood up, went to her chest, and picked up a hairbrush. Slowly, with rhythmic strokes, she brushed her long dark hair.

He started to speak but she lifted her hand. "I'll tell you something, Theophilus. I was looking forward to talking with you this evening. I wanted advice. And I wanted it on some of the very questions you've hurled at me. But when you speak and I hear nothing but words from John Davenport or my mother-in-law, I lose all interest in talking with you." She turned her back on him. "Please leave me alone now."

He stood up. The candlelight shimmered on her long dark hair and outlined her erect form in the thin material of the rail. He sensed a certain rightness in what she was saying. This feeling was quickly buried, however, under a quickening anger that she could so easily manage to put him in the wrong. "Accuse the accuser," he said. "It is ever the way of the guilty."

"Guilty? Guilty?" She put the brush down hard. "You don't know whether I'm guilty or not. You never talk to me or listen to me. All you ever do is hurl accusations at me. You never—"

"Be still," he said. "As you suggested, I'll leave you alone now. Obviously you're too overwrought for rational discussion."

He went out, closing the door slowly and quietly, giving her plenty of time to call out in a contrite voice for him to come back. All was silent. A fine welcome, he thought, a fine homecoming.

LURINDA COLLINGS
AUGUST 1643

Lurinda found, to her surprise, that she liked the Sabbath best of all. Even the long hours at the meetinghouse could not dull the special quality of change after six days of confinement to household tasks.

She was expected to help with the heavy Saturday work when bread was baked, beans were prepared, floors were swept and scrubbed, and fresh sand was put down in the uncarpeted rooms. But at sundown all work ceased. For the twenty-four hours that followed, she was as much a lady as anyone who bore the name of Eaton.

At sundown on Saturday the Sabbath began. The family and all the servants gathered in the great hall and Mr. Eaton prayed and read from his Geneva Bible. He read in a voice so deep and resonant it made Lurinda's spine tingle. It was like hearing the voice of the Lord who, she had come to know, was great in His love but terrible in His anger. Mr. Eaton paused now and then in the chapter and, using the notes printed in the margin of his Bible, explained the more difficult passages.

Lurinda always listened with care, her eyes darting from person to person as they answered questions, noting accents and expressions. When finally Mr. Eaton addressed a question to her, she nearly always answered correctly and was rewarded by a nod of approval. It made her feel almost as if she were one of his daughters.

Some of the chapters were boring and hard to understand; some, like those dealing with punishments for sins, were so horrifying that she trembled for hours afterward. But some were wonderful stories of love. She thought about them as she went about her work and when she lay in bed at night.

Best of all she liked the story of Ruth who, after her husband's death, had said to her mother-in-law, "Entreat me not to leave thee, nor to depart from thee, for whither thou goest, I will go, and where thou dwellest, I will dwell. Thy people shall be my people and thy God my God."

Lurinda felt like that about Mrs. Eaton; she would have followed her anywhere. But when she repeated the words to herself at night, she was really saying them to Samuel.

Later in the same Bible story, Boaz, a well-to-do kinsman, had awakened one night and had found Ruth anointed and in her raiment lying at his feet and had known he wanted her for his wife. Just so, Lurinda was sure, would Samuel one day awaken to all that was pleasing in her. And, being a gentleman like Boaz, he would be most of all pleased by the knowledge that she was a virtuous woman.

When Mr. Eaton was gone on a weekend, as he was this week, it really did not seem like the Sabbath. Old Mrs. Eaton read the Bible and questioned the family and servants imperiously. Lurinda could not properly answer the question that was put to her. She felt annoyed less with herself than with the woman who had deliberately presented her with an especially difficult question.

At eight o'clock on Sunday morning Jarvis Boykin beat a drum in the tower of the meetinghouse and then through the streets of the town. After breakfast Lurinda put on her best petticoat and gown and waited—supposedly meditating and praying—for the second drum, which was beaten at nine. When the drum sounded again, everyone started for the meetinghouse. When Mr. Eaton was home, he always walked first with his elderly mother clinging to his arm. Behind him went his wife, and behind her the young people, and last of all the servants.

Lurinda usually managed—as she did this morning—to take a position not far behind young Samuel where she could worship his straight, gentlemanly back and shapely legs in colorful stockings. He had such a jaunty way of walking. How wonderful it must be to be an Eaton, to know that everyone would automatically respect and admire you.

Once he turned and looked back, his gaze sweeping carelessly past her. She lifted her pointed chin, hiding the disappointment that flooded her each time he failed to notice her.

She suspected that he was not yet ready for love. Her mother had told her that girls were ready at a much earlier age than men. If that were true, then someday he would be ready. Someday she would hand him something or come into a room and he would look at her and suddenly see her as a woman, just as Boaz had seen Ruth.

At the corner the little procession crossed diagonally to the marketplace. The Davenports, who had come up the opposite side of the street, also crossed, and the women exchanged polite conversation. Mr. Davenport, of course, was not with them. He used an exclusive path that led from the back of his house up to the street bordering the square; thus his meditations were not disturbed as he walked.

At the door of the meetinghouse, the group divided. The older people remained downstairs; the younger ones went up to the balcony. The young men sat on one side and the young women on the other.

Downstairs it was very crowded. After the people with assigned seats had taken their pews, with those of highest rank sitting farthest forward, others came in with stools and chairs and filled the aisles. The last rows were taken by the militia who had earlier paraded back and forth outside with a great clanking of arms. Often they were noisy: whispering and occasionally giving forth bursts of laughter. Because they were there for the defense of the people, they were less strictly disciplined than the others. And this summer, fearful of a united Indian uprising, the people especially needed to feel protected.

Mrs. Eaton sat in the first row of the church with her mother-in-law behind her. Mr. Eaton, when he was there, sat in the first row on the men's side. As she looked down at Mrs. Eaton, Lurinda felt a glow of pride. If she was not a member of Mrs. Eaton's class, she was at least her personal servant, and that made her just a little better than any other servant in the plantation.

The church service was long, but parts of it were interesting to Lurinda. She was gradually getting to know some of the people, and she learned more about them as bills were read asking for prayers for the sick, for the recently bereaved, or for those about to make a voyage.

Coming marriages were also announced. As Lurinda listened, she discovered that even when she did not know the people, it was easy to tell by looking around the gallery whose names were being read. When *our* names are read, she thought—Lurinda Collings and Samuel Eaton—I'll sit up straighter and hold my head high like a lady. I won't blush and smirk like a common servant girl.

If they are read. Perhaps it was all just a dream—the idea that some day he would notice her, appreciate her, want her. Perhaps her mother was wrong about young gentlemen. How many, after all, had she known?

Silence fell now except for some murmurs from the soldiers. Mr. Davenport began to pray. He prayed for about fifteen minutes. Following his prayer, Mr. Hooke, the teacher of the church, read from the seventh chapter of Matthew:

"Therefore by their fruits ye shall know them. Not everyone that sayeth unto me, Lord, Lord, shall enter the kingdom of Heaven but he that doeth my Father's will which is in Heaven. Many will say to me in that day, Lord, Lord, have we not by Thy Name prophesied? and by Thy Name cast out devils? and by Thy Name done many great works? And then will I profess to them, I never knew you: depart from me, ye that work iniquity."

Mr. Hooke looked earnestly at the assembly. "Who is Jesus talking about here? He is talking about hirelings and hypocrites who fear God with their lips rather than their hearts. Jesus is saying to them, 'I never accepted you to be my true ministers and disciples.' "

Looking down from the gallery, Lurinda noticed that Mrs. Eaton was rubbing her temple with the back of her wrist. A moment later, she dropped her notebook on the floor.

Mr. Hooke paused until she had picked it up. "And how do you know," he continued, "whether *you* have been accepted? Ah, the Bible tells us: 'By their fruits ye shall know them.' God will prosper you if He has accepted you to be one of his true disciples."

When Mr. Hooke had finished, the ruling elder announced the congregation would sing Psalm Sixty-one. Lurinda rose happily, glad to move her cramped body. The people sang out, though not exactly in unison nor even in the same key: "Hear my cry, O God, give ear unto my prayer. From the ends of the earth will I cry to Thee. . . ."

After everyone had sat down, Mr. Davenport came forward to

preach on the doctrine that Mr. Hooke had explained. He began by telling the assembly that God had decided even before they were born that certain people had been elected.

"Indeed," he said, "as Paul tells us in Ephesians, God chose certain of us for holiness even before He made the world." He looked around the church. "Now some of you may be asking yourselves, 'Why am I not one of the Elect?' But ask yourself these questions: How many lead cows are there in a herd? How many lead geese are there in a flying flock? God knows our natures. He knows that ever since Eve we have been born full of sin. We need leaders among us who are better than the rest, who can guide or advise."

Lurinda tried to concentrate on all he said, for she knew that when Mr. Eaton returned he would question everyone in the family and household on the sermon. She ought to take notes, as so many of the women of quality did.

"We can tell who the Elect are," Mr. Davenport continued, "for God favors their fortunes. They are the ones whose decisions influence people; they are the ones whose business ventures are profitable; they are the ones whose actions are sweet in the eyes of the Lord. Yea, they labor in the vineyards of the Lord and the grapes they produce are bountiful and full of the sweetness of God's love."

On and on he went. Lurinda found herself losing the thread. How was it possible to be sure she was not one of the Elect? Perhaps she had not yet lived long enough to show evidence of God's favor. If she should one day bear the name of Eaton, who would dare to say she was not one of the Elect?

The August heat penetrated the building and people's faces began to shine. Mr. Davenport's voice seemed to melt into the moist atmosphere, increasing its heat and heaviness. Lurinda could feel her skin prickling under the layers of confining garments.

Was someone looking at her, or did she only imagine it? Was it simply the fervent hope that one day she would look up and find Samuel's gaze resting upon her with desire and love? Modestly she turned her head ever so little and cast a sidelong glance across to the other balcony. Samuel, his expression bored and blank, was looking at his fingernails. Down at the other end of the balcony she saw Timothy Evans. When he saw her look at him, he smiled. She smiled back, vaguely, quickly, before turning away.

Sometimes the worshipful way he looked at her made her uneasy. It had taught her something, though, for she had been careful, despite her great longing never to look at young Samuel that way. She glanced back at Samuel. He had stopped looking at his fingernails and was rubbing the back of his neck.

Would the sermon never end? Turning back to Mr. Davenport, hoping she had not missed any of his points, she saw him open his Bible. "One last word from Peter," he said. " Wherefore, brethren, give rather diligence to make your calling and election sure: for if ye do these things, ye shall never fail. For by this means an entering shall be ministered unto you abundantly into the everlasting kingdom of our Lord and Savior Jesus Christ.' "

He closed the Bible. "Now," he said, "does this mean that *anyone* who labors diligently in the vineyard of the Lord shall be elected? No. Notice that the words say 'make your calling and election *sure.*' . . . God means that even though we are elected and this election cannot be changed, we must confirm it by the fruits of our spirit. We must be godly and patient and kind. We do this because we know God's purpose in electing us. And remember this: The principal end of our election is to praise and glorify the grace of God."

Bowing his head, he stepped back. Mr. Hooke rose and prayed. When he had finished, Mr. Davenport again stepped forward. He lifted his arms. They looked, with the black material of his vestments draped down from them, like great black wings.

"Brethren of the congregation, there is time now for baptism of any babes whose parents wish to have them brought into the faith. Will all such parents, with their babes, now come forward."

Two young couples, each carrying a baby, came down the aisle, threading their way among the chairs and stools that filled it. Some of the people rose, noisily scraping chairs, to make way for them.

Mr. Davenport, his face gleaming, took one of the babies and cradled it in the crook of his left arm. Sometimes at such moments babies wailed, but on this day no cries were heard. Mr. Davenport dipped his right hand in the basin.

Suddenly Mrs. Eaton rose. Lurinda saw her turn and start down the aisle toward the back of the church. Again came the noisy scraping of chairs and stools as the startled people made way for her. Heads turned; a questioning murmur arose.

Until the door had closed behind her and the commotion had ceased, Mr. Davenport stood motionless, his hand suspended above the basin, the water running off his fingertips in little glistening drops. Then calmly, as if the ceremony had not been interrupted, he dipped his fingers again in the basin, sprinkled the baby's head, and blessed it in the name of the Lord.

Lurinda had never before seen anyone leave the meetinghouse except for those times once a month at afternoon service when those who were not church members had to leave so that the others could take communion. Alarmed, she looked over at Samuel who was frowning and biting his lip.

What had been wrong with Mrs. Eaton? Was she unwell? Yet she had never looked more healthy. Her cheekbones stained with color, her eyes darkly bright, she had looked younger and lovelier than ever before.

JOHN DAVENPORT
SEPTEMBER 1643

Theophilus and Mr. Gregson had gone this morning to Boston for the first meeting of the commissioners of the United Colonies. John Davenport sat now in his study going over his notes of the meeting held the night before.

The question of what to do with Miantonomo, who was still being held in Hartford, had been carefully considered. How could they decide whether he was a true friend of the English? He had been their ally against the Pequots, but the Pequots had been his enemies, too. In the end, the two commissioners had been given free rein to settle the matter according to the evidence presented.

Miantonomo and a possible Indian uprising were allied with the Swedish and Dutch problems. The English had forbidden all trading with the Indians in arms or any instruments of iron. But, behaving with great insolence, the Dutch had continued to sell them to the Indians. They had also bought goods stolen from the English, harbored fugitives from English justice and filed off their irons, and had driven off some settlers from Connecticut who had begun plantations on Long Island.

Neither the Dutch nor the Swedes had made restitution for their abominable behavior at Delaware the previous year. They had jailed Captain Lamberton and tried to bribe his men to testify against him. Damages from the burning of New Haven's trading houses there were estimated at a thousand pounds sterling. It was probable that this could not be recovered, but protests from the United Colonies might prevent unprovoked attacks in the future.

Davenport had asked Theophilus to remain after the meeting.

They had talked late of many problems, but the one problem that surely must have been as prominent in Eaton's mind as it was in his pastor's was never expressed in words. Getting up now from his desk, Davenport went to the window. The September afternoon was as warm as in summer, but it was far more quiet. The birds and the insects had ceased their calling. When darkness fell, the katydids and crickets would fill the night with their raucous music, but during the day life seemed held in abeyance.

His hands clasped behind his back, John looked up and down the dusty street. He saw Ann Eaton approach her house, a small package in her hand. No doubt she had been at the Widow Stolyon's for needles or for news of the latest fashions from England. Her walk was erect, proud. Proud of what? Proud of causing curious talk about the Eaton family? Proud of making people wonder what was wrong with their chief magistrate that his wife was not circumspect? Proud of making people wonder why she was disdaining proper church ceremonies?

She had walked out of meeting twice now: the first time just before a baptismal ceremony, the second time just before communion was to be served. Theophilus had been away the first time, but the second time, his whole bearing severe with immovable dignity, he had neither turned nor blinked. Was it because he could not control her, or was it because he was planning to handle the matter gradually and quietly?

The only words Theophilus had spoken last night that might have been significant were those he had said when they had parted. "I'm glad that you live so close, John. I can be assured, I know, that your eye is on every member of my family, that you will watch over each of them and give them whatever guidance is necessary."

As John Davenport thought these words over now, it seemed to him that Theophilus had not only been saying he could interfere, but had been implying he hoped he would do so.

"I'll do it," he said softly. "I'll do it now before she has a chance to humiliate us again."

He called out to Elizabeth, "I'm going out to make a pastoral call. I'll be back in perhaps an hour."

She answered goodbye from upstairs and, feeling oddly guilty because he had not told her exactly where he was going, and not even sure why he had not told her, he left the house.

A surprised Ann Eaton opened the door to him. "Theophilus left this morning. Surely you knew?"

"I have come to see *you.*"

Her eyebrows lifted. In a cool, polite voice she said, "Please come this way."

He followed her through the great hall to the parlor beyond. Her back was erect, her tallness emphasized. He was really not much shorter than she was, yet he was glad when she sat down after indicating a chair for him. Her hands rested quietly on the arms of the chair, but her head was held at an imperious angle. Trying not to show irritation at her lack of humility, he said, "I have come to discuss the state of your soul."

"Oh?" The corners of her mouth lifted. "Shall we do it over a cup of beer? Or perhaps some wine?"

"Neither. It would be far better if we did it on our knees. In prayer. You need God's help. I know from experience that He is far more likely to give it if you are humble and supplicating. The Lord loveth a humble person."

"I have never thought you were very humble."

A righteous wrath shook him. It was a moment before he could get his breath. "You're forgetting that I am in a position of leadership. How could I presume to guide if I were not a little better than those I was guiding? But you can be sure that when I meet with my Lord, it is as His most humble servant."

A smile flickered about her lips. Was she mocking him again? It was required that he view all church members as his flock and love and respect each one as he did his own child—yet he found himself actively disliking this woman.

It was not a personal thing, he told himself. It was actually a displeasure brought about because her behavior was such a source of anxiety for her husband. And he was displeased also, and apprehensive even, because she showed signs of being a disruptive influence in the church. If the chief magistrate's wife could walk out of a service without being punished, then anyone could. And might. Worse still, she was openly disdaining the Puritan faith. This could not be condoned.

"Why," he said, "have you profaned our church service by walking out of it?"

Though she still held her chin firmly high, her emotion was reflected in the deepening color of her cheeks. "Because it is not a proper service."

"In what way?"

"Because babies are being baptized in the faith even though they have no knowledge of it."

"They come of godly parents who will raise them in the faith."

"Time enough, then, after they have been raised in the faith, for them of their own volition to join the church—provided they can qualify."

"And the communion," he said icily. "Why did you walk out before that particular ceremony?"

"Because communion is served to those who were baptized before they reached the age of reason."

Her bold statements enraged him. He had expected a few weak doubts, but he had not guessed that she held such definite and outrageous opinions.

"Who has been filling your mind with this? These are the evil ideas held by those people called Baptists. How did you come to know of them?"

"I have been acquainted with them for a long time. No one here has influenced me. You can be sure of that. But being here where religion is so much a part of our lives, I have given much thought to spiritual things. And, meditating, I came at last to think that these new beliefs are right."

"Did you hold these ideas in England?"

"No."

"You began thinking these things here in New Haven, then?"

"No, not exactly."

"Then where?"

"It was in the Bay Colony."

"Someone must have influenced you. Who was it—man or woman?"

"It was a woman," she said finally.

"What was her name?"

"I'd rather not say."

"Why not?"

"I don't want to cause her any trouble."

"It will cause her no trouble. I am concerned only with the people in this town. Boston can handle its own problems. What was her name?"

"Lady Moody."

"What did she tell you?"

"Not much. We just talked."

Never had he had a harder time getting information from anyone. "Talked about what?" he asked.

"About our doubts. Things that bothered us. She gave me a
little book to read."

"By whom?"

"I don't know. It just has the initials A.R. on it."

Anger gathered into a cold, hard ball within him. Someone had
once shown him the book in the Bay Colony. He had thrown it
aside after a glance, considering it subversive and too trashy and
too weak in its arguments to be taken seriously.

"I'd like to see it," he said. "May I?"

"Of course." She got up and left the room, her petticoat rustling
sinuously, like a snake winding through stiff marsh grass.

He waited in quiet anger. Taking the book from her on her return, he leafed through the pages. Yes, it was the same book.

"When you began to have doubts, why did you not observe the
injunction in First Corinthians fourteen: 'If they will learn anything, let them ask their husbands at home. . . .'?"

"Surely you know how busy my husband is?"

"Then you might have come to me, your confessor. You must
also be familiar with Malachi two:seven." As he spoke the words,
a comforting warmth filled him. It was one of his favorite verses.
" 'For the priests' lips should preserve the knowledge; and they
should seek the law at his mouth, for he is the messenger of the
Lord of hosts.' " Again he gave her a long look. "Surely you heard
that verse spoken by your father, the bishop."

She lowered her eyes, shrugged one shoulder.

"You *do* know the verse. Why, then, did you not come to me or
to Mr. Hooke?"

The rich color came and went in her face. "Because—oh, because I was afraid you might be angry."

"Are you mocking me?"

Her gaze was steady. "No."

The thought that she might really fear him had the effect of
gentling him. His anger melted away.

"You must never fear your pastor, my dear—any more than you
should fear your God. Only if your intentions are not pure will either one be angry with you." Watching her fold her hands demurely, he said, "Tell me now exactly why you object to the baptism of babies."

Her fingers moved, twisted. "Well, I used to think that baptism was like circumcision—that both were administered to infants to purify them of natural sin. After I read this book, I began to wonder. After all, when a person is baptized he accepts Christ as his savior. Isn't this a decision each of us should make when we are old enough to know what we are doing?"

"Would you be satisfied if that point were cleared up for you?"

She hesitated. "I . . . think so."

"Then let me take this little book with me. I'll prepare a sermon on the question of circumcision and baptism." He felt a quiet exultation. He knew exactly where to find the answer. It was in Second Colossians. He could have quoted the verses right then, but he preferred to put the explanation into a sermon. That way he would reach any people who had shared the polluting influence of the book.

"Next Sunday," he said, "I shall preach a sermon that should settle your doubts. Right now, I'll pray with you."

She did not move. Did she plan to pray sitting up?

"Come then," he said, "let us kneel here by this large chair." Overcoming a certain revulsion caused by the nearness of one so alien in spirit, he knelt by her side and placed his hand on her back. The material of her gown was unexpectedly thin, and he could feel the warmth of the flesh beneath. The pulse beneath her skin drummed against his fingertips and darted like a rhythmic flame through his body.

Startled, he withdrew his hand. He did it so quickly that she turned and looked at him, her eyes very close and very dark and questioning.

"Why do you stare?" she asked. "Am I so evil?"

His throat choked. Words would not come. He quickly shook his head. Closing his eyes, he waited. The pounding pulse-beat slowed. His breath returned and he cleared his throat. From her body, so close to his in the warm room, came a faint perfume like the scent of incense at a pagan ritual.

"O Lord God of Hosts," he said passionately, "be with us now. Be with us now. Help this woman who kneels at my side. Help her to control the passions that dominate her. Help her to resist the impulses, the proddings of the Devil, that goad her into unrighteous acts. Help her to see the truth, the one sure way to Thy feet. Help her to see that the Puritan faith is the purified essence of Christianity, divested of all but the most necessary rituals."

Once he had begun, the words flowed easily and with more eloquence than he had sometimes displayed in the pulpit. It was really a shame that more people weren't there to hear him.

When he had finished, he rose, his heart full of the grace and nearness of God. Oh, how easy it was to approach His throne if your heart was pure and your motives sincere. As he took Mrs. Eaton's hand to help her up, the flame again flashed through him. He dropped her hand and drew back quickly. Her face was calm. Had she felt nothing?

He swallowed, moistening his throat. "Tell me," he said, "have my words, my prayers, affected you at all?"

"I'm not sure. I'll need time to think over all you have said."

He took his leave, closing the door firmly behind him, yet the memory of that afternoon stayed with him for many days, as earthy and fresh as a newly turned clod in a field. Often as he sat in his study working on a series of sermons that he planned to send to England to be published, he found his mind and senses drifting back to that perfumed moment when the feel of her body beneath his innocent hand had awakened him to the Eve that was within her.

At first he had thought that the moment had been the work of the Devil. But as he ruminated upon it, reliving it in order to understand its significance, it came to him that it had been a sign from Heaven. God wanted him to be aware of the enormous potential of his adversary.

THEOPHILUS EATON
SEPTEMBER 1643

The maples were already aflame when Theophilus sailed back from Boston after the United Colonies meeting. As the boat passed the tip of Cape Cod, he stayed close to the prow, constantly scanning the shoreline. It was probably foolish to fear attack from the Narragansetts. How could they have learned of the secret decision against their chief, Miantonomo? Yet he was uneasy, and continued to scan the shore for a sign of Indian canoes.

His unease was lessened somewhat, however, by the presence of his son-in-law. Both Hopkins and John Haynes, Connecticut's governor for the year 1643, who was also on board, had represented their colony at the meeting.

Edward Hopkins came to his side now. "What have you seen so far?"

"A deer and two foxes."

"No savages?"

"Not one."

"You see very well."

Yes, Theophilus thought, his distance vision was good. But this did not please him. He had known too many old men who, having no other accomplishments, bragged about their keen eyesight. Fifty-three. Not really old, he told himself. And he still had much to do.

Though he saw no savages, he remained uneasy even after they entered the open sea. Now that he could not see the land so clearly, he scanned the sky looking for trouble in the shape and color of the clouds, for the settlers had learned that the storms that hit the coast in September could be sudden and furious.

They had also learned that the area east and south of Nantucket was unpredictably treacherous. It was a place of shifting sandbars, swift and changeable currents, and high seas. Or fog. On this trip it was the fog. When the wind ceased and the sea calmed, fog hung over it so thickly that the stern of the boat was barely visible from the prow. Captain Lamberton knew the Nantucket shoals better than most sailors, but when fog settled around the boat his fingers tightened on the wheel and he spoke hardly at all.

The changing light of the day could not penetrate the fog. Because they were shrouded on all sides, it was impossible to tell how fast they were moving; in fact, some of the time Theophilus had the feeling they were fixed in time and space, as if God were lifting his hand and saying, "Stop! Wait!"—saying it to the sun and to the wind and to all men who forge unthinkingly ahead. It was a time when men are silent, when thoughts turn inward.

After a while the two men began talking. They spoke of trade: of possible products for export, of European markets. Finally Edward Hopkins said, "You seem unusually preoccupied."

Theophilus stared into the fog that seemed to cling to them like a clammy shroud. "I've been thinking of Miantonomo. I cannot seem to put the affair out of my mind."

"We have nothing to fear. I'm sure the Narragansetts have not yet heard of the decision."

"I was thinking of Miantonomo himself. He trusts us. He has always been our friend. Look at the help he gave us against the Pequots."

"Only because they were his enemy, too. As for his trusting us—I doubt if he trusts anyone. He's a powerful and independent man. He didn't become that way through trusting and being trusted. He's arrogant and—"

"We cannot execute him simply because he is arrogant and powerful, because he is not subservient like Uncas."

"No. And we are not." Edward put a hand on his father-in-law's sleeve. "Remember, we are only turning him over to Uncas. Whatever Uncas does will be done outside the settlement . . . strictly an Indian affair. And another thing. It was not the decision of the commissioners. We knew we might have been inclined to look favorably on Uncas, who has always recognized our natural superiority and has always been humble and courteous. That was why we turned the matter over to the clergymen. It was lucky for us that they were meeting in Boston at the same time. It was they, not we, who decreed that Miantonomo must die. We need feel no guilt."

"You are right. Certainly one should not dispute the decision of such godly men."

"And if what the scouts said was true—that Miantonomo had indeed been planning to unite all Indians in a revolt against the English—then certainly the right decision has been made."

"I know." Theophilus sighed. "But when the sources of the information are all Miantonomo's enemies . . . ?"

Edward nodded sympathetically. "But we must trust the same sources of intelligence that have helped us in the past. I see that your conscience bothers you, my friend—my father. But how much more would it bother you if you let Miantonomo go free and then, a few weeks from now, returned from a journey and found the town on fire or in your home the savagely mutilated bodies of your wife, your mother, your children?"

Theophilus shuddered. "You're right. We must consider the welfare of the many. Yet I shall be glad when the whole affair is over. I take no pleasure in it."

"Nor I. But it's not like deciding against a civilized man. Their justice is different from ours. As long as Miantonomo lives, the life of Uncas is in danger; the pattern of vengeance would continue. You must remember that if the English had not been here, Uncas would have killed Miantonomo immediately. Now we are saying: Go ahead with your Indian affairs; we will not interfere. And don't forget, either, what kind of person Miantonomo is. Can we really trust such a man? Have you ever known a more proud, restless, or turbulent individual?"

Half joking, Theophilus said, "I know of only one with a like personality."

"An Indian?"

"No, an Englishwoman."

Edward smiled. "Yes—proud, restless, and certainly turbulent, but at least her turbulence is contained by the walls of your home."

"I hope so. I hope it will continue to be so."

Edward turned his face toward the fog beyond the rail. "At least she is not—she is not like—"

"Yes. I should not complain. Every day, Edward, I pray for you and your trials with your pitiful wife. I wonder sometimes how you can maintain such a balanced temperament, how you can manage so many political duties and carry out so much business."

"These things keep me from thinking, from remembering I have no child to carry on my name."

"Perhaps she will recover. If she were busy with children as a woman ought to be—"

"Perhaps. Even so, I'd be afraid."

"Governor Winthrop happened to mention her to me one day. He feels that too much reading and writing—both such unwomanly activities—have brought on this condition."

Edward shrugged. "It may be. But in her quiet way, my Ann also is headstrong. She has never actually defied me. She nods agreeably every time I suggest too much mental activity may overexcite her delicate intellect, but I know that as soon as she is left alone, out come the books and paper."

"What does she write?"

"Nothing. Just rambling disconnected sentences that reflect the state of her mind. It constantly grows worse, I think."

"It may be that God has sent each of us a cross to bear, lest we become too filled with conceit over our successes."

"It may be." Edward's hands gripped the rail. "Let us talk of other things, things we can control, like trade."

Dryly Theophilus said, "Boston controls our trade."

"Boston would like to control everything. Well"—Edward smiled— "she will control less now that the confederation is formed. Connecticut's and New Haven's votes are just as important as hers. Yet so far as trade goes, it is not entirely her doing. The ships put in there because of her fine harbor and because hers is the largest settlement. They carry more goods for her."

"True. In New Haven we have long needed our own ship—one that will carry our own products to England and bring goods back for us direct, without a stop in Boston. Two days ago I hired carpenters from Rhode Island who will come to New Haven to build one for us." His voice quickened. "This will be our real beginning: the day our direct trade begins."

Almost as he spoke the words the fog began to thin and lift, as if the hope in his heart had dispelled the oppressive shroud.

As they approached Saybrook a few days later, the shallop

moved in closer to the coast. The sight of John Winthrop's fort looking protectively down at them gave them confidence; besides, the Narragansetts were a lesser threat this far west.

At the Winthrop dock a shallop from Hartford awaited Hopkins and Haynes. All the men shook hands gravely. Embracing his son-in-law, Theophilus felt his throat tighten. Two men he loved and trusted completely: Edward Hopkins and John Davenport. It often seemed to him that they had the same feeling of brotherhood and the same common goals that Christ's disciples must have had.

The rest of the journey Theophilus and Thomas Gregson devoted to preparation of a report to be made to the court on the Boston meeting. The commissioners had ratified the articles of confederation drawn up in June. Governor Winthrop was to send a strongly worded letter to the Swedes who had treated Captain Lamberton with such impertinence and injustice at Delaware. Most important of all, it had been agreed that each colony would, if necessary, come to the defense of the others, each supplying men and arms in proportion to its population.

It seemed to Theophilus, as their vessel tacked into the New Haven harbor, that the accomplishments of five and one-half years had been tremendous. The town had increased more than fourfold. The houses were substantial looking, placed on neatly laid out streets. In the center, like the hub of a wheel on which all that was important turned, stood the meetinghouse. Religious strength was what held the people together and kept them moving forward in the same direction.

Beyond the neatly laid out town Theophilus could see to the virgin land beyond: room for new settlements, new people. That the colony might someday extend west all the way to the South Sea was a dream not beyond realization.

Captain Lamberton, once the course of the little ship was set inside the harbor, came and stood a moment with Theophilus and Thomas Gregson. "What a fine harbor this is," he said. "It was made for bigger ships than this."

Theophilus heard the longing in his voice. "We'll have such a ship here," Theophilus said. "Mr. Gregson and I have hired the builders and carpenters. We're going to build a great ship. And you'll be captain, Mr. Lamberton. We wouldn't have anyone else."

And the day, he thought, that our great ship leaves this harbor, laden with our own goods, will mark the beginning of New Haven's place in the new world as a great commercial port.

Was there ever a happier day for a man, he thought, than the one on which the actual shape of his dreams could be clearly perceived?

ANN EATON/FALL 1643

Even before the news about Miantonomo had been announced, Ann had been aware of a sense of unease. The matter had come up when the family welcomed Theophilus home from his journey. He had only said that the English felt they could neither execute him nor set him free.

"Then they will keep him indefinitely in Hartford?"

"No."

"But what will they do? What will happen to him?" Ann had asked at dinner.

His look shut her out. "The outcome is quite out of my hands. I prefer not to discuss it further."

She could feel a throbbing in her veins. Why did he refuse to confide in her? In no time he'd be across the street giving John Davenport all the details of the affair and asking for and listening to his counsel.

"Surely," she said, "they will not return him to Uncas?"

Theophilus gave her a look of silent remonstrance. His mother immediately took the opportunity to say, "It ought to be clear to you, Daughter, that secrecy is required in the matter."

"Theophilus knows he can trust us," Ann said. But something about her husband's reticence troubled and finally silenced her.

Also, although he spent longer hours than usual with Mr. Davenport, he did not mention her absences from church, Davenport's visit with her, or the sermon that had been preached especially for her. She could not be sure whether he knew of these things or whether he had a reason for remaining silent.

Most troubling of all had been his lack of importunity. On the night of his return he had remained in his closet until she grew weary of waiting, all washed and faintly perfumed in a fresh new gown with her hair brushed and hanging soft around her shoulders. She had finally put on a rail and had gone to his closet where she had found him bent over a sheaf of papers on his desk. Two candles burned low in the musty room.

"You are working very late, my dear," she said. "The watch called out eleven o'clock some time ago. It must be nearing midnight." She gave him a soft smile. "You must be very tired."

He rubbed the back of his hand across his eyes. "You're right. I *am* tired. But it's hard to stop when there's so much to be done."

Moving around his desk, she stood next to him and with expert fingers massaged the back of his neck until the fatigued muscles gradually loosened. Her glance fell on the papers in front of him. The top one was headed: *Milford—Compromise Plan.*

"Why, Theophilus, I didn't know you ever even considered compromise."

"My dear, compromise is the essence of political action. You make a minor concession, the opposition makes one, you make another, and so on until agreement is reached."

Suddenly she felt his hand groping in the thin material of her rail as she leaned close to him. In a moment his smooth-fingered touch found her skin and moved over the roundness of her hip . . . sweetly . . . absently.

As she continued massaging his neck she said softly, "But you don't like compromising—do you?"

His voice sounded tired. "A man does what he *must* do, not what he would like to do. Especially when he is leading others."

The tingling of her skin under his touch was a partner to the sudden lively tingling of her intellect. He was actually confiding in her, was letting his feelings poke through the cover of surface conversation.

"Oh, Theophilus," she said, "you just can't know how much I've missed you. A household with nothing but bickering women in it—women who are only preoccupied with gossip about other women or with the details of running a household—you can't imagine how constricting it is. Women live in such a small world. They need men to bring the larger world home to them."

She sensed his withdrawal even before he moved his hand away, leaving her warm and vulnerable skin suddenly cold.

"I have a little more work to do before I go to bed," he said.

"I've annoyed you. What did I say that you didn't like?"

"I'm not annoyed. But I do think you complain too much about your lot. You're better off than any other woman in this plantation. You have a finer home, more clothes, more servants—"

"I wasn't complaining. I was doing just the opposite. I was letting you know how important you are in this household, how much I miss you when you're gone."

"You complain constantly of my mother and my daughter."

She could hear her voice hardening. "I'll wager they complain far more of me. Isn't that true?"

His lips clamped shut, spread out in a thin line as his jaw tightened. She had seen him do this on the bench when he needed more time to come to a decision. She had also seen him do it when he recognized the truth of a statement but did not want to acknowledge it.

She knew she ought to drop the subject, that she could sweeten him and gain far more with a little humility. She wanted to stop talking, but she was like a wind that could not stop blowing until the force behind it was dissipated.

"Isn't it true, Theophilus, that they complain constantly of me?"

In a hard voice he said, "And not, perhaps, without reason."

She drew back quietly. "I'll leave you to your work now."

He looked up as she lifted the latch. "I may be very late. I may not—"

"You would find the door bolted anyway." She was breathing hard. After she had closed and bolted the door of their room, she got into bed. After a little while she got up and slid the bolt back. Not long after that, she heard him walking down the hall. The flickering light from his candle made a pale rectangle around the closed door. He did not hesitate as he passed. A moment later she heard the door open and close in the spare bedroom beyond.

She lay quite still with both fists pressed against her mouth. What made her say the very things that angered him most, just when she wanted to please him? A great sterile feeling of aloneness swept over her. She had known the feeling before, but it had grown more intense in recent months. Sometimes it clung to her all day, like a heavy fog hanging low over the harbor.

She was most aware of it when she was with the women in her

family. She was different and they knew it. They even taunted her with it.

Old Mrs. Eaton liked to preface her remarks with statements like: "I'm sure the *lady* of the household won't agree with me, but . . . "; or, "Someone who was familiar with the running of this household would, of course, *know* that only last week we . . ."; or, "Some people interpret the Bible differently than I do, but . . ."

Ann held her jaw rigid and searched for quick distractions. Sometimes she changed the subject. But sometimes—all too often, in fact—she exploded. When old Mrs. Eaton or Mary had succeeded in making her lose her temper, they looked righteous and self-important, their smugness proclaiming their superiority over a woman who had so little control of her emotions.

Only when she was with Brigid did Ann lose her feeling of aloneness. Inside Brigid's home she was loved for what she was, rather than criticized for what she ought to be. Indeed, the Brewster home had become the only place where she ever really laughed. This past year, however, she had felt less at ease there. Some other women had started calling—Goodwife Leach and her daughter Mrs. Moore. At first they had been somewhat awed at meeting the chief magistrate's wife, but as their awe had decreased, the coarseness of their humor had increased. More and more lately they had subjected her to remarks that she had found increasingly irritating. When they had discovered that remarks critical of the government did not appear to anger her, they had grown bolder. Though some of their remarks clearly mirrored her own thoughts, she did not like hearing them from others.

Miantonomo had been talked about for weeks. Everyone knew that a decision had been made, although it was still secret. Speculation was widespread. News of the outcome was eagerly awaited.

It came about a week after Theophilus had returned. It spread to the marketplace and back to the homes surrounding it almost before Theophilus had paid the messenger.

Ann was at Brigid's that afternoon, as were Mrs. Leach and Mrs. Moore. The talk there had just come around to religion. "Imagine having a sermon preached just for you," Brigid said. "I never knew that to happen before."

"What did you think of it?" Ann asked.

Brigid took her notes from the sideboard. "First he said we are circumcised in a circumcision made without hands. We are circumcised through Christ's circumcision. Then he said we are buried with Christ through his baptism, that through his baptism our natural sins are forgiven. That doesn't prove *babies* must be baptized, and you know it. His text—Colossians two:eleven, twelve—doesn't prove anything. I looked it up. It doesn't say a word about babies."

"I know," Ann said. "I looked it up too."

"His arguments were too weak," Mrs. Moore said. "They didn't even begin to convince me."

Half smiling, Ann said, "If you feel that way, I'm surprised you remain in church during baptisms."

"Ah, but my husband isn't chief magistrate and Mr. Davenport's best friend to boot. I don't have that kind of protection."

Angrily Ann rose, her knitting needles clattering to the floor. "Do you suppose I thought of protection when I walked out of the church?"

Brigid came quickly over, put her hands on Ann's shoulders, and pressed her back down into her seat. She picked up the needles and handed them to her. "Now calm that hot temper of yours. I'm sure you weren't thinking of anything but your convictions when you left the service. You're that way. We're different. Take me, for instance. I'm steadier. I think about consequences. Wait— someone's coming. Oh, it's just my boy."

Joshua, a swaggering youth in his late teens, came in. "Word has come," he said importantly, "about Miantonomo. He's dead." He looked at Ann. "That was what our commissioners decided in Boston."

Everyone looked at her. She could feel the walls of her stomach drawing together in protest. Moistening her lips, she said, "How did it take place? Do you have the details?"

"Oh, yes. They turned him over to Uncas and a small band of warriors who took him away from the town."

"Well, then, it was not Englishmen who killed him."

"But two Englishmen went along to make sure the sentence was carried out. Waweka, brother of Uncas, walked behind Miantonomo. A while after they left Hartford, Uncas gave some kind of signal and Waweka raised his tomahawk and split Miantonomo's head open. He fell to the ground and then"—clearly the boy relished the telling of the story as well as the shock he was creating—"and then Uncas took his knife, bent over, and sliced a piece of flesh from Miantonomo's shoulder and ate it. Ate it raw, just as it was cut."

"Savages!" Mrs. Brewster said.

"Worse than that—he declared it was the sweetest meat he had ever eaten."

"Who's the most savage," Mrs. Leach asked, looking directly at Ann, "the men who killed him so brutally or the men who decreed it should happen? After all, the white man has had the benefit of Christian teaching."

Ann felt a rush of anger at the same time that her mind acknowledged the rightness of the remark. How could she defend her husband's decision when he had never told her his reasons for making it? Why was he so adamant about maintaining silence?

Bending over, she picked up the ball of yarn that had rolled off her lap. Let them think any redness in her cheeks was the result of not sitting upright. After placing her knitting carefully in her bag, she rose. "The sun is getting low. I must leave."

Brigid understood. "Don't be upset, my sweet. It wasn't your doing. Perhaps even your husband had little to do with it. The voice of a little town like New Haven doesn't carry much weight in the Bay Colony."

Ann gave her a grateful look. At the door their hands touched and held a moment. Brigid always smelled faintly of spice, and when Ann left she carried this fragrant impression away with her.

It was not so late as she had intimated; in fact, it was hardly past mid-afternoon. She walked down to the corner, crossed the street and, after a brief hesitation, turned to the left. Why hurry home? No one would expect her so early. Let them talk of the killing, let them turn it over and worry it and chew on it until they had extracted all the juice from it and had quite worn it out; then she'd go home.

She desperately needed to talk with someone—someone special who would listen without rancor, speak without criticism. She wanted to understand the ways of men; she needed to hear a man of wisdom speak of the affair.

Her conscience whispered to her in a pale voice: If you want to understand the ways of man, if you want to speak with a man of wisdom, why do you not seek out Mr. Davenport or Mr. Hooke? Why, instead, do your legs carry you toward the home of Ezekial Cheever?

But I'm merely going to pass by on my way around the quarter, she told herself. If he should happen to be outside, then it will be a chance meeting, not one of my doing.

Someone moved in the Cheevers' yard. Her heart fluttered. Another few steps and she saw that it was Mary. As Ann approached, Mary came over to the fence. She had some herbs in her hand, just picked, and the sweetness of thyme rose from the bruised leaves.

Ann stopped, "Hello, Mary."

"Hello, Mrs. Eaton." Though Ann had several times suggested that Mary call her by her first name, she never did. It was as if she were deliberately maintaining a distance between them.

"Picking herbs for supper?"

"Yes." A pause. "Out for a walk?"

"Yes. The air is very fine today."

"Yes."

What a stilted conversation. Ann never knew what to say to the girl. What on earth did Ezekial talk with her about? Her agitation over Miantonomo was swallowed in momentary boredom. She put her hand on the rough wood fence. The fibers, warmed by the sun, seemed to have more life than this girl with her shadowy face and reserved manner.

Mary was looking at her with slightly raised eyebrows. Finally she said, "Do you feel all right, Mrs. Eaton?"

"Yes, certainly. Why?"

"You look—you seem—well, agitated."

"I'm perfectly fine, thank you."

"Would you like to come in and rest a few minutes? My husband is not at home."

"Thank you. I'd like to. But it's growing late. I think I should finish my walk and hurry home."

"I understand," Mary said. "Good day, Mrs. Eaton. I'll tell Ezekial you were here."

Ann moved away. Had she been so transparent? But Mary had also misunderstood, Ann thought. From the jealous edge to her voice it was clear that she had not understood that her visitor was looking only for counsel.

In her own home, as soon as she opened the door, Ann smelled a chowder cooking. Steam rose from the cauldron over the fire in the great hall. At the table talking were her husband, Mr. Gregson, Mr. Hooke, and young Theophilus. They all rose as she entered, but her son rushed to her. Her heart warmed at his eager, handsome face. Here was a child with all the bright exuberance she had often felt.

"Mother, Mother, have you heard the news?"

"About Miantonomo?" A trembling began inside her but she retained an outward calmness for Mr. Hooke's benefit. "Yes, I've heard." She turned away, slipping her cloak from her shoulders.

"Isn't it exciting? Did you hear what Uncas did after Miantonomo was tomahawked? He cut a piece of flesh from his shoulder and ate it. Ate it raw. And he said it was the sweetest meat he had ever eaten. 'It strengthens my heart,' he said."

Theophilus had come and taken her cloak. He hung it on a peg. Young Theophilus, his face glowing with excitement, remained in front of her.

In a controlled voice she said, "It must have been a savage spectacle."

The boy nodded vigorously. "How I wish I'd been there. There he was walking along, probably thinking that because two Englishmen were there, he was going to be delivered to his own tribesmen. Instead—wham!—down on his head from behind comes the tomahawk, splitting—"

His voice stopped. She could feel his teeth as the back of her hand struck his open mouth. "You little savage," she said. "Is that the way I brought you up?" At one and the same time she wanted to cradle him in her arms and go on striking him. "Are you so much like all other Englishmen that you would happily send a noble man to his death without a jot of evidence against him?"

Again her hand lashed out, but the blow was diverted as a stronger hand took hers by the wrist. She looked up at her husband. "And you?" she said. "Do you also wish you had been there to see that cannibal slice his pound of flesh off the shoulder of a man who has long been a friend of the English?"

He took her other wrist and, holding them both firmly, said, "You do not know all the circumstances, my dear. We had been told he planned to lead a massive revolt against all English settlements. We could not risk letting him go free."

"You did it for the good of the plantation, then?"

"Why, yes."

"I should have known. Everything you do is for the good of the plantation. Individuals don't count."

"My dear wife, it was precisely because of the individuals I am responsible for and the ones I love that—"

"Why bother to explain, son," a voice from the kitchen doorway said. "You can see how she twists everything. You can see how she lets her anger run away with her judgment. Why should she strike an innocent boy who is merely trying to tell her the news?"

Mr. Hooke coughed softly. This sound, reminding Ann of the presence of men outside the family, cut through her anger. She half closed her eyes, letting her body relax. Theophilus, sensing her resistance was gone, released his hold on her.

Immediately she turned and gave the men a falsely bright smile. "Please excuse me, Mr. Hooke and Mr. Gregson. I should not have attempted to discipline our son when guests were present. But I've always felt that when a punishment is put off too long, it loses its meaning." She glanced at young Theophilus, her heart heavy. Old Mrs. Eaton, with much clucking sympathy, was examining the reddened imprint on his face.

"Does it hurt so badly, son?" Ann asked softly.

He glanced at his mother and then back at his grandmother. "It hardly hurts at all." He brushed his grandmother's fingers away. "My mother is only a woman and does not hit hard." Straightening his shoulders manfully, he sauntered out of the room.

His grandmother looked ruefully after him, sorry, Ann was sure, to have been denied a further indictment of her daughter-in-law. The old woman sighed. "Well, then, back to the kitchen. *Someone* has to oversee the supper preparation."

Theophilus said, "Ann would gladly help you, Mother, but we men wish to talk with her."

"Of course." She gave them one of her gracious, great-lady smiles.

"Let's go into the parlor where we won't be interrupted," Theophilus said.

He led the way. Ann followed. Behind her walked Mr. Hooke and Mr. Gregson. Was this the way Miantonomo had felt as the little procession of Indians and Englishmen left Hartford? Had his heart beat with apprehension at the same time that his mind told him there was no cause for concern?

"I'll sit here on the couch," she said. "Why don't you sit over there, Mr. Hooke, and you there, Mr. Gregson. And you, Theophilus—you sit here next to me." Playing the hostess gave her confidence.

"I'll stand," Theophilus said. He stood looking down at her— handsome and stern. This meant that she had to look up at him.

The couch was low, so low that her knees rose higher than her lap. The total effect—including the stern sincerity on the two visitors' faces—combined to make her feel insignificant. "We are here, my dear wife, at the request of our pastor, Mr. Davenport."

Ah, she thought. Uncertainty trembled inside her but she lifted her chin. "What message does the Reverend Mr. Davenport send that he is unable to convey himself?"

Theophilus exchanged a look with Mr. Hooke, as if to say, *You see how she is?* "He is well able. But he feels that I, as your husband, and these two men can perhaps more easily communicate with you and explain theology to you in terms you can understand."

"I see."

"We have here a small book you have consulted and apparently have believed in—more so than the true Word of God."

"I consulted it only because I wanted to understand the Word of God more clearly, more fully."

Mr. Hooke said, "Had you sought the counsel of your pastor, your husband, or a teacher or elder of the church, you would have received answers that would have aided your understanding instead of"—he tapped the book with a long finger—"confusing you as this book has."

"I did not find the book confusing."

"It may not have confused you," Mr. Hooke said gently, "but through faulty reasoning and misinterpretations of the Word, it presents a confused idea of what the Scriptures really mean. A woman—even one so well educated as yourself, Mrs. Eaton—has inferior reasoning powers which make it difficult to separate the spurious and deliberately misleading from the true."

Hot anger flashed through her. Placing her hands flat on the couch on either side of her, she started to rise.

"Please remain seated, my dear," Theophilus said in a firm, cold voice. He stood directly in front of her. Would he actually use force to prevent her from rising? She was not sure. She felt unnerved, uneasy, and, for the moment, undecided about what to do.

When Theophilus saw her half settle back, he took the little brown book from Mr. Hooke. "We plan to show you the weakness of the arguments in the book and the faulty reasoning behind the author's interpretations. Mr. Davenport has found passage after passage of this nature and he has kindly—for your sake alone—

written out clarifications and refutations. I shall read from the book and Mr. Gregson and Mr. Hooke will read Mr. Davenport's explanations and will answer any questions you may have. Is that clear?"

"Yes. Despite my inferior reasoning powers."

"Then we may proceed?"

"I wonder," she said, "if they would dare to treat Lady Moody this way in the Bay Colony."

The men exchanged glances. "Have you not heard about Lady Moody?" Mr. Hooke said.

"She is not . . . dead?"

"No. She has been excommunicated."

And might as well be dead, Ann thought. For anyone who was no longer a part of the church was cut off from both people and from news, and often was avoided by even her closest friends lest they be labeled with guilt by association. "That is very sad," she said.

"Yes. But it could easily have been avoided," Mr. Hooke said. "You must realize, Mrs. Eaton, that we are doing this for *you.* For your salvation. We are certainly not doing it to please ourselves." He gave her a gentle smile. She had always liked him better than most churchmen for he never spoke of himself as God's humble servant.

She returned his smile with a faint change of expression. What did it all matter anyhow? To sit here was as good as to sit somewhere else. She did not have to listen.

"You may proceed," she said in a listless voice.

Theophilus stood in front of her and read from the little book. She had read it so thoroughly that she knew every word before he said it. Instead of listening to what he said, she listened to the inflections of his voice. He had a deep masculine voice—one that had attracted her from the beginning. At one time, she remembered, the voice had spoken warmly and excitingly of love, stirring her unexpectedly to passion. Once it had been full of nothing but admiration for everything she said and did. Once it had been full of humble longing as he had begged her to become his wife.

But this was not the same voice. This was his magisterial voice: a voice of great dignity, a voice from which all personal inflections had been removed, a voice which had faintly accusing undertones.

When Theophilus had finished, Mr. Hooke read Mr. Davenport's explanation and refutation. Though the words were read in Mr. Hooke's gentle, intelligent voice, she could hear overtones of Mr. Davenport's pomposity. Her anger returned.

Her anger grew as the process continued, with Mr. Gregson alternating with Mr. Hooke in reading explanations. After each one she was asked whether she had any questions. Each time she shook her head haughtily. How many of these sessions would there be, she wondered, before they dropped the matter and let her go on living her life as she chose?

They were treating her like a prisoner, and also like a child. She locked her fingers together, trying to control her rising anger. Why should they hold her captive like this? What was wrong with holding her own beliefs? Who was hurt by it when she walked out of church? What would happen now if she got up and walked out of the room? It was her home. Wasn't she free to move from room to room whenever she wished?

She waited until Mr. Hooke had come to the end of an explanation. Then, seeing Theophilus turn a page and hearing him clear his throat as he prepared to go on, she suddenly rose, slid by him, and went to the door.

Smiling at them as she smiled at servants who sometimes overstepped their places, she said briskly, "Thank you very much, gentlemen. Your efforts to enlighten me are indeed commendable. I think, however, that you have expended quite enough effort for one day. And my poor weak feminine mind has absorbed all it can."

Before they could answer or even erase the astonishment from their faces, she had closed the door behind her and was across the great hall and on her way upstairs to the privacy of her room.

LURINDA COLLINGS
OCTOBER 1643

October 26, 1643. Lurinda marked it well in her memory for, as Mr. Eaton said as he stood in front of the crowd, it was a date that would go down in history. In the afternoon a long roll of the drum had summoned the townspeople to the public square. The New Haven Colony had been organized, Mr. Eaton announced, comprising the towns of New Haven, Totoket, Stamford, Milford, and Southold, Long Island.

New Haven Colony, he told them, was strong and was growing. It would some day reach all the way to the South Sea. Its harbor would be full of great ships returning from or leaving for far places of the world. Through its membership in the United Colonies it offered security for all and redress from wrongs inflicted by outsiders and foreigners. Through its leaders it offered the assurance of prosperity for colonists and for their children.

"Moreover"—and these words were offered by Mr. Eaton with great solemnity—"we, as leaders of this colony, shall, with all care and diligence, endeavor to maintain a purity of religion, and to suppress all irreligion according to the best light we can obtain from the divine oracles and by the advice of the elders and churches in the jurisdiction, so far as it may concern civil power."

That last announcement made Lurinda shiver a little. She looked over at Mrs. Eaton, who stood very straight, her chin lifted, her face not changing at all when he spoke of the suppression of irreligion.

But what really excited Lurinda was the news a little later in the day, after all the representatives from the towns in the colony had met, that Mr. Eaton had been elected governor. He would still be chief magistrate of the town, but in addition he would be governor of the colony, presiding over a general court that would meet twice a year. He would be called, so they said in the kitchen later that day as they prepared a feast in celebration, Your Excellency, or Your Grace.

All the important people in town came to the feast as well as the representatives from the other towns. Lurinda helped with the serving. She loved moving among the people, carrying the steaming dishes of buttered lobster and the spicy pumpkin and sweet potatoes, the creamy puddings and jewel-toned preserves. She loved listening to their conversations and absorbing their excitement. Some of the men had even spoken to her, asking her how long she had been in the household. Perhaps they thought she was one of those well-born young girls like Mary Launce, now in the household, who were placed with families like the Eatons for social training and opportunities to meet proper young men.

Only one incident had marred the evening. There had been a lull in the conversation, and Mrs. Eaton, holding her pewter can of wine close to her breast—the can had been refilled more than once—had said, "And so now . . . now that our government covers a broader area, will the kind of justice it dispenses also be broader?"

"What is your definition of broader justice?" asked Mr. Rayner from Stamford.

"A trial by jury—especially for capital crimes."

The governor, who must have heard his wife's remarks as he talked quietly in a corner of the room, now came to her side and put a firm hand on her shoulder.

"Is my wife doing it again? Making jokes about my ability to dispense justice? I sometimes think it is my complaisance about her capriciousness that makes her fear I overlook too much when criminals are brought before me."

Mr. Davenport, who had also quickly joined the group, said, "Mrs. Eaton is noted for her wit."

Mr. Rayner laughed, but Mrs. Eaton only smiled a cool social smile.

"Perhaps it isn't that at all," Mr. Rayner said. "Perhaps your lady fears we will vote away your prerogative. No, my dear Mrs. Eaton, we have no intention of so doing. Your husband will remain the final arbiter of justice without having to bow to the opinion of a group of people who have no knowledge of the law."

Joining the group, old Mrs. Eaton put a motherly hand on Mrs. Eaton's other shoulder. "Unlike many women, my daughter takes a great interest in what goes on in government."

"Very admirable," said Mr. Fowler from Milford.

"Indeed, yes," the old woman said. "Unfortunately, she is, like most women, uninformed about government processes and often arrives at conclusions through misconceptions. She is probably not even aware that they have been having jury trials in the Connecticut Colony for the past two years and have found that it's very difficult to get a group of people to arrive at a common decision. Even with that information at hand, I, who have lived many years longer, would not presume to advise my son, who I think—"

"More Madeira, Mr. Fowler?" said the governor. "I'm sorry, Mother. Did I interrupt you?"

"It's all right, Son. I was just saying—"

"Excuse me," Mrs. Eaton said. "Some more guests have just arrived."

Lurinda watched her walk away, watched the social smile ease as her mistress approached Mr. Cheever.

"Where's Mary?" She held out her hand to him.

"At home. Unwell."

"Again?"

"Yes. I can't stay long, but I did want to offer my congratulations to your husband. And to you."

"Theophilus is over there."

"Yes," he said, but Lurinda noticed he seemed to be in no hurry to move away.

"You're looking well," Mrs. Eaton said.

"You also," he said. "Very well."

Lurinda picked up a tray and carried it to the kitchen. She helped put food away and washed dishes until she heard the guests leaving. When the great hall had grown quiet, she filled a pitcher with hot water and climbed the back stairs to Mrs. Eaton's room. She had turned down the bed, stirred up the fire, and was behind a screen in the corner laying out towels at the washstand when the bedroom door opened.

She waited for Mrs. Eaton to speak to her; instead she heard Mr. Eaton's voice.

135

"What made you ask Mr. Rayner such a question?"

"What question?"

"You know very well what question. About the trial by jury."

"Because I was curious."

"You did it because you knew it would anger me."

"Don't be silly, Theophilus. It was just a light, unimportant question. Besides, he took it as a joke."

"Because he was tactful."

"Theophilus, my darling, don't be angry with me. Don't give me that I-am-the-governor look."

Lurinda held her breath during the pause that followed. Why, oh why hadn't she clinked the pitcher against the wash basin the moment the door opened? Now she could not do so without embarrassing the Eatons as well as herself.

"Then what about this kind of look?" he asked in a voice Lurinda had never heard before. It was tender and gruff and so full of warmth that Lurinda could feel a warmth spreading upward from her own throat.

"You look very lovely tonight, my dear," he added.

Listening to him, Lurinda wondered why Mrs. Eaton should ever try deliberately to anger her husband.

"I have a few things to take care of at my desk," he said in that same voice. "Then I'll be back. Will you be waiting?"

Lurinda did not hear any spoken answer. She waited. As soon as she heard the door close, she came out from behind the screen. Mrs. Eaton, a dreamy look on her face, had sat down in front of her mirror and had begun to take her hair down. Lurinda began talking quickly, explaining that the conversation had begun before she had had a chance to let them know she was there.

"It's all right, Lurinda. Here, help me fix my hair. And did you bring warm water? Good girl."

Standing behind Mrs. Eaton, Lurinda removed the last of the tortoise shell pins and began brushing the long dark hair.

"Is there any gray back there?"

"No, ma'am."

"You're sure?"

"Yes, ma'am."

"It has been a great day."

"Yes."

"Everything went well tonight—don't you think so?"

Lurinda hesitated. "I guess so, ma'am."

Mrs. Eaton looked at her in the mirror. "You *guess* so? Don't you understand, child, that there has to be room in the world for contrary opinion?"

"Perhaps so." Looking in the mirror, Lurinda tried to gauge her mistress's expression before going on. "But I think—I hope you don't mind my saying this—but I think you embarrassed Mr. Eaton. The governor, that is." The word *governor* had a lovely dignity and importance. It made her feel important just to be a member of his household.

"You're fond of him—aren't you?"

"He's been kind to me. Like a father. Ever since I got here, he's—"

"Don't bother to explain." Mrs. Eaton's voice grew soft and melodious. "I'm fond of him too."

"Then why . . . ?" Her eyes met Mrs. Eaton's again in the mirror and she broke off. Mrs. Eaton's eyes quietly told her that she was only a servant, that she had best not overstep.

"Please hurry, will you, Lurinda? And please don't concern yourself with my personal problems. When you're older you'll understand that being a wife in an establishment like this is very complicated."

She really doesn't know why she does these things, Lurinda thought. But she had noticed one thing: though Mrs. Eaton might be concerned about justice and government and interpretation of the Bible, she never said or did anything about her convictions except when her husband spent too much time traveling, or visiting Mr. Davenport, or working in his closet on town affairs.

Lurinda kept such thoughts to herself, however. In the kitchen she was silent when the other women and the servants talked about Mrs. Eaton. They speculated about the reading she did in her room, about what she did at Mrs. Brewster's, about what was said on the afternoons when her husband and the men from the church met with her in the parlor. Sometimes they said she was not really a Puritan. Sometimes they said she deliberately humiliated her husband because she wanted the colony to fail so she could go back to England. Sometimes they said she was like that because she was going through the change; sometimes they said she had always been that way. Sometimes they even said she was crazy—just like her daughter.

Despite all the talk and speculation, the parlor talks with the governor, Mr. Gregson, and Mr. Hooke went on through the deepest part of the winter. Many times at first Mrs. Eaton had emerged looking annoyed and put upon; once or twice she had stormed out with a great swishing of petticoats and had slammed the door behind her. But gradually the atmosphere grew friendlier. Sometimes the men lingered in the great hall after the parlor talks and had beer and spoke of other things: the Indian menace, the building of the great ship, trade. However their conversation began, Lurinda noticed, it nearly always ended with talk of trade.

In the spring the meetings ceased. "Do you suppose she's seen the Light?" one of the young girls asked Lurinda in the kitchen one day.

It was a relief not to have to dissemble. "Of course. Hasn't she been going to meeting every Sunday and sitting through the entire service?" And looking across the aisle every now and then to smile at her husband, Lurinda remembered happily.

No doubt Mrs. Eaton was aware of her more important position now as first lady of a large and growing colony. It was essential for her to set a proper example for all those beneath her. It seemed to Lurinda that her mistress walked taller and spoke with more authority than she had before, and Lurinda, at night in her tiny room, practiced imitating Mrs. Eaton's voice and carriage and dreaming of the day when she, too, might walk to church as part of the Eaton family instead of trailing behind with the servants.

And then one day when summer was borne in on a gentle breeze—and just when everyone in the household was at last convinced that Mrs. Eaton's conversion from the corruption of Baptist influence was complete—Mrs. Eaton suddenly, just before three babies were to be baptized, got up and walked out of the meeting-house.

Lurinda was appalled. Mr. Davenport, who had lifted his arms to welcome the young parents and their babies, stopped in mid-gesture, his hands looking as if they were holding up an invisible object of great weight. The governor, who had returned only the night before from ten days in Southold and Totoket, sat as still as a stone monument.

Young Samuel, Lurinda noticed, appeared to be as uncomfortable as she. He squirmed in his seat in the opposite gallery, glancing at others as if to measure their reactions, and then stared straight ahead with feigned nonchalance. Lurinda felt warmly close to him. Surely they were both feeling the same puzzled shame and reflected guilt.

Behind Samuel and a little to his right was Tim, looking as always directly at her. She smiled faintly, graciously, as ladies smile at servants. Poor Tim.

Little Hannah, who was sitting next to her, slipped her hand into Lurinda's. She was too young to know what was going on; she only knew that something was not quite right. Lurinda smiled at the child and squeezed her hand.

The baptisms were over at last. Lurinda listened restlessly to the final prayer, wanting it to be over, yet dreading the hours ahead that would have to be spent with the other servants. Knowing her loyalty to her mistress, they often made goading remarks that implied she, too, was not guiltless. Lately it had been better; now it would surely be worse.

Mrs. Eaton, of course, sometimes worked right along with the rest of the women in the household, but when she did it was often unpleasant. Although the remarks about her ceased, the attitude remained. When she stayed away, it was hinted that she was shirking; yet when she worked with them she was subtly rebuffed for assuming her rightful position. Her orders were followed with exaggerated slowness or with the response: "The governor's mother told us not to do that." Or: "We did that yesterday. The governor's mother told us to." Or: "*Old* Mrs. Eaton doesn't want it done that way."

They felt safe in acting with an edge of disrespect. Wouldn't His Excellency support them? Wouldn't his mother support them? Wouldn't the church itself support them?

Mrs. Eaton did not, of course, accept such behavior with meekness.

Lurinda dreaded going home after the service. Fortunately, the time spent in the kitchen on the Sabbath was limited, for all the cooking had been done the day before. But Mrs. Eaton shut herself away in the bedroom, and the women in the kitchen filled even the brief time before the noonday meal with speculation and criticism.

Mrs. Eaton appeared for dinner, acting as if the day were like any other Sabbath.

"Who stirred up the fire?" she asked. "It's terribly hot in here."

"You must remember, Daughter, that everyone is not so hot-blooded as you."

Mrs. Eaton's jawline hardened. "The fire is too high."

Old Mrs. Eaton smiled. "I'm afraid you eat too much spicy food. Spicy foods heat the blood. And I strongly suspect they overheat the brain."

"Just what are you implying?"

"Ladies," the governor said. "Let us give thanks for this food and for the warmth as well. It is better to be a little too warm than to perish of the cold."

Lurinda relaxed. How good the governor was. And how wise. He knew how to settle arguments between women; he knew how to calm troubled waters. Like Solomon. Like God.

"You're very quiet, Lurinda," Mrs. Eaton said that evening as she watched her pour water into the washbasin. "Is something troubling you?"

Lurinda shrugged.

"Is it because I walked out of church again?"

Lurinda could feel her heart beating. Softly she said, "It does trouble me."

"Why? Because of your religious convictions?"

"No."

"Then why?"

"Because for a while it was all peaceful. Now—"

"They'll start talking about me again. Speculating. Attacking my motives." She sighed. "I know all about it. And I can do nothing to stop it. Can you think of anything I can do or say?"

Lurinda took a quick breath. "You could stop walking out of church."

"That I cannot do." The voice was firm. "You may not have any religious convictions, but *I* do. For a while I thought I was wrong. When Mr. Hooke and Mr. Gregson explained my book line by line, they made sense. But when I studied it alone again these past few weeks, I realized I was right after all. Now my convictions are deeper than ever. I would be living a false life if I did not act in accordance with my convictions. 'To thine own self be true. . . .' Have you heard that before, Lurinda?"

"I don't think so, ma'am."

"It's by—well, I won't say. The author is considered by the church to be an immoral man." She paused. "It may be that you're too young for any kind of commitment, Lurinda. But when you're older, when your thoughts have jelled and your mind has sifted through all the ideas it's met, I hope you'll develop some strong convictions. And when you do, I hope you won't be afraid to act on them—even if it disturbs a peaceful household or a peaceful community."

"Ma'am?" Lurinda said hesitantly.

"Yes?"

"Couldn't a person just have convictions but keep them to herself? Then there'd never be any trouble."

"No trouble, yes. But no change either." She shook her head and her dark hair rippled around her shoulders. "Some people can keep their convictions to themselves. My conscience won't let me do so."

Her conscience must have continued to prod her, for on two more Sundays during that month, whenever a communion or baptismal ceremony was about to take place, Mrs. Eaton rose from her seat and made her stately walk down the aisle. It was never a quiet affair. Murmurs rose, chairs scraped, and in the rear where the soldiers were crowded, firearms and swords clanked. Up in the gallery, some never-identified boys stamped their feet in rhythm with her majestic footsteps. And in the pulpit the Reverend Mr. Davenport's lips hardened into a righteous and angry line.

The undercurrent of unpleasantness at home grew stronger. When the governor was there, the women for the most part treated each other with restrained courtesy. When he was not present, they deliberately said the words most likely to stir Mrs. Eaton to anger.

And as the days went by, it became clear to Lurinda that Mrs. Eaton was more easily stirred to anger than before. She had always been quick-tempered, she had always spoken her mind, but she had usually known when to retreat.

One day after listening to a particularly heated exchange, Lurinda, distressed and helpless, slipped out of the room and went into the cool dimness of the parlor. Pressing the palms of her hands against her eyes, she managed to hold her tears back. Why, oh why, in this beautiful home could there not be peace?

A voice came from a shaded corner. "Are you crying, Lurinda?"

Her hands dropped. She rubbed them against her petticoat. "Samuel. What are you doing in here?"

"Resting. My father thinks I'm out at the farm helping, and the man at the farm thinks I'm at home helping my father. It's nice and quiet in here. I don't have to listen to the women. Is that why you're here, or have you come to dust?"

"It isn't important. I can come back later." For months she had dreamed of being alone with him, of impressing him with her glittering conversation. Now she was too distraught to speak.

She fled from the room and went upstairs. In Mrs. Eaton's bedroom she smoothed the feather bed and spent a long time straightening the utensils on the chest. When she finally left, she saw old Mrs. Eaton and Miss Mary coming down the hall toward her. Old Mrs. Eaton stopped to tie her hood.

"Lurinda, if anyone should ask where we are, we've gone to see Mr. Davenport on a very important matter."

Lurinda nodded. Behind her back she knotted her fingers together. "When shall I say you'll be back?"

"We'll be back when we've received certain assurances. And you, child—I'd advise you to be very careful. Don't emulate the wrong people, or you may find yourself in trouble."

"She means not to imitate people who are themselves headed for trouble," Mary said. Her mouth closed—tight, pure.

Lurinda stood still, feeling the hard hammer strokes of her heart as they walked down the hall, their heads lifted at a godly angle, their backs righteously straight.

JOHN DAVENPORT
JULY 1644

John Davenport paced back and forth across the floor of his study, plowing his way through the steamy night air. A few moments earlier he had closed the window—too late—against the mosquitoes. Now a large June bug hurled itself against the brightness of the window like a sinner seeking the Light.

As he paced, he scratched. How did the mosquitoes—so delicate that the slightest touch would crush them—manage to penetrate his clothing? He had not even dared to loosen his band though the skin on his neck was chafed and uncomfortable. The mosquitoes, he reflected, were like sinful habits: at first appearance they seemed ephemeral, harmless, and easily overcome, but if ignored, they generated evil results out of all proportion to their size. Mosquitoes. They were discomfiting, to be sure, as were the sultry heat and the heavy air. But his real discomfort ran far deeper.

How long did that woman think she could openly defy him? With God's help he had been more than patient with her. He had given her time. God knew he had given her time to rectify her errors. He had given her the counsel of learned men. For a while she had seemed almost humble, listening in church so attentively he had felt sure God was truly working through him to save her soul.

But in the spring it had begun again. First he had noticed nothing more than a restlessness in her, a shifting in her seat, a rustling of the pages of her psalm book, a changing of expressions that bore no relation to the order of the service. Then early in the summer she had once again walked out of church. While he was still trying to decide how to handle that regression, she had, on the Sunday of this past week, committed the act that made him realize he had been hesitant and patient for too long.

Not only had she insulted the worshiping, believing congregation, the elders, and the Puritan service, but she had also insulted him—personally insulted a consecrated man of God just as he was about to clarify the words of God as told to Moses.

"Let me explain this to you," he had said. "I will be brief."

And from her seat at the front of the meetinghouse she had murmured loud enough so that he heard it clearly, "I pray you will."

God had so filled him with anger that he had hardly been able to go on, but it was an anger that made him realize that despite his love for Theophilus, he could no longer postpone positive action against his wife.

He looked at his clock, as always with a certain pride, for he was one of the few in the colony to have one. It had been a gift from a wealthy parishioner in London. It was nearly nine. Soon Theophilus would disentangle himself from all the apron strings that threatened to immobilize him and cross the street.

I must find the right words, he thought.

A moment later a knock sounded and he opened the door to his friend. A smell of salt marshes floated in on the humid air. Lately the townsmen had given four days each to digging a channel across the mud flats so boats could be brought at low tide to a proposed warehouse at the foot of one of the streets. The digging had added the smell of rotting vegetation to the air.

Theophilus gave him a tired smile as he entered. "Sorry to be so late. I had to deal with a messenger from Stamford. The savage who assaulted the woman in Stamford with a hammer has been caught. I made arrangements for him to be brought here for trial."

Waving him to a chair, Davenport said, "And the woman—how is she? Will she ever recover her reason?"

"It's unlikely. The blows were enough to kill most people."

They sat down. Theophilus shook his head tiredly when he was offered Madeira.

"Do you suppose," Davenport asked, "that this is the same savage who murdered that man between Stamford and Fairfield?"

"Who knows? So many of them are murderous by nature. And most of them can't differentiate between an Englishman and a Dutchman. They're just at war with white men, and when they see one who's helpless, they attack."

"I wonder—when the Dutch asked us for help last winter—would these attacks have been prevented if we had helped?"

. Sighing, Theophilus shook his head. "I don't think so. If we had joined the Dutch in a general war against the Indians, we'd then be open to attack on all sides and from all Indians. As it is, we do have a good relationship with the Quinnipiacs. Besides, if the situation were reversed, I'm sure the Dutch would refuse us any kind of help. They wouldn't even offer food and grain as we have." Again he shook his head. "They brought a great deal of this on themselves by selling the Indians arms and ammunition they hoped would be used against us."

"You're right. Your appraisal is completely realistic. You have acted for the best interests of the town. So far as our town and colony go, my friend, you are a fine, even an irreplaceable leader."

Theophilus gave him a sharp look. "And elsewhere?"

"Elsewhere?"

"I thought you qualified your statement. Perhaps you did so without thinking." His lips, his nose, his whole face suddenly seemed thinner, sharper. "Were you perhaps implying that I do not display leadership in my personal life?" His voice had the taut pitch of controlled anger.

John Davenport could feel his own muscles and nerves tightening in response. Obviously, he had made the wrong approach. Despite all their years of closeness, all their years of looking at problems together and working out solutions, they were at this moment further apart than the Dutch and English settlers.

"Good friend," he said in a conciliatory voice, "you must admit the Eatons—both men and women—are strong-minded and independent. And apparently they seek mates of the same kind. It's stock that breeds leaders, but it also breeds . . ." He paused, hoping Theophilus would fill in the necessary word.

But Theophilus merely sat with his head inclined a little, his face closed and unresponsive.

"It is stock," Davenport went on, "that, when its independence of thought veers in the wrong direction, breeds trouble. I've taken no public steps because of our friendship, but I can put off such action no longer."

"Public steps against whom?"

"Surely, my friend, you must know that I'm speaking of your wife and of all her transgressions and, especially, of her public repudiation of our service of worship. Believe me, I have never taken action with a greater reluctance, but after long discussion with the elders, it has been agreed that tomorrow—"

At his last word Theophilus seemed to come alive. "Oh, not tomorrow. Let me talk with her first."

"You have already talked with her many times. As have I. And the best minds in the church."

"She means no harm. She is misguided."

"Misguided, yes. But you must admit she scorns all proper guidance. We have exhorted her, counseled her, prayed with her. You know that. It has done no good. She goes her own way, openly flouting our convictions and influencing goodness knows how many of our less strong-minded communicants."

Theophilus stared at him for a long moment. A deep and deeply tired sigh escaped his lips. "You cannot wait even a few more weeks?"

"If I do, can you assure me of her absolute reform?"

Theophilus pressed his lips together. His shoulders slumped.

"And that is not all," Davenport said. He went to his desk and got out a long sheet of paper. "Your mother and your daughter— your daughter Mary, that is—visited me one day recently. Here are their charges, charges that indicate a profound lack of Christian behavior in the home. And all these acts—lies, unfounded accusations against your daughter, lack of respect for an older woman, and so forth—were witnessed also by other than members of your family."

Theophilus quickly skimmed the paper, shaking his head as he read. His fingers trembled a little as he handed it back.

"Do not be sad or upset, my friend," Davenport said. "The lack is not in you. You have done your best, I know."

Theophilus rubbed his forehead. "You will have a trial?"

"Yes. After the offering tomorrow afternoon."

"And what will your recommendation be—censure?"

"No."

"Not excommunication?" His face was white.

It was hard for Davenport to stay firm. "Yes."

"Could you not merely suggest censure?"

"I could. But knowing her wilfulness . . ."

"To excommunicate her—" Theophilus shuddered. "You don't really know her, John. Underneath her air of confidence is a loneliness. She needs the Sabbath—the people, the news, the intellectual stimulation of the sermon."

"We all do. That is why we have set the day aside for worship. That is why we must weed out those who would prevent others from worshiping in our way."

Rising, Theophilus said, "I see I cannot move you."

"Wait. Sit down a minute." Davenport waited until his friend had again eased himself into the chair. "Have you ever changed a political decision because of me?"

"No. But you never asked me to."

"Correct. I gave advice freely when you came to me for it, but I never tried to dissuade you from a decision already made."

"Your inclinations have been reflected in most of my decisions."

"Only because you came to me freely for advice." He paused. "We made an agreement when the town was organized. Do you remember?"

Theophilus briefly pressed his fingers against his eyes. "Yes, I remember. But at that time I never envisioned anything like this. Except, perhaps, for my brother Samuel. And once he was gone, I felt all possibility of dissension arising from my family had been removed." Again he sighed and the sound was so full of melancholy and fatigue that Davenport felt almost moved to pity, almost moved to reverse his decision.

"Perhaps," Theophilus continued, "I've been too busy with colony affairs to see what was happening. And I've been away far too much."

"Yes. And your wife does need a strong guiding hand."

Silence fell. After a moment or two Theophilus said, "You are right, however. We did have an agreement." He smiled. It was not his usual spontaneous smile. It was an intellectual smile, a smile that said his mind knew he must be agreeable even if his heart still felt resentment. "You must, as the leader of our church, do what you feel is right."

"Theophilus, my friend. My dearest friend." Davenport went to him and put a hand on his shoulder. "Do you have any idea of how hard a decision this was to make? To try the wife of my best and oldest friend, to risk losing his friendship—a friendship that means more to me than any other earthly friendship?" He saw Theophilus look up at him, his eyes no longer quite so cold. "Theophilus, I cannot do it." He shook his head. "I realize as of this moment that I cannot do it. I cannot risk losing our friendship. I must find some other way."

"No." His friend's voice was suddenly firm. "You must do it.

We made an agreement long ago: the town was to be mine to run, the church yours. She is undermining your work; you cannot do otherwise than excommunicate her. And do not fear that I will think less of you. In a way I will think more. For I cannot help admiring a man who follows his conscience at the risk of losing what he truly values."

John let his hand fall from his friend's shoulder. "Friends still, then?"

"Friends always."

They clasped hands as Theophilus rose. "About recommending censure rather than excommunication," Davenport said, "I'll sleep on it tonight, pray on it."

"You must do what you feel is right." Theophilus went to the door. "I must go now. It's been a long day."

"Good night, my friend." Davenport held the candle in the open doorway so Theophilus could see his way to the street. A mosquito hummed near his ear, but he paid no attention to it. After he had closed the door and had put down the candle, he clasped his hands across his stomach and let his breath out in a long, unburdening sigh.

ANN EATON / JULY 1644

It was going to be another hot day. The air, when Ann awakened about an hour after sunup, was soft and still and laden with mist. No horses' hooves beat on the hard-packed road; no children's voices rose from the yards. It was the Sabbath, and it was as peaceful and quiet as it must have been on the Lord's first day of rest after He had created the world.

She always looked forward to the Sabbath, to the change from the tedium of the daily routine: the new ideas, the different faces, the talk, the special clothes.

For a while she lay quietly in bed. The smell of the sea came in her window mixed with the spice of the gillyflowers. From somewhere in the tall trees a bird song rippled through the stillness with three rising, chordlike notes, a pause, three more rising in a different key, and then three descending. It reminded her of the music that had been played in the churches of her childhood. Was this God's way of saying He did not disapprove of music on the Sabbath?

Stretching lazily, she wondered what Mr. Davenport would say if she suggested such a thing. Nothing, perhaps. Lately he seemed less concerned about her behavior. The last time she had risen to walk out of church, he had not even looked up from the communion table. Perhaps he had decided to accept her for what she was, realizing she was sincere. Or perhaps he had concluded that he could not afford to antagonize the wife of a man who, as governor of their growing colony, was becoming increasingly powerful in the new world. Last night Theophilus had spent no more than an hour with him. And he had spent an hour with her beforehand. John Davenport, she thought, your influence may be waning.

Feeling pleasantly stimulated, she slipped out of bed and went to the washstand where she washed her face and rinsed her mouth with clove-scented water. As she was putting on her pink-and-white rail, she heard the first of the Sunday morning drum rolls. A moment later a knock, like a miniature drum roll, sounded on her door.

She opened it to her grave-faced husband, still wearing his nightshirt. He had not returned to her the previous evening, but she had known he was very tired. She also knew that a man of middle age who is deeply fatigued in the evening is sometimes full of vigor in the morning, and, feeling excitement suddenly stir her blood, she lifted a happy face for his kiss, glad that her breath and skin were fresh.

His kiss was brief and chaste. Drawing away, she said, "Why, then, did you come in your nightshirt?"

"Because I wanted to talk with you first thing today. Alone, uninterrupted." He latched the door. "Sit down." He waited. "Sit down. Please."

She sat down.

"I went to see our pastor last night." He paused and then spoke steadily. "You will be tried in church today at the end of the afternoon service."

Her skin began to prickle. "For what?"

"For your behavior in the meetinghouse . . . and at home."

"At home? What does my behavior in the home have to do with the doctrine he preaches?"

"You do not behave like a Christian. You are impatient, subject to fits of temper."

"And who would not—?"

He lifted a hand to silence her. "You make unfounded accusations. You lie. You do not show proper respect for women who are older than you."

Rising, she went to the window. Once again she heard the organlike bird song. Closing her eyes briefly, she said, "Now I understand. It is your mother who has stirred up sentiment against me. And because of her, your wife will stand trial." She turned and faced him. "Don't you have any pride? Think what they'll say in the other settlements. Can you not control your mother?"

150

After what seemed like a long time, he said softly, "Can I control my wife?"

She smiled. "You could, Theophilus. Oh, you *could* . . . if you treated her as you once did, if you made her feel she really was your helpmate." She stared at his expressionless face. Was it possible that he could stand by with complete calmness and allow this to happen to her? Didn't he want to do anything about it or . . . couldn't he?

"It is true," she said. "You cannot control your wife and you cannot control your mother. Nor can you, obviously, control events outside your home. It is completely clear that it is the Reverend John Davenport who is really governor of New Haven."

His lips whitened. "You are wrong. I am governor in every sense. *Every* sense. Not once has he ever interfered or tried to influence me."

She had spoken impulsively. Half of her knew it. Half of her realized her words were calculated to hurt and should not have been said. The other half of her exulted in having been able to find the words that could anger him most. They were on equal footing in an argument, for her mind was as quick as his. But she gained nothing by making him aware of this. Why, then, did she do it? Why did the need to assert herself temporarily banish all common sense?

Yet more unbidden words came. "He has no need to interfere," she said. "You consult him ahead of time and he advises. All the decisions are actually his decisions."

Theophilus opened the door. "This is always your way, my dear. When you have done wrong, you never seek to right the wrongs. You never admit your guilt. Instead, you fling accusations in every possible direction."

She realized that he was leaving, leaving her to face the day completely alone, completely unaided. And it was her fault. What had driven her to taunt him so? Speaking softly now, hoping he would realize that the sound of her voice was a kind of apology, she said, "Theophilus, what will happen to me?"

"I don't know."

"You must know something. Surely he confided in you, told you his intention."

"He said only that you will be tried today."

"But it's ridiculous. He spoke to me once about some of the

charges. They're all nonsense. And you, as governor of this colony, can stop this whole silly affair." She went to him, put her hands flat on his chest. Underneath her palms she could feel the hard beating of his heart, the heart that had so often beat against hers. They were close: man and wife, one in the sight of God. He could not let this happen to her. "You can prevent it," she said. "Just tell him that you are the governor and you will not stand for having a member of your family humiliated in this way."

She looked up at him, waiting for him to melt and put his arms around her. Instead he smiled thinly. "But you have said that I am only a puppet, that I have no power." Taking her hands by both wrists, he removed them from his chest, turned and went out of the room.

Ann stared at the closed door. He would come back; surely he would come back. But he did not. Nor would she pursue him. She had humbled herself enough.

Briskly she dressed and fixed her hair. She chose a dark-red silk gown and wore a white lace furbelow with it. The clothing gave her confidence. When she arrived at the meetinghouse she was able to greet people with her usual assurance.

After dinner, she returned to her room. Sitting in the gathering heat, she leafed through the book Lady Moody had given her, wondering whether at this last moment she could detect any arguments that seemed illogical. But she was so distracted now that the book seemed nothing more than a mass of words that defied understanding. While she sat there, the afternoon drum roll rumbled from the public square. Once again, as she had for her first service in this land, she fastened a red rose at her waist.

Her heart beat with a strange loudness as she followed her husband and mother-in-law in the procession headed for church. Hannah came up from behind and slipped her hand in hers. Perhaps some feminine intuition told her that her mother was in trouble. Ann squeezed her hand. "Run along with your friends now," she said.

She walked with measured step as Nepaupuck had on the day of the first execution in the colony. "It is *weregin*," he had said. But this was not *weregin*. It was unnecessary, uncalled for, unfair.

For once she hated her seat in the front of the church. She could feel hundreds of eyes focused on her back. Did they like her and sympathize with her, or did they envy and hate her? How would they vote if Mr. Davenport asked for a show of hands?

She hardly heard the prayer or the scripture. When the psalm was announced, she rose but did not sing with the others:

I called unto the Lord in my trouble, and he heard me.
Deliver my soul, O Lord, from lying lips, and from a deceitful tongue.

Clearly, the psalm had been chosen for her. She closed her ears to the rest of it. Nor did she take notes when Mr. Davenport preached his afternoon sermon.

At the end of the sermon Mr. Hooke said, "Brethren of the congregation, wherefore as God hath prospered you, so freely offer."

Theophilus rose and went forward with his offering of some pieces of silver. Following him came the magistrates, the elders, the married men, the single men, and, at the end, the widows. Ann watched impassively. After the contribution—that was when the trials were held.

When the last of the widows had returned to her seat, Robert Newman, the ruling elder, came forward. He cleared his throat.

"Some of the brethren have been waiting to hear what issue the matter concerning Mrs. Eaton is brought to. We elders have not been neglecting it, but have been preparing matters for your hearing. If you are willing that she be now called forth and have the particulars read to you, we will do so. We will take your silence for consent."

Was it possible for a church to be so silent? Were they all so anxious to see her humbled? Ann took a breath. The air had grown oppressive. The smell of sweat lay heavily on it, and barn smells, and fisherman smells, and a sharp new scent that seemed to come from her own body.

"Mrs. Eaton, you will come forward."

Slowly she rose, rubbing the palms of her hands against her gown. From their seats behind the altar the elders looked disapprovingly down at her. Only Ezekial's face had any kindness in it.

The ruling elder nodded to Mr. Davenport who began a recounting of her transgressions against the church: how, though she had known it was an offense to all, she had departed from the assembly whenever baptism or the Lord's Supper was administered; how she had fallen into this error through reading a book given to her by Lady Moody of the Bay Colony; how she had shown it to several friends, thereby further spreading the infection; how she had failed to seek help and light from either her husband or her pastor according to biblical injunction.

She tried to close her ears to his words, to divert her mind with old memories: her first husband fastening a necklace around her throat; Maud brushing her hair and talking about May Day. Yet she could not avoid hearing most of it. He spoke of talking with her, of preaching a special sermon for her, of writing out answers to all the points in A.R.'s book, and of having them explained to her.

"After that," he said, "I waited. When I saw that she continued as she was and did not propound any questions, I marveled at the hand of God therein, fearing that, as before she would not seek Light, so now God would not give her a heart to receive Light."

He paused. Was that to be all? Ann looked at Theophilus. It was said that if you stared at a person long enough, he would feel your eyes on him and would turn toward you. But he was staring straight ahead . . . detached . . . uninterested.

"While I was thus sadly exercised," Mr. Davenport continued, "divers rumors were spread up and down the town of her scandalous walking in her family."

In all, he told the congregation, the church had seventeen particulars against her, each of them documented by two witnesses. He had admonished her about these, he said, and she had refused to give satisfaction for any—to deny, to admit, or to repent. She had barely deigned to listen.

Ann moistened her lips and tried to stand straighter as Mr. Davenport read the seventeen charges against her. Her feet hurt. It had never occurred to her that her feet would hurt. To her side she could hear the rustle of taffeta petticoats as women settled themselves comfortably to hear about the scandalous goings-on in the home of their governor.

She heard him say that she had struck old Mrs. Eaton on the face, thus in her sinful rage and passion breaking both the Fifth and Sixth Commandments;

that she had unjustly charged Mary, saying her belly was great and her breasts big, and she looked blue under the eyes, and vomited, and that she feared her sickness would be an ill sickness— slander of a high nature, contrary to the Ninth Commandment as well as to Romans III:8;

that she had accused Mary of ruining the souls of other young women who came into the house—slander, contrary to the Ninth Commandment;

that she had called her maids wicked wretches—an unpeaceable speech contrary to the Ninth Commandment as well as to I Peter II: 21, 22, 23;

that in a kitchen argument with Mary over who was responsible for some spilled milk she had said, "Oh for the Lord Jesus Christ's sake, hold your peace"—a sin against the Third Commandment as it is a taking of God's name in vain, and against the Ninth Commandment as she would not let her daughter clear herself;

that she had accused Miss Mary of having wrought with the Devil—a false accusation of a very high nature and a sin against the Ninth Commandment;

and that she had said old Mrs. Eaton was not really her mother—a sin against the Ninth Commandment.

Off to her side Ann could hear whisperings. A heat spread over her skin. How embarrassing it was to have her family's personal life spread out for all to see, like stained clothes bleaching in the sun.

On and on he went documenting her breaking of the Third, Fifth, Sixth, and Ninth Commandments. He finished by saying that one morning she had complained to Mr. Eaton because their manservant Anthony had not brought water; then because the governor did not choose to reproach Anthony, she had suggested with much heat of spirit that both men get out of the house.

"And this," Mr. Davenport said, "is a breach of the Fifth Commandment, violating her relation to her husband and her servant, and against the Sixth Commandment in her distempered passion, and so a scandal by her ill example. Also, her desire of getting from her husband is against the covenant of marriage, contrary to First Corinthians seven:ten."

He stopped. After a moment she heard Robert Newman saying, "Do you, Mrs. Eaton, have anything to object to in these facts charged upon you?"

She took a breath. "Yes, I do. I'd like to say that the evidence is flimsy and the charges much exaggerated. A woman's maids are likely to be lazy and resentful of direction. They are hardly reliable witnesses. Most of the charges are based on the sort of exchange that goes on in many large households. When women spend hours working together in close quarters, tensions arise and things are said without anything serious being meant. It is my feeling, therefore, that I should not be censured."

Mr. Davenport said, "Such things may go on elsewhere, but since these evils have been brought out in public, they cannot pass without the church's rebuke. The rule is: Those that sin openly must be rebuked openly. Do not sit down, Mrs. Eaton. Stand right there, facing the church." He nodded to Robert Newman. "We await the decision of the church."

"Are you satisfied," the ruling elder now asked the congregation, "that these facts have been sufficiently proved? If so, please signify by raising your hands."

With her shoulders held as rigidly as if they were clamped in the pillory, Ann stood and watched. Mary and old Mrs. Eaton were the first to raise their hands. Vindictive, lying women . . . Others followed until it looked as if all hands were up.

"Having heard these facts charged and proved," the ruling elder continued, "you must now consider whether Mrs. Eaton should be cast out for these facts or whether she is deserving only of an admonition."

Several people said they were afraid she'd never change if she were only admonished; others said she had already been given enough time to change her ways.

Finally Mr. Davenport spoke again. "Brethren, the charges against Mrs. Eaton are many and great." He looked toward Theophilus who remained motionless, still staring straight ahead. "Yet," Mr. Davenport went on, "I feel they are not of that nature that calls for a cutting off from the church. I am not sure they proceed from a habitual frame of sinning in her. I recommend . . . I recommend a public admonition."

Ann could hardly believe she had heard him correctly. She had been sure he would ask for excommunication. Why hadn't he? There could be only one reason. He obviously did not feel he could, on such flimsy evidence, go that far in humbling the wife of the governor. Anger surged through her. If he dared not excommunicate her, why even admonish her?

He turned now to her, the piety on his round, sweating face mocking her. It was as if he were saying, "See how magnanimous I am? I could have had you excommunicated, but I chose instead to give you another chance."

In a sonorous voice he said, "In the name of the Lord Jesus

Christ, and with the consent of this church, I do charge thee, Mrs. Eaton, to attend unto the several rules that you have broken, and to judge yourself by them, and to hold forth your repentance according to God, as you will answer it at the great day of Jesus Christ."

After he had dismissed the congregation, Ann returned to her seat and wiped her forehead with her handkerchief. When Theophilus came to her now, what should she say? How should she greet him? Glancing across to his seat, she saw that it was vacant. A coldness moved against her heart. He had gone. He had not even cared enough about her feelings to escort her out.

She knew what it would be like outside with people standing around in little groups exchanging gossip. They would have plenty to gossip about now. And the look on her face as she came out of the meetinghouse would add the final touch to their accounts of this day. If she had gone out on the arm of the governor, it might have silenced them a little. But to be alone. . . .

The elders had come down from their seats behind the pulpit and were filing out behind the last of the members. One of them stopped at her side.

Gratefully she turned to him. "Well, Ezekial, it's been a fine day—hasn't it? A fine day for our pastor and for the elders."

"Not for all of them."

"Are you saying there were some who didn't agree that this should be done?"

"I know of one. One only."

Softly she said, "You do not believe the charges?"

A faint smile flickered around his mouth. "Oh, I believe most of them were probably based on actual incidents. But I know how great the pressures on you are. And I also know how impetuous and quick-tempered you are. These, I feel, are not so much sins as faults that you should strive to control."

"Yes. I must try harder." Suddenly, she wanted to cry. She blinked rapidly as her eyelids began to burn. How ridiculous. She never cried. And she had not been excommunicated. Why should she cry? Evidently his gesture of sympathy, his understanding, had made her drop the tight control she had put on her emotions.

"Don't," he said. "Don't cry. They'll be looking at you when you go outside. Remember, you're still the governor's wife."

"Much good it has done me."

"You weren't excommunicated."

"Yes. Perhaps the object was merely public humiliation."

"Wipe your eyes. Quickly now. That's it. Lift your chin. Good."

She held out her hand. "Thank you, Ezekial. For everything."

His clasp was firm. Warm. A moment before, she had felt his mind touch hers with understanding; now their fingers were clasped together. They were standing near the pulpit in the house of God, their hands joined, just as couples had stood during their wedding services in the days before the Puritans had outlawed such papal pageantry and had decreed that marriages were to be solemnized in a civil ceremony.

As their hands dropped, Ann saw a figure enter the meeting-house and come down the aisle toward them, hesitating in the dimness.

"Is that you, Ezekial?"

"Yes. I was just . . . counseling with Mrs. Eaton."

"So I see."

"Good afternoon, Mary," Ann said.

"Good afternoon, Mrs. Eaton." The voice was calm, more assured than usual.

Ann found herself unable to think of anything to say. Mary's eyes, large and shadowed in her thin white face, rested a moment on her, then moved away.

"Are you coming, Ezekial? The children are waiting."

"Yes, I'm coming."

They preceded her out of the meetinghouse, hurrying away. Ann stepped outside, her body stiff and strange. As she went down the steps, she saw people still gathered in clusters. Most talking ceased as she approached.

She nodded, tried to smile. They nodded back. Most of them reserved comment until she was beyond hearing, but she did catch the last words of one woman saying, ". . . smiling just as if nothing had happened."

The air was heavy and moist, laden as it moved sluggishly in from the harbor with a low-tide smell of rotting vegetation. She walked slowly. Her two-storied home would be cooler than most places, yet she felt she'd rather put her head down on a chopping block than go home to the smug triumph of her mother-in-law and stepdaughter.

Someday, John Davenport, she thought bitterly, I'll have my revenge for this. Someday you'll know what it is to be publicly humiliated. And when that time comes, I'll stand by and smile.

But the thought brought little comfort. With her fingers on the latch, she hesitated outside the door of her home, closed against the summer heat. No woman, she thought, ever has anything harder to face than the triumph of another woman.

Don't let them know how you feel. Lift your chin. Good.

Although her stomach felt as if it had been drawn up tight with leather thongs, she knew her expression was pleasant and unconcerned as she stepped into the coolness of the great hall.

THEOPHILUS EATON
SUMMER 1644

Theophilus felt he would never forget the look on Ann's face when she came into the house after her censure. He had walked home earlier with the children to save them the embarrassment of any questions. The younger children had hardly seemed aware of the implications of what was going on. Hannah had asked only, "Why was Mama standing in front of the church?" When he had said the elders had wanted to ask Mama some questions, she had been quite satisfied. Young Theophilus had been quite indifferent to the whole matter; Samuel, though he looked concerned, said nothing.

His mother, however, could speak of nothing else. Just before Ann came in, she had been suggesting that only the intercession of someone very highly placed could have prevented the excommunication she had been expecting.

"If it was you," the old woman had said, "—and who else could it have been?—you'll be sorry. I know. She'll think now that she can get away with anything. Watch her come in with her head in the air and a brazen smile on her face."

And Ann had done exactly that. She had come in with her head at a haughty angle and her smile confident. Looking at her, he had been torn between admiration and revulsion. God knew her every word and act made his job as family leader and colony leader ever more difficult and more frustrating. Yet like this defiant, untamed land, she challenged him and stirred him with excitement. These were feelings, however, that he must carefully conceal.

Sternly, he said, "Where have you been?"

"At the meetinghouse."

"All this time? What delayed you?"

"I was talking with one of the elders."

"Seeking counsel?"

Her lips twitched. "We weren't discussing trade."

"A typical disrespectful answer," old Mrs. Eaton said. "She has no more respect for you, Son, than she has for the church."

Ignoring his mother, Ann said to Theophilus. "Your question was unnecessary. After my afternoon's experience, what else would I be discussing with one of the elders but my personal life?" In a gentler voice she added, "Do you not suppose that I am by this time of day tired of standing in front of people and being both accused and questioned?"

The appeal in her voice softened his heart. "Then why do you not sit down? We will speak of other things. And soon we will have supper."

"I'd rather go upstairs. I'd like to rest. It's been so hot. And I don't think I want any supper."

"Very well, my dear. Perhaps Lurinda will take something up to you a little later."

She nodded and left the room.

Almost before the door to the stairway closed behind her, his mother said, "Spoiled. She came to you spoiled by an indulgent husband and by her father before him. Instead of reversing the process, you have continued it, indulging her every whim, letting her feminine ways befog your mind."

"You're forgetting she did not come to me as a young girl, Mother. She was already quite set in her ways."

"You are a leader, Theophilus. You should know that it is never too late to help someone change and grow more acceptable in the eyes of God."

His chest rose and fell and his breath came out in a long, harsh sound that reflected the weariness deep inside him. The day had not been an easy one for him. The most tiring days, he had discovered, were those during which his mind and heart were drawn in opposing directions. While a part of him had sat back like a magistrate and acknowledged the need for today's trial, another part of him had stood beside his wife and shared her pain. He had even asked himself whether such humiliation was necessary. He had been beset by the same conflicting feelings that had caused him inner anguish in the early days of the colony when he had decreed the execution of Nepaupuck. Do we have the right to do this? he had asked himself then. And then, as now, the answer—unpleasant though it was—had been that it must be done for the sake of the well-being of the rest of the people in the colony.

Today, as he had sat impassively in his assigned seat in the church, he had reminded himself that his best friend John Davenport—a man who was closer to God and to an understanding of right and wrong than anyone else in the colony—had seen the need for the trial. John must have hated the role his office had today forced upon him. No man could be anything but disturbed at having to try the wife of his best friend.

His mother stood up. "Since you have told the governor's lady that she may rest, I can see that it is I who will have to supervise the preparations for supper. Again."

He started to speak, but she lifted her hand. "I predict that her behavior will continue to be as scandalous as before and that she will never show a sign of repentance—if she isn't doing even more scandalous things."

She swept out of the room: tiny, dignified, and all too wise. But her words remained with him during the weeks that followed like partially digested food that sent up sour reminders now and then of its presence.

Added to his mother's disapproval was, he noticed, a coolness in his wife's manner toward him. She was pleasant but reserved, never quite herself. During the first weeks after her trial she did not go out at all, and when he finally went to their room one night and found her sitting on the edge of their bed fastening the ribbons on her nightgown, she greeted him with what seemed almost like pleasure. It was clear that she had been lonely.

Sitting down beside her, he put his arm loosely across her shoulders. She drew away only a little. "So," she said. "So now you're ready to be my husband again."

"I've always been your husband."

"Except for the one time when I really needed you."

"But," he said gently, "what happened to you was your own fault. You courted that admonition. You did it deliberately." The skin of her shoulder was excitingly pliant under his fingers and a faint perfume drifted from her body, making his breath quicken. "I had no choice but to stand aside and let the matter take its course."

She looked earnestly at him. "But you did use your influence to see to it that I was not excommunicated."

"Well . . ."

"Of course you did."

"Perhaps being governor—"

"Yes. Anything you said would carry some weight." Sighing softly, she turned her body sweetly against his. "Ah, well, it's all in the past. It's all behind me."

He wanted to remind her that a case of censure is not over until repentance is evident, but as her face lifted toward his and her lips came close, the admonition slipped from his mind. Another time, he thought. This was not the moment to upset her or risk angering her.

Yet though she had been sweetly pliant for a little while, the trouble in the household continued. When he asked his wife about it, she was always angered. "You don't understand how it is with women. When I join your mother and daughter in work, they remark with surprise. When I reprimand one of the girls, they defend her. When I respond to this, they accuse me of being hot-tempered. They are constantly either inciting me to anger or scorning me for becoming angry."

He wanted to believe her. When his arms were around her and he was enveloped in her softness and her voice was like honey in his ear, he was convinced of her gentleness and defenselessness. Yet when his mother or his daughter began a beguiling recital of facts, quoting exact words said, he found himself swayed in their direction. He often wondered what Solomon would have done, but a careful rereading of the wise king's words yielded no help. His wisest move, he finally decided, was to remain unmoved. When the women came complaining, he listened, he counseled, he preached patience and calmness. Beyond that, the whole affair was in the hands of God.

Though she never mentioned it when they were alone, he felt sure that Ann must be pondering on all she had been accused of during her trial. It was like her to work in secret. One day she would surely emerge from her room with a formal statement of acknowledgment and repentance for the elders. After waiting and watching for several weeks, he finally broached the subject one evening when they were alone in the bedroom.

"Have you spoken or written to the elders yet?"

"About what?"

Patiently he said, "About the charges against you."

"They have tried me and humiliated me. They have had their day of triumph; what more do they want?"

"Evidence that their labor has borne fruit. Evidence that you acknowledge your transgressions and repent of them."

"And if I do not?" Her head tilted angrily. "If I cannot acknowledge that all the petty backstairs gossip about me was the immortal truth—what then?"

"Each of the charges was supported by proof in that each one was witnessed by two people. If you refuse to take the charges seriously, you must understand that the elders will probably take further steps. So far they have been very lenient with you—"

"Lenient—" The word exploded from her lips. Her color rose and her eyes grew fiery. At times like this he was irresistibly drawn to her. It took a great deal of moral strength to keep his back straight and his expression stern.

"Lenient," she repeated. "Harassing me in my home, humiliating me before the church—you call that lenient? Why do they choose *me* for all this? I am no different from dozens of other women in this town."

"You *are* different, my dear. As the governor's wife, you set an important example. What you do is far more likely to be followed as an example than what some goodwife of inferior birth and breeding does. Furthermore, you are brighter, quicker to think and act, more emotional—"

"These are sins?"

"Perhaps not. But they lead to irresponsible acts."

She made a little face, like that of a child who pretends she cannot understand the complexities of adult ways.

"In the past," he continued, "you have seen others censured. You know that after a few weeks they have either presented writings to the elders or appeared before the Assembly to acknowledge errors and give evidence of repentance." He paused. "I should think the former would be easier. Would you like me to have writing materials sent to you?"

She gave him a hard look. Abruptly she moved away and, turning her back, began unpinning her hair.

Usually he loved watching the hair fall around her shoulders as the strands were freed. It was part of the treasured intimacy of the bedroom. Now he felt he had been dismissed as peremptorily as a servant, and the impatience he had felt earlier crystallized into anger. Without speaking again, he left the room, closing the door carefully and quietly behind him. Door slamming was for women.

Using the same willed control, he was able to close his mind to her actions most of the time. Sometimes it did not even take much willpower, for as fall waned into winter he was busier than ever before with the increasing responsibilities of the governorship.

Fortunately for the colony, the Dutch had such problems with the Indians that they had neither time nor men to harass the English. The Dutch war with the Indians extended from Manhattan to Stamford as well as deep into Long Island. In both places it was too close to settlements of the New Haven Colony, but the United Colonies had proved a powerful deterrent against Indian attack. Savage though they were, the Indians apparently understood that an attack on one colony would now constitute an attack on all four. They were also no doubt aware that each colony now had a well-trained and completely armed militia, for many of them were present on the four days a year when the troops were mustered and reviewed.

Theophilus had decreed also that no man should go out to the fields unarmed and that the soldiers should always wear their arms to church. When he heard the clank of their arms during the service, he never thought ill of them, for his people were being protected.

His greatest source of optimism was the great ship that would one day—perhaps within a year—ply a profitable trade back and forth across the ocean. The skilled workmen from Rhode Island had already begun work on it. Piles of lumber had been cut and were seasoning at the water's edge. The rhythmic sounds of sawing and the fresh smell of newly cut wood had, all summer, been borne into town by the breeze from the harbor. During the months after his wife's censure, the sound of a saw or the clear ring of a hammer were always sure to brighten his outlook.

The work seemed slow, however, perhaps because his hopes for a speedy building had been so great. He had hoped the ship would be ready for the summer of 1645, but as the winter of 1644 approached—and it came very early, with blustery snowstorms arriving in mid-November—he began to fear it would not be ready.

It was on such a stormy day, when he was snug in his closet working on accounts, that Lurinda knocked timidly on his door.

He was well pleased with Lurinda. Though she appeared to be delicate, she had not had a sick day since she had been with them. Her behavior was irreproachable. Despite being his wife's personal servant, she cheerfully performed tasks anywhere in the house and she was unfailingly courteous to the other women in the family. When young—or even older—men were present, she always kept her eyes modestly lowered, never flirting, never trying to call attention to herself. She was so conscious of her duties that she did not even seem aware of the presence of young Samuel, who was not far from her age.

Her decorous behavior was in pleasant contrast to that of servants in many other homes. Hardly a session of the court occurred without a recalcitrant servant coming up before him charged with lying, stealing, slander, or speaking sharply to master or mistress. And the offenses continued despite the severe and humiliating punishments: irons, locks worn on the body, public whippings, even banishment.

"Yes, Lurinda. What is it?" He gave her a friendly smile. He was determined that he would find a good husband for her when her term was concluded—someone of her own class, of course, but with a reputation for hard work and high morals.

"Some of the elders are here to see you, Your Grace. And to see Mrs. Eaton."

"I see." Rising, he said, "Have you summoned her?"

"No, Your Grace. I'm on my way."

"Thank you. Tell her we'll be in the great hall."

He went quickly down the stairs and met Mr. Hooke and Brother Lupton in the hall where they were brushing snow from their cloaks and large-brimmed hats.

"Well, gentlemen, what brings you out on such a blustery day?"

Mr. Hooke looked past him. Turning, he saw Ann entering from the stairway, smoothing her dark hair as she came toward them.

"You received my writing?" she said pleasantly.

Theophilus felt a leap of joy. Underneath all her defiance lay, after all, a feminine compliance.

"Gentlemen," he said, "let us sit down at the table—here by the fire where you can warm yourselves. Right here, my dear." He held a chair for his wife, feeling warm and expansive. What better

166

news could there be than that she had acknowledged her faults in writing and they had come to lift the censure? No longer would he need to feel that vague shame that came from having someone close to him under the disapproving shadow of the church.

It was only as he, too, sat down that he noticed that the elders were not smiling, that their foreheads were creased with concern. For a moment no one spoke. Some sleet crackled against the window and the rosy logs in the fireplace behind them crackled a warm answer.

"Yes, Mrs. Eaton," Mr. Hooke said, "your writing has been received and studied. We find it defective."

"In what way?" Her face was that of a gently affronted woman, but in her voice Theophilus heard a familiar gathering of stubbornness.

"It neither comes up to acknowledging the particulars for which you were admonished nor holds forth repentance according to God."

Brother Lupton frowned, cleared his throat, and nodded.

Drumming her fingers on the table, she made a faint exasperated sound. Theophilus leaned toward her, covering her drumming fingers with his large quiet hand, and said, "It might be well, my dear, to ask what your next step is."

"And what is my next step?" She sounded as a child does when forced against his will to speak.

Giving her a stern look, Brother Lupton spoke up. It was evident that he had missed neither the stubbornness in her voice nor her growing hostility.

"First you must acknowledge the facts as they appeared in the admonition. Secondly, you must hold forth your repentance, confess your sins and judge yourself for them. And thirdly"—he gave her a look so remonstrative that even the hardest of sinners would have shrunk from it—"you must correct your scandalous miscarriage to the extent that those who formerly testified against you can testify to your complete reformation."

"That's ridiculous. Ridiculous." She pounded her fists on the table in a fit of temper that was shamefully like those that had been described at her trial.

"My dear—" Theophilus said.

But she had jumped to her feet, scraping her chair back across the floor. "Don't you understand anything about what's happened?

Those who testified against me will never testify for me no matter how I behave."

"Are you saying they are liars?" Mr. Hooke asked quietly.

She blinked. Theophilus could see that she understood that by agreeing she would be adding yet another well-witnessed libel charge and breach of the Ninth Commandment to the long list of charges against her.

She rubbed her hand across her eyes. "I am saying that I do not believe they can be induced to change their testimony."

Mr. Hooke and Brother Lupton looked at each other, exchanging unspoken signals. Together they rose. In a formal voice Brother Lupton said, "In the face of your continued obstinacy, no further talk seems reasonable at this time. The church awaits your reconciliation with it. Meanwhile we will bewail the hardness of your heart and shall mourn for you in secret."

In a less formal voice Mr. Hooke said, "We shall discuss what you have said with the remaining elders."

She rose. "Is that quite all?" When they nodded, she said, "Thank you, gentlemen." With her head high, she walked gracefully out of the room.

"Thank you, gentlemen," Theophilus himself said. He felt as if his chest were filled with lead. "I wish I could—"

"Do not blame yourself, Your Grace," Mr. Hooke said kindly. "We know that her behavior grieves you as it does us. We did not wish to visit your home on such a mission. But it was our duty, unpleasant though it may be."

"I understand. The duties of my position are not always pleasant either." He was thinking of the day when he had been forced to try the daughter of one of his fellow magistrates for filthy dalliance with a man in her father's employ. Though her father had neither moved nor spoken when she was sentenced to a public whipping, Theophilus had understood how he must have felt. "Will you have some wine to warm you before you leave, gentlemen?"

"No, thank you, Your Grace. It's time we left."

As they went to the door, a gust of wind rattled the window and sleet snapped against it like great handfuls of thrown sand. Theophilus held their cloaks. "What is the next step?" he asked.

"That is up to your wife. We will await another writing from her, one which the church hopes will be more satisfactory than the first."

And if she does not write, thought Theophilus, or if she does write but it is not deemed satisfactory . . . what then? He did not ask that question aloud, however. It was better to pray for the best than to anticipate the worst.

As he held the door open for the men, he had to fight the wind which threatened to wrench it out of his hand. The swirling snow was so heavy that he could not see the home of his friend on the opposite side of the street. Afterward he went quickly to the fire. The chill from the wind had seeped through his clothing and settled against his skin. What next? What would she do next? She was so mercurial, so unpredictable. So unmanageable.

Young Samuel came in and slouched into the high-backed chair in the corner.

"Sit up, boy," Theophilus said sharply and, surprised, the boy straightened, a respectful look on his face. Had he been too easy with him, too easy with his wife? And the two younger ones— were they already spoiled too? A sigh, echoing the wind outside, escaped from his throat.

Theophilus noted Samuel's height and the breadth of his shoulders. He really wasn't a boy any longer; he was sixteen and on his way to being a man.

"We're going to have to start thinking about Harvard for you one of these days, Son. We've all been sending our gifts of wheat and corn to support it, you know."

"Yes, sir. Of course."

"Your Latin is good?"

"Mr. Cheever says so."

"It will be like starting a whole new life," Theophilus said. With a pang he remembered his mixed emotions when he had left home to go to Magdalen College. But he had begun more than one new life since then: the two marriages, the years in the Low Countries, the move to America.

The boy nodded in a guarded way, as if he sensed his father was only making conversation.

"You'll probably be glad," Theophilus said, "to get away from this household full of women."

"I don't know, sir." The thickening eyebrows lifted and Theophilus glimpsed the man soon to come—a man sure of his attraction for women. "They're all pretty good to me."

"But the dissension. Doesn't it bother you?"

"Not too much—not so long as it doesn't concern me. I think of hens cackling and fighting over a grain of corn and I tell myself that, after all, they're only women."

"We must always respect women, Son. After all, God made them, formed them of man."

"Of course, sir."

Theophilus gave him a long look. Was he mature enough for a really manly talk? He longed for his brother Samuel whose mind had been so keen, whose judgments had been so incisive. Close as John Davenport was to him, he was still, first of all, a man of the church, and his judgments could never be wholly objective. Finally he said, "About this business with your mother and the church— what is your opinion?"

Samuel's eyes moved thoughtfully sideways and then back again to his father's face. "I pity her and I admire her. I wish she had sense enough to hide her convictions. Then I remind myself that she's only a woman and cannot help being guided more by emotion than by intellect."

"And what of the future? Do you think the censure imposed last summer made enough impression on her intellect so that she will cease to be a problem?"

The boy shook his head slowly. "I can't believe that any more than you can. I think that when she's in the presence of men with their stronger intellects, she almost believes she's wrong. But when she's alone again, her own convictions come to the fore."

"You don't think she'll ever apologize to the Assembly?"

"No, sir. No more, sir, than you do."

"And will she again sometime walk out of meeting?"

"If the spirit moves her."

Theophilus closed his eyes against the scene, but the very thought of it made his stomach tighten. In the quiet the wind again hurled sleet against the window. The boy had spoken thoughts he himself had hardly dared acknowledge.

Yet despite this reinforcement of his fears, he still, after that, found himself hopefully watching his wife for signs of repentance. Always, whether he was working on plans for the great ship, for expanding trade, for dealing with the Indians, for increasing the size and number of the settlements that were a part of New Haven, overlaid on his mind was the consciousness of his wife's differences with the church and the hope that these would somehow be resolved.

Perhaps if she did not disturb the elders further by flaunting her doctrinal objections, and perhaps if no further complaints were lodged against her, they would drop the matter. Eventually, everyone would forget about it. The elders had not actually, he reminded himself, threatened further action.

Apparently, Ann had come to the same conclusions. She attended meetings regularly, walking with slow grace down the aisle to the foremost seat, her acknowledged place as first lady of the colony. Theophilus could not help feeling a pride in her—in her ripe beauty, her elegance of dress, her queenly carriage. On the wintriest days, when icicles sometimes formed on the inside walls of the meetinghouse and the other women huddled down into their shawls or cloaks, she sat as regally straight as ever, with the pure white column of her neck rising coolly impervious from the lacy ruff at her throat.

As spring approached, and as plans for renewed activities occupied his attention, the overlay of worry about his wife thinned and parted like worn-out gauze. He thought of her transgressions less and less, and when they did come to his mind, it was with the realization that he had spent too much time worrying about and searching for solutions to a problem that gradually was being solved by time itself.

Soon work would begin again on the great ship. He conferred with the chief carpenter on a Saturday afternoon in March and was told that, if all went well, the ship might make its first journey across the ocean in the fall. Soon after supper that same day, Theophilus crossed the street. Ordinarily he did not visit Davenport on Saturday nights, for it was then a pastor usually worked on final preparations for the next day's sermon. But Theophilus knew his friend would want to hear the good news about the ship.

John seemed to receive the news with less pleasure than Theophilus had expected. His manner was remote, his full attention lacking.

"I'm sorry, my friend," Theophilus said. "I knew I should not have interrupted your work on a Saturday night. You have a sermon to finish."

John made a quick gesture with his hand. "It isn't that. My sermon is finished. Everything that will take place at tomorrow's meeting has been prepared for completely." He paused. "If I seem distracted, it is because I grieve inside."

"For what?"

John gave him a long, solemn look. "For you. For my oldest and dearest friend."

Theophilus could feel his heart beating like the measured roll of the drum that called all souls to worship.

"What is it?" he asked. The words fell softly amid the drumming heartbeats.

"Your wife will be tried again tomorrow. The elders want it, the Assembly wants it, and I—"

"You want it too."

"Do not put it that way. Let us say only that I know it must be done."

Theophilus sat very still. His hands were icy.

"Once we made a pact," John said. "We said that your decisions would be final in the civil realm, mine in the spiritual. But that was when we were only a tiny plantation and you were merely its magistrate. Now you are governor of a growing colony. If you should decide to interfere, it would be within your power to do so."

"You did not say this the first time you tried her."

"I know. I have reconsidered."

Theophilus studied him a moment. He's putting the responsibility on me, he thought. He wasn't entirely sure he liked the idea. At last he rose heavily and went to the door. The two men shook hands soberly. "Thank you for telling me about it," Theophilus said.

"Pray about it. Go into your closet and pray all night if necessary. Let the Holy Spirit guide you."

His steps heavy, his mind in turmoil, he crossed the street. Ann, who had just bent to stir the fire, was alone in the great hall. Hearing him, she straightened and turned. The glow from the fire lit her face and glimmered in her dark hair. Though he wanted to reach out to her, he let his arms hang loose at his sides.

"What's the matter, Theophilus?" Putting down the poker, she came toward him. "You might as well tell me. You've heard something at John Davenport's. What did he tell you?"

Theophilus took a deep breath. "He told me that you will be tried again tomorrow."

She took the news calmly. "And what did you tell him?"

"I? Tell him?"

"Yes, Theophilus. You are the governor of the New Haven Colony. What did you tell him?"

172

He took off his cloak, hung his hat on its peg. Turning, he gave her a solemn look. "I told him nothing."

"In other words you were silent, letting him—as usual—make all the decisions for the colony."

"For the church."

"For *everything*," she said. Her mouth hardened. "Let me tell you something, Theophilus. That man hates me. He always has. And he is jealous of me. He wants to humiliate me, to defeat me, to put me in the lowest position possible. He has wanted it from the first; and I know why he wants it."

"He wants a colony dedicated to the glory of God."

"No. He wants a colony dedicated to the glory of John Davenport. And I stand in his way. He is fearful that I may have some influence on you. He doesn't want that. He wants to be the only one who can influence you. He will never rest until he has ground me under his heel."

Theophilus sighed. "What they say about you is right. You have just made the most slanderous and sacrilegious statement I have ever heard."

"You are on his side. Always his side. Never my side."

"I try only to be on God's side." Moving to the stairway, he said, "I am going upstairs now to pray. I wish you would do the same. I want to help you, my dear, but you seem to have no desire to repent or to help yourself in any way."

"Wait," she said. She spoke now with a quiet, slow steadiness. "I'm not stupid, Theophilus. I know that if I am tried again tomorrow, the outcome will surely be excommunication. He wouldn't bother to go through with it again for anything less. I also know that you have the authority to prevent it." She paused. Her eyes were dark, her jaw firm. "I want you to take this one thought with you. If you willingly allow your friend to do this to me, I will no longer consider you my husband."

After a long moment he nodded, picked up a small candle, and went upstairs. Setting the candle on the corner of his desk, he sat down, but he had no desire to work. He put his head in his hands and tried to pray, but no words came to his mind and no guidance came from God.

How long he had sat there he did not know, but when he suddenly became aware that someone was knocking on his door, the candle was out and the room was filled with a gray light. His heart jumped. Had she prayed and thought? Had she repented her harsh words?

The knock had been very light. If he had not fallen asleep in an awkwardly uncomfortable position, he might not even have been awakened by it. Now the door opened quietly and his mother stuck her head in.

"Oh, you're there, Son. Praying?"

"Yes and no." He tried to erase the fatigue and worry from his voice. "Come in, Mother." He rose quickly and pulled out a chair for her.

She stepped inside—small, erect, imperious. "You look exhausted, my boy. It's nearly dawn. Have you slept at all?"

"Some, I think."

She scanned his face with a mother's sharp eyes. "Why are you so unhappy?"

His chest rose and fell. "You know about the trial? You know they're going to try her again?"

"Yes, I know."

"Then can you not see that I am unhappy for her? She is too highly strung to have to go through this."

"Perhaps. But perhaps she hides behind her nervous nature and uses it as an excuse. I know, Son—you think I do not like her, that I have never liked her. That is untrue. I was prepared to love her. I opened up my heart to her until I saw that she sought only to hinder you and subject you to ridicule. Surely she knows that tomorrow will be as hard—perhaps far harder—on you than on her. All she has to do is go to the elders before the service tomorrow and assure them of her guilt and her repentance and they will surely cancel the trial. But she will not do so. She would rather see you humiliated. Is that love? I think not."

"You may be right."

"Have you ever known me to be wrong?"

"Not really." He sighed. It seemed to him that he sighed a great deal lately. It was as if he had difficulty getting enough breath into his chest. "This will be a very humiliating day for me . . . indeed, for all of us."

24

EZEKIAL CHEEVER
MARCH 1645

The March wind came at him in a punishing gust. Despite its harshness, Ezekial found it less chilling than the dank cold within the meetinghouse, a cold intensified by the chill of unsmiling faces.

When the wind eased, the marketplace became strangely quiet. No living person was in sight, for he had been the first to leave the meetinghouse. On this sunless afternoon the square with its muddy ruts and rotting tree stumps had a ravaged look. It was as the land might be on the Day of Judgment, just before the Lord ordered the graves to burst open.

As he passed one of the little Sabba'day houses where the farm people warmed themselves between Sunday services, a horse tethered there broke the silence with a long whinny. A shiver passed over Ezekial's rangy body, like the shivering chill that came with the ague. And, indeed, he did not feel well. A malaise that began in his heart crept leadenly through his body. It seemed to him that a sickness had penetrated the colony, a sickness that had become a part of him also.

After the repressions of the Church of England and the injustices of the Star Chamber, he had expected a freedom here, an opportunity for growth. But it seemed now that what had begun as a protection for the church had grown into its main reason for being.

At the end of the square he crossed the street, glancing down from the corner to the Eaton home. *Domus sua cuique tutissimum refugium.* He shook his head. Surely Mrs. Eaton's home had not been her safest refuge.

As an elder of the church he had not at first questioned the church's right to be interested in people's private lives. But for some time now he had been convinced that it was wrong, and when he reached his home and had carefully bolted the door behind him, he was glad that no church member was looking over his shoulder or peering into his heart or mind.

Quietly he tiptoed through the hall where he daily labored to teach the fundamentals of Latin to the colony's future leaders. At the door to the kitchen he stopped a moment, listening. He found himself hoping that Mary was asleep. She had given birth to their fourth child only two weeks before. Still weak, she had not gone to any of the services today.

While he hesitated, he heard her voice, soft and whispery. "Are you all right then, my little one? Have you had enough for now?"

Ezekial started to sigh, checked himself, and, calling out her name so he wouldn't startle her by suddenly opening the door, he pulled up on the leather string that released the latch. The door swung open.

Mary's hand flew to her mouth. "Oh," she said, "you startled me. I didn't hear you come in."

"I tried to be quiet. I thought you might be sleeping."

"How can I sleep? She's so delicate, I'm almost afraid to—"

He bent and kissed her, stopping the flow of anxious words. He did not know who was the more delicate, his wife with her transparent, fine-drawn skin and fragile body, or the tiny, almost ethereal-looking baby.

Mary moved the baby away from her breast and closed her bodice. "It seems as though you're very late," she said, but now she smiled as he smoothed her hair back from her damp forehead. "They didn't try Mrs. Eaton again, did they?"

"Yes, they did."

His feeling of uneasiness returned. He went to the bedroom and saw that their three-year-old daughter and two-year-old son were quietly napping. Softly he closed the door so their voices would not disturb them. Behind him he could hear Mary saying, "Surely the trial came to naught. The governor's wife. Surely they would not dare to censure her twice within a year."

Carefully he took off his waistcoat and hung it on a peg in the corner. Why was it so difficult to get the words out? When he finally turned and spoke, his voice had a strained sound. "They didn't censure her. They excommunicated her."

Her eyes widened and grew strangely bright. "Surely not. I cannot believe it. Was the governor there?"

"Yes."

"What did he say?"

He really did not want to talk about it. He could tell by the curiosity in his wife's voice and eyes that the conversation was going to increase his feeling of discomfort.

"Let me help you with the supper," he said.

"It isn't a man's work."

He took trenchers and spoons from the shelf and put them on the table. "You haven't been well. Otherwise I wouldn't."

Rising, she put the baby in the cradle. A whimpering began. She rocked the cradle and made crooning noises until the baby grew quiet.

"You haven't answered my question, Ezekial. After all, when I'm not able to go out . . ."

He went to the chimney, took the beans from the oven, and set them on the table. "What question?"

"I asked you what the governor said."

"Oh. As a matter of fact he didn't say anything."

"Did he do anything—frown, seem upset?"

"I didn't notice."

"Perhaps you were looking at someone else at the moment," she said. Her gaze was intent, probing.

"I don't remember."

She smiled.

They sat down and automatically bowed their heads. Ezekial asked the Lord's blessing on the food they were about to eat. Afterward, he served his wife and himself.

She did not begin eating immediately. Instead she tipped her head to one side and said thoughtfully, "It seems strange that the governor should sit there in silence while his wife was being tried. Can it be that our pastor has more power than he?"

Ezekial was surprised by her question. Power was an issue he had not considered. Yet it was true that Governor Eaton had risen from chief magistrate of a small plantation to governor of a colony that might possibly some day be larger than Europe. Did Mr. Davenport feel he needed to prove the governor's power had limits? Such a thought, he realized guiltily, was very close to being sacrilegious.

"It does seem strange," Mary continued, "that everyone should unite against Mrs. Eaton. I don't know how she felt—she's always seemed so assured—but if it had been I—well, I don't think I could have endured having the whole church against me and no one, not even my husband, willing to speak for me." She gave Ezekial a clear-eyed look. "How can you speak of it with so little passion? Didn't you feel any pity when no one came to her defense?"

Ezekial poked a piece of salt pork to the edge of his trencher. He did not like fat. "I don't think I said that no one came to her defense."

"Oh?" Her voice was alert. "Who spoke for her?"

He chewed and swallowed some beans. They were unusually dry and tasteless, completely unlike the moist, deep-flavored dish served at the Eatons.

"It was I who spoke for her," he said.

She stared at him until he looked away. "Oh?" she said. "And what did you say?"

"I said I felt the charges were too flimsy for censure, much less excommunication."

"I see."

The baby began whimpering again. Moving around in her chair she rocked the cradle until quiet returned. Ezekial went on eating, chewing, swallowing.

Finally she turned back to him. "I see some things very clearly now."

"What do you see?" he asked wearily.

"I see now what I've always suspected. I see that you have a special feeling for Mrs. Eaton."

"I have no special feeling for Ann Eaton. I spoke in her defense because I felt she was being treated unjustly."

"You even refer to her by her first name."

"Mary, having the baby so soon after—" He stopped and began again. "Your being so weak—I think it's made you overly sensitive. You never felt this way before about Ann—about Mrs. Eaton."

The skin on her face tightened and the tight look hardened around her eyes. "I have always felt this way about your Mrs. Ann Eaton. I have never liked her. I have always been uncomfortable around her. I have always felt that you had a special feeling for her and that she knew it and took pleasure in it. Why don't you admit it? Admit that you have a special feeling for her."

"All right, I do. I have a special feeling for her. And that feeling is pity. I pity her because she is an intelligent, high-spirited woman who is forced to keep a tight rein on all her thoughts and feelings."

Mary smiled. "Tight rein? There would have been no trial if she had kept a tight rein."

"The tight rein is the one that breaks."

She was silent. After a moment he saw that she had begun to cry. With relief, he watched the tears slide down her cheeks, for tears were a sign of her surrender.

He got up and put more wood on the fire. Then he walked around the table, knelt by his wife's chair, and took her hand. It felt fragile, pathetically weak.

"I pity her, but it's you I love."

"And isn't pity very close to love?"

"It's entirely different."

"In what way?"

He stroked her wrist. "Let's not talk about it any more right now. Later, when you're feeling better—"

"Ezekial." Her fingers tightened around his. "What will happen now?"

"I suppose she'll go away. Or perhaps the governor will straighten everything out. Or maybe nothing at all will happen."

"I wasn't thinking of her." Again the tight look hardened around her eyes, making her seem less pitiful, less in need of tenderness. "I was thinking of you, Ezekial. What will happen to you now?"

"Why should anything happen to me?"

"Remember what happened to the governor's brother?"

"Nothing happened to him. He went back to England to look for people who would be willing to begin a new settlement east of here."

"And never returned. Don't you remember, Ezekial? He was the only one to speak against Mr. Davenport's resolutions the day the government was organized. You told me about it yourself. He must have left because he knew he'd never get any cooperation from Mr. Davenport." She moved her chair back and stood up. "It doesn't matter whether you're the governor's brother, the governor's wife, or one of the seven ruling elders of the church—it doesn't pay to go against Mr. Davenport."

"You're being very silly."

"No, I'm not. You wait and see. He'll find a way somehow, sometime, to discredit you."

He stood up then and took her in his arms. He could feel her slight body trembling against his. "Don't be silly," he said. "The church thrives on opposition. It always has."

"You never credit *me* with having any intelligence."

"Oh, I do. I do." He brushed her cheek with his lips, found her mouth and silenced it with his.

THEOPHILUS EATON
FALL 1646

Surely Ann had not meant that silly threat she had thrown at him the night before her trial. Yet why did she isolate herself from him? Why did she refuse to discuss anything with him? Why was she so quiet and subdued?

Why wasn't he able to keep her out of his mind?

Theophilus looked around the meetinghouse where the court was being held and noted the concentration on the other men's faces. Clearly, they were fully occupied with the problem of the Dutch and Indian war.

It was strange. During all the years that she had been a problem, constantly meddling in affairs that were quite beyond a woman's calling, constantly criticizing his every act and decision, constantly rousing the other women of the household to argument and anger, he had been able to handle her with a certain effectiveness. And after he had dealt with her, he had always been able to put all thought of her and of all the problems she engendered into a separate compartment in his mind so that he could give his full attention to his work. But now that she seldom spoke, now that she spent most of her time in her room, now that she apparently had no interest in what was going on in the household or the colony, he found himself constantly aware of her presence and even more aware of her when she deliberately absented herself from him.

With a distinct effort and with the knowledge that he had missed a part of the discussion, he turned to Stephen Goodyear.

"Will you present for the court, sir, your latest communication from the governor of New Amsterdam."

In his quiet, cultured voice, Goodyear said, "Our honorable neighbor is a bit less arrogant than before. I think that as his problems with the Indians increase, he grows more aware that it is to his advantage to be on friendly terms with us."

And is it not to Ann's advantage to remain on friendly terms with me? Theophilus thought.

Someone asked, "Has Stuyvesant yet offered restitution for all the goods seized in the raid on Delaware?"

"He will settle, I am sure, but his pride will not let him do so quickly," Goodyear answered.

Pride. Perhaps it was only pride and not anger that was making her so aloof. If so, he could surely overcome it. With a somewhat easier mind, he turned to Goodyear. "Then you feel we can begin to make plans for another trading post and for renewed trade in the Delaware area?"

"I'd say so. But let's not move this time until we're sure they won't molest us."

Goodyear was cautious. He was learned and a good diplomat, but though he was interested, his dreams of expansion and trade did not equal those that had so long lighted up the mind of Theophilus.

Theophilus made some notes. "What is the status of the great ship?" he asked now.

The chief carpenter, who had been waiting near the rear of the meetinghouse, was motioned forward.

"My men have been working from dawn to dark, Your Grace, but the interior work is not yet finished."

"I am aware it is not finished. But what we all want to know is, when *will* it be ready?" He looked around at the expectant faces of the other men. "We hoped for readiness last summer. Then this spring or early summer. We expected surely it would be ready to sail in late August or early September. Now it's October and still no ship."

The man shrugged. "It's only a matter of weeks, Your Grace."

"But the ocean grows more dangerous as winter approaches."

"The hull will rot if the ship doesn't set sail soon," one of the magistrates said.

"We'll go down and look at it after court closes." Theophilus started to rise. "Is there any other business?"

Mr. Goodyear touched his arm lightly—lightly as a mosquito touches.

"The slander case," he whispered.

"Oh, yes. Of course." Slumping back in his chair, he sat quiet and grave while the offenders were summoned. Agitation whirled in his stomach. Why was it that the most intimate aspects of his family life had to be constantly brought into public view? Was not the family of the governor of a colony entitled to any privacy of thought or act?

The four people were brought in and identified: Goody Susan Ball, her husband Allen, Mr. Richard Pery, and Dorothy Ball. Trying to hide his aversion, Theophilus said to Stephen Goodyear, "Perhaps you would question them."

Nodding, Goodyear turned to the defendants. "The charge against you is a serious one. You all know it is a breach of the Ninth Commandment. You all know also how slanderous gossip of this kind can harm the people who are put in a ridiculous or unpleasant light." He looked down at a paper in front of him. "The charge says that when returning from the Bay Colony on a pinnace last week you all stated that Mrs. Eaton, the wife of our governor, had removed her bed to another room and had refused to lie with the governor since her admonishment. What have you to say to this?"

They looked at each other, fidgeted, looked away.

"Did you or did you not make this statement?"

Susan Ball, who was apparently the boldest, said, "We may have said something like that."

"Loud enough so everyone on board could hear?"

Her head was bent. With calloused fingers she picked at her petticoat. "I guess so . . . yes."

Theophilus tried not to listen. Yet any attempt to separate his thoughts from what was going on in the meetinghouse resulted only in his recollections of the aspects of his home life that had led to the ugly gossip.

For she had removed not only her bed but her self and every personal belonging. She had done it, with Lurinda's help, on the night of her excommunication. He had not known about it until Hannah had met him in the great hall and had asked, "Papa, why is Mama moving all her things to the blue room?" The child had looked disturbed.

By the time he had confronted his wife in the upstairs hall, the removal was nearly complete. She had been carrying the silver ewer down the hall.

"Where are you going with that?"

"To my room."

"You are taking it from your room. From our room."

"No. That is no longer my room. It is now exclusively yours— to go to whenever you tire of your work and need a change."

"But you will not be there?"

"Exactly."

"Now just a minute." He grasped her by the arm and, to his surprise, found her flesh soft and unresisting. "Certainly you are not going to carry out last night's foolish threat?"

"Please, Theophilus." She looked at him with eyes as soft and weary as those of a very old woman. "Please do not try to detain me. I'm very tired and I need some rest."

Her voice, too, was soft and weary, its vigor, its imperiousness, its arrogance gone. If she had demanded in the old way, he would have felt the need to assert himself and demand his rights; instead, she had begged, and her humility so enchanted him that he removed his restraining hand from her arm.

"It hardly seems necessary for you to remove all your things simply because you need temporarily to be alone. I could have slept in the next room, as I so often have, until you were more rested."

She closed her eyes a moment; her body swayed slightly. "Please, Theophilus, do not—"

"Very well. I can see you are not feeling well. I will allow this temporary change."

She had smiled then but it had been like a smile borrowed from someone else. And when she did so, she had looked at a point a little to the left of his eyes, as if denying his existence.

Perhaps if it had not been such a long and emotionally exhausting day for him also, he might have noticed the almost masculine determination that lay beneath her gentle words; he might have understood that her humble air was yet another way of trying to manage him.

For the change had not been a temporary one. A year and a half had gone by and she had shown no signs of returning to his bed. In various subtle ways, either by having Lurinda or Hannah with her, or by pleading illness, she had managed to maintain their separateness and to make good her threat of the night before her trial. Although it had never come down to an outright request and an outright refusal, it had worked out exactly as Susan Ball had said on the pinnace, and just as she had repeated only a moment before: Mrs. Eaton no longer allows the governor to lie with her.

"Clearly," Stephen Goodyear said sternly, "you have no way of knowing whether or not such a situation exists. And even if you did have proof, can you not see how damaging and humiliating the spreading of such intelligence could be for our respected and beloved governor?"

Susan gave Mr. Goodyear an almost flirtatious look. "But it was not I who began the story. It's only what everyone in the Bay Colony is saying." She turned to her companions. "Isn't that true?"

As Theophilus watched them nod vigorously, the skin of his face stretched taut with the effort to maintain an indifferent expression. It was bad enough to be denied the warmth of a wife's bed; it was worse to be subjected to ridicule—and ridicule by the lowest class of person. Anger smoldered inside him.

Stephen regarded the group with severity. "Loyal citizens of a colony would not listen to such gossip, much less repeat it. Perhaps a fine of three pounds each will remind you of the value of silence."

The four exchanged looks and nervous whispers.

"But, sir," Allen Ball said, "we do not have that much. Not one of us."

"Then you will be given a month to earn it. You may leave the court now. Consider yourselves fortunate that you're not spending the next few days in the stocks."

Rubbing the back of his hand across his damp forehead, Theophilus said, "A rather high fine, my friend. Not one of them is a worker."

Goodyear nodded. "True. But a development of industrious habits may allow less time for tongue wagging. A few of our residents need to be shown that the dignity of our elected leaders is not to be taken lightly."

Theophilus stood up, his hands flat on the table before him, and suggested adjournment and a walk to the docks to check on the progress of the great ship. As the little procession of officials walked across the square and down to the harbor, the sunlight slid through the dark red leaves of the oaks near the water's edge. In the late afternoon glow the ship took on a golden cast.

Golden indeed. Theophilus could feel the hastening beat of his heart. It was always so. Just as a man's first child can be the beginning of a dynasty, so also can a country's first ship be the beginning of a fleet. He could see this ship, and all the others it would lead to, sailing into the famous ports of Europe and the Mediterranean countries, greeted with the respect due a ship from a strong, prosperous, and godly state.

Hammers rang against nails. The carpenters called back and forth to each other. Some working on the interior of the ship used language that caused Theophilus and Stephen Goodyear to glance uneasily at each other. It was really best, though, to close one's ears to such language—especially since no women or young people were present—and keep the men working. Clearly they were nearly finished.

Theophilus called the master carpenter over. "It looks further along than we were told. Can it be ready to sail by the end of the month?"

"I doubt it, sir."

"Next month?"

"Perhaps. But do not forget, sir, that after it is finished it must be loaded. Careful loading takes time."

While they had been talking, a pinnace had been approaching. Looking out across the water, Theophilus could see that it was Captain Lamberton's.

Excusing himself from the others who were still inspecting the great ship, he stepped out onto the dock.

"So, you are back." He greeted Captain Lamberton. "I am more than glad to see you. Were you able to get to Barbados?"

"Yes."

"Any troubles?"

"This time none. The Dutch are too occupied with the Indians to have time for further aggravation of the English. I even made a brief stop at Delaware. I have skins, tobacco, and some fine exotic fruits from the island."

"Good. The fruits we can use. My wife especially likes sweet ripe fruits. The rest of the cargo will be fine for overseas trade."

Lamberton instructed his sailors to begin unloading.

"I'll take a little of the fruit right now," Theophilus said, obeying a sudden impulse. The words about his wife had brought her image to his mind, sweet and ripe. The idea of going to her with a gift of exotic fruits seemed laden with possibilities.

While they waited for the fruit to be unloaded, they discussed the great ship.

"It may be ready in a month," Theophilus said.

"Don't rush the men too much. She must be seaworthy."

"I'm not rushing them." Theophilus resented the faint criticism in Lamberton's words. "But I feel sometimes that these men are making the job last. They don't appear to be trying to get it finished."

"Patience, my friend," Lamberton said. "Your ship will be built in good time. And I will sail it to England for you. Here"—he filled a shallow basket with red and gold fruits—"take this, and let it sweeten your hopes."

A heavy summer ripeness rose from the basket. How lush and fertile the island must be, Theophilus thought as he walked back toward his home, to produce such fruits. He had never been there, but from descriptions from seagoing men, he gathered that in appearance, at least, it was a little like the garden of Eden. Sunlight and warmth had gentled the fruit, just as love and warmth gentle a woman.

Ann had grown pale lately, her cheeks thin. Was it not partly his fault? The gossips were saying she had refused him her bed. But could he not, after her withdrawal, have tried to win her back? Instead he had allowed himself to be drawn further into the details of government and trade. It was she who had closed the door, but it was he who had left it closed. He had been as arbitrary with her as he had been with the Dutch. But it was not too late.

Hannah was playing at the gate. A dark-haired, bright-eyed child, she grew each day more like her mother in looks and temperament. Leaping up, she gave him an impetuous hug as he passed her.

"Look what I've brought you," he said. "An orange."

She looked beyond what he had in his hand to what was in the basket. "I'd rather have one of those," she said, pointing to a banana.

"No. They are hard for children to digest. Take the orange."

"I don't want either one." She turned sulkily away.

"Very well." He had reached the door when he heard her small voice behind him. "Papa?"

"Yes?"

"I *will* have the orange."

"No."

"Please?" she said prettily.

It was hard to refuse her. Yet she must learn. "No," he said. "You said you wanted neither one."

Lurinda met him at the door. She started to take the fruit from him but he quickly said, "No, never mind," and gave her his hat instead. "Where is Mrs. Eaton?"

"Which Mrs. Eaton, sir?"

"My wife, of course." Was it not clear that he was bringing a gift to his wife?

"Upstairs in the blue room."

As he walked upstairs and down the hall, his heart beat with anticipation mixed with self-doubt. He knocked lightly on her door.

In the past she had always called out, "Come in." Now she said almost cautiously, "Who is it?"

"Theophilus." His voice had an odd sound as if it had been affected by the heady odor of the fruit; in fact, he had felt nearly the same heady uneasiness when he had first approached the beautiful Widow Yale with marriage on his mind.

Had she heard him? Against the solidity of the door he repeated his name and now, softly, she said, "You may come in."

She was wearing a rose-colored rail. Her hair was down, but braided, and its severity accentuated the recently formed hollows in her cheeks. Her skin looked like old ivory. Not even the faintest pink touched her cheeks.

"I've brought you some fruit." He put the basket down on a table and, selecting an especially round and golden globe, held it out to her.

She looked at the fruit, then at him. A slow smile came to her lips. "It is beautiful. I am very tempted."

He had feared she would be cool, or arrogant as only she could be. It was going to be easier than he had expected.

"Then take it," he said warmly. The perfumed warmth of a southern island rose seductively between them. Outside he could hear Hannah calling to her brother, "Theophilus, guess what Papa brought home."

"Take it," he said again. Later he would touch her and speak of love, perhaps even of forgiveness—if it seemed necessary. Now he needed only to have her make the gesture of receiving his offering.

She started to reach out; then drew her hand back. "Isn't this a rather odd reversal?"

"Reversal? I don't know what you mean."

"Isn't it supposed to be Eve who tempts Adam—tempts him with a piece of ripe fruit, tempts him into an awareness of sensual pleasures?"

Rarely was he stirred to real anger. Now his fingers tightened around the orange so that his nails dug into it, releasing the bitter-sweet oil of the skin. He stared at it and then at the glittering mockery in her eyes. Slowly he lifted his arm, turned his hand over and in one powerful stroke hurled the orange to the floor with such force that the skin split and the segments came apart and opened up like a flower.

Looking down in dismay at the evidence of his loss of control, he felt the beginning of a headache grinding up through his temples.

"I had no thought of tempting you," he said. "I thought only of—"

"Yes?"

"Only of—" He rubbed his temple. The pain was growing. "How do I know what I thought of? A woman like you drives all rational thought from a man's mind." Giving her a hard, cold look, he added, "I will not bother you again."

ANN EATON/NOVEMBER 1646

At first it had given Ann a great deal of satisfaction to move into the blue room and shut everyone out.

She went to the great hall at mealtimes and, for the sake of the children, presided with remote graciousness at the opposite end of the table from Theophilus. But she did little work in the kitchen, washhouse, or brewhouse, and, when guests came, she allowed old Mrs. Eaton to be chief hostess. It was what the old woman wanted and what, apparently, Theophilus wanted. Though she never hoped for the colony's failure, neither did she actively wish for its success. It had rejected her ideas, her beliefs, her self; now she willfully and willingly existed apart from it.

In her room she brooded and read. The fast days observed in sympathy for the Puritans in England were like all other days to her: every day was a deprivation. She rarely took out her Bible. Now that she was free to worship in her own way, she felt hardly inclined to worship at all. After all, she was no longer exposed to the Sunday and Thursday night services at the meetinghouse or to the Saturday night services Theophilus held at home to herald the Sabbath. Perhaps all of these had kept a constant interest in religion alive in her, even though they had aroused contradictory thoughts.

Much of the time she lived in the past, dreaming of the happy days of her first marriage and the happy early days of her second. She remembered all the times Theophilus had approached her with ardor, all the times she had responded by moving toward him with tremulous eagerness. But overlaid on this was the memory of his impassive face on the days when she had been tried, the two days when he had failed her.

She thought, too, quite often of the day he had brought her the fruit. What had bothered her more than his lack of apology had been her own instinctive response. A few kind words, a smile, and a gift, and she was ready to walk into his arms and forget all her injuries. But she had noticed a look on his face, an awareness of her weakening resolves, a satisfaction almost, and suddenly her heart had hardened. Right or wrong, she had deliberately courted his anger. She had widened the gap between them and had increased her feelings of isolation and loneliness.

The days passed more quickly than the nights. Hannah came in every morning for lessons in reading and writing, and in the afternoon young Theophilus came to recite his Latin verbs and his noun declensions. He hated school and talked only of going to Ireland where fortunes could, he was sure, be made.

Sometimes he spoke of Ezekial. Less than a year after Ann's trial, the Cheevers had added still another child to their family. The crying of babies often interfered with the boys' lessons.

"How does Mr. Cheever look?" she asked her son one day.

"Like always. Sterner, maybe."

Of course the boy would see Ezekial only as his teacher rather than a friend, as she did. The feeling she had for Ezekial was unique, totally unlike what she had felt for either of her husbands. She felt gratitude and warmth and confidence. He had risked a great deal for her on the day of her trial, daring, because of his sense of justice, to defy the powerful Mr. Davenport—daring more, even, than her husband had. He had stood to gain nothing from his gesture and this made her value it even more highly. It would be good, she thought, to hear some news of him now and then. Or news of anyone.

Sometimes she felt that Mary and old Mrs. Eaton actually conspired to keep news from her. You couldn't possibly be interested, they seemed to imply; otherwise you would have done what was necessary to remain in the church.

Lurinda brought Ann what news she could, giving her mistress a sketchy idea of what the Sunday sermons were about, and what bills had been read from the pulpit. But even though she had been in New Haven for three and a half years, she still could not remember the names of all who were involved.

One day at dinner, however, old Mrs. Eaton said to Theophilus, "You must have had an interesting morning in court."

"No more so than usual." He picked up half a pigeon and began to gnaw on it.

"Was not this the morning you were to try Mrs. Brewster?"

"Yes."

Ann's stomach knotted. All desire for food left her. There was silence until she said, "What were the charges?"

Theophilus put the pigeon down and wiped his fingers. Without looking at her he replied, "Sundry vituperative speeches concerning the church, its pastor, and the magistrates."

"Speeches made where?"

"In her own home."

She seemed to have difficulty breathing. "Who witnessed against her?"

"Her maid. Conversations with her son and with her friends were reported. She is said to have torn up her sermon notes saying the words of her pastor made her stomach womble. She is also reported to have been highly critical of punishment meted out by the magistrates for filthy practices. She particularly objected to the whippings."

"She's the one who ought to be whipped," old Mrs. Eaton said.

Ann drew in her breath quickly. "Will she be?"

"No. She was fined instead."

With a knowing, superior look on her face, Mary asked, "Were there not other crimes also?"

"Oh, yes." Theophilus looked directly at Ann now, his eyes hard. "She spoke to Mrs. Moore, Mrs. Leach, and the governor's wife of trying to seduce other women with their malicious tongues, turning them away from church and town. She even suggested they have themselves banished so they could start a new community in Rhode Island."

Hidden by the massive table, Ann's fingers clenched into fists. "But that was only a joke."

"So Mrs. Brewster said."

"A fine kind of joke," old Mrs. Eaton said.

A sourness rose in Ann's throat. Putting her hands flat on the table, she half rose. "May I be excused, please?"

"But you have eaten nothing," Theophilus said.

"I have had my fill."

The sourness thickened in her throat. Her stomach wombled as Mrs. Brewster's had. "Please do excuse me—all of you." Quickly she left the room. All afternoon she remained quiet upstairs, sitting by her window. Nor did she go downstairs for supper. When Lurinda was sent to inquire, Ann told her she was unwell.

"Again, ma'am? Should we not call a surgeon?"

"No. It is not that kind of sickness."

Lurinda knelt down by her and took her hand. "Oh, ma'am. I hate so to see you like this. You're heartsick—isn't that it?"

Ann leaned back, closing her eyes. "Yes, I am heartsick. I feel sure Mrs. Brewster would never have been brought to trial if she had not been a friend of mine."

Alone again she tried to rest, but she kept seeing Brigid's open merry face and remembering all the happy afternoons they had passed together. Since her trial she had not had the heart to go calling—nor had anyone called on her—but now she knew she must shake off her apathy.

Her eyes stared back at her in the mirror from hollowed eye sockets. Her cheeks, too, had a hollowed look. She placed her hands on her stomach. Nothing could match the hollowness inside her. I look old, she thought, and the thought did not bother her. But enough of the old spirit remained so that she pinched her cheeks and put on a frothy pink furbelow to brighten her face. Leaning toward the mirror, she could see a fine network of lines just touching her skin with cobweb hesitancy. A tilt of the head, a smile, and they disappeared. What she needed was some laughter—honest laughter, earthy laughter—and she knew it could be had only at Brigid Brewster's. Why had she waited so long?

The air outside was sharp, but it had the feel of life. The cold penetrated her clothing and made her realize suddenly that she was still alive, still able to feel. She found Brigid out in her tiny yard putting dry leaves around her flowers. As she raked furiously with her fingers, almost like a chipmunk digging, she murmured words that could not be distinguished but that in their rise and fall had an argumentative sound.

"Be careful, my friend," Ann said, leaning against the fence, "or someone overhearing you will accuse you of casting spells."

Brigid turned, frowning. When she saw who had spoken, brightness spread over her face. Awkwardly, she got up off her knees and came to the fence. Her light-blue eyes glowed with pleasure.

"Ann, my dear. Oh, how I wish I could cast a few spells." She held out her hands across the fence and Ann squeezed them hard. "I've missed you so. You can't imagine. But you're so thin. You look . . ."

"Terrible."

"Not terrible, but . . . so thin, so sad. What have they done to you?"

"Nothing. They leave me alone and I leave them alone. But what have they done to you?"

"Enough. It could have been worse." She looked earnestly at Ann. "I'm not sorry, though—are you?"

"About what?"

"That we defied them. We showed them—didn't we?—that even though we're women we're able to hold our own opinions."

"Don't forget they threw me out of the church."

"And is that so bad? With winter coming on, I often think of you with envy as I close the door on my nice warm hearth, knowing I'm going to spend the next few hours shuddering in the cold. And I shudder even more when I think of listening to that mealymouthed—"

"Careful," Ann said, but she could feel a smile spreading over her face.

"Except for hearing the news and seeing whether anyone has any new clothes, what are you missing?"

"Why, I miss—" Ann hesitated.

"Do you know what I think? I think you miss the opportunity to defy Old Pudding Face, to walk out on him, to humiliate him."

Ann heard herself laughing now. "Oh, Brigid, it's so good to see you again. Until this moment I didn't know how much I had missed you."

"Yes . . . I, too."

All at once Ann felt as exhilarated as if she had been freed after having been held against her will. The laughter had stirred up an old warmth inside her. Moving along the fence toward the gate, she said with the assurance of one who knows she is welcome, "Aren't you going to ask me in?"

Brigid moved to the gate. Ann waited. Brigid seemed to be having trouble with the latch.

"What is it, Brigid?"

Brigid gave her an anguished look.

"Is it your husband?"

Brigid nodded. "It was the fine. He said I would not have been fined so much if I had not been your friend. He said he had never felt the friendship was right, but had never before had any real reason to stop it."

"I see." The hollow feeling returned.

"You can't know how I feel . . . to have to say this."

"Oh, I know. I know."

Ann turned and started down the street. Her throat was so swollen she could not manage a goodbye. Looking back once, she lifted her hand in a silent wave. With tears sparkling against her rounded cheeks, Brigid returned the gesture. Then suddenly she called out, "Wait!"

Ann turned. Brigid hurried down to the corner of her yard. "I almost forgot. My husband's going back to England to get some backing for a new business—if the great ship ever sails. When he's gone, come back."

Ann nodded. "I will."

"You do understand?"

"Of course I do. It probably won't sail until spring, but I'll see you then." She hesitated. "Unless your husband leaves you strict orders about not seeing me. Is that possible?"

Brigid looked embarrassed. "I—don't know."

"Send me a message," Ann said.

That night at supper she asked Theophilus when the ship was likely to sail.

"December," he said, "or, at the latest, January."

"But what if the harbor freezes?"

"It isn't likely."

"You wouldn't really send a ship off in the dead of winter, would you?"

"Why not?" he said. "They'd be sailing into spring weather."

"It seems foolhardy."

Lifting his eyebrows, he said, "Do you really consider yourself a competent judge?"

Ann saw Mary and old Mrs. Eaton exchange satisfied looks. They made fewer remarks these days. It wasn't necessary for them to call the attention of Theophilus to his wife's weaknesses and

195

defects. Since the day she had refused the fruit he had brought her, he had gone completely over to their side.

These days nothing seemed to bring her any real satisfaction. One cold afternoon she picked up the little book by A.R. and again read through the section on baptism. Several times she found herself looking away from the book, yawning or glancing outside to see who was passing.

At last she closed the book and sat still in the gathering dusk. The low fire sent enough glow into the room so that she did not need to light a candle. Across the public square a drum rolled at the watchhouse as the first two men on watch were called to their evening duty. Careful watch was still kept, even though an Indian attack was most remote. Until snow covered the ground, settlers were, however, doubly watchful.

She stared out into the growing darkness as the wind rose. What had ever made her think the teachings in the little brown book were so important? Why hadn't she been able to read it as a dissenting view, and then put it aside and forget it? Be honest, she told herself. And she knew that if she were, she would have to admit that if she had not wanted to do battle with the Reverend Mr. Davenport, if she had not hoped to humiliate and annoy him, she would never have embraced the Baptists' teachings. Brigid was right: the religion itself was not really so important.

As she continued staring out into the darkness, snow began falling, sifting gently at first and then after a while coming down so heavily that it made a thick, cold curtain between herself and the world.

EZEKIAL CHEEVER
DECEMBER 1646

It was the earliest and most severe winter New Haven had yet
seen. The cold had begun early in November and by late in the
month the ground was covered with snow. The weather held and
gradually the harbor began to freeze. Permission was given for
wine to be drawn to help the carpenters work in the paralyzing
cold. In December the ship was at last declared finished.

Ezekial often walked down to the harbor in the afternoon to
watch the loading. He was a deputy of the general court now and
he knew how important the success of this voyage was to the town.
Yet to him the process of loading seemed singularly unplanned. As
merchants and agents brought goods to the docks, the goods were
loaded on board. The West Indian hides went in first, then beaver,
and then the peas and wheat. The plate, all heavy silver, would be
last.

When they first began to stow away the cargo, it had seemed to
Ezekial that the ship listed slightly to one side. One day when the
governor was watching with him, he called his attention to it.

The governor didn't say, "Stick to your Latin verbs," but his
amused expression indicated what he was thinking. "I've seen
many a ship loaded," he said. "I've been on hand when they sailed
away and when they returned with new cargo. The men know
what they're doing."

Captain Lamberton, who was to be in charge of the vessel,
seemed less sure. Ezekial, shivering down by the windy harbor,
talked with him the day before the sailing.

"Look at how walt-sided she is," Captain Lamberton said, shaking his head. "That ship will be our grave."

Thoughtfully Ezekial said, "The governor knows ships. In England he fitted out many of them. Why doesn't he see that there's something wrong here?"

"Because he doesn't want to. All his dreams of the future are tied up in this vessel. He and I have spent hours talking about it. Besides, I've been sailing for him since this colony was founded. I've managed against Indians, Dutch, Swedes, tropical storms, rip tides, and fog—and I've never lost a ship. He thinks I can do anything."

"Maybe you can."

"With God's help. If we have it."

"Surely He *is* on our side."

Just then the governor joined them. "Our own ship," he said. "Can you think what it means? We can ship what we want, when we want, where we want. And this is just the first of many. A few years from now you'll see this harbor crowded with ships. You'll see the town spread all the way back to the red rocks. And the area it controls will stretch far, far beyond."

"I hope so, sir," Lamberton said.

"You hope so? Believe in it, man. Believe. Have faith."

"I wish I did have your faith, sir. I wish I had the faith to believe I can sail that ship to England."

The governor clapped him on the back—a gesture foreign to his usual reserve. "You're too modest. You lack faith in yourself. You're the best sailor, the best captain, I've ever known. Isn't it true, Cheever, that the colony could not do better than have Captain Lamberton in charge of its first ship?"

"Yes, I believe so. But perhaps for so good a captain we should have prepared a better ship."

The governor looked irritated. "She *is* a good ship. What can you find wrong with her?"

"Isn't she a bit walty, sir?"

And Lamberton said again, "She will prove our grave, sir."

"Nonsense. They haven't finished loading. The plate will balance her. So will the passengers and trunks."

"Perhaps if we waited until spring—"

"Nonsense." The governor's voice was edgy. "If we wait until spring, the hull will rot."

"Yes, sir. You're right about that." Lamberton strode away.

"He's all nerved up," Theophilus said to Ezekial. "He's like this before every trip. The longer the trip and the more valuable the cargo, the more nerved up he is."

"Is that a good thing?"

"Yes. I wouldn't give a farthing for a man who didn't worry himself almost sick before such an important journey. But I know Captain Lamberton. The minute he gets on that ship and shouts his first command, his nervousness will cease and every instinct of a skilled manager of men and ships will take over."

Ezekial felt as if a weight had slipped from his shoulders. The governor's sure knowledge gave him confidence. For a while he stood in silence watching the loading. Finally he said, "Do you think Cromwell will grant us a charter?"

"Certainly. Mr. Gregson never fails in his missions. He has long dealt with people of importance. Cromwell will doubtless be pleased to have a strong Puritan state supporting him on this side of the Atlantic. And, of course, we may at some time need his help against the Dutch."

"I hate asking for a charter," Ezekial said. "We bought this land from the Indians. It's rightfully ours."

"Yes. But don't forget England is laying claim to the whole continent and might well, in a capricious moment, grant a charter to some other group for the very land we're now cultivating."

"What bothers me is that we'll no longer be completely independent."

"True. But how much control can they exercise from across the ocean? We have more to gain than to lose."

Another silence fell as they watched a huge chest being hauled up onto the ship. Ezekial broke it by saying, "How is Mrs. Eaton?"

The governor looked straight ahead. "She is well. Fairly well, that is."

"I have not seen her for months."

"She stays in her room much of the time."

It was hard for Ezekial to imagine so much vigor contained within one room day after day, month after month. "Will she be coming out for the launching?"

"Perhaps so—though it is very cold."

He hasn't asked her, Ezekial thought. They really must be

estranged. What an unlikely pair they were—the governor all dignity and control and she all warmth and openness. How had they ever expected to understand each other? Was the governor happier now that she remained in her room much of the time? At least she was not creating dissension and causing people to question what their leaders did. Yet the governor did not look happy. The skin on his long bony face grew taut when his wife's name was mentioned. And his dignity jelled into a coldness that widened the distance between himself and other people.

Quickly seeking another subject for conversation, Ezekial asked, "How far out is the harbor frozen?"

"Three miles. We will have to chop a way out for the ship."

How bitterly cold it would be on board ship, Ezekial thought, on the open sea with the high winds and the freezing spray.

After a moment Theophilus asked, "And Mrs. Cheever—will she come to see the launching?"

"I'm not sure. She is rather delicate, you know, and seldom leaves the house in winter."

"This will be an important historical moment for our town. You really should encourage her to come."

"Yes, I will." And I know the first thing she'll ask me, he thought. She'll ask whether Mrs. Eaton is going to be there.

And that was exactly what she did ask, her soft gray eyes searching his face, trying to discern his feelings.

"Probably not," he answered. "She hasn't emerged from the house in months. I asked the governor today and he said she was confined to her room much of the time."

"Oh . . . you inquired?"

He clenched his fingers, helpless against her uncontrollable jealousy. "Mary, will you never forget that I befriended—?"

"Befriended? Always before you have said *defended*."

"Defended. That's what I meant to say. I defended her for one reason only, and that was because I thought the case against her was unjust. As a man of honor, I could not fail to do that."

"And the others? The governor and our pastor and all the elders—they are *not* men of honor?"

He who could argue well at court, he who could write learned discourses on Latin, was quite unable to deal with such devious feminine logic. He reached out for her. She stood light and delicate as a wicker basket in his arms. How could so much jealousy be contained in such a fragile cage of bones?

"Mary, Mary, it is you I love. How many times do I have to tell you? What must I do to make you believe? Why can't you try to understand?"

"Oh, I do try. Over and over I tell myself it's nothing." She pressed her face against his chest so that her voice was muffled. "Then I think of her—of that swinging walk that almost forces a man to stop and look, of her eyes, her smile, her voice, all so full of life, and her wit, and the way you used to turn and look at her with admiration when she said something rare and intelligent."

He spoke soothingly. "But don't you see, my dear Mary, this was admiration only for what was said, not for the person saying it."

"How can you separate the speaker from the speech?"

He was surprised by the percipience of her question. Sometimes in the midst of her emotional wanderings she stumbled on a truth.

"Just believe me," he said. He patted her and released her. "Come now, let us eat our supper. It grows dark very early. We do not want to waste our candles. You know how scarce they are."

She said no more, remaining subdued through the evening meal, speaking mostly to the children. He was not sure what her decision was about the launching until he was getting ready to go the next day.

"Will you be coming?" he asked.

"No. I have too much to do here."

"You really should come. This is our first ship, the beginning of a whole new era for New Haven."

"It's much too cold out. You know that I've been coughing for days."

"Well, then, stay here where it's warm." As he put a heavy log on the fire, he added, "I'll tell you all about it when I return."

"You really have to go?"

"As a deputy of the general court I certainly should be there. Besides, this is an occasion—"

"When you might see her."

Sharply he said, "Then come along to make sure I don't."

She shook her head. Without bothering to argue further, he put on a heavy cloak and left the house. She was only like this once in a while. Most of the time she was loving and sweet.

Her utter dependence on him had been flattering at first. It still aroused all his protective instincts, but in the past few months he had occasionally felt a faint irritation. She had a way of making him feel guilty even when he had done nothing, had not even thought of doing anything, to upset her. As he went down the street, he wondered what it would be like to have a wife who stood straight and independent, who thought for herself and acted for herself, who did not ask for constant declarations of love.

As he turned the corner and passed the Eaton house, the windows stared hollowly at him. Was she behind one of them, still languishing, perhaps not well—sick from some undisclosed ailment or sick at heart? Mary was right; he *was* interested in Mrs. Eaton. But it was not a matter of love; it was simply a matter of pity and admiration.

Though he was tempted to linger, hoping the door might open, he walked swiftly on, picking his way among the frozen ruts. Other people were also headed for the harbor, some carrying leather bags. Seventy of the townspeople were making the historic trip to England.

The sun glared on the ice of the harbor. People were crowded around the ship, blinking and smiling and stamping their feet. Vapor rose like smoke from their mouths as they called out greetings to each other. Many of the men with axes and saws had already begun cutting the ice ahead of the ship.

To Ezekial it seemed that the ship still listed to one side. He stopped and spoke to Mr. Malbon, a prominent and experienced merchant who should surely have known about such things.

"How does it look to you?"

"Fine," Malbon said. "She's a seaworthy vessel."

"Doesn't she list a bit to one side?"

Malbon smiled knowingly. "She's not fully loaded yet, with passengers or cargo. Some people are still taking on plate."

Ezekial thought a moment. "Wouldn't it have been better to have loaded the plate first?"

"Well, perhaps. But most people didn't want to part with it earlier. Don't forget it represents most of the wealth of the colony. It wouldn't have been a good idea to leave it here with so many strangers around."

"Yes, I suppose you're right."

Excusing himself, Malbon moved away to speak to another of the merchants. For a while Ezekial stood alone. Someone had built a huge fire on the beach. Occasionally people moved to it to warm their hands and the comforting smell of wood smoke drifted across the ice.

"All aboard!" The words reverberated across the ice. The last of the seventy passengers said their final goodbyes and boarded the ship. Those who had been helping them get settled in the cabins scrambled off.

As the crowd separated and changed, Ezekial saw her. She, too, was standing alone. After a moment's hesitation he moved casually to her side. Her face, surrounded by a dark beaver hood, was paler and thinner than he remembered. The delicate color that had so often suffused her cheeks in moments of excitement was gone. Only the tip of her nose was red.

Giving him a smile that was as warming as the fire on shore, she said, "Oh, Ezekial, I *am* glad to see you."

"And I you. You are alone?"

"I . . . did not decide until the last minute that I would come down. By that time the rest of the family had gone." She pushed her hood back a little. "Is Mary with you?"

"We both felt it might be too much for her. She's been coughing a great deal lately. She has always been delicate, you know."

Silently they watched as the ship's sails were unfurled. They hung limply in the expectant quiet.

The Reverend Mr. Davenport came forward, Bible in hand. "Prayers and faith will fill her sails. Come, my brothers and sisters, let us walk beside the ship as the channel is cut for her."

Axes rang against the ice, breaking it enough so that the ship could move through. Slowly the sails gathered wind and bellied forward. The ship began to move.

"She moves with great dignity, does she not?" Ann said.

"Yes." Excitement made a quiver in his voice. He was beginning to catch the feeling the governor had expressed. It really was an important moment, this beginning of greatness for New Haven Colony.

"Doesn't the ship lean a little to one side?" Ann asked. "Or is it because the channel is so narrow that she has not yet had a chance to gain her natural balance?"

"I think that is it."

"She does not look to be as good a ship as the one we came over from England in."

"I am not an expert," Ezekial said, "but I have asked many who are and they say she is a good ship."

They followed the people out onto the ice behind the slow-moving ship. The crowd began singing Psalm 136: "Praise ye the

Lord, because He is good: for His mercy endureth forever. Praise ye the God of Gods: for His mercy endureth forever."

At this point Ezekial glanced at Mrs. Eaton and saw that she was not singing. She was frowning.

"I wonder," she said, "what Captain Lamberton thinks about the ship."

Ezekial did not answer. Only too well did he remember Lamberton's words: *That ship will be our grave.*

"Some of our best men are on that ship," she said thoughtfully. "Captain Lamberton, Captain Turner—how ever will we run our military affairs if something happens to him?—and Mr. Gregson." She sighed. "And most of our wealth, too. If the ship goes down—"

"She will not go down," he said firmly.

"I know." She turned her head a little and gave him a sideways smile that had some of the old Ann Eaton in it. "Prayers and faith will fill her sails. The wind from Mr. Davenport's prayers and sermons alone could carry her to England and beyond."

In a chiding, schoolmasterish voice, he said, "That is not a proper way to talk."

"Of course not. Whoever said I was proper? Ask anyone— anyone in my family, anyone in the church—and they will tell you what I am."

He gave her a long look. A sudden sweep of wind made him shiver. "And they'll be wrong," he said.

Her face sobered. "It's good to know I have one friend."

"Of course you have," he said, "and probably many more."

As they continued to walk behind the ship, they talked less, for the wind had grown more sharp and, as they moved up into the tightly packed group of people, the sound of the singing drowned out any words. The walk out to the point where the ice thinned was a long one. Once she stumbled and he quickly took her arm.

"Are you sure you're up to such a long walk?" he asked her.

"Of course. Why shouldn't I be?"

"The governor intimated you had not been well."

She shrugged. "I am well enough."

The ice was thinner now and thunderous cracking sounds split the air as the ship plowed ahead. The men with axes stood back at last and, as the ship entered open water, a great shout went up.

Raising his arms for silence, Mr. Davenport uttered a final

prayer. He ended with the words: "Lord, if it be Thy pleasure to bury these our friends in the bottom of the sea, they are Thine. Save them."

"Oh God, oh God," Mrs. Eaton said, but her voice was quickly drowned as the people cheered. And though she raised it once again in protest, the wind lifted the sound and carried it away from the ears of all who believed.

LURINDA COLLINGS
MAY 1647

Spring came late. To Lurinda, the confinement of the long, bit-terly cold winter had become almost unbearable. A winter life-lessness seemed to have seeped into the house. Old Mrs. Eaton and Mary no longer argued much with Mrs. Eaton, largely because she stayed in her room most of the time. The governor spent long hours in his study, or, when men came to see him on colony busi-ness, in the great hall at the table in front of the fire. They kept their voices low, but not low enough to conceal the undercurrent of worry.

Lurinda often heard them speak of the great ship, but she was too much taken up with her own concerns to be interested in town problems. She was nineteen now, and skilled in the workings of a household and in knowing how to dress and how to put up her hair. She was ready and eager for marriage.

"I used to think your mother was pretty, but you're far pret-tier," Mrs. Eaton said one day. "I'm surprised some young man hasn't come asking for your hand."

"Some might, ma'am, but I've let it be known that I'm not in-terested."

"Why is that?"

Lurinda had hidden her real motives for so long that dis-sembling came easily. "Why, I've another year to serve you. A year and a few months."

"Lurinda, you know that I'd give you your freedom very quickly if I thought it meant your happiness. How about the young man who came over on the boat with you? Is he one of the interested ones? I used to see the young man who works for Mr. Goodyear looking at you on the way to church, too. What about him?"

Lurinda hid her annoyance. Much of the time Mrs. Eaton treated her like an equal. But when it came to marriage, she never thought of considering anyone for Lurinda but another servant.

Half indifferently she said, "Perhaps, ma'am, it's just that no one has really struck my fancy yet."

"Yes. Well, spring is coming. Perhaps that will bring a change in all our lives. Samuel will be coming home at the end of May. That will brighten the household."

Lurinda stirred the fire. "Will he stay all summer?"

"Yes, of course."

Now that she had something to look forward to, the days sped by. The weather changed abruptly early in May and the season leaped from winter into summer.

And then like a second burst of summer sunshine, Samuel came. Everyone in the house lined up to greet him, and he went down the line shaking hands, patting cheeks, and occasionally bestowing a kiss. Though he did not kiss her, he did say, "Why, Lurinda, how pretty you've grown."

His attractiveness had increased. College, however, had given him an air that seemed to widen the distance between them. Later that day when she happened on him in the parlor, she tried to bridge the distance.

"How was Harvard?" she asked.

"It was fine. Not Oxford, of course. But fine."

"What will you be doing this summer—studying?"

"No. Working father's farm." He turned a page.

"Will you like that?"

"I suppose so. Anyway, it will mean more freedom than I'd have here in town."

So, he wouldn't even be around the house. She waited a moment. Why wouldn't he put down that book and really look at her? "Samuel—or should I call you Mr. Eaton now?"

"Samuel's all right," he said.

"Samuel, I'm worried about your mother."

"She's not really my mother, you know."

"She's been like a mother to you ever since you were a baby. Besides, she adores you. You know that."

He looked up now, indolent charm lighting his face. Clearly he was pleased to be told he was adored.

"Why do you worry about her, Lurinda?"

"Because she's changed. She doesn't have any spirit any more. She stays in her room most of the time and almost never goes out. Your father—oh, please forgive me for saying this, but he does nothing to lift her spirits."

He closed his book, keeping a finger in the place. "Perhaps he's relieved that her spirits are lowered. At least she isn't stirring up trouble and embarrassing him."

"She meant well. She was sincere in her feelings."

He looked amused. "So was King Charles, I suppose."

She began to feel a little angry. "Well, if you don't care about your own people—"

"You care, don't you, Lurinda?" He looked at her thoughtfully.

"Yes. They've been like mother and father to me. I care, yet I'm not really free to speak. After all, I'm only a servant."

He stood up then, came over to her, and grasped her by the arms just above the elbows. "You're much more than a servant, Lurinda—much more. But I can understand how you feel about interfering. I'll see what I can do." His fingers were warm and strong on her arms. "You really are quite lovely, Lurinda. Or did I mention that earlier this afternoon?"

"Yes, you did." She hoped he couldn't feel the quiver that shook her body.

He gave her a long look and then abruptly dropped his hands and went back to his book.

Although it was clear he didn't want to talk any more, she couldn't resist saying, "It's nice that you got back in time for the fair."

"Yes. Will you be going?"

"Oh, yes. Your mother has given me the day for myself. The whole day."

"That's nice."

He did not say he would see her there; still, she was encouraged at the way the conversation had gone. And at supper she noticed he was hardly more communicative with his father.

"In Boston," the governor said, "they have heard no word of the great ship? No rumors even?"

"No word, Father. I told you that this afternoon. Two ships

have come from England these past few weeks. They report no ship and no sighting of any ship—not even of any wreckage."

"Let us not speak of wreckage," the governor said gravely.

Old Mrs. Eaton said, "We must have faith. No doubt it was a slow passage. No doubt our ship arrived in England right after the second ship sailed for Boston. We'll get word any day now."

"There will never be any word," Mrs. Eaton said. "It takes more than prayers and faith to sail a walt-sided ship all the way to England."

"Your mother," old Mrs. Eaton said to Samuel, "knows more about shipbuilding and sailing than all the experienced men in the colony."

Ignoring the remark, Mrs. Eaton pressed her hands together and held them up in an attitude of prayer. "If it be Thy will, O Lord, to consign them to a watery grave, take them—they are Thine."

Mary leaned forward. "She's making fun of our pastor again."

"I am not making fun of your pastor. This is no joking matter—playing with people's lives and resources."

"Can't you stop her?" old Mrs. Eaton said to the governor. "Are you going to let her stir up a quarrel on the very first night Samuel is home?"

"Ladies, ladies," Samuel said. "Please don't stop. It wouldn't seem like home if the three of you weren't bickering. No dining table in Boston equals this one for diverting conversation. Our Lurinda, when she marries and has her own home, will be able to demonstrate exactly how the top level of society behaves at table."

Lurinda was not pleased. It seemed to her that he was implying she would marry into a lower level of society.

Nor did the governor seem pleased. "That will do, Samuel. Let us speak of something more pleasant. Did you know you arrived home just in time for the fair?"

Before he could answer, Mary asked, "Were there new goods from England on your boat?"

Lurinda went to the kitchen for more corn pudding. She was less concerned with the goods that would be offered than with her day of freedom and the possibility that Samuel might walk with her. She prayed for sunshine and a mild day so that she could leave her heavy, unattractive cloak at home and go in her one pretty muslin dress.

And the God who had possibly ignored Mr. Davenport's prayer

chose to answer hers. The day could not have been lovelier. Before she left, Lurinda stopped at the blue room. Mrs. Eaton sat by the open window, her arms stretched out on the window sill.

"How beautiful it is outside today." She turned and looked at Lurinda. "You look lovely, my dear. You're sure to have a fine day."

Lurinda glanced down at her dress. It was everything that a pretty figure and careful sewing could make it, but it had been impossible to hide the strips of unfaded material where the seams had been before it had been made over. Still, she looked fresh and pretty, and she knew it and took pleasure in it.

"Aren't you going to the fair, ma'am?"

"No. I think not."

"Why not come and walk around just once? It isn't good for you to be alone like this."

"I've been alone like this for a long time."

"I know, and you need to be out where you can see people. You need to talk to someone besides me." Persuasively, she added, "I hear they're going to have more booths than ever before and many new and pretty things to buy."

"I'd like to go, but . . . oh, I don't know."

"I know what it is, ma'am. You've stayed in so much, it's hard to break the habit."

"Perhaps you're right. In the old days I couldn't get out often enough. Now I just can't seem to push myself."

"Then let me push a little. Please come. It would make Samuel happy. Only the other day he mentioned his concern about you."

"Did he? Well . . . but I'd have to fix my hair and find something special to wear."

"Let me help you look." She found a gown and got the hairbrush.

"This isn't right, Lurinda," Mrs. Eaton said as they left. "I give you the day off and then you spend it with me anyway."

Lurinda smiled. "Don't worry about it, ma'am." She wouldn't have admitted it, but she was still a little frightened by large gatherings of people. Being with her mistress gave her a feeling of confidence.

The marketplace had come to life. Tables and booths were set up in loose concentric circles, each one displaying a distinctive color. Some booths were decorated with gaily waving banners;

others attracted attention with the merchandise itself. Many people were selling articles they had made during the winter—yarn, cloth, kerchiefs—while others had articles that had come in on the first spring boats from England.

Sales were brisk but conversation was brisker. Some people had not had a chance to talk with each other since that bitter winter day when the great ship had sailed. They would wave and nod at church, but it had been so cold that few had lingered long after the services.

People nodded and spoke respectfully to Mrs. Eaton, but no one sought to detain her in conversation.

"You should be with the young people, Lurinda," Mrs. Eaton said. She gestured toward a table where some servant girls were giggling together as they fingered the new ribbons.

Lurinda felt infinitely superior to them. "They're a little silly, ma'am."

"Yes, I suppose they are."

"Perhaps because I've spent so much time with you, ma'am, instead of giggling and gossiping with the others in the kitchen all day, I'm different."

Mrs. Eaton looked thoughtful. "That may be. But I'm sorry if I've deprived you of friendships."

"Ann!" a voice said.

Mrs. Brewster was facing them, her eyes, blue as the harbor, crinkling with pleasure.

"Brigid. How good to see you. You cannot know how many times I've thought of you. Each day with no word from your husband must indeed be a long one."

Brigid's face sobered. "Long ago I gave up expecting to hear. That was a funeral service Mr. Davenport held the day of the sailing—nothing else."

"Oh, Brigid—"

Mrs. Brewster lifted her hand. "Don't fill me with false hopes. No friend would do that. I am quite resigned. But I did think you would come to see me."

"I did once."

"I mean after . . ."

"I thought you would send a message. I wasn't sure—"

Beyond Mrs. Brewster Lurinda suddenly saw Timothy Evans. She felt her heart leap. It wasn't the thundering excitement she felt when Samuel was near; it was the leap of old warmth, old friend-ship. She lifted her hand in a tentative wave. He waved back en-thusiastically. He had about him a surprising air of substance and could easily have been taken for a young freeman.

She turned back to Mrs. Eaton who was listening to Mrs. Brew-ster talk about Mrs. Stolyon's display.

"She has everything: thimbles, pins, silk thread, the latest pat-terns," she was saying. "Her prices are outrageous, of course. Over this way. I want you to see. Then later we can go to my house for beer."

Mrs. Eaton hesitated.

"Please go, ma'am," Lurinda said. "It will do you good. Be-sides, I see someone I know."

Tim came to her the moment Mrs. Eaton walked away with Mrs. Brewster. His air of confidence melted as he approached.

"Lurinda," he said, "I—oh, it's good to look at, to see you." The last step he took nearly catapulted him into her arms as he tripped over a perfectly visible root. Righting himself, he stared mutely at her, his face reddening, his arms swinging.

With her chin lifted, she sunned herself in his gaze. She knew exactly how he felt. When she was with Samuel, her feet and tongue often behaved just as awkwardly.

"What a boo—beautiful dress," he said. "You look"—he hesi-tated and said the word with care—"beautiful."

Smiling, she lifted her hand in a careless gesture she'd often seen Mrs. Eaton make. "Clearly you don't know much about dresses or materials, Timothy. Otherwise you'd see how many times this has been turned."

"You still look beautiful," he said. The redness was fading from his face. Straightening his shoulders with a sudden surge of con-fidence, he said, "Come and walk around with me. I've been watching you. You haven't seen much yet."

As she walked with him, Lurinda noticed some of the other girls looking at her with envy. Tim was certainly better looking than most young men of his class. He carried himself better and spoke better. For a girl with no special hopes, he would be a fine catch.

But not for me, she thought. He's good and he's kind, but he's not for me. And as people gave them sidelong glances that seemed to sum up their relationship, she thought: They'd better not think that we belong together, that I'm his intended or anything like that.

And as if to reinforce her thought, the next time he pointed out something attractive, she said disparagingly, "It's pretty enough, I guess. It might well appeal to some uneducated servant girl. But a lady would never wear it."

"I expect you're right, Lurinda. It is a little gaudy." He nodded agreeably, admiring her even when she was rude. "You do have good taste. I suppose it comes from being around the governor's family."

A girl shouldn't have so much power over a man, she thought. It makes her want to use it, to test it. But I won't be unkind to him. I must remember how kind he has always been to me.

"Now here," he said, stopping at a table loaded with laces, "are these not pretty?"

"Yes." She picked up a wide band of creamy linen lace. "This is an example of real beauty, simple and lasting. See how finely it's made?"

"How much is it?" Tim asked the woman.

Lurinda laughed. "Don't be silly, Tim. I have no gold, no wampum, nothing to trade. I'm not going to buy anything."

"But *I* am."

She put the lace down and turned. "Come away."

"No." He stood firmly in front of the table.

"Please come." She took a few steps, sure of her power to make him follow, only to turn and see him leaning toward the woman. From a leather pouch he had drawn from his pocket, he took some wampum, counted it out and gave it to the woman.

"Here." He handed the lace to Lurinda.

She held it, protesting. "I cannot accept this."

"Why not?"

"It makes it as if—don't you see?—as if I were your girl."

"You are—as far as I'm concerned."

It was hard to say the words she knew would hurt him, but finally she managed. "But not so far as I'm concerned."

He was quiet a moment. "That's all right. You like me, don't you? I know you do. I could tell by the look on your face when you saw me today."

"Tim—yes, I do like you. But I don't feel about you the way you feel about me."

"That's all right. But keep the lace. I know you like it."

She held it, winding it gently around her fingers as she walked. "It's new, you know," she said. "No one has ever used it before." It was impossible to keep the pleasure out of her voice. "No one has ever washed it or mended it or taken it off something old and put it on something new. It's as if all the time it was being made, it was being made just for me."

"Didn't you ever have anything new before?"

"Not that I can remember."

He gave her arm a quick squeeze just above the elbow. "I'm glad I was the one," he said.

Again she felt that quick leap of the heart. Oh, it was nice to be admired and cared about.

They stopped at a booth displaying the latest muslins from England: soft, flowered, and fresh as springtime. She could not help fingering them, those remote beauties she could not hope for until her indenture was over, and then only if she married a man of means. One length of material in particular caught her fancy. It had a snowy background strewn with violets.

"How much do you need for a gown?" Tim asked.

Quickly she drew away from the booth. Though she was awed by his gesture, she said severely, "You've already done too much. I should not even have accepted the lace. I positively will not accept a piece of goods for a gown."

"I want you to have it," he said. "I want you to have a dress that's all new, that has never been turned or made over, that isn't streaked, faded, or patched."

"But don't you see, Tim?—if I accept it, it's the same as saying I'm promised to you. And that isn't what I want."

"I don't care," he said stubbornly. "If you want to marry me some day, that's fine. If you will not have me, I still want you to have it, for I would rather give it to you freely than spend it at the ordinary."

She felt shamed by his goodness. "Where are you getting the money, Tim?"

"I've been doing some trapping. And some trading. Mr. Newman has helped me. I'll be able to begin a real business of my own by the time I've earned my freedom. Please, Lurinda. This is the first real money I've earned in my life—let me spend it in a way that gives me pleasure."

Finally she nodded assent. With excitement simmering inside her, she waited while he made the purchase. Returning to her side, he handed her the folded cloth. "Remember," he said, "I give it to you freely."

Some of the tables were piled with foodstuffs, the specialties of various women. Tim bought a small round of crusty bread at one table, some ripe cheese at another, and some cake at another.

While they ate, sitting on two empty stumps at the far corner of the square beyond the guardhouse, he told her of his plans for trading in skins, and for, possibly, setting up a leather-worker's shop with several apprentices. "I plan to be somebody someday," he said. "Somebody to reckon with."

And I also, she thought. More than you know. She turned and sniffed a breeze from the sea. It swept away for the moment the prevailing smell of horses and beer and sweat and food.

"I like your profile," he said, "but not so well as your full face. Your profile shows your intelligence—it's sharper—but your full face shows your sweetness."

She gave him a fond look. "You're too good, Tim, to see me as I am. I'm neither intelligent nor sweet."

"You are. I know."

He was so good, she thought, that he saw his own goodness in her. She could not help, though, being warmed by his words.

After they had finished eating, they made another circle around the square and then took a walk down by the harbor. Companionably, they relived their voyage and spoke of all that had happened since. When they were at a distance where no one could see, she even allowed him to hold her hand as they walked.

Late in the afternoon, when he left her at the Eaton gate, she said honestly, "Thank you, Tim, for everything. It's been a wonderful day."

"May I call on you, Lurinda?"

"Oh, Tim." Now came the feeling of obligation and of guilt. "Please don't ask. You said—"

"Yes, I did. Then I won't ask. If you want to see me, you can give me a sign in church."

Upstairs in her room, she hid the cloth and lace in a drawer. Dear Tim. He really was good. Ambitious, too. Already he was making money. She could do worse than let him call on her. And certainly he would be a loyal and loving husband. With him she would not have the kind of life her mother had—unloved, unpraised, and overworked. She remembered the leap of pleasure she had felt when she had seen him and the warmth his look and touch had stirred inside her. Perhaps this was what married love was like: something warm and gentle instead of a thunderous, tearing passion.

It was foolish to go on dreaming about Samuel. He had not even bothered to look for her today. He thought of her as a servant—nothing else. Next Sunday she would give Tim a sign in church.

Feeling tremulous and happy, she went down the stairs. She was glad she had made her decision, given up her impossible dream. She thought with excitement of the snowy, violet-strewn material and imagined herself wearing a gown made from it—full-skirted with a flounce and with ruffles at the wrists. Feeling almost as if the dress were already made and she was stepping forth in it, she opened the door to the great hall.

Samuel was standing with his hands behind him, gazing at the fire. Turning, he looked at her. But instead of looking away again as he usually did, he continued to stare.

"Lurinda, what's happened to you?"

"Why do you ask?" Her self-possession immediately deserting her, her fingers leaped nervously to her hair.

"Nothing's wrong. It's just that you have a kind of glow. You look like a girl who's just been kissed. Have you?"

She should have been angered by his boldness. But she wasn't. She merely said demurely, "No."

"Honest?"

"Honest."

"Then you look as if you ought to be kissed—or want to be."

She stepped back, bracing herself against the door.

He laughed good-naturedly. "Don't be afraid. I won't force myself on you. But you do have a look I've never seen on you before and it makes you very attractive. Seductive even."

"Please don't talk like that."

"All right. Where have you been?"

"At the fair."

"I didn't see you there."

"You weren't looking for me," she said.

"Of course I was."

"When? Where?"

"All day. Off and on. Here and there."

She knew he was lying. She had seen him lie to his parents. A twitch at the side of his mouth always gave him away. But it didn't matter. What mattered was that he was taking the trouble to lie to her in order to impress her, to show his interest.

He moved closer to her. "Did you know that I'm going to the farm for the summer?"

"Yes. You told me." The shorter her replies, the less likely she was to stutter or trip over her words.

"I'll miss you," he said.

She lifted her eyebrows.

"All winter long," he said, "I've been looking forward to spending the summer in the same house with you and now I'm going to be at the farm." He lowered his voice. "Some night during the summer, I'm going to have a venison feast out there. Will you come?"

"Who will be there?"

"Not the family. Just some young people. You'd be my girl." He said the last words slowly, caressingly. "Will you come?"

She stared at him, swallowing. Was it possible, after all this time, just when she had nearly given it up, her dream was really going to come true? *You'd be my girl,* he'd said.

"Will you come?" His words were an urgent whisper.

"Yes," she said breathlessly. "But how will I get there?"

"I'll arrange it later. Meanwhile, don't say anything to anyone."

29

JOHN DAVENPORT / JUNE 1647

Ann had begun going out again, and she had stopped wearing black. She had never had any reason to wear black anyway. From his study at the front of the house across the street, the Reverend Mr. Davenport noted her comings and goings, the variations in her costumes, and the quality of her step. He could do this and write a sermon at the same time—such was the ability of his mind to handle two threads of thought and keep them disentangled.

As he stared out the window on a sultry June afternoon, puzzling over the explication of a particularly obscure point of Scripture, he saw her come out of the house. She was wearing a cool-looking blue gown. Over her arm was a large basket from which knitting needles protruded. Davenport loosened the band at his throat. Even inside his study the air was thick and stickily warm.

How did she manage to look so cool and untouched? It was as if her confidence produced such self-containment that not even the intensities of heat or cold could penetrate her awareness.

Lifting her hand to shade her eyes, Ann stood still a moment looking toward the harbor. The fate of the great ship hung heavy on the minds of all. It had become a habit for eyes to first glance out to sea.

Soon, Oh Lord. Send us word or give us a sign. How often had he prayed thus, both publicly and privately.

She turned and began walking up the street, her hips swinging with delicate rhythm. Leaning toward the window to get a better view, Davenport frowned. Could she not do something about that walk of hers? Surely a woman could control such things. If she followed a straight course and thought virtuous thoughts, her hips would doubtless respond by abandoning that tantalizingly suggestive movement.

It was said that she was once again visiting Brigid Brewster. Well, at least it was a comfort to know that the town no longer need fear the fruits of their gossiping and criticism. Both had been discredited. No one would listen to them or care to be involved with them.

He could never understand why Hooker up in the Connecticut Colony was so reluctant to try the malcontents in his community. Hooker had censured only one member of his church and excommunicated only one. A meager record. The day would surely come when he would find that nothing but evil could result from failing to keep his church pure.

The Lord said: "Cast out the serpent that is among you." It was the only way. To ignore ungodliness, to fail to punish it, was to condone and encourage it. Get the bad apples and their rottenness out of the barrel and the rest would remain sweet and pure, ever a tribute to the God who had made them.

How hot it was. He dipped his quill in the ink and wrote down a carefully worded sentence. There. He ran his finger around under his band as he read over what he had written. His felicity with words was a recurring source of pleasure to him, a gift from God that could not be discounted.

The door across the street opened and closed again. He looked up and saw Lurinda come out. Without stopping to look out across the harbor, she crossed the yard, picked a bunch of gillyflowers, and took them back into the house.

The girl was exceptionally well dressed and she carried herself like a lady. He would have to speak to her. More humility in dress and carriage would better suit her age and station.

He rubbed the back of his hand across his moist forehead. The air grew more sultry and still with each passing moment. Leaning forward to look at the sky, he saw that it was tinged with copper. In the distance, off beyond the red rocks, came a faint rumble. As the moments passed, the rumbles increased and rolled ominously closer. A yellow streak of lightning split the coppery sky.

During the next rumble of thunder Theophilus came out of his house and crossed the street. Davenport greeted him warmly and led him into the shadowy room. Moment by moment it grew darker, as if candles somewhere were being blown out one by one. Thunder shook the house as they took their accustomed seats.

"So," Davenport said, "you have come to sit out the storm with me."

"Yes. I could tell that I soon would not be able to see to work. It seems a pity to use candles in the daytime."

Elizabeth came tremulously into the room and settled her soft bulk into a chair close to her husband. He patted her arm. "Don't be nervous, my dear. God will protect you. He cares for his own."

She gave him a tight-lipped smile. "I still feel safest when I am close to you."

"Perhaps," Theophilus said, "that is because he is so close to God."

Thunder growled furiously and lightning snapped at its heels. It was followed almost immediately by an even louder crash of thunder.

Elizabeth winced and covered her face a moment. "Please excuse me. Tell me, Your Grace, does your wife fear storms?"

In the shadowy room the hollows and lines in his face were bitter and dark. "So far as I know," he said, "my wife fears nothing. Nothing."

"I am saddened that you must make such an admission, my friend," Davenport said. "Remember the words of Solomon: 'The beginning of wisdom is the fear of the Lord,' and 'Favor is deceitful, and beauty is vanity, but a woman that feareth the Lord, she shall be praised.' "

"I am sure she fears the Lord," Elizabeth murmured.

"And I am just as sure she does not," Davenport answered emphatically.

Theophilus started to say something, but his voice was drowned by a deluge of rain, pounding on the roof, slashing at the windows. The wind roared and behind it, as the atmosphere darkened, the thunder rumbled and crashed and reverberated with an ever increasing anger. At intervals, brilliant flashes of lightning illuminated the room.

It was a strange storm. Instead of sweeping in and then sweeping on out again to sea, it seemed caught in the bowl between the red rocks and the harbor. Caught there, it boiled and roiled and rumbled like a huge and evil brew.

When at last the storm was over, late in the afternoon—when at last it had ceased with strange abruptness and the sun had returned—everyone went outside to see what damage had occurred.

One huge tree near the end of the street had been split and felled, but no frightening columns of smoke rose over the town.

"God has been good to us," Davenport said. "He has spared us again."

The sky was now miraculously clear except for one last cloud that lingered low on the horizon near the mouth of the harbor. As they looked at it, the cloud began to take on the shape of a ship. Its sails were full, and it sailed in a northerly direction against the wind.

"My God," Theophilus said, "it looks like the great ship—like Lamberton's ship."

"Yes," Davenport said. His breath came hard as if he had been running a long time.

For nearly half an hour the shiplike cloud was visible. Many townspeople, seeing it, came to tell their governor and pastor and remained to watch it with them. Ann had come, too, but she stood a little apart from the others, listening to the comments. She did not speak.

"Is she Lamberton's?"

"Oh, yes. She is. I can tell by the rigging."

"But is she real?"

"Isn't it just a cloud?"

"Why is she sailing away from us and not toward us?"

"Why is she slightly above the water and not on it?"

"Be quiet, my children," Davenport said at last. "This may be a message from our Lord. Be quiet and watch. Surely God has a reason for showing us this."

And as they watched, the main topsail of the ship seemed to blow off. It was left hanging in the shrouds. Then the mizzen-top blew off, then all its masting. After that the ship careened and vanished into a smoky cloud. In a few moments the cloud had dissipated and the air over the harbor's mouth was brilliantly clear.

"What does it mean, sir?"

They were all looking to him for guidance, for answers, for a glimmer of hope that they must surely know he could not give.

"God," said Davenport, "has condescended, for the quieting of our afflicted spirits, to give us this extraordinary account of his sovereign disposal of those for whom so many fervent prayers have been made."

"My God," Theophilus said in a low voice as the crowd silently dispersed, "seventy of our best men and women. Five thousand pounds of plate. How can we withstand the loss? How can we survive?"

Davenport, shaking his head, looked past him to Ann who had remained there, standing a few yards away. She was staring at Theophilus, her face hard and cold. But just as she turned to walk away, Davenport saw a glitter of tears in her eyes.

LURINDA COLLINGS
JULY 1647

Every Sunday Samuel came in from the farm for church, yet week after week passed without a message for Lurinda. Finally, early in July, he caught up with her as she was walking home alone across the public square after the service.

"An Indian has promised us some fine venison for next Friday and our Maker has promised us a fine moon." He smiled down at her engagingly. "Do you still want to come out to our feast? Or have you changed your mind?"

She could not keep the joy out of her voice. "Oh, no, I haven't changed my mind. I was afraid *you* had." Immediately, she wondered whether she had said too much, seemed too anxious. When she was with Timothy, she didn't worry about saying the right thing. Why was it so different with Samuel? Why, even though Samuel had at last shown a definite interest in her, did she still feel unsure and puzzled?

"Of course I haven't," he said. As they neared the edge of the square, he told her to wait by the bridge right after the nine o'clock watch was called. "Someone on horseback—probably me if I can get away—will pick you up. But remember, even if someone else picks you up, you'll still be my girl."

My girl, my girl. She hugged the words to herself all week and was so full of singing joy that even Mrs. Eaton noticed it.

"You act as though you have a beau, Lurinda. It must be wonderful to be young and full of plans."

Lurinda heard the sadness in Mrs. Eaton's voice. How horrible it must be to live without love. Yet she knew that it was her mistress herself who had banished her husband from her bed. It was something Lurinda could not understand. The governor was the most wonderful man she had ever known. She had never seen him anything but gentle, kind, and just. He was very human, too. Sometimes he made little jokes, though never the kind that would hurt anyone. But lately he had smiled less and joked hardly at all— especially since the image of the great ship had appeared in the clouds after the thunderstorm.

"Really, ma'am, I have no special plans."

"Well, there's something different about you. If you're not in love, then you must be ready for love."

Lurinda smiled and thought of the violet-strewn gown hanging behind a curtain in her room. It was as beautiful as any of Mrs. Eaton's gowns. Only a little more work remained to be done on it. The buttons had to be sewed down the front to the waist, and the flounce around the bottom must be gathered and attached.

By Friday, it was finished. Each morning during the week she had slipped out of bed at the first streak of dawn and had worked on her dress by the window until she heard others rising.

On Friday evening as she was brushing her mistress's hair after supper, Mrs. Eaton said, "Are you all right, Lurinda?"

"Of course, ma'am. Why do you ask?"

"Your fingers are trembling. And you look flushed. I hope you don't have that awful fever that's taken so many of our friends?"

"I'm sure I don't. But I . . . I do feel tired."

"Why don't you go along to bed."

"Perhaps I will."

"Would you like me to come to your room later to see how you are?"

Lurinda's heart sank. "Oh, no, ma'am," she said quickly. "I don't feel really sick. I know I'll go right to sleep."

The concern in Mrs. Eaton's eyes made her feel guilty. She really does care, she thought. And she felt almost like sharing her plans with her. Mrs. Eaton would probably understand. She, too, had broken rules to do what she believed was right for herself.

"Well, go along," Mrs. Eaton said. "Sleep well."

Lurinda carried warm water to her room. She undressed, washed carefully, and dressed again, at last slipping the new gown over her head. The wonderfully fresh smell of new material was headier than perfume. Breathing deeply, she savored it. It made her think of everything that was at last to be new in her life.

If only she had a large mirror in her room so she could see herself, remember herself, as she looked at this moment. But she knew she looked beautiful, knew that—better still—she looked as much a lady as any of the women in town whose husbands were entitled to use *Mister* in front of their names.

With a long cloak on and her skirts tucked up beneath so they wouldn't be caught on the brambles, she stood calmly in the darkening shadows of her room until the nine o'clock watch was called. When the last sound had faded into the distance, she hurried down the back stairs, and out the back door.

As she darted diagonally through the underbrush beyond the gardens, she lifted her cloak slightly and held it tight against her body. How bright it was out, yet how different everything looked. The moon, though less bright than the sun, cast deeper shadows. And the noises, so familiar in the sunlight, were now startling and mysterious. Her heart beat like a muffled Indian drum, making her breath uneven and her walk rapid and nervous.

By the time she reached the bridge, she was thoroughly frightened. He shouldn't have asked me to come out like this at night, she thought. For the first time she began to wonder seriously why, if Samuel really liked her and wanted her to be his girl, he hadn't told his parents. Why hadn't he asked to sit or walk with her on Sunday evenings? Did he suspect they might be reluctant to encourage a relationship between son and servant? Perhaps, after all, she was wise to meet him this way. She'd capture his interest completely and then let him argue it out with his mother and father.

After almost running across the bridge, she moved quickly to the sheltering shadow of a huge oak. She loosened the hem of her tucked-up skirt and felt its newness flow around her ankles. Excitement stirred in her as she heard the sound of approaching hoofbeats. Shrinking against the trunk of the tree, she waited.

The horse stopped, snorting. A voice whispered, "Lurinda?"

"Yes." Her heart lifting, she came quickly out of the shadows. "Is that you, Samuel?"

She heard a dry laugh that she didn't quite like. Holding her cloak very tightly around her, even though it offered no protection, she watched the man get down off the horse. It was Will

Harding who worked for Mr. Malbon and had an unsavory reputation for his attentions to young girls.

"Come on, girlie," he said. "You don't want to spend the night standing here."

"Did Mr. Eaton—young Mr. Eaton, that is—send you for me?"

"That he did. And he said to hurry."

He lifted her up onto the horse and got on in front of her. Her face was so close to his that she could smell his sour, beery breath.

"You'd better hang onto me," he said as the horse started to move.

It seemed as though she could not bear to do it, but as the horse gained speed her precarious balance forced her to put her arms around him. Grasping his leather jerkin with both hands, she tried to hold herself erect so their bodies would not touch.

"So you're Sam Eaton's girl," he said.

"Yes."

"Funny thing. I saw you at the fair with Tim Evans. Even got the idea he was buying something for you. If anyone had asked me, I would have said you were Tim's girl."

"Well, I'm not."

"Maybe you're anybody's girl." Expertly he doubled the reins over his left hand and suddenly she felt his right hand on her leg, trying to push its way up under her petticoat.

In a furious voice she said, "Stop that or I'll report you to Mr. Malbon. And Samuel. And the governor."

"You wouldn't dare," he said, his fingers still insistent.

"What makes you think I wouldn't?"

"Because you'd have to admit you sneaked out to a forbidden feast. They'd punish you, too."

"I don't care. Even if I had to be publicly whipped, I'd do it for the pleasure of seeing you whipped. And don't think the governor wouldn't believe me. He's been like a father to me."

"Have it the way you want it," he said roughly, but he did take up the reins with both hands again.

She felt a little guilty about using the governor's name, but, after all, the governor was fond of her. She knew he'd take her word over that of someone like Will Harding.

Will rode faster now so that it was all she could do to maintain the small distance between them. What a horrid way to start her beautiful evening.

226

At last she saw a reddish glow through the trees. In a moment they were at the farm and Samuel was lifting her down. The ride, after all, had taken only a few minutes.

The area in front of the farmhouse was bright with pine-knot torches. Their aromatic smell mixed with the richness of the roasting venison to fill the air. In the glow of the torches and the fire of red coals that smoldered under the venison, she could see more than a dozen young people. Most of them were sitting around a long trestle table singing a bawdy air she remembered hearing at her father's pub. As Samuel led her closer, she saw that many of the best young men of the town were there. William had gone over to the pit where the venison was turning on a spit. She was pleased to discover that he was a worker there rather than a guest.

As she gradually made out the faces of the girls, however, it was as if someone had placed a cord around her stomach and was drawing it tighter and tighter. The girls were *all* servants. Why? Why? She had thought Samuel had invited her because, despite being a servant, she acted like a lady. But these girls, these girls who were joining in the singing of the bawdy air, who were throwing their heads back and laughing raucously, who were leaning toward their male companions and sometimes flinging careless but familiar arms across their shoulders, in no way resembled ladies.

She looked up at Samuel, hoping for some kind of reassurance. His look was warm with interest.

"Let me take your cloak," he said. "It's warm tonight." As he took it, he added, "What a lovely gown. I've never seen it before—have I?"

"No. It's new. Even the material is new."

He looked amused. "Come, let me show you off."

Drawing her close to a group that was standing near the pit, he said, "Look, people, at my Lurinda in her beautiful new gown. Note the new material and the latest styling. Note the intricate ruffle at the neck." He bent close as if to examine the ruff. Suddenly she felt his lips pressing against her throat.

Some laughed, some clapped. One of the young men said, "They must have taught you well at Harvard, Sammy. That's the way to do it, all right. Always take them by surprise. Never ask."

Lurinda stood very still, smiling tremulously, hardly knowing whether to laugh or to cry. Or to show her anger. In an effort to regain her composure, she turned and gazed at the pit. The man turning the spit looked up at her . . . at her face . . . at her dress. For a few seconds her heart seemed to stop beating. The man was Timothy.

Once on board ship when she was sicker than she had ever remembered being, when she had thought she was dying, when she had even wanted to die, Timothy had held her gently and had eased the moment past. Now once again, she wanted to die. He could not ease this moment for her, however; nor could she do so for him.

Through dry lips, she said, "Hello, Tim."

"Hello, Lurinda." He smiled at her just as he always had.

She wanted to say something, to explain, to try to make him understand. But what could she say with Samuel standing right there beside her? Besides, she told herself, she had told Tim that she didn't want to be his girl.

"Is it ready?" Samuel asked.

"I think so, Mr. Eaton," Tim said.

The meat was carved and placed on the table. It was good. Everyone was gay. Next to her Samuel was being devoted and interested. But Lurinda found it hard to eat and hard to join in the gaiety. A pervading sense of uneasiness dulled her pleasure. Whenever she looked up, she saw Tim watching her. His expression was always thoughtful, never angry. It would have been better if he had been angry.

Gradually, as the food was finished, couples began getting up and leaving the table. Lurinda didn't notice where they went. She was much too interested in all that Samuel said and did. When at last he picked up her cloak and said, "Let's go for a walk," she was glad to get away from the raucous group still sitting there, and even more glad to get away from Tim and the guilt aroused by his uncritical gaze.

The moon hung like a polished copper plate in the sky, familiar and reassuring. Lurinda found her uneasiness ebbing away. With Samuel beside her, the shadows of the night were no longer menacing.

"You've been very quiet tonight," Samuel said. "Aren't you enjoying yourself?"

"I am now," she said. "I suppose I'm not used to parties like this. All that loud talk and laughter. All those jokes. I didn't even understand some of them."

Stopping, putting his hands on her waist, he turned her so she faced him. This was what she had dreamed of—just the two of them far away from everyone else. Her heartbeat quickened as he looked warmly down at her.

"Is this what you wanted—just to be alone with me?"

"Yes," she whispered. Was it bold of her? But he didn't act as if it were. Dropping his hands from her waist, he took her hand and they continued walking. A warm happiness filled her. It seemed to her that they understood each other perfectly. It almost seemed as if they had understood and perhaps even loved each other for years in this same silent way.

After they had walked until the sounds from the farm were as indistinct as the shapes of the bushes and trees around them, they stopped. Samuel spread her cloak on the ground and drew her down onto it.

"There," she said, spreading her skirts around her. "Now we can talk."

His voice was husky. "We'll talk later."

Without knowing how it happened, she found herself in his arms. He was holding her close. His lips were on hers, so warm and insistent and sweet that all her reserve slipped away and she could feel herself melting unashamedly against him, responding, aching to be kissed like this over and over.

Suddenly, a strange cry split the night. It sounded all too human, like a hoot of derision. Startled, she drew away, only to have Samuel pull her close again.

"Wait," she said.

But he did not want to wait. "It's only an owl."

"You don't know. It could be an Indian. It could be someone listening to us. It could be a wild animal waiting to pounce on us."

For a moment they sat still listening. Samuel's fingers gently caressed her arm while she held back, waiting. No new sounds were heard, but she found herself all at once remembering her mother's words as she had told her about that long-ago May Day evening: Oh, they can kiss you and touch you until your blood is singing and you think that no one before has ever known such sweetness. And then it's all over and nothing is left but pain and shame and a lifetime of ill-treatment.

This was not the path a lady took to the kind of marriage that the Eatons had. This pathway could lead only to a forced marriage, or worse still, the shame of no marriage at all. The singing excitement inside her was stilled, and when Samuel again reached for her, she leaned back saying again, "Wait, please wait."

But his arms were tight around her and she could hear the impatience in his voice as he pressed her now unwilling body against his. "Don't be such a silly," he said. "It's only an owl."

Disillusionment came quickly on the heels of wisdom. With his lips fastened on hers, his hands moved on her body. Feeling him touch her breast, she twisted her face from his. "Stop. Oh please stop."

Ignoring her plea, breathing hard, he began fumbling with her skirts and, just like Will Harding—oh, worse than Will because she could not seem to stop him—his fingers were moving upward along her leg. At the same time, he was trying to force her down on her back. And he was strong, very strong.

Angry, hurt, full of shame, she struggled against him, but her resistance only seemed to increase the urgency of his desire. For a moment she pretended compliance; then, catching him off guard, she wrenched away from him and jumped to her feet. He was as quickly on his. Reaching for her again, he said in a voice now grown hoarse, "Don't tease me like this, Lurinda darling. Don't play games with me."

His hand was on the ruff at her throat. He was trying to unbutton her bodice. With a twisting movement she freed herself. At the same time she heard the rip of material as her beautiful new dress was torn.

Holding the bodice together, she began to run.

"Wait," he called out. "Don't go back to the farm yet."

She continued to run, not toward the farm but back toward the town.

"Wait," he said again. "You've forgotten your cloak. Wait, Lurinda. I didn't mean—"

But she kept on running, running. As she ran, stumbling now and then, feeling the branches at the sides of the path tearing at her dress, she sobbed. It was like running in a nightmare, running, running, and never reaching a familiar spot. She had lost her sense of direction. Perhaps she was running away from the town instead of toward it. Perhaps she would run on and on into the wilderness until fierce savages caught her and cut off her fingers to make bracelets from the bones.

Surely she could not run any longer. Her side began to ache and her breath rasped in her throat. Rest a minute, she thought. She stood still and, looking ahead, saw that she had reached the bridge where Will had picked her up. Oblivious now of any sound she might make, she hurried across it. This time she did not go through the woods. Instead she followed the darkened street.

As she was about to turn the corner to go up the street that ran past the governor's house, she suddenly saw two moving figures coming toward her, made grotesque by the flaming pine-knot one of them held above his head. The night watch. She had forgotten about them. Turning, she began to run in the other direction.

"Halt!" She heard a musket click its readiness.

Still clutching her torn dress, she stopped and faced them. Their long black shadows leaped toward her.

"So. What wench is this?" They held the burning wood close to her.

The acrid smoke and the smell of pitch seared her nostrils. As the flames leaped and played on the faces of the two men, they began to look like two grinning devils. Surely this must be the way hell smelled and felt and looked. Terror encircled her chest, making every heartbeat, every breath, an agony.

"And where have *you* been, Miss?" one of the leering faces asked.

"Nowhere."

"Nowhere, is it? Just been standing here letting the wind tear your dress and scratch your face. Looks to me as though you've been out having more than a little fun. Who are you, anyway? Who are your parents?"

"I have none . . . here."

"I know who she is now," one said to the other. "She's a servant girl. I've seen her in church. Most of them have no morals, you know. They'll go with any man who looks at them."

"That's right. And right now she's going with us."

Each of her arms was gripped by a hard, strong hand. Was this mad, frightening evening never to end? As she tried to pull herself away, their fingers tightened painfully. In her absolute helplessness, the terror inside her exploded and came out in a high, thin scream.

THEOPHILUS EATON
JULY 1647

A light knock sounded on the door of his closet. Theophilus lifted his head, not quite trusting his hearing. His wife had been in and out of his thoughts all evening long, lurking on the edge of each of his problems. Was it possible that on this golden moonlit night she, too, had been thinking of him? Missing him? Was it possible that after all the long, long months of separation she was ready at last to extend her soft, white, forgiving arms to him, ready to welcome him back to her bed?

The knock came again, a more peremptory sound now, but still with that same familiar rhythm. Despite the fatigue that had been plaguing him, lying heavily in his chest all evening, he reached the door quickly and opened it in a swift, youthful motion.

It was his mother, tiny—tinier every year—but still straight-backed, vigorous, and knowledgeable. Her white hair was down and braided.

"You looked pleased to see me, Son. It's been a long time since I've seen such a welcoming look on your face."

"Sit down, Mother." He held back a sigh. What kind of fool had he been to think *she* might have been thinking of him, simply because he had been thinking of *her?* How could he have been so mistaken about the rhythm of the knock? "I'm always glad to see you, Mother. You know that. But aren't you up very late?"

"That's what I came to see you about. You're burning too many midnight candles, my son. If the Lord had meant us to work at night, he would have made the moon much brighter."

"The Lord gave us reason so we could invent candles. But I agree, Mother. I should not be so profligate with them." He rubbed the back of his hand across his eyes.

"What's wrong, Son?"

"What's wrong? Nothing." He paused. "No, everything. I've been sitting here wondering how we can sustain all the losses of the great ship. Should we build another ship, I ask myself? Should we concentrate again on another settlement in Delaware, or should we just try to increase our coastal and island trade?" He sighed deeply. "Or should we stop trying to grow?"

"I think you should try all three, Son. Don't let a few setbacks turn your eyes backward. Perhaps God was testing you to see whether or not you're really serious about setting up a kingdom for his glorification."

"Then there's Southold. They're still flouting the fundamental agreement. I'm not sure—"

"Put your foot down, Son. They're getting protection from us. The least they can do is respect the rules we've laid down."

"Yes, you're probably right. That's what I should do." He began stacking papers, straightening his desk. "I am despondent, too, about the deaths of our friends. Word has come from Hartford that Thomas Hooker was sick no more than twenty-four hours. It seemed no more than a cold and a light fever at first. I fear for the church there now that he's gone. They haven't anyone strong like John Davenport to hold it together."

His mother nodded. "It's sad. And it seems worse because it happened so suddenly. They say Margaret Winthrop went as quickly."

"Yes."

"Such a fine woman."

"Yes. She was very good to us during the year we were in the Bay Colony."

"I was thinking of what a fine wife she was. She honored her husband. She thought only of him. She stayed unobtrusively in the background and never did anything to undermine his authority in the colony. A wonderful wife."

"Are you perchance talking about me?" a voice said from the doorway.

"Ann." Theophilus jumped to his feet, his heart thudding. His premonition about her visiting him had not been wrong after all.

His mother inclined her head, smiling faintly as if to greet—but in a not too friendly way—someone of inferior station. "We were talking about Margaret Winthrop, a fine and loyal wife, content to run her home and to give her children love and attention, and discourage them from abnormal tendencies—"

"If you're referring to my daughter—"

"Please," Theophilus said. His chest tightened and a jagged pain coursed across it. By the light of the guttering candle he could see the anger playing on his wife's face. "Let's not irritate each other with painful references."

"We also," said his mother, smoothly changing the subject, "were talking about colony affairs. My son was discussing some of his problems with me and seeking my advice."

"I see," Ann said. "I'm sure, then, that the colony will continue to move forward as profitably as it has for the past year or so."

His mother's lower lip jutted forward but she made no reply. After a moment Theophilus said to Ann, "Did you wish to see me about something?"

"I could not sleep. Earlier this evening Lurinda told me she wasn't feeling well so I went to her room to see how she was. She wasn't there. I looked downstairs, too. Finally I thought I'd come to ask you what we ought to do. She seemed feverish earlier. I'm afraid she may have become afflicted by delirium and wandered off."

"If she's wandered off," old Mrs. Eaton said, "she's wandered off with some wenching fellow. I've seen the way they look at her."

"Lurinda is a sweet and pure young girl."

"I must agree," Theophilus said, not looking at his mother. "Lurinda has never given us any cause to question her behavior."

Ann smiled at him. Was there a chance, just a bare chance, that the rift between them might be healed? With an ache that went all through him, he longed for the oblivion, the surcease from trouble, that he had never been able to find anywhere but in her arms.

In the street outside a long, thin scream tore through the darkness.

"That's Lurinda," Ann said. "I know her voice."

Looking out the window, Theophilus saw the three figures outlined by the red glow of a pine-knot. "She's in some kind of trouble, I think."

"What did I tell you?" his mother said. "Went out looking for it—you can be sure of that."

With Theophilus lighting the way, they went downstairs to the great hall. Theophilus unbolted the top and bottom parts of the door and the two watchmen led Lurinda in. Her eyes were red and swollen. A scratch made a crimson tracery from cheekbone to chin. Tangled with twigs and grasses, her pale hair hung in complete disarray around her shoulders. Her dress was soiled and torn, with the bodice shamelessly ripped open so wide that she had to hold it together in one clenched hand. Sobbing soundlessly, she could only stand and look at the floor.

"A sorry sight," old Mrs. Eaton said.

Theophilus said, "What happened to you, Lurinda? Where have you been?"

Lurinda shook her head a little. Tears spilled down on her face.

"Let the girl sit down," Ann said softly.

"Prisoners always stand in the presence of the governor," old Mrs. Eaton said. "Even at a pretrial hearing."

"Let go of her," Ann said to the two men. "She's not a prisoner. She's a member of this family. Besides, she's not well."

"Let her sit," Theophilus said. He had been about to suggest it himself, but felt a flicker of irritation at having Ann do so. Must she always interfere?

Theophilus sat down behind the long table. Lurinda sat facing him, flanked by the two watchmen.

"Now," said Theophilus, "I'd like to know exactly what happened."

One of the watchmen spoke. "We had just gone down the street by your house, Your Grace, and had turned to the left and were walking in an easterly direction, when we heard someone running across the bridge. In a few minutes we saw this young woman coming toward us. When we told her to halt, she tried to run the other way. We caught her and she struggled and screamed."

"Is that how her clothing became so disheveled and torn?"

"Oh no, Your Grace." The other watchman put his hand over his mouth to conceal a knowing grin. "She was in that sorry state when we apprehended her."

"Where were you tonight, Lurinda?"

She sobbed, murmured something he could not hear.

"Speak up, Lurinda. Where were you?"

235

"At one of the farms."

"Which one?"

She did not respond.

"Which one?"

Her lips remained tightly closed.

"Look at me, Lurinda." He waited until she had lifted her head. "Do you refuse to say where you were?"

She nodded.

"But you were at one of the farms?"

"Yes."

"Were you alone there with someone?"

She shook her head.

"It was a gathering, then?"

"Yes."

"Of young people?"

"Yes."

"Many of them servants?"

It seemed to him then that her face became sullen. "Many of them? Yes."

"And you were with a special young man?"

"Yes." She had bent her head again. One hand still held her dress together; the other, resting in her lap, opened and closed convulsively.

"His name?"

Her eyes darted from side to side as if looking for answers in the shadowy corners of the room, but she did not speak.

"His *name?*" Theophilus let his voice grow sharp.

She shook her head.

"You will not say it? Look at me. Speak up."

She lifted her head. "I will not say it. I will *never* say it."

Behind him, his mother drew in a shocked breath. "It will go hard for you, my child," he said, "if you are as defiant as this during your trial." He paused. "Why did the young people gather?"

"For a feast. A venison feast."

"And for what else?"

"I don't know what you mean."

"For what other kind of activity? Eating venison does not tear clothing and scratch flesh."

"I went for nothing else." Her face was blank, but her mouth set stubbornly.

He regarded her carefully. "Did you or did you not go with the intention of dallying with some young man in a filthy manner?"

"I did not!"

"Whether or not that was your intention, did you engage in filthy dalliance?"

"I did not!"

"Then how does your clothing come to be in such disarray?"

Looking downward, she moistened her lips. "Because I refused. Because I ran from it . . . from him."

He was inclined to believe her. No one needed to tear the clothing of a compliant maiden. Only one who struggled and resisted would look as she did. He glanced at his wife. With her back against the door that led to the upstairs, she was watching him intently, hopefully. She lifted her eyebrows a little in an unspoken question.

He turned back to Lurinda. Her breath still came convulsively, but she had stopped crying. She looked wretched. Pity filled his heart, blurring his reason. Why not tell her to go off to bed and rest and pray? Why not instruct his wife to soothe her and treat her wounds?

But, as if she had guessed the softening of his heart, his mother behind him hissed, "Don't forget the watchmen know about this. If you let her go with only a word of admonishment, all the young people in town will feel free to break the laws of God and man. She's lying. She won't even look at you. Servants always lie. This one especially. I never did trust her."

Theophilus inhaled slowly, then held himself still as he felt his breath catch in a flash of pain. Within seconds the pain was gone and his breath slowly eased out. He inhaled again. No pain. It was as if he had only imagined it.

But another pain remained: the pain of always having to judge, of having to punish, of having to set the example. His mother was right. He must put all personal feelings aside.

"You do know," he said to Lurinda, "that such gatherings of young people are forbidden?"

"Yes."

"Yes, Your Grace," his mother prompted.

"Yes, Your Grace."

"And you refuse to name the person or the people you were with?"

She nodded, her eyes not meeting his.

He rose. "Well, then, you will be tried before the court on Thursday, three days hence. Prior to that time you will submit to an examination by a midwife. She will testify as to your innocence or guilt. Even if you are innocent of filthy dalliance, however, it will go hard for you if you refuse to name your companion for the evening."

LURINDA COLLINGS
JULY 1647

Lurinda was dusting the parlor beside the great hall. Earlier this morning with roughened, hurtful fingers the midwife had invaded the privacy of her being, joking as she probed for evidence of fleshly guilt. When she had finished, she had said, "So far as I can tell, the maid is innocent. Unviolated."

Unviolated? As she passed the feather duster over the top of a highboy, Lurinda shuddered. Surely today her modesty had been violated in the ugliest manner possible, for it was a violation that pretended at neither love nor help. And where was her innocence? Was anything left of it? Innocence was believing in goodness. Innocence was trusting in the goodness of others. Innocence was feeling that if you did what you were sure was right, no one would think ill of you.

The hinges squeaked as someone opened the door to the parlor. Lurinda turned, her body tensing as she saw that it was Samuel. He closed the door behind him and leaned against it. With a defensive movement, she drew back, holding the feather duster in front of her like a shield.

Standing very straight, he regarded her with faint amusement. "You don't need to protect yourself, Lurinda. I won't attempt to come near you."

"Why are you here?"

"Because I want to apologize. You had a rather bad time of it the other night, I know. Were the watchmen considerate of you?"

"Considerate enough to drag me along the street against my will and to bring me before the governor. I was in a sorry condition and was much ashamed to have him—and your mother and grand-mother—see me like that."

"Were they rough in their handling of you?"

"No more so than you. In fact, not as much so." Pleased at seeing his cheeks redden, she added, "Apparently gentle birth is no assurance of gentle manners."

"I did not mean to be ungentle, Lurinda. It was only that I was . . . not quite myself. Perhaps I had drunk too much beer. I thought—please believe me—your resistance was part of a game. Girls do that sometimes. They pretend to struggle, pretend a young man's attentions are unexpected and unwelcome."

Girls do that sometimes. The words were not lost on her. They settled like a lump in her breast. "I struggled for one reason only," she said. "I struggled because you were attempting to take liberties I could not permit."

He looked puzzled. "But then, why did you come? Why did you agree to come out to the farm?"

Outside a wagon rumbled past and in its wake the clear voice of a child calling to another rang through the sunlit air. She looked at him steadily. "To be with you."

"To be with me—yes. But what did you expect? What did you think?"

It was her final chance. Looking at him standing so straight, so much in appearance and mien like his father that he must surely also have the wisdom to match, she was encouraged to say, "What do you suppose I thought, Samuel? What does any young girl think of or dream of or hope for when a young man she has long admired suddenly notices her?"

He looked faintly puzzled, faintly worried.

"Is it so difficult to understand me, Samuel?"

He opened his mouth to speak but no words came. Looking at his frozen, open-mouthed face, she was reminded of a fish washed up on the sand. His utter surprise was a measure of the foolishness of her dreams.

Cruelly, he put it into words. "Lurinda, I never dreamed—"

"Of course not." Was she actually smiling at him? "I was just a servant. You hardly knew I was here, much less dreamed of me." Turning her back to him, running the duster over the top of a carved cabinet, she said, "Please go away now."

"I'm afraid I've hurt you badly, Lurinda. What can I do to make it up to you?"

"Nothing. Just go away."

"Perhaps I should go to my father and tell him I am responsible for what happened the other night."

Was this what she wanted—a kindness born of guilt? She was tempted, but only briefly. "No," she said. "Please just go away."

"It might save you from being whipped."

Calmly she said, "The governor is just. I do not fear him. He has always treated me like a daughter. I'm sure he'd never let me be whipped. Please go away now, Samuel. I do not want your help."

"Then so be it," she heard him say.

It seemed like a long time before she heard the hinges of the door squeak again as he went out. She stood still then, waiting for the dammed-up tears to spill over. Nothing happened. Her eyes remained dry and aching as if, along with her heart, the tears had frozen solid.

Tears tried to fall when they were least welcome; men were most importunate when women were most indifferent; bad luck came when good luck was most needed. Was all life like this? If so, why dream, why hope, why try?

What good even was honor? The foolish flight to save her chastity had led only to her capture. What good was honor when she could not even be honest with herself? She told herself she did not love Samuel, that she did not want him to come forward to defend her, that she trusted in the governor's justice. All were lies—lies to bolster her courage, to cover the fear that clutched at her heart.

The fear would not go away. That night, when she was brushing Mrs. Eaton's hair, she asked her, very hesitantly, how she had felt when she had been on trial. "Were you frightened?" she asked.

"Frightened? No. I think anger is what I felt. Or a kind of shocked outrage that this should happen to me."

Mrs. Eaton tipped her head back and closed her eyes. "How I love having you brush my hair. Sometimes, when we were first married, Theophilus used to brush my hair." She sighed. "He's a kind person, Lurinda. You need not be frightened. I'm sure if you throw yourself on the mercy of the court and tell the whole truth—name the young man who lured you away from here—it will not go hard for you."

Lurinda did not answer.

Softly Mrs. Eaton said, "It was that young man you came over on the boat with—wasn't it?" She paused. "After all, the midwife has found you innocent. You have only to tell where you were and to name the young man. They would probably drop the case and let you go free—provided, of course, that you and the young man marry."

"And if I won't say?"

Mrs. Eaton opened her eyes and stared up at the flickering shadows on the ceiling. "My trial was different from yours. It was a church trial and yours is a civil trial. But the principle, I think, is the same. You must not challenge their authority. Oh, they expect certain sins, for it is human to stray from the paths of righteousness. They expect them and they punish them accordingly. But the greatest sin in their eyes is to challenge their authority. Think about it carefully before you decide to remain silent."

It seemed to Lurinda, however, as she thought it over later in her room, that her case was very different. She had not questioned any of the beliefs of those in authority; she had not insisted on making her own rules. She had done something wrong and was willing to acknowledge that it was wrong. She expected to be punished in some way—perhaps with a small fine—but the midwife's testimony ought to ensure her against severe punishment. She was fearful, but less about being punished than about the act of standing before the magistrates for questioning.

She had imagined it hundreds of times, yet when at last she actually entered the meetinghouse and saw the row of magistrates awaiting her, it was even more terrifying than she had thought.

The air was still and warm. It smelled like an unaired feather bed. She found it hard to breathe and, as she waited her turn, her stomach churned so sickeningly that she wondered whether she would be able to stand up for long without being embarrassingly sick.

Hers was the fourth case. Before that, the magistrates made decisions on the man who ran the ordinary and who had been accused of selling beer and allowing noise too late in the evening; on Mrs. Stolyon who was accused of selling goods from England at too high a profit; and on a woman who had slanderously called a contumacious neighbor a witch. All had been admonished and fined. It was a good sign. When Lurinda was called, she stepped forward, feeling, beneath her trembling fear of the moment, a confidence that she also would be dealt with sternly but fairly.

One of the magistrates read the case against her: "Lurinda Collings is accused of leaving the governor's home at night by stealth, of spending the evening at one of the farms in the company of a young man with the intention of dallying with him in a filthy manner."

"Now then," the governor said, "what do you have to say for yourself?"

He sounded as matter-of-fact as he did at home when he asked her if there were more clam chowder. Why should she be uneasy?

"It is true, Your Grace, that I left the house by stealth and went to one of the farms. The intention ascribed to me, however, is not true."

"Which farm did you go to?"

"I cannot say."

"Who invited you?"

"I cannot answer that question either, Your Grace."

"Why did you go?"

"He said there was to be a feast."

"Is it not true that you went mostly because it gave you an opportunity to be with this young man away from the surveillance of those who are responsible for you?"

She hesitated, trying to be honest. "Well, perhaps, Your Grace. I didn't think of it that way at the time but—"

"In other words"—the accusation was snapped out—"you went because you hoped to engage in filthy dalliance with this young man?"

"No!" The word came out so explosively that two of the magistrates who had been studying papers jerked their heads up as if startled by a musket shot. "No, that was not what was planned. And I have been examined and found to be innocent."

Another of the magistrates said, "We are not trying to establish your innocence but your intention. The intention of sinning, even the desire to sin, is as black in the eyes of God as the sin itself."

Wearily she said, "I did not intend to sin. I hoped only for a better acquaintance that might lead to marriage."

"Are you not aware," the governor said, "that a young man with intentions of marrying asks permission to call on a young woman? He does not arrange to meet her by stealth."

She looked down at the rough flooring of the meetinghouse. "I know that now, Your Grace."

The governor was looking past her. "Will the young man involved please come forward."

Her heart lurched. Had Samuel, after all, confessed, or had the governor, after all, suspected the truth? Slowly she turned her head and saw, not Samuel, but Timothy Evans taking his place beside her.

"Do you know this young man?"

"Yes, Your Grace."

"Has this young man ever asked you to marry him?"

"Yes, sir. More or less."

"And did you accept?"

"No, Your Grace. I did not."

The governor looked intently at her. "Is it true that on Fair Day you spent many hours with him, walking with him, talking with him?"

She nodded, puzzled. What was he getting at? Was he trying to get Tim in trouble? Her stomach felt queasy.

"And isn't it true that he gave you gifts—some cloth and some lace?"

Again nodding, she tried to swallow. Her throat was dry with sudden fear.

The governor's voice lost its fatherly, kindly quality. "And are these the kinds of gifts a young woman accepts from a young man she has no intention of marrying?"

"Not usually, sir. But—"

Tim broke in. "If I may interrupt, Your Grace, I gave her those gifts freely."

"Then you did not intend or wish to marry her?"

"Oh, I did, Your Grace. That is, I hoped. But if she would not have me, I still wanted her to have the gifts."

"Would you marry her still?"

Lurinda could not look at Tim now. What would he say, what *could* he say after all he had seen at the farm?

"I would be glad to," Tim said in a firm voice.

"Very well, then," said the governor. "If we can have a marriage, perhaps we can settle the whole matter with a small fine. For though you did meet by stealth, the young woman has retained her chastity, and an engagement gift had already been rendered and accepted." He turned to Lurinda and said gently, "You will have this young man?"

It took her a long time to answer. The governor was trying to make the whole episode logical and without evil intention, but his logic was based on a false idea: he really did think it was Tim she had met. Beside her she sensed rather than saw Tim's stalwart form—his courage, his strength, his goodness. His pity. If she said yes, he would marry her and would remain always by her side, strong, kindly, good, and with a nobility that transcended his birth. Shame flooded her as she thought of all his kindnesses to her from the day they had sailed from England to this last moment of supreme kindness. It had to be nothing more than kindness; surely now that he had seen her with Samuel, seen the familiarity she had allowed, he could no longer love her.

"The court requests that you answer the question." The governor paused, waited. Finally he said, "Please—we have other business to take care of. Please answer the question. Will you have this young man?"

She lifted her head. "No, Your Grace, I will not. I did not promise myself to him. Nor was he the young man I spent the evening with."

The governor shook his head, turned to the other magistrates and spoke to them in a low voice. Turning back to her he said, "Are you ready, then, to tell us whom you met?"

"No, Your Grace. I cannot."

"We have here then," he said precisely, "a young girl who accepts gifts from one man with absolutely no intent of marrying him and who meets another at night, a girl already set in the ways of dishonor and sin." His look was so cold that Lurinda had to lower her eyes. He leaned forward. "For the last time: who was the young man?"

Lurinda closed her lips tightly.

"Do you refuse to answer? Do you dare to defy the authority of this court?"

She gave him an anguished look. Ignoring it, he turned to listen to the comments of the magistrate to his left.

"So be it," he said at last. He rose and with great dignity and even greater coldness said, "This court sentences you to an hour in the pillory on Saturday next with a writing over your head to tell of your guilt. At the end of the hour, you will be whipped."

Lurinda drew in her breath sharply. It caught in her throat and made a noise like a sob. Next to her Tim said softly, "You and your pride. Your foolish pride." Louder he said, "If I may be permitted a word, Your Grace—she is too frail for a severe whipping. Could not I be whipped in her stead?"

"It is she and not you who needs to profit from punishment. Be assured the whipping will not be so severe as to be disabling." He nodded to Lurinda. "You may return now to your duties . . . and to contemplation of your sins and your punishment."

At that moment and in the three days that followed, she often wished that her duties in the Eaton home were heavier than they were—duties that would so occupy her mind and tire her body that she would be too busy to think during the day and too exhausted to worry during the night.

As it was, she endured the humiliation of the pillory and the pain of the whipping a thousand times before they happened. The imagination that had once led her to picture herself as a second Mrs. Eaton, stately and beautiful, first lady of the New Haven Colony, now led her to imagine herself with head and hands awkwardly trapped, a target for bold stares and insulting remarks. And the whipping. She had seen whippings, had heard the pitiful cries, had seen the blows go on and on even after the blood came. How could she endure it? When at night she did finally drop off to sleep, it was to awaken all too often with a start, her body moist with sickly smelling sweat as she emerged from a dream of devils with slashing whips.

On Saturday the marshal came for her. Numbly she allowed herself to be led away. It was a blessing, the numbness that had come over her this morning. She had not counted on it.

At the marketplace she was fitted into the pillory, her head bent forward in a position more awkwardly uncomfortable than she had anticipated. As the townspeople strolled by, some merely glanced at her, some stopped to stare or to whisper as they read the writing over her head. Always she had moved quietly around the town. Unnoticed. Sometimes she had thought to herself: one day you'll notice me, look up to me, realize that I'm here.

And now they *were* noticing. It was better, she realized, to be ignored, to be so unimportant, so colorless, so little known, that gazes slid thoughtlessly past you, leaving you whole and untouched. Now the stares came at her from all sides, converging on her face, making her skin flame.

How many moments had gone by? She could not tell. Her shoulders began to ache. Though the sun beat hotly down on her, she could not tell how much it had moved. At midday it was always hard to gauge the passage of time. Her body felt prickly with heat, and from underneath her upraised arms a trickle of perspiration slid like a crawling insect down her ribs.

A fly lit on her cheek. She gave her head a shake—as much as her confinement would allow—and it flew away. A few seconds later it was back. Again she shook her head and again it flew. It was not long, however, before it had learned that no hand was free to slap it away. As her irritation increased and her skin grew more moist, another was attracted. How could she stand it? She kept moving her head in quick little jerks, but it did little good. Would it never end—this long, long hour?

The air was motionless. The smell of rotting cow dung rose up, challenging her to tilt her head or to walk away. A mosquito bit her on the wrist and the need to scratch the bite seemed more urgent than any need she had ever experienced. To be free of this horrible confinement, to be able to scratch at an itch, to be able to wave a fly away, or turn from a smell—these were all she wished for, even though being free of the pillory meant being free for the whip.

Something hit her with a sharp sting just above the eye. Moving her head slightly, she saw a group of young boys giggling as they fitted an object into a slingshot. She closed her eyes. Perhaps it was only a currant. It was better not to look. Besides, she did not want to lose her sight.

Hearing a cry of pain and surprise, she opened her eyes quickly again and saw Timothy Evans with the boys. He was holding the slingshot in one hand. With the other he held the wrist of one boy and was talking severely to him. She heard the last words: "Now go. All of you."

They went. Tim came over and, standing close in front of her, looked up and said, "I'm sorry I couldn't get here sooner. Has it been very bad?"

"I can stand it."

"Did any of them hurt you?"

"No. Not really." She moistened her lips, gave her head a quick shake to dislodge a fly. "Tim . . . how much longer?"

"Soon now." He waited a moment. "Lurinda, it's not too late."

"For what?"

247

"To tell them who—"

"No." Her voice was sharp.

"Then let *me* confess. Let me say it was I who lured you against your will—"

Her eyes welled with tears. His goodness softened her tight hard defenses more effectively than all the misery of the pillory.

"No, Tim. They will only whip me. You're a man. They would do worse to you."

A man. Funny, she had never thought of him before as anything but a boy. But now, as he stood so straight in front of her, she saw and felt, in a disturbing way that came like a fresh new surprise, how she was attracted to his manliness.

"I wouldn't care what they did to me," he said, "if only they'd let you go."

She was tempted. She could not help being tempted.

"No, Tim." She said the words firmly.

A drum roll reverberated across the square. The planks on which she stood trembled with it and her heart echoed its pulsing beat. The crowd began to gather for the week's most exciting event.

Tim turned as one of the deputies approached. The man was young. A friend? Tim said something; the man shrugged and shook his head. Returning to her, Tim said softly, "Do not stiffen your body. It hurts less if you do not brace yourself."

The crowd moved in so close it had to be told to step back as the fastenings on the pillory were loosened and she was released. Her freedom, however, lasted only a moment—a moment in which the knots in the muscles at the back of her neck and in her shoulders had no time to lose their aching stiffness before she was led to the whipping post and was bound there by wrists chafed from the pillory.

She kept her head high. At least she could do that. How many times had she seen people cringing and resisting, crying out with pain and fright, begging to be spared. Such piteous behavior only increased a victim's humiliation. She had stood an hour in the pillory without shedding a tear or asking for relief. The whipping would be more painful but briefer. She could stand it. She *would*.

Turning her face away from the crowd, she awaited the first blow. When she heard the whip whistle through the air, she could not help bracing herself against it. It lay across her back like a streak of fire, like a branding. Clamping her teeth together to avoid crying out, she squeezed her eyes shut as the whip lashed down on her back again and again.

Each slashing blow burned more painfully than the one before as her flesh grew more tender. It seemed to go on forever. She was a mass of pain—seared, burned, raw . . . hurting, hurting, hurting. Again the whip struck, again, again, again. She heard laughter—oh, how could they laugh? How could they not feel even a little of her pain. Again. Again. Again.

And then there was a silence. She waited. Seconds went by. The flesh on her back crawled and stung and recoiled from anticipated blows. None came. The whistling sound had ceased, but the pain went on. Someone loosed the ties at her wrists and she looked down at the chafed redness. She lifted her hand to her mouth and it came away with blood on it.

She had moaned softly; she had whimpered a little to herself; but she had not cried out. She had not begged for mercy.

Mrs. Eaton came out of the crowd and, holding out her hands, helped her down from the platform.

"Come, child." Very softly she said, "Keep your head up. Don't let down now."

Walking slowly beside Mrs. Eaton, Lurinda lifted her chin defiantly. Each step she took jarred her body and pain flowed and flashed across her back like a vibrant echo of the whip.

The crowd parted. Suddenly she was faced by the governor and by the pastor of the church.

Mr. Davenport fixed her with a lordly stare. "And have you learned a lesson, my child?"

Lurinda looked at the two impassive faces, at the two all-powerful humans whom hurt could not touch nor feelings disturb, the two humans who deliberately dispensed pain and humiliation, calling it justice, and inside her all the pain and humiliation gathered into a great ball of anger and hatred.

"A lesson?" she said. "I have indeed."

"Come." Mrs. Eaton drew her away. To the men she said, "The child has had enough to bear for one day."

Mr. Davenport continued staring at Lurinda. Before he turned away he said, "Perhaps not. I heard an insolence in her voice that the whip did not reach."

At the edge of the square Lurinda saw Tim waiting. Silently he walked beside her to the gate in front of the Eatons' house. Again she was aware of his strength, his goodness, his manliness, his feeling for her—a feeling so foolish that he had been willing to offer himself for punishment in her place. Fool, fool, she thought; why didn't you have sense enough to recognize real love when first it stirred your heart? She would not, she decided, say no to this man again.

When Mrs. Eaton had gone inside, leaving them alone together, Lurinda said to him, "Thank you, Tim, for coming. Having you there made it a little easier."

He smiled at her. It remained only for him to speak, to say, one last time, that he wanted her to be his.

"You don't need to thank me," he said. "It was no more than any good friend would do."

Good friend? Only that? She waited tremulously.

Reaching out, he took her hand and squeezed it gently; then dropped it. "I hope everything works out better for you, Lurinda. I wish you much good luck."

Before she could answer he had wheeled around and was walking briskly away. He did not look back, nor did he wave. Quickly, uncaringly, he walked out of her life. And why not? she thought bitterly. The wonder of it was that he had tried to help her at all.

Upstairs in Lurinda's room Mrs. Eaton was waiting. She helped her undress. Lurinda lay down on her stomach and Mrs. Eaton gently spread a soothing salve across her back. She drew the curtains, making the room dim and restful.

"Do you want me to sit with you a while?"

"I wish you would." Now that the uncaring world could not see her, she wanted to let herself go in tears, but now the tears would not come. Inside her was a coldness, a hardness, a hatred of all who had caused her so much suffering. Beyond this, occupying a separate place inside her, was the memory of Tim's face as it had been in that last moment: friendly, but casually indifferent to the sudden call of her heart. Oh God, God, she thought, why do we not see what is true until it is too late?

Mrs. Eaton took her hand. "Did he ask to call?"

"No, why should he? He helped me only because we have long been friends."

Friends. She thought of his kindness during the long Atlantic crossing when she had been so sick and frightened. She thought of the way he had looked at her on Fair Day. How proud and happy he had been because he had been able to give her something new and beautiful: the snowy white, violet-strewn length of goods. And she thought of the dress that had been made from it, soiled now, and torn by the hands of a man who had not cared for her at all.

Oh, Tim, Tim, she whispered silently; why was I so foolish? And then, at last, the tears began to come.

THEOPHILUS EATON
AUGUST 1647

"She was too delicate a girl for such a severe punishment."

Ann told him this repeatedly during the weeks that followed. A few times she said it aloud; most of the time she merely looked at him with eyes so full of accusation that even though he was sure he had treated the child with complete justice he felt a gnawing of guilt.

For several weeks Lurinda had lain in her room—feverish, weak, sometimes in a mild state of delirium. The surgeon had come and bled her, but it was nearly a month before his treatment did her any good. Theophilus went once to visit her. A faintly acrid odor of fever hung in the warm, moist air, mixed with the scent of herbs. She had grown thin, but even in its thinness her face did not look like the face of the girl whom he had met in Boston four years before. It was a face shadowed now and marked by experience.

"I'm sorry you're feeling so poorly, Lurinda," he said.

She had been lying on her side staring at the wall. It was a moment before she slowly turned to look at him. But once she had, she fixed him with a gaze so cold, so full of hatred, that he had to brace himself against it. A chill passed over his body. How was it that a mere servant girl could make him feel this way?

Ann came in with a tray of delicacies for Lurinda. Looking at him as if he were an intruder, she said, "If you will leave us alone . . . ?"

He nodded, almost grateful for the dismissal. "I hope you will soon be better, Lurinda," he said. Yet he could not help adding, "Perhaps this quiet time will give you a chance for penitence and for planning a future that will have no room for frivolity or sin."

She inclined her head briefly. The gesture was meek, but the look in her eyes had not changed.

Had the punishment been to no avail? He mentioned the incident later to John Davenport when they met in the evening.

"She is very bold," John Davenport said. "The chastising should have humbled her." He paused delicately. "And your wife—is she as concerned as you are about her servant's attitude?"

Now it was Theophilus who hesitated. He was so conscious of his friend's disapproval of Ann that he preferred to leave her out of their conversations.

"She . . . hasn't said."

"You don't suppose"—John got up and closed the window—"you don't suppose they are somehow joined together in defiance of our church and our civil laws?" He stopped. "I'm sorry. You're angry."

"No."

"Then annoyed. I shouldn't have let my thoughts form into words. We must keep our private lives separate from our public ones." After several reflective sips of wine he added, "But what is one to do when private lives begin to affect the public good?"

"I know. It is this that is my problem. Which, I ask myself, is more important?"

John gave him his full gaze. "You really have to ask?"

Theophilus felt a tightness in his throat. "No." He exhaled slowly. His chest felt weighted. "No. I'll speak to her as soon as an opportunity presents itself."

"Perhaps you can even make the opportunity. Remember, a man's rule begins in his own home."

Theophilus felt a flash of anger. It was as if his friend were saying: *A man cannot rule a colony who cannot rule his own home.* But the anger, he realized, was really an anger directed at himself. And another part of his anger was directed at Ann, for it was her attitude and behavior that had reflected on his ability to rule. Even so, he had to acknowledge that her public behavior had been circumspect ever since her trial. Until the incident of Lurinda's misbehavior, he had not had any grounds for criticism of his wife.

But now she was obviously once again sowing seeds of discontent. She was pampering Lurinda, giving her so much attention that the girl could only conclude she had been treated unjustly. No wonder she was so boldly impenitent.

As he crossed the street to return to his home he made up his mind that he would not let his wife best him, that he would speak to her before the matter went further. Determinedly he went to her room and knocked peremptorily on the door.

"Who is it?"

"Theophilus."

"Oh." For a moment he heard no sound. Then she said, "Well, then, come in."

As he stepped in, she was fastening a lacy rail across her bosom. The brief glimpse of the whiteness of her breast made his heart thud sharply in memory of all the nights of intimacy they had shared. Very deliberately putting his hands behind him, he went toward her. "I came to you about Lurinda."

"Good. I, too, had something about her I wanted to discuss with you."

Her expression was matter-of-fact. The cold, accusing look was gone from her eyes. Perhaps she had begun to see that other viewpoints than her own were also important. Perhaps she would now be receptive to his counsel. Perhaps later she would even—his heart, anticipating his thought, began to thud again. With an effort he checked the thought before it took shape.

"What is it that you wanted to discuss?" He drew a straight-backed chair close to the couch where she half reclined and sat down. Leaning toward her, he was close enough so that the scent of her skin stirred his senses.

"It wasn't terribly important," she said. "It's only that she wants to stay on here after her five years of service are up."

"Certainly she may. But I had thought she would be thinking about marriage."

"She does not intend to marry."

"Well, even though nothing could be worked out with Newman's servant—what's his name?"

"Timothy. Timothy Evans."

"Then perhaps we could find someone else. How about that boy who works for Mr. Malbon?"

"Theophilus! Don't you ever listen? I told you she does not intend to marry."

"Why not?"

"Lurinda keeps her own counsel. I only suspect she was in love with the man who tried to lift her skirts that night. I think she was disillusioned by his treatment."

"Then why didn't she report him?"

"Perhaps she's still in love with him. Or perhaps she's trying to protect him."

"Who is he?"

"I don't know, Theophilus. I told you she keeps her own counsel."

"Of course you know. You spend hours together. You talk about everything—I'm sure of it. You cater to her and lead her to think what she did could not have been wrong or it would not have led to such favorable treatment."

Ann swung her body around and lifted her legs off the couch. "I'd hardly call a brutal whipping favorable treatment."

"I'm speaking of her treatment here." He tried to be calm and rational. "Mainly, my dear wife, I'm speaking about your attitude toward her and her sin. As a matter of fact, that's why I came in to speak with you."

Folding her arms, she stared straight ahead, giving him a view of her unyielding profile with its proud, strong nose. "Go ahead," she said.

"I don't even like your attitude at this moment," he said.

"You have nothing to reproach me for. I told you to go ahead and speak."

"You have no humility." Rising, he moved to the end of the couch so he could face her. Immediately, she swung her legs back up and turned, exposing the other side of her face.

"Look at me," he said.

She did not move.

"Look at me!"

"I will listen," she said through lips that barely opened to release her words. "I will listen. That's all."

"Yes, you will listen," he said. "You will listen with great care, and you will do as I say. You are my wife and you are required to obey me. You will stop treating that girl like a martyr who has been unjustly punished. In public you will start acting like the wife of the governor of this colony—a woman whose responsibility it is to support the ideals and laws of the leaders rather than to flout them. In private you will start acting like a wife—like the wife defined by our Bible, a woman who respects and honors her husband instead of striving to dishonor and humiliate him at every opportunity."

She turned now and allowed him to gaze on the cool beauty of her full face. "And what of you?" she said in a deceptively gentle voice. "Are you not required to love and honor me, to respect me?"

"Of course. I am your husband, your protector—"

But she had jumped to her feet. She stood before him, so close that her warmth and fragrance encircled him, enveloped him, stirred him with wanton desire.

"Protector? When have you ever protected me? When have you ever defended me? When have you ever thought about my needs, my rights, my feelings? When have you ever shown any evidence of love for me?"

"This home that I built for you is—"

"This home that you built, you built as a monument to your position, your importance."

In a steady voice he said, "Our children are evidence of my love."

"Of your *lust.*"

"It was not lust. The marriage bed is consecrated."

She lifted her head and laughed. "Our marriage bed was consecrated to your lust. It is lust and not love when a man thinks of a woman as nothing more than an object to be used, or as a person whose only function is to honor his weaknesses and obey his unreasonable commands." She lowered her voice. "And how can a woman honor a husband who is nothing but a shadow of another man? You probably would not even have come to my room tonight if he had not suggested it."

It was hard now to keep his voice steady. "That is enough. I'm beginning to think my mother may be right about you and the precariousness of your mental state, the weakness you have evidently passed on twofold to your daughter."

Ignoring his comment about her daugher, she said, "Ah, your mother. She, too, hates me and tells you how to treat me. Between those two—your mother and your confessor—practically every move you make is either dictated or suggested. Tell me"—she gave him a mocking smile—"did they even tell you when you were to take me to bed?"

256

He stood and stared at her, not trusting himself to move, not trusting himself to speak. He had been judge at many trials for crimes of passion; he had heard many tales of violent acts. Now, for the first time, he understood what it was to feel a murderous impulse. For the first time he realized that, godly or not, intelligent or not, self-controlled or not, rage could awaken a primitive violence within him.

Was he no better than all those who came before him to be judged for their impetuous acts? Well . . . perhaps a little better, or a little more blessed with grace, for he did at last summon the strength to turn away from her and walk out of the room.

LURINDA COLLINGS
SEPTEMBER 1647

"The governor thinks I pamper you too much," Mrs. Eaton said to Lurinda a few days later.

"Does he? It's strange . . . he's harder than I thought. I always felt he thought of me almost as a member of the family—"

"Yes, I believe he did. But you must understand this, Lurinda: if one of his daughters had been caught under the same circumstances, she would have received the same punishment."

"Even little Hannah?"

"Especially little Hannah. For the Lord chastiseth those whom He loveth." Her eyes seemed to darken as she looked away. "And you must remember he made no move to prevent his wife from suffering humiliation."

"Out of love?"

Mrs. Eaton looked back quickly. "No, certainly not out of love in that case. Not unless you could take his feeling for the colony and call if love." Her voice was bitter and husky with hurt.

Lurinda reached out for her hand. Always she had looked up to her mistress and wanted to be like her. Now as she realized the depth of her hurt, she felt a bond between them. She thought of the expressionless look on the governor's face when he had sentenced her—the same look that had been on his face when his wife had stood helpless before the church.

"He does it," Mrs. Eaton went on, "to keep the people unified and intent on the purpose for which the colony was founded."

"And what about Mr. Davenport?"

Mrs. Eaton's eyes flickered. "My experience has taught me that he is not one to be crossed."

"I'll never forget the way he looked at me after my whipping. I'd like to see him brought low—really low. Wouldn't you?"

"Thoughts like that have crossed my mind. But it's not anything I'd ever actively seek." She smiled a little. "Perhaps all I want is the satisfaction, eventually, of knowing I'm right."

"About your religious beliefs?"

Mrs. Eaton hesitated a long time before speaking. And when she did speak, Lurinda didn't quite understand her answer. "No, I'm thinking about the use and misuse of authority." She rose. She had been making sure that Lurinda rested every afternoon even though it was now nearly six weeks since her whipping. "I have some things to do right now. Why don't you try to sleep."

After she had left, Lurinda lay quietly on her bed. The bruises on her back were now healed, but the night of the venison feast burned livid in her memory, and every horror that had followed it still seared her with hurt.

A knock sounded on her door. Thinking it was Mrs. Eaton returning for a last word, Lurinda called out from her bed, "Please come in."

The door opened quietly. Young Samuel stepped in and quickly closed the door. He stood with his back against it, staring at her.

Lurinda leaped angrily to her feet, tugging at her disarranged clothing, poking at her hair. "Why did you not—why did you not—?"

"But I did knock," he said, "and you invited me in."

"You did not say who you were. You shouldn't be here."

He shrugged, lifting one shoulder in an elegant way. He had his father's elegance but not his stateliness. At least not yet.

"It does not matter. No one is at home except for a few in the kitchen." He seemed to enjoy looking at her. "How lovely the color in your cheeks is. It becomes you to be surprised on your bed."

"Leave here at once. Before I scream."

"Please—no. I shouldn't have said that. I'm not here to take advantage of you, Lurinda. Please don't be fearful. I came only to talk to you."

It was true that he had not taken a step toward her. Perhaps he did mean no harm. "I can think of nothing we might have to say to each other," she said.

"Very well. I won't waste words. I'm leaving for Boston very shortly. I'd like to marry you and take you with me. After thinking it over, I've decided you would be a good and satisfactory wife for me. I would try to be the same kind of husband to you."

"Surely this is some kind of joke?" she said. "But even if you were serious—"

"I am serious. I want you . . . for my wife."

She stared at his face—the face of a man who is earnestly doing his duty, rather than the face of a man passionately declaring his feelings—while her mind sped from one thought to another. Then suddenly, without having planned it, or ever even having dreamed of it, she turned away from him, quickly unlaced her bodice until it fell away from her body, exposing her back from the waist up. She heard him gasp as he saw the places where the whip had left its marks.

"Do you see those scars?" she said. "Well, the scars inside me are deeper and even more hurting. My back is nearly healed, but the scars on my heart will never heal." Whirling around, she faced him, holding the bodice up in front of her, but holding it, she knew, in such a way that some of the sweet curve of her young white breasts was revealed.

"I will always hate you," she said. "I will always hate you and I will always hate all those men who never gave a thought to what I was going through. All they thought about—you included—was the exercise of their whims and rights and authority."

He took a step toward her, his arms outstretched. "Lurinda, my dear—"

"Take another step," she warned, "and I'll scream and scream. I'll say you surprised me in my room and began removing my clothing against my will. Go quickly now."

"But I"—he was breathing hard—"I really do want to marry you, Lurinda."

And he really looked as if he did.

"Take another step," she said, "and I really will scream. I'm going to count to seven and then begin screaming unless you are out of the room. One . . . two . . . three . . ."

"Lurinda, please—"

"Four . . . five . . ."

"I *love* you."

"Six." She paused, giving him time.

After a brief hesitation, he lifted the latch and went out.

"Seven," she said.

The door closed. She stared at it a moment before flinging herself down on the bed. Her cheek burned against the cool coverlet. Whatever had possessed her? No lady would have cheapened herself so. It was as if I tried to entice him, she thought, while refusing him. It was a revenge of sorts. Refusing him, she had tried to make him doubly aware of what he would never possess. Oh, cheap, cheap—the cheap trick of a servant girl. What a long time it took to become a lady.

As her breathing slowed and she grew calmer, the scene repeated itself in her mind. He said he wanted to marry me, she thought. He actually said it. I *am* good enough for him. Slowly, with great care, she rolled onto her back. It hurt only a little as she did it, and after she had moved into position, it hurt even less. She clasped her hands behind her head.

A light breeze stirred the tree outside her window and the shadows of the moving leaves floated back and forth across the ceiling. Her thoughts moved freely in the same way. I could marry him, she thought. I could go to Boston with him where people probably have not heard of my punishment. By the time we came back here, most people would have forgotten. Even if they did remember, they wouldn't dare say anything because by then he'd surely be somebody important.

Images flashed through her mind. She saw herself standing by his side receiving important guests. She saw herself sitting at the opposite end of the table from him. She saw herself walking to the meetinghouse with him. She sighed. It was a pleasurable, satisfying feeling. Confidence flowed through her. I could marry him, she thought. I could be young Mrs. Eaton. She lay still, letting the thought hold, listening to her quiet, even breathing and the steady beat of her heart.

And all at once it came to her that the old excitement was gone. Long ago when she had thought of marrying him, she had thought first of their private moments together, and when she had thought of them, her heart had pounded and her breathing had become quick and passionate. No longer. Now she thought of him only in terms of public appearances and when she thought of him, she thought of him quietly, critically, and dispassionately.

She didn't love him.

She didn't love him at all. It was wonderful to know that he really did feel she was good enough for him, but she didn't love him. Carefully she took the thought a little further. Being good enough for him, she was then good enough for anyone.

Tim. It was almost as if she had hardly dared to let herself think of him until this moment. *Tim.* The name vibrated in her mind as if a stringed instrument had been plucked. She remembered all the times he had been kind to her: the way he had stood by her when she had felt deserted by everyone, his offer in court to marry her.

Wasn't it possible that he still loved her even though he had said nothing when he had left her by the gate after her whipping? He had probably known that day was not the time to speak again. Besides, how many times had she refused him? Perhaps he had not wanted to risk another refusal.

Sitting up, she got out the hand mirror she had brought across the ocean with her. For the first time in weeks a softly smiling young girl returned her gaze.

All she had to do now was somehow get a message to him.

THEOPHILUS EATON
OCTOBER 1647

The family gatherings, Theophilus reflected, had lost their savor. For a long time the innuendos, the sarcastic remarks, and the outright accusations and quarrels had made mealtimes almost unbearable. Now an uneasy truce existed among his women. Their excessive politeness was almost worse than their earlier conflict. That, at least, had been an honest expression of feelings.

The relationship between himself and his wife could hardly be called a truce. It was more like a stalemate. Stale mate, he thought. Things have gone stale between me and my mate. It was not often he created a play on words, but this one was so bitter in its implications that he could take no pleasure in it.

She sat regally now at the end of the table, her head as always held high, hardly bending even to meet an overfull spoon. Her coolness both repelled and attracted him.

He had returned from a confederacy meeting in Boston only the day before. In the past the news he had brought had usually brightened the table for several days. Now everyone sat spooning up the pigeon pie in glum silence, as if families gathered for no other purpose than to eat.

Of course, it was never quite the same without Samuel there. His teasing of the women helped make the table cheerful. But he had left this morning on the same shallop that had brought Theophilus back from the Bay Colony. Samuel had not yet decided what he would do with his life, whether to become a cleric or whether to stay on in the New Haven Colony. It was hard, Theophilus thought, waiting for young people to make up their minds.

Finally his mother spoke. "I heard a rumor the other day that Robert Newman is thinking of returning to England. Have you heard anything of this, Theophilus?"

"He's spoken to me of it. But it isn't definite yet and won't be until he's established new business operations in London."

"How can he set them up in England if he's in New Haven?"

"He sent that boy—that young man of his—to make some investigations."

"That boy?" Ann said. "What boy?"

"Tim. Timothy. What's his name?"

"Evans?"

"Yes, Evans. The servant boy. The one who came over with Lurinda. Only—mark my words—I don't think he'll be a servant for long. That young man is slated for success. He's smart and thrifty and industrious. And he's ambitious. Already he has some business interests of his own. He'll probably develop others while he's in England." Glancing toward the kitchen, he saw Lurinda standing still in the doorway.

"Well, Lurinda," he said, "are you going to bring in that pudding?"

She still stood unmoving.

"Lurinda!"

"What, sir?"

"Are you going to bring us that pudding?"

"Yes, Your Grace." She brought it in and set it clumsily in front of Ann.

"I hadn't heard any of this," Ann said. "When did you find all this out?"

Theophilus passed his trencher to her for some pudding. When she had put a generous portion on for him, he said, "We traveled together to Boston—the boy and I. I was much impressed by all he had to say. Mark my words, he'll be a wealthy, influential man some day."

Lurinda moved noiselessly away from the table, wraithlike, her face pale. It was taking her far too long to recover from her day of punishment. It was almost as if she were trying to make him feel guilty. He was sure she was healthier than she pretended to be. As soon as her indenture was over, she would, he hoped, change her mind about not marrying and would find some other young servant who appealed to her. It would be a relief to have her out of the house.

After supper Theophilus retired to his closet above the great hall for prayer and work. He was immersed in a new statement to send with a delegation to Southold, when a light knock sounded on the door.

"You may enter," he said.

The door opened and Lurinda came in hesitantly.

"Oh, Lurinda." He half rose. "Please sit down."

"No, thank you, Your Grace. I'll only be a minute. I just wanted to ask you—how long will Tim be gone?"

"Tim?"

"Mr. Newman's boy."

"Oh. A year or two, I'd imagine."

"That long?"

"Certainly. Perhaps longer. It's a long journey, both ways. And you don't make business connections in a matter of days."

"I suppose." She stood hesitantly as if waiting. Outside the katydids chorused interminably, heralding the end of summer.

Lurinda half smiled at him, puzzling him. What did she want? His puzzlement grew as she continued to stand there. Finally he said, "Was there something else you wanted to ask?"

"No, sir. I thought perhaps you had something to tell me."

"About what?" He was trying hard to be patient with her, but he was still tired from his journey, disillusioned by his indifferent welcome, and beset by problems and affairs of state.

"I just thought . . . I just thought perhaps Tim might have said something to you about me."

"About that night?"

"Oh, no, Your Grace. I meant"—she was trembling now—"I meant perhaps about calling on me."

"I see." For a moment he pretended to be occupied with his papers in order to give her time to compose herself. He felt sure she was on the verge of a confession. Looking up, he said quickly, "Was he the one you were with that night?"

"Tim?" She gave a short, nervous laugh. "Oh, no, Your Grace."

Her answer had come so quickly he felt sure it was the truth. "Then what makes you think he'd want to call on you?"

"He said something about it once—something about speaking to you about it."

"I see. My child, he may have said it once, may even have

meant it at the time. He was even gallant enough at your trial to say he'd marry you. But you must remember that he's now on his way to becoming a rich and important man. Do you really think he's likely to be interested still in a servant girl who was so loose morally that she had to be publicly whipped?"

Even in the dusky dimness of the room, he could see her face whiten. Though his heart stirred with pity, he was careful not to let it interfere with the stern expression on his face. This girl had been too defiant; she had never shown any indication of remorse. As his friend John Davenport said, she needed some humbling.

"You'd be wise, my child, to retire to your room and to spend some time in prayer—that is, if your work is all done. The Lord will be merciful to you if you approach him with humility."

She did not speak or move.

"Did you hear me, Lurinda? I said you had best return to your room."

"Yes, Your Grace."

She turned awkwardly, stiffly, as she had right after she had been whipped, as if every movement of her body were painful.

He had only been honest with her—honest in the facts he had given her, honest in his appraisal of the situation. Why, then, long after she had left his closet, did he continue to think of her stricken face? Why, even though he tried to concentrate on the papers on the desk before him, were his thoughts shadowed by a faint sense of guilt?

ANN EATON/NOVEMBER 1647

When it had finally been accepted by all that the great ship had truly gone down, and after the commemorative days of humiliation and fasting had been held and the estates of the victims had been settled, Ann went once again to visit Brigid to offer her condolences.

In the months since the fair her friend had changed. The merriment was gone from her eyes and her shoulders sagged. Ann knew that Brigid and her husband had never been well matched. It was hard to find appropriate words to say.

For a time she sat quietly knitting while Brigid prepared a small lunch. "You've lost a good man," she said at last.

"Yes. And one who was always good to me. He always provided for me. I don't know what I'll do now." Her eyes were bleak. "Just about everything we had went down with the ship."

"You have your son."

Brigid waved her hand as if brushing away an insect. "What can I expect of him? He criticizes the government; he consorts with those who are not church members. What chance does he have of succeeding in this colony?"

Ann leaned toward her. "Would you have him any other way? Aren't you glad he questions and rebels? Isn't this something he learned from you?"

"Yes . . . more's the pity. I made the mistake of speaking too freely too often. I thought it was safe. I thought it was rather funny. I even thought"—her gaze caught Ann's now and held it with hypnotic blue steadiness—"I even thought there was a kind

of integrity in saying what you believed—no matter how dangerous."

"And isn't there?"

"Not when you're about to become dependent on these very
same people. Principles and poverty make poor bedfellows."

"Perhaps you'll remarry."

"It isn't likely," Brigid said.

Even as she had spoken Ann had realized how few opportunities
existed for her friend. Most of the older men were married. Several
matches had already been made between men and women who had
lost their respective mates on the great ship. And though it was
true that many young men often married older widows, they did so
because of the financial advantage. But Brigid had little to offer a
young man seeking a start in life.

"Let's talk of other things," Brigid said as they sat down to eat
the food she had prepared. "The problems of a poor widow are far
from your ken."

"But I do understand."

Brigid's expression was almost hostile. "Please don't try so hard.
It would be better if you didn't."

Ann looked away. The trouble was that she knew Brigid was
right. Their positions were different, and when she tried to pretend that it was not so, she was being false to a once-honest relationship. But after a moment she turned back. "Brigid," she said
softly, "do you remember the day we met—down by the creek?"

"Yes, I remember."

"We became friends almost instantly. Why was that, I wonder?" She waited a moment. When Brigid did not answer she went
on, "It always seemed to me as if we had a real understanding, as if
we could almost read each other's thoughts. Didn't you feel that
way too?"

"Yes, I felt that way."

"Then why should it change? Why should we not understand
each other just as well today? Shouldn't we, after our years of
friendship, understand and sympathize with each other even better
than before?"

Brigid took a long drink of beer. She put the pewter can
down—put it down hard. "No," she said. "No, not at all. And I'll
tell you why. Back in those days, and all during the time of our
friendship, we were united by two ideas: our feelings about the

church and our feelings about the government. We talked about these things, speculated about them, even laughed about them. Finally you rebelled. You've settled your score; you have nothing more to rebel against."

During the time of our friendship. Trying to ignore the implications of the words, Ann said, "But I can still understand any feelings you might have."

"Can you? Perhaps so. But can you understand that I have much more to lose, more even than you ever did? They will do nothing more to you. After all, you *are* the governor's wife. But they will continue to harass me. My husband was right. He said that as long as I remained a close friend of yours, they would make things difficult for me. I thought he was foolish then, but I know now that he was right."

Ann gave her a diffident smile. If only she could make her friend laugh again in the old merry way. "Come now, Brigid, you know you're exaggerating—just imagining things."

Brigid got up and took a piece of paper from her writing table. "Read this and tell me how much I am imagining."

As Ann read, she could feel a chill creep over her skin. It was a notice, dated several weeks before, to appear before the court for selling wine by forbidden small parcels and for suffering company to come in to drink wine by quarts and pints.

Shaking her head, she handed it back. "You were tried for this? I didn't know. What was the punishment?"

"A fine. Far more than my profits. Do you see now why I dare not rebel? They are watching for me to do something wrong. I must be circumspect, careful. I have no one to protect me."

"I see." Ann picked up her knitting and bent her head over it. She felt a shame for the court that had brought the charges and a shame for herself who was immune to such harassment.

"I need the money," Brigid said in a tired voice. "That's the hard part of it. But the part that really angered me is that even some of those who were connected with the court—Mr. Goodyear, Mr. Malbon, and Mr. Evance—had often sent servants to my back door for little parcels. Because of that, I didn't think they'd ever touch me. It was almost as if they were laying snares for me."

"Do you really need money badly?"

"Not enough to accept anything from their fund for widows and orphans. Or from anyone else."

The hostility had returned to her face. Oh, how proud she was. But I'd feel the same way, Ann thought—and had to bite her tongue to keep from saying so.

After she had knitted a little longer, Ann picked up her work bag and rose. "I must go now. The sun tells me it's time to prepare supper."

Brigid went to the door with her. "Thank you for coming," she said. "Please do come again some time."

The words sounded hospitable but they fell false and cold against Ann's awareness.

"I should like to," Ann said, "but it might be better for you if I did not come too often."

Brigid's light-blue eyes were full of a sadness and resignation that made Ann's heart ache. "Yes," she said softly, "it would be better that way."

After that Ann did visit occasionally, but the old closeness was gone. They talked of food and fashion and of happenings in the town, but their comments were always guarded. Sometimes on cold winter days other women came with their wheels and, as they spun, they gossiped. But their talk remained general; it carefully skirted affairs of government and church.

Ann talked and listened and exchanged innocuous opinions, but when she left she felt not one whit less lonely. She began to feel as if she had no one at all to talk with. Lurinda, too, had withdrawn into herself, and guarded her thoughts and dreams and opinions with passionate care. Women couldn't enjoy a real friendship, it seemed to Ann, unless they were able to speak freely about their feelings.

Now and then in the afternoon she would pick up her wheel or her knitting and start out of her room, only to hesitate in the hall and at last turn back. It was easier to stay by the fire in her own room, to let the days slip by into weeks and the weeks into months.

Other times, especially during the warm weather, she would leave by the back door of the house, walk out through the garden and orchard, down through the still unused lots which had been assigned to David Yale and old Mrs. Eaton, to the creek. There she would sit on a rock watching the water flow steadily and quietly to the sea. Its floods in spring, its low waters in summer, and its icing over in winter, marked out her days.

Sometimes in the early fall, when the air was still and the birds and insects quiet, a great restlessness came upon her. It was like the old impatience that had beset her when the colony had been founded and she had discovered she was to have no real part in its planning or its activities. Now, as then, she was filled with an urge to do something—now, before it was too late. She felt an urge to be important, to be wanted, to be necessary.

Frequently at times like this she went to see the Cheevers. As the 1640's drew to a close, delicate Mary Cheever's life was flickering out. Ann visited her often during the last months. Even though Mary had always been cool to her, she felt a mysterious compulsion to do things for the younger woman. Nearly every day she could be found there dusting, cooking, scrubbing, wiping noses and comforting the hurts of small children, and, especially, doing everything to make Mary as comfortable as possible.

Ezekial usually hovered in the background, his face shadowy and cheerless, helpless as men often are in the face of illness or death. Ann's heart ached for him. Often he sat with his fingers pressed against his forehead. He had very bad headaches. None of the herbals she suggested seemed to help.

Ann was one of the watchers at Mary's deathbed. In the months that followed, she continued to visit at the Cheever home, though less often, to make sure the children were receiving proper care. She was preparing to go there one afternoon when Lurinda came into her room with a freshly pressed gown.

"Will you be going out this afternoon, ma'am?"

"Perhaps." She felt almost as if she had something to hide—for surely this restlessness that had plagued her for so long was an unhealthy sign. She was too old for such dissatisfaction. Women of middle age were supposed to be settled, content, happy with their home tasks. Even Lurinda, it seemed to her, was more resigned than she to her place and condition. It was as if she had done all her living in one night and all her paying for it in one afternoon.

As Lurinda held the gown ready for her to slip into, she said, "Are you going to the Cheevers', ma'am?"

"Probably."

"Those children really love you."

"They'd be grateful to anyone who was kind to them right now."

"You're very good, ma'am."

"No. It's only that I want to help. And Mr. Cheever and I have been friends for a long time. Sometimes I think he's my only friend in this town."

"Well, ma'am, if you have one friend, you have one more than I have—outside of you."

Ann gave her a quick look. "You're still young, Lurinda. You haven't yet had a chance to go out and make friends."

Lurinda didn't answer and, looking at her quiet face, Ann was struck all at once by her beauty. These past two years of quiescence had softened her face. She was still delicate-looking, but the sharpness that had once been a part of her features had been replaced by a rounded maturity. She stood and held her head with a certain poise. For a moment it was hard to decide what had happened to her, and then it struck Ann that Lurinda had become a lady. Not just a woman, but a lady.

After picking up some ribbons for the little Cheever girls, Ann left the room. Feeling lighthearted and purposeful, she started down the hall. As she passed his study, she saw that Theophilus was home and had left his door open.

"Oh, there you are," he said. Something about his voice detained her and she hesitated. "Were you going out?"

"Yes."

"Where?"

"No special place. Well, that's not quite true. I just happened to see some ribbons in my drawer that I thought would give pleasure to the little Cheever girls. I might stop by there."

She felt faintly guilty. What was there about her husband that seemed to delve beneath her most innocent of motives and unearth a quality of guilt?

"Come in, please," he said. "Sit down. You are well?"

"Yes."

As she sat down she noticed that he looked oddly embarrassed. "For some time, now," he said, "I have felt the need to speak to you of something."

It took him too long to get to the point. She was restless and eager to leave.

"It has been called to my attention," he said, "that you—well, perhaps I should simply ask you. How often do you visit Ezekial Cheever's home?"

"Perhaps two or three times a week. Why?"

"Why do you go?"

"Isn't it obvious? I go to see to the children. I do the little things for them that are a woman's province—things like mending and helping them with their reading and writing. And on baking days, I often take them cakes and cookies."

He nodded. "All that is quite commendable, I'm sure. But have you ever stopped to think that people might start gossiping? After all, he is now a widower."

She felt like laughing at him, at his seriousness, his air of morality. "Good heavens, Theophilus, he's in his classroom most of the time when I'm there. And most of the time I take Hannah with me. Surely you are not implying I might be guilty of immoral behavior."

"No. Whatever you"—he paused delicately—"whatever you may *not* be, at least I am sure that you are a virtuous woman in both action and intent. You do, however, give the appearance of evil."

"How could I possibly do that? I am a married woman—the governor's wife."

Standing up, he put his hands behind his back. "Yes. But certain private details of our marriage are not unknown to the townspeople. And the fact also remains that you are not a member of the church."

"And in the eyes of the godly, I am therefore ungodly? Perhaps even immoral?"

He seemed relieved that she had put it so clearly. "Exactly."

She stood up. It gave her more assurance. "Let me tell you this, my dear husband. I may not be godly and moral as you and Mr. Davenport and the elders of the church and the members of your court view such things, but I have never knowingly injured anyone; I have never sacrificed one person for the sake of many; and I have never said the words decreeing that possibly innocent people should be humiliated, whipped, or executed."

As she spoke the last words, she saw him flinch, but he only said, "You do not change at all."

"What do you mean?"

"Any attempt to make you aware of your shortcomings or the evil appearance of your actions always has the same result. You hurl accusations at everyone you can think of, and especially at those who are the most godly and most dedicated to the welfare of this town."

"In your opinion."

273

"Let us end this discussion," he said. "It is clear that you do not plan to be reasonable."

"Let us not end it," she said, her voice rising in anger, "not until you tell me who of the townspeople called my evil behavior to your attention."

Folding his arms defensively, he said, "That is quite beside the point."

She came up close to him. "It is not beside the point . . . because I know who it was. It was the same person who has made trouble for me since the moment our marriage began. It was she who had me summoned before the church, she who saw to it that my friendships were destroyed. She will not rest until she has deprived me of every last privilege and prerogative and has completely removed me from this house."

In a controlled voice he said, "You will stop talking about my mother in this way."

She gave a triumphant laugh. "But I had not even mentioned your mother. It was quite clear to you, though, what person I was talking about—wasn't it?"

"We will not discuss this further. I will just make one final statement. You are not to go to Ezekial Cheever's house again. That is a command. I *forbid* you to go again to Ezekial Cheever's house."

The chill of the room settled down on her. "Are you giving that order as husband or as governor?"

"As both. As your husband and personal guardian of your morals, I forbid you; and as governor and guardian of the town's welfare, I forbid you."

"If I defy you—?"

"I will call you before the court." He put his hands on her shoulders. His fingers felt hard and bony. "Do you doubt that I would?"

"No, unfortunately I do not." She sighed softly. "But I promised the Cheever children some cookies today. And there's mending to be done."

"Have young Theophilus take the cookies over and pick up the mending after classes tomorrow. You can do it here as easily as there." He released her. "Please believe that I am doing this for your sake, my dear. You are far too susceptible to female emotions. You are very impulsive and quite incapable of looking ahead to the possible consequences of your actions."

274

Her sudden strange feeling of emptiness was so great that she could not even muster any anger. "One favor, Theophilus. May I go today—this one last time—just to explain that I will be very busy in the future and perhaps unable to visit? Please—just this one last time?"

"No. I forbid it."

She gave him a long look. "Are you aware of how few places I can go where I feel welcome?"

His lips thinned. "That is a condition you have brought on yourself."

"Theophilus, I believe I sometimes hate you."

He turned away from her. "I shall pray for you."

When she returned to her room, Lurinda was just leaving. "Did you forget something, ma'am?"

"No. I just . . . changed my mind." She sat down heavily.

Lurinda lingered in the doorway. "Are you sure you're all right, ma'am? Your face looks—well, so pale."

"I'm all right." She had to pull the words up out of her. They came reluctantly. She was not all right. "I just want to be alone to rest."

Lurinda stepped to her side and touched a cool hand to her forehead. "Call me if you need anything. I'll let you rest."

Ann sat very still. After a while she reached into her work bag and took out the ribbons. She smoothed them out across her lap and then rolled them up one by one. How the little Cheever girls would have loved them. How much it would brighten their sad little faces to have received them. She could imagine them tying up their hair, laughing, admiring each other.

And behind them, his face also a little brighter, would be Ezekial, his eyes lovingly following their every move. His eyes also watching . . . *her?*

Her breath came a little quickly and her fingers trembled as she rolled the last ribbon. Could it be that he had sometimes watched her with more than friendly interest? Could it be that his gaze had warmed with more than the warmth of friendship? Could it be that old Mrs. Eaton had actually scented a feeling, almost before it was born?

And what of you? she asked herself. Have you ever felt a lift of joy when he came in sight? Is your mind stimulated to exciting talk when you are with him? Do your thoughts dwell on him when you're not with him?

No. No. *No.* No to all three questions. I'm happy to see him because he's a friend; I like to talk to any intelligent person who thinks my conversation worthwhile; I never let my thoughts dwell on him.

Never? What about right now?

Well . . . sometimes.

And never *any* joy in seeing him? Never *any* feeling of stimulation when you talk to him?

She swallowed, her throat oddly tight. Well, she admitted to herself, if I ever have been guilty of any of these, it was in complete innocence. I always thought of it as friendship only.

She thought of him now: tall, broad-shouldered, kindly-faced, with his pointed beard and intense dark eyes. She thought of his sudden smile, his fine hands. His fine hands. She imagined them firm at her waist, sliding around her, urging her close. She felt them on her cheeks lifting her face to his. Oh, Ezekial, Ezekial, she thought, and raised her own hands to her face. Her cheeks were hot.

Had the feeling been there all the time, like a spring plant that was suddenly revealed when the leaves were raked away? Or had Theophilus today planted a seed that had fallen on fertile ground and had sprung magically into bloom?

Whatever it was, however it had begun, she knew it had to be pinched back. But a plant pinched back thrives all the more. She must uproot this feeling. She must put him completely out of her mind. She must fill her mind with godly thoughts and she must busy her hands with godly occupations.

Theophilus had said he would pray for her. Little did he know how badly those prayers were needed.

EZEKIAL CHEEVER
MARCH 1650

From his uncomfortable perch on a high rock, Ezekial stared at the swollen waters of the creek that ran across the eastern end of the square where he lived. The turbulent spring flood matched his feelings, yet at the same time soothed them. He hadn't lost everything, he told himself: at least he had the children. They gave his life meaning, and they gave him something to plan for. But he had no one now to confide in or to share his doubts and feelings.

In the first weeks after Mary's death Mrs. Eaton had come often to visit. She had walked diagonally across the gardens and orchards behind the governor's home to the garden behind his home, appearing at the back door with a basket of bread or sweets or small gifts for the children. Her maternal presence had transformed his bereaved household into a place of warmth. He had not realized how much her visits had meant to him until she'd stopped coming. This past winter had been the loneliest winter of his life.

How could he speak to his children of the meeting with the church elders today? They were too young to understand.

It was just as well, he thought, that they did not understand. It meant less pain, less suffering for them.

Behind him a twig cracked. Startled, fearing Indians, he turned quickly. It was Ann Eaton. She was turned a little away from him, bent to remove a bramble caught on her skirt.

Leaping off the rock, he called, "Mrs. Eaton!"

Sudden color stained her cheeks. "Why, Ezekial. Where were you? I didn't see you."

"On that big rock—where it flattens out a little on the other side."

"I know the spot. I sit there often."

"And I. Come then, and sit down. Tell me how things have been with you these last few months."

She sat down on the rock, smoothing her red petticoat around her. Moving several feet away, he sat on the ground, Indian fashion. After an odd and lengthy silence, he said, "So, you come here often?"

"Yes."

"I come here often too. It's strange that we've never met here before."

"It may be that I come when you're busy in the classroom."

"Perhaps you do so deliberately?"

She did not answer. After observing her silently for a moment, he said, "It may be that you are trying to avoid me?" He studied her face—unhappy and still. "Tell me, what have I done to offend you? I or the children? You were so good to us, so kind in our sorrow. I feel you would not have stopped coming unless we had done something that made you feel your kindnesses were not appreciated. Did we fail to thank you?"

"Of course not. And if you had, it would not have mattered."

"Then did you feel perhaps that it was time we learned to do for ourselves?"

"Oh no. No, of course not. I just—well, we have such a large house. So many tasks pile up that have to be done. I did more spinning than usual this past winter and began my spring cleaning earlier than usual."

"Then you have just been busy."

"Yes."

"And we didn't offend you?"

"No."

"Not in any way?"

"No." She smiled. "I don't offend easily. I'm not one of those sensitive women."

"I think you are."

She shrugged.

"Well, then," he said, "if we have not offended you, perhaps we can count on a visit from you soon. The children have really missed you. They still say every morning—at least one of them says it—'I wonder whether Mrs. Eaton will come today?' "

Almost imperceptibly she moved so that she was looking at the water. He could see only her profile now. And even though he looked at it critically and noted the bump just beneath the bridge of her nose and the faint softening under her chin, it seemed to him that she was as attractive as any woman ever needed to be. What bothered him, though, was the stillness of her face, the closed look of it.

At last she said, still without looking at him, "Perhaps it would be best if you gave them my love but told them I am very busy and unable to visit."

"Very well." He changed position, sitting now with his knees bent in front of him, his arms around them. "But would you tell me why?"

Facing him again, she gave him a look of anguish. "You are very persistent, Ezekial. I had hoped not to tell you this. I had not really thought my little neighborly visits were so important to you and your children. It's like this." She lifted her hands, palms up, in a helpless gesture. "Someone misinterpreted the motives of my visits. As a result, Theophilus forbade me to visit you."

"Misinterpreted? In what way?"

She tipped her head a little to one side. "The governor's wife is not a church member and therefore does not live by God's grace. When such a woman visits the home of a man who no longer has a wife, the reasons for her visit are speculated upon. The result is gossip."

He felt a sour taste in his mouth. "Ugly gossip."

"Yes."

Anger roiled inside him. Couldn't they see how good she was? How kind? He stood up, clenching his fists. "Perhaps I should talk with the governor. Do you think he'd listen to me?"

She gave him a funny little twisted smile. "I doubt it. He listens to only two people that I know of."

"It probably wouldn't do much good at that," he said. He had become so interested in her problem that he had actually forgotten his own. For a moment he had almost believed that his words would still be seriously considered by those in authority. He shook his head.

"Ezekial, do you have one of your headaches?"

"Not right now."

"Then what's wrong?"

"What makes you think something is wrong?"

279

"I felt it from the moment I saw you today. You're upset or worried about something?"

She wasn't just asking a casual question. Yet he found it hard to speak. Picking a blade of grass, he rolled it back and forth between his fingers.

"You can't help, but I will tell you," he said finally. "I've been critical of some of the other church leaders. In my opinion they're too powerful and too prone to use their power. I've disagreed with them on several occasions—"

"Beginning with me. You said at my trial that you felt the charges were flimsy."

"Yes. I still do. And I've been as outspoken on other occasions, both in church and at some of the private meetings of the elders. A delegation of them came today and asked me to make a public statement clearing them of all the various charges I have made."

Her face was full of concern. "Are you going to?"

"No. Would you? Ah, that's a foolish question. I know you wouldn't. I tell you, Ann, my statements were made only after careful consideration. To retract them would be like telling a lie."

"Do they no longer want you as an elder?"

"Worse than that." He could hear his voice deepen as his throat tightened. "They hope to expel me from the church. I go on trial tomorrow following the afternoon meeting."

"Just for differing with them?"

He got up and moved to a tree, hit his fist against the trunk. "Oh, they've added a few charges." Turning, he rubbed his temple. "They accuse me of unseemly carriage in church, of peculiar expressions on the face, and of rubbing my forehead."

Now she slipped off the rock and came over to him. "But don't they know about your headaches?"

"I told them. I don't think they believe me."

"But, Ezekial, you were one of the original founders of the church, one of the twelve who selected the seven pillars. You've been a member of the court. You've taught the sons of all of the best people in town. You've been an elder for years. They can't possibly excommunicate you."

He looked down at her. How pleasant and warming it was to see her concern, to feel her interest in him. "It seems that way to me, too. But they're certainly going to try."

"They will fail."

"Perhaps. But if they did not fail in their attempts to bring the governor's wife low, surely they will have no difficulty in defeating a poor schoolmaster."

"Oh, my dear. My poor dear Ezekial." She stopped, apparently dismayed by her words. "It's just that you've given so much to the town. I don't see how they can be so unjust."

She was standing very close to him. A faintly spicy scent came from her skin. He had to force himself to let his arms hang loose at his sides, so powerful was his sudden urge to put them around her, to take comfort from her womanliness. How could the governor fail to appreciate such a woman? She was everything a man could want. Everything.

Her eyes met his in a long look. How much she could read of his thoughts, how much she could sense of the urge that had so suddenly possessed him, he could not tell.

She moved away, smoothing her dark hair. "Something must be done," she said.

THEOPHILUS EATON
MARCH 1650

Life has its good times and its bad times, Theophilus reflected as he prepared for bed. A long letter had arrived earlier that night from Harvard, where Samuel had stayed on a year to teach after earning his master's degree.

Theophilus had long been concerned about what the boy would do with his life. Now Samuel had written that he wished to return to New Haven.

"I want to go into business with you," he wrote. "And I hope to serve in the government, too, eventually. I've also been thinking a great deal about Delaware. I don't see why we can't reestablish a settlement there."

How could Theophilus fail to have been delighted by such a letter? In an age when all too many sons flouted their fathers' advice, his son was paying him the compliment of genuine interest in everything that was important to him. Theophilus wanted desperately to share his pleasure with someone who would understand what the news meant to him—that his dreams and plans did not have to end with his own death.

After supper he had mentioned Samuel's plans to his mother, but she had merely said, "Of course. What else would the boy do except take up what you've begun?"

She hadn't quite understood.

Ann? He had been tempted to tell her, but he had refrained because he felt she *would* understand. She would shrewdly guess at the response he hoped to receive . . . and then taunt him with the opposite. Was ever a woman so hard to live with?

Yet despite her deficiencies, her foibles, her stubbornness and emotional outbursts, he still foolishly yearned for her. The habit of holding her close, of feeling her heart pounding beneath his, of tasting the sweetness of her lips had been too long a part of him to be easily dismissed, even after years of deprivation. Although he went to sleep many nights with hardly a thought of her, other nights the desire was strong enough to keep him awake for hours.

Tonight, he feared, was going to be one of those nights. The happy news about Samuel had stirred him and made him feel almost young again. Together, father and son—strong, intelligent, well educated—what could they not accomplish?

As he fastened his nightshirt, he glanced toward his bed. Although it had been turned down, he could not persuade himself to lie down. Instead, he sat on the edge of the bed, turning the pages of his Bible by the light of one candle. Perhaps one of the psalms would soothe him and cool the heat of his blood.

A faint knock sounded on his door, so faint he at first thought it was farther down the hall. The knock was repeated and Ann's voice said softly, "Theophilus, are you there?"

Cautiously opening the door, he saw her standing in the hall as lovely, ethereal, and dreamlike as if he had imagined her. Her dark hair flowed around her shoulders, and her eyes reflected the very short, flickering candle she held.

"I'm nearly out of candles," she said, "and I cannot sleep. I want to read for a while. Do you have any extra?"

"Come in. I'll look."

She glanced toward the bed where he had been sitting. "You weren't asleep, were you?"

"No. I was restless tonight."

"I, too."

Her voice was almost a whisper. Was this the same woman who had quarreled so angrily with him last winter when he had forbidden her to go again to Ezekial Cheever's?

"Sit down. I'll only be a minute." He fumbled in the top drawer of his chest, deliberately taking more time than was necessary. Why had she come? Why had she come? Was it possible that she had somehow sensed his need and had come to assuage it?

Glancing over his shoulder, he saw that she had sat on the edge of the bed. Wasn't that in itself significant? He went over to her with the candle in his hand. Her rail was opened at the throat revealing the shadowy line between her breasts. A yearning to bury his face there nearly overcame him. As he looked down at her it seemed to him that she was a little nervous, as well she might be if she had chosen to be the aggressor in love.

But supposing he was wrong? Supposing she had come for nothing more than a candle and was nervous merely because she feared he might take advantage of the intimacy?

Caution then. Keep her there until she made some gesture that would let him know whether his attentions were welcome.

As he handed her the candle, he said, "Would you like some wine? Sometimes it quiets a restless mind . . . or body."

"Yes, that might help." She gave him a faint smile, possibly one of encouragement. It made him feel like a young man in the throes of courtship doubts and delights.

When he had poured the wine and had handed her the small pewter can, she smiled again. It gave him the courage to sit down beside her.

"I had a letter from Samuel today," he said. "Tonight, rather. A pinnace came in just before dark."

"Oh? What did he say?"

"He has made a decision about his future. He's going to come home and join with me in all my enterprises."

She turned her face toward him. He could not doubt her sincerity when she said, "Oh, I am glad for you, Theophilus. I know how much it will mean to you to have him with you."

"And to know that someone will carry on the future I've tried to build. He's as interested as I am in recovering our losses in Delaware. He is also interested in trade and government." He tried to speak matter-of-factly, not daring to reveal the extent of his joy.

"When will he be coming?" she asked. "We'll have to prepare a celebration."

"In another month." He put down his wine and lightly placed his arm across her shoulder. It did not seem as though he could wait much longer. "Finished with your wine, my dear?"

"Almost." She regarded him seriously over the rim of the can. At last she handed it to him and, stretching a little, he placed it on the nightstand next to his Bible. Without appearing hasty, he turned back to her and suddenly, as if the idea had just struck him, bent and pressed his lips against the soft, scented hollow between her breasts. At the same time he let one hand casually rest against the side of the rounded curve.

284

After a moment he raised his head. Her eyes were very dark. She moved a little so that her head rested against his shoulder. As his hands moved to hold her with more firmness, she did not demur. Could he really believe in her compliance? What had finally brought her to his room? She went, of course, to few places. Perhaps in the long quiet hours she spent alone she had sometimes had second thoughts about the move she had made to the blue room.

It must have been very difficult for so proud a woman to make a move that was tantamount to admitting she had been wrong. He decided to protect her pride by pursuing the fiction that she had come to him for nothing more than a candle and had been inadvertently softened by love. It was a challenge, this handling of a proud, high-spirited woman. He was glad now, though he had experienced doubts at the time, that he had forbidden her to visit the Cheever home. Evidently the deprivation of this last important social contact was what had finally moved her to return to him.

Almost as if she sensed what was going through his mind, she said suddenly, "I heard some rather distressing news about Ezekial Cheever today."

"You did? What was it?" Speak of it quickly, he urged silently.

"I heard that he is going to be tried in church this Sunday."

"Yes, that is true. He is certainly greatly changed from the man who was once so dedicated to the ideals of our church."

"How has he changed?"

"He has become contentious, overly critical. Though younger than the rest of the elders, he dares to question their decisions and the motives behind them."

His hand moved across her back, up under her hair, gently trying to turn her head so he could kiss her.

"But surely," she said, "as a godly man he is entitled to his opinion. Isn't there as much chance he is as right as they?"

"One against several?"

"Why not? All through the past men have fought singly against the group for what they felt was right and history has eventually proved them right. Even Christ himself—"

His hand grew still. "Surely you are not comparing Ezekial Cheever to Jesus Christ?"

"I only meant that often people with the best of intentions are misunderstood and sacrificed."

"Intentions," he said scathingly. "Whatever his intentions, no matter how sincere his motives, he could at least listen to reason. Besides, there's more. In church he makes peculiar gestures—rubbing his temples, shaking his head, grinning peculiarly at certain points in the sermon."

"He has very bad headaches, you know. Perhaps what you're seeing are not grins but grimaces prompted by pain."

"I doubt it. The gestures don't just occur at random moments as pain does; they occur when our pastor has made certain succinct statements."

"Perhaps he hears a false note that causes him pain."

"You haven't been at church for a long time. You don't know."

It was hard to be patient with her. Once again he began caressing her, at the same time drawing her closer. Bending his head, he stopped her next argument with his lips. He had almost forgotten how exciting her mouth was, yielding and sweet and tasting faintly of wine. In his mind they had already begun melting together when she suddenly drew away.

"You could stop all this nonsense, you know," she said.

"I don't want to stop," he said huskily, trying to draw her close again.

She laughed—a small abrupt sound. "I don't mean *this*. I mean the business about Ezekial. You could easily stop it. All you have to do is go to John Davenport. Tell him—"

"I'll tell him nothing. I didn't stop your trial. My own wife. If I didn't do that, I wouldn't stop the trial of someone who meant so much less to me."

"But it would be logical. I can see now that if you had stopped mine, people would have said you did so because I was your wife, not because I was innocent. But if you stopped Ezekial's, you would clearly be doing so because you felt he was not guilty."

His breath came out impatiently. "But I don't happen to feel so."

She twisted in his arms. "But you must. Don't you remember, Theophilus?—he was one of the original founders of the church. He made real scholars of your sons. He has served the town honorably. How can the church elders—and you—accuse such a man of misconduct?"

A sudden coldness quivered along his spine. A thought, ephemeral and tenuous drifted in and touched his consciousness like a snowflake that stings and chills before it melts.

"Whose house did you visit today?"

"No one's."

"You must have gone somewhere. Don't lie to me now. Did you disobey me and go to the Cheever home?"

"No, I did not."

"You are lying. You visited him and you talked with him. Otherwise you would not know of the trial. Only the elders and Mr. Davenport and I know. And of course Cheever. No one in this house knows. So be honest. Tell me where you went today."

"I went for a walk. Out through the woods behind the house. Down to the creek. I often go there."

"What for?"

"Just to sit on a rock and think." A faint smile warmed her eyes. "And dream a little."

"Such idleness is hardly commendable," he said dryly. As the head of the household, he always felt duty-bound to remind those under his charge of the dangers of frivolity and idleness.

"I know. But at times I feel a kind of turmoil. I need—"

"That is when you should seek the Lord in prayer."

"Perhaps that is what I'm doing. Meditating. Praying, in my own way."

"Well . . . perhaps." Suddenly he realized how far they had strayed from the subject they had been discussing. How clever, how devious she was. "You still," he said, "haven't told me how you learned about the trial. Did you meet someone by the river?"

"Yes."

"Who?"

"Ezekial."

For a few seconds he was too astonished to be angry. All kinds of thoughts began pelting him like hail propelled by a sudden high wind. He remembered how on shipboard she and Ezekial had often stood talking near the rail; he remembered how at their Sunday evening gatherings they had talked and laughed together separate from the others; he remembered how Ezekial had defended her at her trial; he remembered how they had walked out on the ice together the day the great ship had sailed. Worst of all, he remembered her anger, and also what he now realized must have been her anguish, on the day he had forbidden her to go to Ezekial Cheever's home. How right his instincts had been.

"You met him by prearrangement," he said. It was a statement, not a question.

"I did not."

287

"You said you went there often. How many times have you met him there before?"

She pulled away angrily. "What is this—the Star Chamber?"

"How many times?" he persisted.

"Never before today. I swear it."

He gripped her shoulders. "Don't lie to me."

"I'm not lying. Never before today." She looked a little frightened.

"Just answer one more question for me. Did he touch you? At all? Or you him?"

Her eyes were dark, mysterious, like deep, sweet wells where a man could drown.

"No. Absolutely not."

He had been holding his breath waiting for her answer. Now he let it ease out. But he felt no peace. "I don't believe you," he said. "You came to me tonight like the whore of Babylon, a part of your body bared, all perfumed and sweet. You came to offer yourself— to sell yourself—in exchange for a favor for the man you love."

She stood up. "I may have come here seeking justice, but I sought it for Ezekial as I might have for anyone who was being treated unfairly. Was I in love with Nepaupuck, with Miantonomo, with any of the townspeople who've been severely whipped for petty reasons? Of course not. And let me tell you something else, Theophilus. When you began making love to me tonight, my passions were much aroused. I could feel my body coming to life, trembling with the excitement a woman can only feel for the man—"

"Stop it! You're talking like a whore. Good women don't say such things."

He heard her sharply indrawn breath. The candle on the nightstand made, at the same time, a guttering noise. It had burned low now and gave such a feeble light that her features were mostly shadowed.

"Theophilus," she said in a strangely hard voice, "that's twice tonight you've called me by that unspeakable name. I'm going to ask you to apologize."

His fingers clenched into fists. Although his body felt completely limp and drained of strength, he was able to manage one last strong and harsh but perfectly modulated statement.

"A . . . woman like you neither needs nor deserves an apology."

He looked away. In a moment he heard the door open and close. After a long time, he got into bed. As he blew out the candle, he saw the other one—the one she had not taken, lying on the night-stand.

EZEKIAL CHEEVER
MARCH 1650

Twelve years, Ezekial thought as he walked heavily toward the meetinghouse. Six children, one dead. A gentle wife, neither strong enough for life in a new land nor for childbearing and other wifely duties. His heart stirred when he thought of her. He missed her sweet, plaintive voice, her gentle loving ways, her jealousy that had once made him feel important.

He missed her, but he was glad she was not here to witness what was going to happen today.

Rumors had reached him that Mr. Davenport had said that for a man who had come to the new world with an estate of only twenty pounds he had grown too self-important. That was far from true. He was not self-important. He merely tried to look behind acts, tried to calculate motives, tried to see that justice was done.

He nodded at people as he entered the meetinghouse. Some looked at him with more than the usual interest; some, embarrassed, pretended not to see him. With a certain dignity he took his seat on the platform behind the pulpit with the other elders. He tried to sit without stirring through the long service, but his headaches were always worse on Sundays. His head felt now as if someone were pounding on it with the blunt end of an axe. It took a great effort of will not to put his head down on the table in front of him. No matter how hard he tried not to, he simply had to rub his hand across his forehead from time to time.

The service, which lately had often seemed to last far too long, today seemed far too short. While pressing his fingers against his left temple to quiet the throbbing pain, he suddenly heard his name read and realized his attention had strayed. He was asked to stand in front of the congregation while the accusations against him were read. He did so, letting his arms hang free at his sides, trying hard to ignore the pain.

Mr. Davenport spoke. "For a long time Ezekial Cheever has been guilty of uncomely gestures and carriage before the church. He has rubbed his forehead, shrugged, and sometimes even smiled, always at inappropriate times. Also, these gestures have often occurred during our church trials, when we were solemnly trying to root out evil and indifference to God.

"His unseemly gestures," Mr. Davenport continued after a pause, "have made light of God's work." He turned to Ezekial. "Do you have a statement to make in defense?"

"Only that sometimes my head aches and to hold a hand against it makes it feel better. As for the smiles and shrugs—I was not aware of them. Perhaps my thoughts are too easily mirrored on my face."

"In other words," Mr. Davenport said—and each syllable had the crisp sound of chips of ice falling—"your thoughts during worship of our Lord are often facetious? Do you find our service humorous? Do you perhaps ridicule it in your mind?"

A murmur rippled across the assembly. It passed over Ezekial like a chilling breeze. He longed to press his fingers against his temples, to sit down and place his forehead on the communion table. At the same time, he felt an impulse to smile, for surely the situation had comic aspects. That he should be on trial for unseemly carriage was ludicrous. Surely in a few minutes this trial, that was so much like a distorted incident from a dream, would be over and he would be able to go back to his home where he was so much needed.

Trying to speak with complete honesty, Ezekial said, "Sir, I never find the service ridiculous. But sometimes—perhaps as a result of fatigue—my thoughts wander a little."

"In other words you do not concentrate with us on worshiping the Lord?"

"I do. Most of the time. But once in a while—"

"We quite understand," Mr. Davenport said. He pulled his lips together like a miser tightening a purse. "There are other charges," he said, "that are even more serious." Facing the Assembly again, he said, "Mr. Cheever has failed to vote either affirmatively or negatively to clear the elders of charges of usurpation and partiality, thus leaving them injuriously under suspicion. He did not condone the execution of Goodman Playne of Milford for unnatural filthiness as he said there was never more than one witness at a time to his acts. In addition, he has claimed unfairness to Mrs. Eaton." After a pause, he turned to Ezekial again. "What have you to say?"

Without thinking, Ezekial rubbed his hand across his forehead in what must surely have been an unseemly gesture. His skin felt hot and sticky and the pounding beneath it vibrated against his fingers. He knew he had only to say that he had been mistaken, that he knew the elders had been acting for the good of the people. But, beginning with the trial of Ann Eaton, he had seen too many people tried and censured for what had seemed to him to be flimsy charges.

He reminded himself of all he had to lose by insisting on his own opinion, by differing from the others. Perhaps they were right. Perhaps if what they did was for the general good, it didn't matter if a few individuals were sacrificed.

"What have you to say?" Mr. Davenport asked. "Speak and be heard."

He had much to lose. He was a magistrate, an elder, a schoolmaster. All of these would be denied to him if he were censured. The thought of his wife came to mind; even her memory would be dishonored. And his children would suffer.

"Do you still feel the same way?" Mr. Davenport asked. "Do you still feel that all the good elders, as well as your pastor, who have served long and faithfully, have acted in ways that were not just and impartial?"

For a few seconds Ezekial closed his eyes. He felt himself trembling. Then, taking a deep breath, he firmed his shoulders.

"I do," he said.

He was tempted to go on, to say why he thought they had been partial, to talk about power and its tendency to corrupt. Before he could decide whether to speak, Mr. Davenport said, "That will be all. You may be seated."

Ezekial sat down. A faint musty smell emanated from the walls, threatening to sicken him with its suggestion of corruption. Head in hands, he listened to a summation of the case against him. His stomach twisted as if giant hands were wringing it.

"And even now," Mr. Davenport was saying, "he sits with his head in his hands, indifferent to respectful behavior and procedure. I ask you to consider this man's behavior and decide for yourselves whether or not he should continue to be a member of our church." He paused and Ezekial looked up. "Do any of you," Mr. Davenport continued, "have any questions to ask Mr. Cheever?"

In the silence Ezekial could hear only some faint whisperings and shufflings of feet.

"No questions?"

No one rose. That, it seemed to Ezekial, was a good sign. A very good sign. Or perhaps a very bad sign, for it might mean no one had any doubts.

"Let us vote, then, on whether or not to censure this man. Will you rise, please, Mr. Cheever. Now then, will those in favor of censure please rise."

Ezekial could feel his Adam's apple move dryly in his throat as he saw no more than a half a dozen people getting to their feet. His heart lifted. Only six. Only six out of several hundred. But then a few others stood up. And then others. Chairs in the aisles creaked as people pushed them back so they could stand up and be counted. Mr. Davenport fixed his gaze on those who were still sitting. A few shifted uneasily and then rose; a very few remained seated.

Only a very few.

Ezekial could hardly believe it. Among those standing were many who had come to him in praise of all he had taught their sons; others who had entertained him and visited in his home; and many others who had at times asked favors of him.

"So be it," Mr. Davenport said. "Please remain standing if you further agree that, upon serious consideration of all his miscarriages, he be cast out of this body until the proud flesh be destroyed and he be brought into a more memberlike frame."

Ezekial waited. No one moved.

Davenport turned to Ezekial. "You have heard the opinion of this body?"

"Yes."

"Do you have any statement to make now in your behalf?"

Solemnly and with dignity Ezekial said, "I would rather suffer anything from men than make shipwreck of a good conscience."

He stood still while Mr. Davenport dismissed the congregation.

After everyone had left, he walked slowly out, every footstep like the sound of a hammer that was forever nailing a door shut behind him.

His life in New Haven was over.

40

ANN EATON/OCTOBER 1650

In the fall Ann felt the same troubling restlessness of the previous year. Again she tried to work it out of her system by undertaking a thorough housecleaning. She gave orders and then worked harder than those who worked for her: scrubbing, polishing, shaking, dusting, washing, moving furniture, and cleaning out corners.

When she had finished, it was late October and the house had the smug glow of a moral woman. She began to spin then, and to knit, and to bake fruitcakes, and to make mincemeat for Thanksgiving. Rarely still, she forced her thoughts to revolve around her activities. Even old Mrs. Eaton was impressed by her industry and interest in her home. Several times she even made kind remarks that made Ann glow inside like a young girl praised for her first efforts. Perhaps, Ann thought, we can get along after all; perhaps we're both mellowing.

Yet her restlessness did not cease. In November a light snow fell. It melted in a day and was followed by a golden "Indian Summer." It was at this time of year, when their tracks could not be traced, that Indians often made their final raids of the season. The fear of attack lasted through three golden weeks and then the cold settled in. The air turned gray with it.

Ann could feel the grayness and the coldness seeping into her very heart. The eager vitality left her as she thought of the unendurable winter ahead.

News reached her that Brigid Brewster was going to remarry and leave the colony. Ann visited her again and their relationship was now almost as it had been in the old days, for Brigid no longer feared the authorities. But in a few weeks she had gone and Ann found herself completely alone. She had, she realized, nowhere to go. Some afternoons, when all her work was done, she paced her room trying to stir her blood, her mind. Surely her life was not meant to end within these walls, her stomach leaden, her breath slow, her every move restricted.

On one such day in December the snow began to fall. It fell thinly, with snowflakes fluttering and drifting in the air like milkweed fluff, barely noticeable when they finally came in gentle contact with the ground. Soon, she knew, days of heavier snows would come when she would not be able to leave the house.

Impulsively, she put on a heavy merino cloak and tied a gauzy new hood onto her head. Without being seen, she went down the backstairs, out the kitchen door past the washhouse and the brewhouse to the orchard.

Despite the falling snow, the air had a gentle feel to it. A few apples still clung to the trees, wizened and small, but a bright and cheerful red. From under her feet a few rotted apples sent up the musty smell of old cider. The snow struck her cheeks with delicious little stings as she moved toward the woods.

A noise halted her. Turning, she saw Ezekial leaning against a tree trunk, gazing at her without smiling. Had she come so close to his home without realizing it? Or had she come here instinctively? The sight of his serious, intelligent face gave her heart a sudden joyful lift.

"Well . . . Ezekial," she said.

His face brightened. "I knew you could be the only one foolish enough to come out on a day like this."

"Or lonely enough," she said.

He studied her face, saying nothing.

Finally she said, "Have you been well, Ezekial? Are you still having those bad headaches?"

"No. They are better now—especially since I have come at last to a decision."

The wind rose a little and some flakes of snow cut sharply now across her cheek. "A decision?" Why had her heart already begun such an ominous thudding?

"Yes. I'm going to leave New Haven Colony."

"On a . . . visit? A trip somewhere perhaps?"

"No. Permanently."

"Where will you go?"

"Somewhere in the Massachusetts Colony, I suppose. Probably Boston."

"I'll miss you," she said. In the silence that followed, they looked at each other for a long time. After a while she added, "Sometimes I think you're the only real friend I've ever had in this town."

"I, too, have few friends. Especially since my trial."

"Well—" She shrugged. It was strange how little they could find to say to each other.

"Have you ever thought of leaving?" he asked.

"To go where?"

"Somewhere. Anywhere."

"Alone?"

"No. With someone of the same mind—someone you could trust."

His look was so penetrating she at last had to look away. "No, I have not thought of it."

"Already we have shared a great deal."

"Yes." Her heart was really pounding now.

"Why are you here, talking with me now, when your husband has forbidden you to see me?"

"We met by accident."

"You did not need to linger."

"I know." Why did she stay? Why not turn now and leave? Why not?

"Tell me something," he said. "When a man has practically cast a woman out, when he refuses to defend her, when he will not allow her to communicate with her friends, when he allows another woman to usurp her prerogatives in her own home—how does such a woman, even if she had loved him once, feel about such a man?"

She pulled her hood forward on her cheek even though the thin material was little protection against the sharpening wind. "She . . . just doesn't think too much about it. After all, what can a woman do? It is men who rule this world."

"Not all men. Remember that it was because of other men that we in this plantation were forced to leave England."

"Ah, yes. But being men they were able to leave and start a new life. And even you—you will make a new life somewhere. That *I* could never do. I have learned that much in these past few years. Before that, I thought I could do almost anything. After I realized I could not, it was as if part of me died."

He moved close to her. "It shouldn't have. It didn't. You are still a whole person. Sometimes I think of your husband and I wonder about him. How can he not see that you are everything a man could want? Everything." His face was very close to hers now. "The Bible says one must not covet another's wife," he said. "But it does not say how one should feel about a woman who has been almost cast out as a wife."

She began to tremble. "Are you saying——?"

"Yes, I'm saying I love you. I'm saying I want you to go away with me. I'm saying I want to spend the rest of my life with you. I leave by shallop tomorrow at dawn. Will you come?"

"You are forgetting," she said softly, "the difference in our ages. I must be—oh, as much even as eight or ten years older than you." She knew she was at least ten and probably more years older than he, but it seemed enough to admit as much as she had.

"I don't care if you're twenty years older. I love you. My children love you. Come away with us. Far away—perhaps even Barbados. I will even delay the shallop an extra day if you need the time."

"But what about *my* children?"

"Only Hannah is still really dependent on you. She can join us later."

"But what kind of life could we make if we left here in disgrace? How could you be a schoolmaster anywhere after running away with a married woman?"

"I don't have to be a schoolmaster. I can farm, or hunt, or do anything necessary to put food in our mouths." He hesitated. "Perhaps you are reluctant because, even though outsiders think otherwise, you and Theophilus still, in the privacy of your—"

"No," she said quickly. "No. Not for years. We have nothing left. We maintain a relationship for appearances. That is all."

"Was I wrong to think you had a fondness for me?"

Her voice was tremulous. "No, you were not wrong. I have never seen you that my heart has not lifted."

"But you will not go?" His eyes were dark, intense.

"I have not said that."

He drew in his breath. "You *will* go?"

The moment stretched out, threatened to snap.

"I will go." She gave a brief harsh laugh. "Perhaps they will not even notice I have gone."

"Oh, Ann." Coming closer, he reached out and touched her hood. "Do you know what they call these hoods in New Amsterdam?"

"No.

"They call them love hoods."

She smiled. He reached for her, but she backed away. "Not yet, Ezekial. We have so much time . . . later. Let's save all the joy. I must go now."

"Then let's make some quick plans. You won't be able to take much, I'm afraid. Some light bags, no trunk. Pack two or three and put them out by that stump at the end of the garden after dark tonight. Then you can slip off unencumbered before dawn."

Why, despite the joy, did she have such a feeling of foreboding? Was it because she no longer dared to believe in happiness?

"What if something goes wrong?"

"Nothing will go wrong," he said firmly. "Not if we don't let it."

"Before dawn, then," she said. She moved away, looked back. He lifted a hand. His face looked as young and bright as it had on that day when he had stood beside her as their ship entered the harbor.

In her room she began emptying drawers, piling clothes on her bed. This, this, and this. Something for cold weather, something for hot weather, something for rainy weather. Her prettiest nightgown and rail. Her hairbrush, some scent, some laces, some ribbons. Petticoats, bodices, gowns, cloaks, shawls.

She stood back, surveying the growing mounds. It was too much. She could not possibly take so much. Suddenly the air in her room seemed oppressive. Leaving the clothing in heaps on her bed, once again she left the house. When she returned, she decided, she'd choose what she must take.

She went down the street toward the harbor, holding her cloak tight against her as protection from the wind and stinging snow. Far out, through the falling snow, she could see a shallop coming in. Her heart quickened. No doubt it was the one Ezekial had hired for next morning.

She went close to the shore, watching the boat approach. Did ever Cleopatra watching one of her barges on the Nile greet it with a greater feeling of excitement? Tomorrow, she thought, with happiness leaping like a flame inside her—tomorrow, tomorrow. Why had she never realized before that you only had to make one final, irrevocable decision to find happiness suddenly within your grasp?

How would Theophilus react? Stoically, she decided. His routine would not change, nor his habits. He would, as always, put the town and the colony first. Once the initial embarrassment was over, he would proceed with business and government in his usual manner.

As the shallop came closer, she could see that it had several passengers on it. A man on board stood up and waved. Squinting a little, unsure of his identity, she waved back. His seated companion had a peculiarly defenseless slope to her neck and back. As the shallop came closer, she recognized her son-in-law, Edward Hopkins. And rising shakily, assisted by her husband, was her daughter Ann.

She was almost speechless as they got out of the boat and came toward her, Edward smiling genially—always the smooth trader and politician—and her daughter, with shoulders rounded and head bent forward, gazing at her with the eyes of a frightened fawn.

"We hadn't planned to come," Edward explained, "but some things went wrong." Turning, he directed a sailor to take their belongings from the shallop. They had brought, Ann saw with dismay, a great deal. Well, if they planned to stay, they would simply have to make the best of her leaving.

Edward now drew her aside a little, while her daughter stood alone, drooping, uncaring. "She's very bad. So defeated, so depressed, she rarely even speaks now or acknowledges other people are present. I have to go to England, and I may be gone as long as two years. It did not seem right to leave her at this time with anyone but her mother."

Ann went over to her daughter and put her arms around her. The young woman regarded her seriously for a moment and then moved a little closer and pressed her cheek against her mother's face. Ann felt her heart constrict.

Edward said soberly, "That's the first spontaneous gesture, the first sign that she recognizes or cares about anyone, that she's made in weeks. You are the only one who can help her."

LURINDA COLLINGS
JUNE 1652

The most important part of being a lady, it seemed to Lurinda, was learning to hide your feelings, even from yourself. For years now Mrs. Eaton's bedroom had shown no evidence that her husband ever visited it. Yet their behavior in public remained unchanged. If anything, they were more polite to each other than they had been in the past.

It was through observing their behavior that Lurinda learned to hold her head high and to present a contented demeanor to the world. When people teased her about marrying, she always answered calmly, "Me? I haven't really thought about it. I am happy here."

She waited, not knowing or really caring whether the waiting was worthwhile, but if a young man approached her, she quickly and firmly put him off.

After two years of teaching at Harvard, young Samuel had returned to New Haven. He had changed. Teaching, or the process of growing older, or perhaps simply the fact of being an Eaton, had given him dignity. These days he never tried to be alone with Lurinda. He treated her much as he treated his sister Mary: with a semi-teasing respect. It was as if the night at the farm had never happened.

Nor did she still have any feeling for him. In the rare moments when she let herself dream, she thought only of Tim. She remembered his kindness, his goodness, and the admiration and love that he had once felt for her. Over and over she asked herself how she could have rated him so low.

He would probably never return to New Haven. If he did, she told herself, it would be with some London miss with knowing ways and the latest fashions.

Yet sometimes when she was wearing something pretty and her hair shone and her skin glowed, she liked to pretend she saw him coming toward her, his eyes full of surprised delight. He was always a success in this daydream—a gentleman—and longing to find her again.

On the day when she finally did see him again, however, she was wearing a faded gown and her hair was straggling away from its pins. Mrs. Eaton had looked at her that afternoon and had said, "Lurinda, you look like a bedraggled I don't-know-what. What you need is to get out of this house. You need some fresh air to stir up your blood."

Lurinda had felt a tug at her heart as she had looked at her mistress half lying on the couch, a book held listlessly in her hand.

"I think that's what *you* need, ma'am."

Things had never been the same with Mrs. Eaton since that December day the winter before last, when she had come home from a walk strangely excited. After spending an hour or so putting many of her clothes and possessions in a pile on her bed, she had suddenly, as if seized with an even greater restlessness, gone out for another walk. She had returned with her daughter and Edward Hopkins.

Lurinda had thought at first that her mistress had been about to move her possessions back into the governor's room, but if that had been her intention, she had changed her mind.

Young Mrs. Hopkins had stayed for nearly a year before leaving to go to her brother in Boston. Mrs. Eaton had cared for her devotedly, calmly putting up with her peculiar behavior, trying to draw her out of her black moods. At the time, Lurinda had thought her mistress's quiet air was due to fatigue. But even after her daughter had left, Mrs. Eaton had remained subdued and remote. These days she sat silent at the table, her thoughts, it seemed, at a great distance. She gave fewer orders about the house, quietly letting the other women take over. She read incessantly. Every new book that came from England was immediately carried to her room.

"Do you really enjoy all those books?" Lurinda had asked her one day.

"Enjoy? I read, and when I'm reading, I'm not thinking of anything else. If by enjoy you mean temporary relief from painful thoughts, then yes, I enjoy them."

"That isn't what I meant, ma'am."

For a moment they had eyed each other. Sometimes it seemed to Lurinda that they were as close as mother and daughter; at other times the gap between them was too broad ever to be bridged. When moments like these last ones widened the gap between them, a faint look of hauteur sometimes tightened Mrs. Eaton's face and Lurinda realized she had said or suggested too much. Sad as she was, Mrs. Eaton preferred to bear her sadness alone.

And am I, Lurinda thought, so different? Carefully she had kept her secret about the night at the farm. When she looked at Samuel at the table engaged in serious conversation with his father about government and about the new effort of some Branford men to settle Delaware—an expedition which Samuel himself would lead—it was hard to believe he was the same man who had surprised her in her bedroom and passionately begged her to marry him.

The drabness of her life sometimes struck her with a pain that came fine and sharp, like a sliver entering her heart. Much of the time the drabness seemed to be reflected in her face, her skin, her eyes. Everything about her seemed dull. How could a girl be anything but dull when no shining hours ever enlivened her days?

And it must have been apparent to others, for it was on such a day, when she had felt almost smothered by the way she lived, that Mrs. Eaton had suggested she take a walk.

"I really have nowhere I want to go, ma'am," Lurinda finally said.

"Then take this book over to Mrs. Malbon's house for me. When the governor brought it to me he said I should send it to her after I had finished it."

"Oh . . . well, I'll have to change."

"No. Go just as you are before I change my mind and decide to put you to work. Don't worry about how you look. All the respectable young men are busy working at this time of day."

"I wasn't thinking about young men, ma'am."

Mrs. Eaton gave her a look of almost motherly tenderness. "I know you weren't. That's your trouble. You're beginning to think and act like a spinster. And you're much too young. It's high time you put that one bad experience out of your mind."

"I have," Lurinda said flatly.

"No, you haven't. Otherwise, you wouldn't try so terribly hard to live completely without emotion. You hardly dare let yourself even laugh."

Lurinda held herself still. "Just as you say, ma'am. I'll go out for a while. May I have the book, please."

The house had been cool. As she stepped outside, the June air touched her skin with a light caress. Her arms were bare to the elbows and the breeze ruffled the faint golden down that covered her skin. Something alive within her responded. Taking a deep breath, feeling the air expand her chest, she began to walk briskly down the street.

After leaving the book with Mrs. Malbon, she continued walking just for the pleasure of it. She was entering the marketplace on her way back when she saw him coming toward her. At first she felt nothing but a vague curiosity. Who was he—this strange young man with the confident step and the jaunty silver-buttoned waistcoat? Was he . . . ? The beat of her heart reverberated through her body. Feeling strangely off-balance, she stood still and watched him approach.

He was smiling. This young man with the jaunty air, with the look of success, was smiling at her, and, shaky and dizzy though she was, she saw clearly that his smile was not just one of greeting but of genuine gladness.

He held out both his hands. "Lurinda!"

Lifting her hands to his, she felt his fingers close hard over hers. His roughened skin was faintly abrasive and its touch against the delicate smoothness of her wrists sent a tremor up her arms.

"So you're back." She tried to smile, but her cheeks felt strangely stiff and her lips could not hold the proper shape. What was the matter with her? In the old days she had smiled easily when she was with him. Now she felt as she felt with highly-born young men: awkward and uneasy.

Drawing her hands from his, she straightened her body. No matter how unsure she felt, she must try very hard to hide it with a ladylike coolness.

"I often wondered whether you'd ever come back."

"I always meant to. I never felt there was any place for me in England. New England is where I have always planned to live and work."

"And make your fortune." She was surprised at how normal her voice sounded.

"I hope so. I've made some connections. I know exactly where and how to dispose of furs and other goods. Now I need to find more sources."

"You sound very—oh, very decided, as if you know exactly where you'll be going."

"I do. To a certain degree." He gave her a searching look. "Could we go for a walk, or would it make you an object of gossip?"

"We're old friends." She smiled. Her smile felt natural now. "If people want to talk—well, I've been talked about before."

His eyes flickered. It had been the wrong thing to say, reminding him of her error and her shame. Was he remembering that night when Samuel had led her up to the guests at the farm in her new dress? Or was he remembering her rejection of him in court? Or was he thinking of some girl he had met in London, someone untouched by scandal and the sting of the whip?

"You're sure it's all right?" he asked again.

"I am quite trusted. And I have a few minutes before I have to get back to my duties."

They walked along the street where Ezekial Cheever had once run his school. Rose bushes had been planted along the fence, and some of the blossoms, pink and fresh, peered over the top rail like the innocent faces of children. She longed to reach out and touch one.

After they had rounded the corner and had started down the road toward the creek, Tim stopped. "Let's sit under this tree here. I want to hear about you, too—what you've been doing, what your plans are."

They sat down on two rocks, a little apart. Around them the June world pulsed with life: insects hummed; a pair of chipmunks flashed by in playful chase; birds called out to each other. But Lurinda's heart beat with a slow, hopeless quietness. Near her feet a small, lilylike flower poked its cheerful yellow head up through the dead leaves of other years. Suddenly shy, she bent and picked it. Without looking at Tim, she said, "What have I been doing? Well, I work in the house. I go to Thursday lectures and to Sunday meetings. I fast when the Eatons fast, pray when the Eatons pray. Actually, my life has changed very little."

"But *you* have changed."

She looked up, surprised. A bird—bright blue with a wash of rose on its breast—flew by with a straw crossways in its mouth, disappearing in the tender green of the shrubs across the road. For a few seconds she closed her eyes. "I am older," she said.

"That wasn't what I meant. I was thinking of the way you suddenly drew yourself up tall a moment or so after we met. I couldn't help thinking how much you seemed like an Eaton."

"Being around them for so long, I suppose I was bound to acquire some of their gestures."

"Yes. And being an Eaton."

She stared at him. "*Being* an Eaton?"

"I mean being married to an Eaton. Being married to Samuel."

"But I'm not married to Samuel. I'm not married to anyone." She heard herself laugh, felt the laugh disintegrate into the softness of the air. "What is it, Tim? Did you want me to be married? Are you sorry I'm not married to Samuel?"

The muscles in his face had tightened and an angry red seeped into the line where his light hair grew back from his forehead. "All this time I've thought of you with Samuel for a husband—happy, having what you always wanted, being what you always wanted to be."

Quietly she said, "I wanted that once, yes. Once when I was young and very foolish."

He still looked angry. "He promised me," he said. "He swore he would go to you and ask you to marry him. And he swore he'd always be good to you. I'm—"

As he started to rise, she reached out with both hands to hold him back. "Tim, wait. What makes you think he didn't ask me to marry him?"

"You just said . . ."

"Tim. You didn't listen. I said I had only wanted Samuel when I was young and foolish. He did come to me. I didn't know you had sent him. I'm glad I didn't. Because I refused him anyway."

"You refused? But why?"

"Because I had decided that someone else meant far more to me, someone who was far too good for me. And I told myself that if I couldn't have him, I didn't want anyone."

He sat down again, his shoulders slumped. "I didn't know you had your sights set on anyone else. But whoever he was or is, he couldn't possibly be too good for you."

He was the good one. It made her want to cry. But she mustn't. She mustn't even think of it.

"Let's stop talking about me," she said. "Tell me about yourself . . . about your family."

He shook his head. "You know I never had any real family."

"Not even now?" She waited, holding her breath. "No children? No wife?"

"Children? A wife?" Turning slowly, he faced her. "Lurinda, don't you know I couldn't ever think of marrying anyone but you?"

She felt an easing inside her, a sweetening. Once again she reached her hands out to him and this time he took them both and held them. For a moment she could not find the right words; then slowly, hesitantly, she began to explain.

THEOPHILUS EATON
JANUARY 1658

The relations between them had been strained for so long that to treat each other impersonally had become a way of life. As the hate had dissipated along with the love, they accorded each other the courtesy of strangers.

Had a guest or stranger been ill in his home, Theophilus would have been courteous enough to stop by his room to show his concern. Could he do less for the woman who was his wife? Besides, the watchers—a few servants and a woman who lived close by—were in her room. It was wise always to present a picture of domestic harmony when such people were present.

Ann had been prepared for the night. The women who had been sitting quietly about the room rose and greeted him deferentially when he entered.

"How is she?" he asked.

"Better, I think," one of them said, obviously wanting to encourage him.

On an impulse he said, "Why don't you all leave for a while? I'll sit with my wife for a time."

Ann's head turned on the pillow. Her dark eyes met his. As he sat down by her bed, her eyebrows lifted appraisingly.

"How do you feel?" he asked.

"Better. Really. I think the fever has lessened—perhaps gone. I feel weak, but it seems to be the kind of weakness that comes after an illness." She smiled with old-time bravura. "I'll survive, Theophilus."

"I'm sure you will," he said.

But the pallor of her skin made him uneasy. Too many who had seemed indestructible were now gone from his life. A year ago, in 1657, Edward Hopkins had died in England where a business trip had been extended by his appointment as Admiralty Commander by Cromwell. In his will he had left the money for a grammar school to be established in New Haven in his name, a gesture that had meant a great deal to Theophilus. He felt his loss deeply, almost like that of a brother.

Not long before that his mother had died. Except for his daughter Mary, who had married Valentine Hill several years before, his mother had been the one woman in his life on whom he could always depend for love, admiration, advice, and help. Though he missed her deeply, he was, because of her age, reconciled to her death.

But he did not think he would ever, ever, be completely reconciled to the tragedy of Samuel's death. The thought of it even now was enough to make him bury his head in his hands. In his mind he repeated the words: *The Lord hath given and the Lord hath taken away. Blessed be the name of the Lord.* He had told himself over and over that he must submit patiently to the Lord's will, but it was not an easy submission.

"Stop it," Ann said softly.

He looked up. "Stop what?"

"Stop thinking about your son."

"Samuel had so much, such a great future. A magistrate only three years after his return to New Haven, a good marriage."

"I know," she said. "He seemed ready to carry on all your dreams."

Delaware. Samuel had led an expedition of fifty-nine Totoket men down there. This again had been thwarted by the Dutch, but another had been planned. Samuel had seen the great value of a settlement at Delaware and Theophilus had been sure the young man would eventually succeed in establishing one.

But Samuel and his wife had been stricken with a strange fever on a trip upriver to Connecticut. That she had died within three days was not a great surprise, for she had been a wealthy widow twenty years older than Samuel. When word had come of her death and of Samuel's illness, Theophilus had retired to his closet and prayed. Surely God could not, would not, take this beloved son of his. For two days he had fasted and prayed. Word came then that Samuel, too, was dead.

Sometimes it seemed to Theophilus that, like Job, he was being continually tested. For distraction he had thrown himself into codifying the laws of the colony, a task that had occupied his mind for months. But the successful completion brought him no real satisfaction. Young Theophilus had, as he had long wished, gone to Ireland. No son remained to carry on his name, his work, his dreams in New Haven Colony.

With a harsh tearing sense of loss that bore down like a great living weight on his chest, he remembered his son's liveliness, his youthful humor and escapades, as well as their later close relationship as they had seriously planned for the future of the colony. It had never, never occurred to him that Samuel might die before he did.

And now as he looked at his wife, he remembered also how it had been with her in the beginning: the way she used to smile at him, the misty look in her eyes when she was ready for love, the sound of her laughter. If she were to die tonight . . .

Without thinking about what he was doing, he suddenly took her hand. If she were to die tonight, what he would remember, he realized now, would be all the early times, all the moments of warmth, of love.

Her eyes glinted. "I'm not going to die, Theophilus. Was that what just crossed your mind?"

"Of course not."

With a wry smile she said, "Of course it was. Why else would you hold my hand if not to be sure your conscience would not bother you later? You could always say to yourself: 'I was kind to her at the end.' "

He dropped her hand. "Your illness has not changed you."

"No." Putting her hand under her head, she lifted her hair to one side. It was still thick and dark. The few gray hairs were imperceptible in the candlelight. "No, my illness did not change me. I changed before that. It was lack of love that changed me."

Her mocking look was maddening. Though it was hard to control himself, he knew he must. He was not sure how serious her illness was and he certainly did not want to excite her unduly.

"You have always been . . . cherished," he said.

Her face softened a little. Then the slow maddening smile

began. Before she could repeat his words and twist them into her own definition of what it meant to be cherished, he hurriedly added, "I have always respected you and provided for all your needs. I have also provided you with luxuries many women do not have: a personal servant, books, fashionable clothing. And up until the moment you locked me away from your chamber, I loved you with all the warmth and affection of which I am capable." He regarded her seriously. "Can you deny any of this?"

"No. In many ways you have been a very good husband."

"Well, then . . ."

"Well, then," she repeated. "All that remains to be considered is that one moment in time, that one moment when you needed only to raise your hand or speak out to save me." She moved her head so that now he could only see the strong lines of her profile, the nose with the faint bump just beneath the bridge. "That one little moment, Theophilus, was the test of your love. And you failed the test."

All at once he realized how tired he was. The Indians and Dutch were no longer serious menaces, but problems still beset him on all sides. The most irksome now were the murmurings of non-church members who wanted a voice in the government and the chance to become officers in the military. A delegation of such upstarts had been to see him that afternoon. Pressures, pressures. His chest seemed filled with lead, and his fatigue was so great that even the act of breathing was an effort.

Slowly, speaking with calm control, he said, "It was your decision that led you to that moment. I did everything in my power ahead of time to talk you out of your stubbornness."

"You were the stubborn one, not I."

"No, it was you."

Turning back, she caught him in her dark-eyed gaze. "We sound like children."

"Yes."

He did not realize she had reached for him until her fingers closed around his.

"Why do we always quarrel, Theophilus?"

"I don't know."

She was silent a moment. "*I* know. It's this damnable raw, rough new country. We never quarreled in London. Oh, maybe I was a little dissatisfied at the way your mother refused to let me be the mistress in my own house, but outside of that I was happy. We had many wonderful moments. We *were* happy—weren't we?"

Those days in London were so long ago he could not remember details. Memories of the last years there were all bound up with difficulties with the King, problems connected with Puritanism, and the outfitting of the ships to be sailed to America. But he could remember her compliance, her submissiveness, her way of melting against him when they were alone and, remembering this, he pressed her hand in silent acknowledgment of the past.

"And another thing," she added, "that man across the street—he had less influence with you then. He didn't interfere with our marriage when we were over there."

"He still doesn't. He is concerned with church matters only. After seeing what has happened in Hartford since Hooker's death, he feels very strongly about keeping all of our people together, all of one mind."

"Theophilus, how can you be so naive? That man hates me."

"You're mistaken."

Her voice rose as she lifted herself partly up from the pillow. "I am *not* mistaken."

Releasing her hand, he placed his palms against her shoulders, gently pressing her back down. "Please. It's best that you stay quiet."

"All right. But just think, Theophilus, how many of our quarrels have begun with this man. He comes between us at every opportunity."

Theophilus wanted to tell her she thrust Davenport between them. But he could see it would do no good to argue with her. He sighed and the weight in his chest shifted. He needed rest, a good long rest. That moment or two of understanding tonight, he realized sadly, was just a mirage in the midst of a vast desert of dried-up love and hopes. They would always quarrel. Every intimate conversation always led back to his fancied betrayal of her. He thought of all their quarrels of the past, and then all those that had not yet flamed up in the future, stretched out before him like a fatiguing journey over a plain covered with boulders.

"I think I'll go to bed now," he said. "Until I sat down here, I didn't realize how tired I was."

"You *do* look tired."

As he started to rise, she once again caught at his hand. "Oh,

312

Theophilus, let's go back to England. We were happy there. You've set up the colony here. You've increased its size and you have everything running smoothly. Why not go back?"

"No," he said.

Her fingers slipped from his. "You will not go?"

"No."

"Not under any circumstances?"

Opening the door, he beckoned to the watchers before turning back to say, "No. You may go if you wish. I shall die here."

In his room he undressed tiredly and got into bed. The leaden feeling still filled his chest and now and then a jab of pain shot across it. Obviously he had eaten either too much or too quickly. Perhaps if he lay very still the discomfort would cease.

Putting his wife out of his mind, putting town and colony business out of his mind, putting everything out of his mind except thoughts of his Maker, to whom he whispered a fervent prayer, he drifted off to sleep.

He awakened to a strange sound. It was his own voice making a low moan. The leaden weight in his chest had become massive. It was as if the combined tonnage of his home, the meetinghouse, the great ship, the *Hector,* St. Stephen's Church in London—everything he had ever valued—was pressing on his chest. With a wrenching movement that tore him with pain, he tried to free himself, but the leaden weight had become a mass of molten metal.

As if from a great distance he heard a faint voice asking, "Are you ill, Mr. Eaton?"

He tried to lift his hands, to open his eyes. His lips were numb as all sensation was rolled back by the enormous hard burning pain in his chest. With almost no breath at his command he was able at last to get out the words, "Very ill."

The heavy weight ripped through his chest like the ball from a giant musket. Relief came. And silence. And peace. He could not now hear even the sound of his breathing, or of his heart beating.

43

EZEKIAL CHEEVER
JUNE 1658

As the Ipswich sunshine streamed through the open windows of the schoolhouse, it made angelic aureoles around the heads of the perspiring young scholars. Drifting in, warmed by the June sun, was the smell of lilacs, fading now and oversweet.

Ezekial stood in front of the class, his birch rod held lightly in his hand. "Try the next verb," he said, this time calling on his own young son.

"Vinco, vincas, vincat; vincamus, vincatus, vicant."

After nodding his approval, Ezekial turned to the next boy. "And now the past tense." Ezekial had called on him because the boy's attention had strayed. Instead of following the lesson, he had been looking out the window that faced the street. Now he was staring at the doorway behind Ezekial.

Stroking his beard and tapping the rod lightly against his desk, Ezekial said, "The past tense, John. Quickly now. Stop the wool-gathering or you'll find yourself gathering something less soft."

The boy began to stammer out the conjugation, but as he did so his eyes kept straying back to the doorway. Other boys were staring also, and at last Ezekial turned to see what they were looking at.

It was a woman. As she stood in the doorway framed by sunshine, its brilliance made such a dark silhouette of her head and erect body that her face was not recognizable. Yet something about her stance made Ezekial feel he knew her.

"Yes?" he said, and then before she could answer he added,

"One moment. I was about to give the boys a written assignment." Turning back to the class, he said, "Open *The Accidence* to page nineteen. Copy and translate the first six sentences."

Before turning back to the woman, he tried quickly to decide who she might be. She had entered without compunction about interrupting a class. She must be someone of note, someone he ought instantly to have recognized.

Feeling half uneasy, half curious, he approached the woman. As he walked toward her, he saw that despite the youthfully erect posture and the bright red of her gown, she was a woman in late middle age. She was smiling. Suddenly, like the crash of surf on the beach, recognition came, stunning him, leaving him breathless and, for a few seconds, speechless.

When he had left New Haven eight years before, he had been bitterly unhappy. After their moments together at the edge of the garden, after seeing the promise of love in her eyes, he had been positive that Ann would go away with him. Difficult though it would have been to find acceptance in any of the Puritan colonies, he was sure they could have gone somewhere and begun a new life together.

Her note had been a blow as shattering as the sudden death of a loved one. Had she really been so concerned for her daughter? Could she not have found someone else to care for her? Or had she, alone and in the cold light of reason, changed her mind? The brusqueness of her note, despite its indefinite promise, had led him to think the latter was true.

The first months had been painful because he had still hoped. He had resolved, at last, to put her completely out of his mind. But he hadn't really succeeded. For months after he had arrived in the Bay Colony, and even after he had gone northward up the coast to Ipswich, her image, her words, her smile hovered at the edges of his mind. In between was a vast emptiness that even his love for his children could not fill.

"Oh," he said now with complete inadequacy. Glancing back over his shoulder, he saw the class staring at him. He glared at them, stroking his beard, until every last head was bent over his work. And then he turned back to her.

"Oh, my dear," he said.

Her smile was gone. "You did not know me."

"Only because your face was in the shadow."

"It was because I've grown old. Even when you came close, it was a few seconds before you recognized me."

"No. It was because I thought you might be the mother of one of my boys. And it was because I long ago put the thought of your coming here out of my mind."

"You couldn't have taken me for one of your young mothers," she said. But a smile was wistfully lifting the corners of her mouth. "I have changed—haven't I?"

Her face was the same except that it seemed to have slipped downward a little, as if the bones were growing tired of holding up the skin. Her eyes, however, were still bright even though the hollows beneath them were wrinkled and faintly discolored. The high color that had once made her seem so much more alive than other women was gone.

"Changed?" His gaze rested gently on her face. "Perhaps. It is a condition of life. Unless we die young, we cannot avoid aging."

"Last winter I was not well," she said.

A muffled sound behind them, a whisper, a smothered laugh, made him turn. Again he stroked his beard until the boys returned to their work.

"Let us step outside the door here," Ezekial said, "where we can talk with more privacy. I have so much I want to ask you."

"You have heard about Theophilus?"

"Yes. I am very sorry. He was a good man."

As he spoke, he wondered about the honesty of his words. Yet he was sorry. Eaton had always seemed like a good man, but a man so good, so devoted to the church and its leader that he was blind to the possibility of prejudice, hypocrisy, or injustice. And though Ezekial felt it was commendable for a leader to subdue his personal feelings for the common good, he did not feel that he himself would have behaved with such cold indifference had his own wife been on trial before the church.

She nodded. "He was a good man—yes. And during his last years he suffered many blows. His mother died and young Samuel. Edward Hopkins, too. He died in England."

"I knew about that. I didn't know about Samuel. I'm truly sorry." After waiting a moment, he said, "And what of Edward's wife?"

In her eyes was an old anguish. "She did not stay long with me. Less than a year. And then she went to Boston to be with her brother. When Edward died, he committed her in his will to her brother David's care." Looking away, she paused. "She is no better. I think now that she never will be, that no amount of loving care will make any difference." Her eyes met his with a piercing intensity. "I feel now that no sacrifice, *no* sacrifice made in the past ever made any difference."

He was held by her eyes. For a moment the time that had passed was compressed into a series of meaningless events that served only to link this meeting with that last one eight years before.

Finally he said, "How did you happen to come to Ipswich?"

"I came with David. He had some business to do here and he said there was plenty of room in the shallop."

"You knew I was here?"

"Yes. I inquired when I first came to the Bay Colony." The old animation brightened her voice. "It was a lovely trip, weaving in and out among all the islands. What a beautiful country this is."

Again they were silent—silent as two people are when they have too much to say, but do not know where to begin. Should he ask her if she were planning to live in Boston? Should he make some inquiries about New Haven? Should he tell her of his life since he left New Haven?

It was she who resumed the conversation. "You have a fine schoolhouse here."

"Yes. The people here are very generous. One man, a Robert Payne, donated this schoolhouse and a dwelling and two acres for my use."

"Apparently you're doing very well."

"Yes, the school is prospering."

"I'm glad, Ezekial."

Another silence fell between them. He was thinking of how much magnetism she still had. He was remembering and trying not to remember.

"Are you happy here, Ezekial?"

"Yes, I am happy here." He watched her closely. She had an air of expectancy, as if she were waiting for him to ask her something. "And what of you?" he asked finally. "Are you happy? What are you planning to do now? Will you go back to New Haven or will you stay in Boston?"

"Oh, Ezekial." With sudden nervousness, she laughed. "Can't we stop all this foolish talking, all these words that haven't said anything? Can't we talk about what we're both thinking about? For the past eight years my heart has been so full of—" Abruptly she broke off. "Here comes someone. Probably one of the young mothers you took me for. How pretty she is, Ezekial. I find I'm a little jealous."

He turned. But even before he turned, he knew. For no one in town was so pretty as Ellen.

She came up to them, her eyes blue and sparkling like a sunlit summer sea, her step, her bearing, her face all animated by a barely contained vibrancy. It struck Ezekial how much she and Ann Eaton were alike, not in looks but in the way they responded to life.

"I saw from the window that you had a guest," Ellen said, "and I couldn't contain my curiosity any longer."

"Ellen, this is Mrs. Theophilus Eaton, wife of the late Governor of New Haven Colony."

Ellen executed a graceful half-curtsy. "I felt sure it was someone important."

"And this is my wife," Ezekial said to Ann, trying not to let the words come stiffly out of his mouth, "the former Ellen Lathrop."

He felt her astonishment even before he saw the quickly concealed reflex that made her body go rigid. Yet, after only a few second's hesitation, she held out her hand with ease and dignity. "How nice to meet you, my dear. Have you been married long?" Her manner was calm and friendly, but her jaw was tightly set and a muscle twitched near the corner of her right eyelid.

"Six years," Ellen said.

"And you have children?"

"Oh yes. Four so far. And Ezekial's other children, too, of course. It makes a big family. You'll want to see them—won't you? Please do come over to the house. Dinner is nearly ready."

"I'm not sure I—"

"Please come," Ezekial said. "The older children will be disappointed if they miss seeing you. They still remember their old life and old friends. And especially you."

Ellen began to move away. "I'd better run back and see to dinner. Please don't be too long."

"I'll just show Mrs. Eaton the school," he said.

She nodded. Half running, half skipping, she hurried back toward the house.

Ezekial watched her a few seconds and then watched Ann watching her, dark eyes strangely dull as if a candle behind them had stopped flickering. Once again at a loss for words, he stepped through the doorway and said to the boys, "School is dismissed. For the day."

Shouting, glowing with unexpected happiness, the boys rushed out the door. When all was quiet, he said gently to Ann, "Come inside."

In the schoolroom the smell of fading lilacs still came in through the window, mingled now with the primal smell that always drifted up from the salt marshes at low tide. He put his hands on her arms just above the elbows. "You didn't know?"

She shook her head.

"I was sure you knew," he said. "News travels quickly from settlement to settlement. More than once I had word of you."

"You're forgetting that I went out very little, that because I did not go to church, I missed much of the news. And Theophilus saw to it that your name was never spoken in our home."

"But you said you had inquired about me in the Bay Colony."

"Yes. But as soon as I found out where you were I changed the subject." An uneasy laugh sprang to her lips. "I didn't want to appear too interested. And a good thing, too."

"Your son didn't say anything?"

She shrugged. "I suppose he thought I knew. After six years such information is no longer news." Drawing away from him, she sat down at one of the small desks.

He stood in front of her, the birch rod loose in his fingers as he slid it absently from hand to hand. Conflicting emotions and wishes simmered within him. Her shoulders were slumped forward. He felt an immense urge to comfort her, to put his arms around her and whisper soothing words to her. But through the window he could hear the lilt of his wife's voice as she called to young Ezekial and he found his heart leaping in response.

"If you knew, if you only knew," he said, "how disappointed—how bitterly disappointed I was the night when I waited for you and you sent someone with a note instead of bringing your bags. If you only knew how lonely I was during those first two years."

"Do you think *I* don't know what disappointment is, what loneliness is? I do, my friend. I have lived with little else for fourteen years."

He dropped down into the chair across from her. When he spoke, his words were weighted with remorse.

"My dear, if I've caused or added to your unhappiness—"

"Don't feel sorry for me," she said. "Please, please don't." She was silent a moment. Watching her intently, he saw a subtle change come over her. Though she had not apparently moved, her spine looked straighter; the angle of her chin became more confident. "I can manage," she said. "Really. And your news wasn't entirely a surprise. Certainly I had considered the possibility that you might have remarried. I was prepared for it."

"You're being very—"

With a gesture she silenced him. She rose and stood as she once had stood greeting guests at the Eatons' Sunday night entertainments.

"You never promised me anything, Ezekial. I was the one who promised that I would come to you when I was free. Well, I have done so and I'm delighted to find that you're so happily situated. You have a charming wife."

"Thank you." Feeling as if she had now put a great distance between them, he said in the voice of a polite acquaintance, "What are your plans now?"

"I'll go back to England, probably. Theophilus and I were discussing it the night he died. Hannah plans to go this summer, but I'm not sure I'll go right away. David and his family will be going when his business permits him to do so."

"It would be nice for you to travel with them."

"Yes."

He heard Ellen calling out to them in her sweet, clear voice. "Perhaps we should go now."

"Yes."

At the doorway of the schoolhouse, in their last secluded moment together, they stopped briefly and looked at each other without speaking. He remembered that cold December afternoon when, her face framed by a gauzy love hood, she had looked at him with dreams in her eyes: he remembered how badly he had wanted to kiss her. Was she remembering?

"Come," she said. "We're taking too long."

All through dinner he watched her. He did not see how Ellen could suspect anything, for Ann Eaton so beautifully acted the part of an old acquaintance. He found himself almost believing in it.

He found himself searching for sorrow on her face, listening for heartbreak in her voice.

None. None at all. Perhaps he had not, after all, been of much importance to her. He felt a quiver of longing, of longing to recreate that moment when love and longing had warmed her whole being and turned her face toward him as if he were the sun.

As he walked to the dock with her after dinner, he found himself wishing for some word, some sign, that would indicate she retained even a few sparks of warmth for him. He could not say why he felt the need so strongly when only a short while ago he had been grateful that this very warmth had not been revealed.

Just before she got into the shallop, he took her hand and pressed it firmly. "The Lord look between me and thee—"

"When we shall be departed one from another." She returned the pressure of his fingers. "When we shall be departed one from another—for the rest of our days."

For the rest of our days.

He did not want to release her hand. Looking at her face, he wondered why he had thought, on first seeing her today, that she had seemed old.

As she withdrew her fingers, he found himself saying, "I hate to see you go."

She gave him one last, very bright smile. Her son helped her into the boat. "Over here, Mother, where you'll be out of the wind."

"I n did mind the wind," she said.

The river breeze whipped at the sail. Ezekial watched the boat glide away toward the sea, watched the effortlessness with which the space between them was increasing. He watched until he could no longer make out her features or the shine of her eyes.

At home, Ellen came quietly into his arms, her face subdued. "I liked Mrs. Eaton," she said, her face against his chest. "She must have been very lovely once."

"Yes, she was." He stroked her back. "She's going back to England."

"She has a great deal of courage."

"Yes." Ellen was light and tender in his arms.

ANN EATON / JUNE 1658

"Are you all right?" David asked her as the shallop sailed down the river out of Ipswich.

"Yes. Why?"

"You look pale."

"I'm tired, Son. I'm no longer young, you know."

"You? You'll never be old."

Flattery even from a son was pleasant. His kindness made a glow inside her. But it was not enough to erase that chilling moment when Ezekial had walked toward her. He hadn't known her. She had changed so much that he hadn't known her at all.

She looked down at her colorful dress. Suddenly it seemed too bright, too youthful. Oh, silly, foolish old woman, nourishing the idea that she was still attractive, that someone loved and wanted her. All the way to Ipswich she had told herself that she expected nothing; now that she was headed for Boston again, she realized that she had expected everything.

She wanted to bury her head in her hands, to throw her sorrowful cries to the wind, to share her tears with the sea. She wanted to let go, to come apart, to stop trying to maintain an appearance of wholeness and dignity.

But gradually the impulse passed. Drawing her shoulders back, she lifted her head and let the wind blow against her face. She sat very still. If her punishment for opposing the church fathers of New Haven had taught her nothing else, it had taught her that maintaining an outward calmness helped to bring about an inner peace.

She was even able, upon returning to her son's home on Beacon Hill in Boston, to talk with her daughter-in-law about her visit to the Cheever home.

"I had forgotten he had married again," Ursula said. "How nice that he's happy now—after so much sadness. And that silly trial." She frowned. Neither she nor David were Puritans, and they were not in sympathy with Mr. Davenport's policies.

Ursula was vigorous and unruffled, a good tonic for her moody, depressed sister-in-law: kind but not overly solicitous. Yet the presence of Ann Hopkins with her strange foibles and her withdrawn air placed a strain on the household.

Ann felt she must stay and help. She let Hannah, who was always intent on getting her own way, return alone to England to stay with her uncle Samuel.

She lived from day to day, sometimes, in warm weather, sitting outside her son's house looking out across the water. As she knitted or mended, it was surprising how pleasant many of her memories were. Even the image of Theophilus had mellowed. At his best he had been a husband who loved her with tenderness and passion; at his worst he had been less himself than a tool of John Davenport.

When she thought of John Davenport, a coldness settled in her chest. He had too much power—too much power and too little humility. Even now, bitterness rose into her mouth as she recalled her hours before the church. She thought of Mr. Davenport's questions, his accusations, his self-righteous smugness. Someday, she thought, someday.

In the spring of 1659 a letter came from Hannah saying that she would be marrying William Jones of London on the fourth of July and that they planned to come to America the next year to settle in New Haven. Hannah had inherited the big house there from her father. "William is a devout Puritan," she wrote, "and he feels that life in such a godly place would be much to his liking— especially since the Royalists here are steadily gaining in power."

Ann was not sure how well she would get along with William, nor was David. When the Joneses arrived the following July on the *Prudent Mary*, however, William turned out to be a pleasant though very serious man, full of adoration for his spirited young second wife. He reminded Ann a little of Theophilus. And would the day come, she wondered, when he would look disapprovingly at Hannah and frown whenever she spoke her mind?

The *Prudent Mary* had also brought word that the Stuarts had been restored to the throne. The son of the executed King had been brought back from France and had been crowned Charles II. The news spread like the plague through the marketplace, infecting the people with uneasiness.

They were remembering that in 1633 King James had attempted to administer the affairs of New England people through a governor-general. The colonists had vigorously opposed this appointment. Only the stress of internal affairs had prevented the King from enforcing his edict. Would the new King try to renew this effort? Would the colonies now lose the independence they had come to take for granted during the years of Puritan rule? It was said that Charles II was a reasonable person. He had even been willing to grant amnesty to all who had conspired against his father, and had, in fact, left the entire question up to Parliament. But would he remain reasonable once he held the reins of power firmly in his hand?

William and Hannah were not optimistic. They spoke often of their relief at having an ocean between England and themselves. They also, when discussing their voyage, spoke with obvious pride and pleasure of their acquaintance with two other passengers: Edward Richardson and William Stephenson. Rumors quickly circulated that these men were actually Edward Whalley and William Goffe, the two judges who had sentenced Charles I to death.

One evening near the end of their first week at the Yale home, David confronted William and Hannah with the rumor.

"You were well acquainted with these men," he said. "Are they really the King's executioners?"

"Executioners?" William said. "That's rather a strong word. They are Whalley and Goffe—if that's your question—men who made a rational judicial decision, a decision, I might add, that reflected the will of the people."

"I see." David looked very grim.

"You don't seem pleased."

"I never was pleased by their decision. I did not consider it rational or a reflection of the will of the people. Englishmen do not kill their kings."

Ann could feel tension rise around the table as William said complacently, "They did this one."

"And it will forever be a blot on the history of a civilized people."

"You talk like a Royalist," Hannah said, her dark eyes glittering.

"Please dear"—William touched her hand—"your sentiment is appropriate, but I'd prefer you let me carry on this argument."

To Ann's surprise, Hannah, with a submissive smile, merely said, "Very well." What would have happened in her own marriage, Ann wondered, if she had been as deferential? But these two were apparently in basic agreement about issues while she and Theophilus . . . oh, what was the use of looking backward?

"It is not my intention to argue with you," David said evenly. "I merely wanted to confirm a suspicion."

"And I'd like to do the same," William said. "I'd like to know how you felt about our Lord Protector."

"I felt he was an excellent military man but an ineffectual ruler. And his son Richard was a poorer one."

The two men stared at each other a moment like fighters trying to decide where to jab next. Finally William said, "I agree with my wife. I think you *are* a Royalist."

A muscle twitched near David's eye. "Perhaps so. By your definition. I merely think of myself as an Englishman. As such I prefer not to have every aspect of my life dominated by Puritan thought."

"Then I'm surprised you stay here in the Bay Colony where so few people share your views. Many people here have been very happy to entertain our friends Mr. Richardson and Mr. Stephenson."

"I'm aware of that. They're taking a chance, I think, even though the men have not, so far, been accused of anything. But as for me, William, I do plan to return to England, perhaps the year after next."

William's face had darkened. "Good. We don't need people like you here in America."

"You just got here. What do you—?"

"Please!" Ann found herself interrupting. "This is only rousing your spirits. Nothing can be gained by any further discussion." In the brief silence that followed, she found herself remembering other family arguments, arguments of long ago, arguments that had surely never led to any gain. And who had started many of them? She could feel her cheeks flush as David looked at her with slightly upraised brows.

"You're right, Mother," William said. "But at least we've clarified our positions." He rested his hand on the top of Hannah's silky dark head. "As soon as my wife is completely rested from her voyage, I'll hire a pinnace to take us to New Haven."

Hannah lifted her chin. "I'm quite rested now."

After William and Hannah had left the room, David said to his mother, "In the old days you always seemed to enjoy an argument."

"Only if something could be accomplished by it. This one was getting nowhere." She paused. "I hope you'll try to forget your differences and make the rest of their stay pleasant. I may never see Hannah again."

His eyes were kind. "You're mellowing, I'm afraid. But I'll be pleasant, of course. She's my little sister."

Hannah and William's visit lasted only five days more. During that time polite relations were restored as David helped William arrange for the departure. The night before they sailed, Hannah came to her mother's room.

"I'm glad you came," Ann said as Hannah sat down beside her on the bed. "We've hardly had a moment alone." She felt a sadness that she tried not to show. When Hannah had gone to England, she had let her go reluctantly but with the knowledge that she would be joining her before long. Now Hannah was going to New Haven and she herself to England. "Do you realize," she added, "that we may never see each other again?"

"That's why I came to see you. William and I would like you to visit us before you return to England. We'd even like you to live with us—if the idea pleases you. William and I don't see how you can be really happy living with David, having to listen to all his Royalist ideas."

Faintly amused, Ann said, "Isn't your William aware that I am an outcast from the Puritan church?"

"Oh, yes. But we feel your ideas at the time were probably influenced by your age. Many women of middle years behave strangely but regain their senses later on."

"I see." Ann was no longer amused. "So, on the basis that I have regained my senses, he has agreed to allow me to live in his house."

"Yes. Especially if you'd . . . if you'd get up in front of the church and say a few words. You understand."

"I do indeed." Sudden anger made Ann's voice hard. "All he wants me to do is publicly humble myself, admit my sins, beg for mercy. Your William sounds like another—"

"Please. Don't say it. No more dissension. Please. I didn't realize you were still so bitter." She put her soft-skinned hand over her mother's. "That's why I wanted you to come," Hannah continued. "So you could see how he is in his own home, so you could see why I love him. He's not really himself here. He feels the undercurrents too strongly. Oh, please, please come, even if for only a few days."

Ann was already ashamed of her outburst, she who only a few days ago had been told she was mellowing. "All right, my child, I'll come. But just for a few days."

She had told herself she'd never go back. Until she said the words *I'll come* she had not realized how much she did want to set foot once more on New Haven's soil. Homesickness and a kind of bittersweet nostalgia beckoned to her now almost as warmly as the promise of a bright future had done nearly thirty years before.

"Yes," she repeated, "I'll come. Especially since it seems to mean so much to you."

ANN EATON/OCTOBER 1662

Almost two years passed before Ann went to New Haven. Much happened during that time. Parliament decided that amnesty did not extend to the two judges who had sentenced the King to death. The regicides went into hiding. It was said that for a while they were sheltered in New Haven, first by Mr. Davenport, and then by Hannah's husband, William Jones, and later in a cave.

Lurinda wrote to Ann about one of Mr. Davenport's sermons preparing them for possible questioning about the judges. "He as much as told us it was all right to lie in this case."

Ann read the words with amusement, remembering that he had once accused her of breaking the Ninth Commandment simply because she had said the governor's mother was not her mother. Apparently a lie, if it served his chosen purpose, was not a breach of the Ninth Commandment.

Change came even more rapidly after that. In August of sixty-one Connecticut Colony sent John Winthrop to England to secure a charter from the new King. Winthrop succeeded. But to Ann's consternation, the much-publicized charter that arrived the following spring granted Connecticut all the land from Narragansett Bay on the east, Massachusetts on the north, Long Island Sound and the ocean on the south, and all the way to the South Sea at the west—territory that included New Haven Colony.

Rumors abounded: New Haven was refusing to honor the charter; some of New Haven's dissidents were being received as citizens of Connecticut; reprisals from the King for sheltering the still-missing regicides were imminent.

By now David had nearly completed the closing of his business in America. But even as she prepared to sail back to England with him, Ann made plans for a last visit to the beleaguered colony that had b̶e̶e̶n̶ her home for so many years. She had promised Hannah she would come. She wanted, too, to see her son Thomas and his family one last time. Lurinda also. And there was something else, something indefinable. Even though it was surely too late to realize any of her dreams, she was lured by a dim possibility of satisfaction, a sense that somewhere between the red rocks and the sea lay the answer to a question that had long lain heavily in her mind.

David objected to her making the trip—a woman alone, getting on in years.

"I intend to go one last time," she said stubbornly.

He finally agreed, but only after she had agreed to take young Elihu with her. She was glad to have his company, for he was still at an age when he thought his grandmother and all her experiences were interesting and important.

William and Hannah welcomed them warmly into Ann's old home. A runner was sent for Thomas Yale and his family, who came in from their farm. Thomas was especially happy to see his nephew Elihu before he left for England. At noon they sat in the great hall and had a meal of pigeons from some of the flocks whose fall migration had recently darkened the skies.

As she looked around the room, warm and comfortable with family feeling, Ann found herself constantly slipping into reverie. Hadn't it often been pleasant like this? The old quarrels and differences seemed unimportant now. She realized wryly that she did not fully approve of the way Hannah was running the household. If she lived here, she might herself be as critical as old Mrs. Eaton once had been.

Afterward, Hannah suggested she rest. Ann declined, annoyed at the implication that she was no longer young. Almost immediately she set out alone.

At the corner she stood for a moment looking up the street toward Brigid's house. A great longing welled up inside her as she remembered the laughter, the warmth, the friendliness she had known there. Brigid never wrote. Ann would never know how the new marriage in a new settlement somewhere south and west of New Amsterdam had turned out.

Then very deliberately, as if facing something sure to bring her pain, she turned her gaze toward the house where Ezekial Cheever had once lived. Memories leaped against the long-closed door of her heart: Ezekial smiling at her with understanding, Ezekial frowning as he advised her, Ezekial defending her before the church, Ezekial steadying her as she walked out on the harbor's ice, Ezekial reaching out to touch the love hood that framed her face—all the unfinished gestures, all the words and moments that had led to nothing, all the sweetness, all the sadness. Hearing herself sigh, she turned abruptly and walked briskly across the public square to Lurinda's.

Lurinda, presiding proudly over her home with its floors covered with fresh, sparkling sand, had grown matronly after the birth of five children. Her cheeks round and satisfied, she looked little like the fragile, timid servant of long ago.

"Tell me what is really happening in New Haven," Ann said after they had talked of their families. "Neither William nor Thomas would say much. Like Theophilus, they think some things simply aren't women's business."

Lurinda picked up her smallest child and held him in the curve of her arm. "What is happening? Everything. Everything we've worked for these past few years is happening now. Mr. Davenport thinks he can hold out against union. But he can't. Except for a few church members, most people want to be part of Connecticut. Some have already joined. Men like my husband want to be treated fairly, to be allowed to vote and to hold public office. A man should be appointed head of the guard because he's qualified to lead, not just because he's a member of the church."

"But surely you realize the fundamental agreement—"

Lurinda snapped her fingers. "Who gives a fig for the fundamental agreement? It was made up by a little body of men who happened at the time to hold the purse strings. It's time now for those old men to step aside."

"You sound rather hard, Lurinda."

"I am." Gently she drew her child close. "I'm soft and warm with Tim and our babies, but when it comes to the men who rule this town, I'm hard and cold. It was they who made me so. All I want to see now is their defeat."

"Even if it means there will never again be a New Haven Colony?"

"Especially if it means that."

Ann did not answer. She knew she would not be able to make Lurinda understand what New Haven had once meant to her. Lurinda hadn't come here when nothing lay between the red rocks and the sea except a few tiny buildings and some cellarholes dug in the banks along the creek. She hadn't watched the town grow and achieve an identity. She hadn't seen it expand into a colony of like-minded towns. Most of all, she hadn't known of the dream Theophilus had so long nurtured of a huge, prosperous, independent colony stretching far to the south and west. It was a magnificent dream, and all who had been a part of its beginnings had been touched by its magnificence.

"Wouldn't you like to see men like my husband in the government, young vigorous men who would treat everyone with justice?"

Why, Ann wondered, did she feel this strange reluctance to agree? Why was it so hard to shed old beliefs? Was it possible that these men, many of them former servants without birth or breeding, really were fit to decide how a government should be run? All the political leaders she had ever known had been educated, cultivated men.

Lurinda regarded her thoughtfully. "I'm surprised you have any feeling for New Haven. Here it was that they made an outcast of you and humiliated you—all because you dared to think for yourself."

"That's true."

"I'll never *never* forget what they did to me. I still have marks on my back."

"You have?" As she looked at Lurinda and remembered her pain-racked ordeal, her thoughts swept backward in a bitter rush. It was not just her own trial and all the desolate years when she had been so effectively kept from seeing her friends. It was Lurinda's cruel whipping, Ezekial's shattered career, Brigid Brewster's unfair harassment. It was her own helplessness—she the wife of the governor, who had not had the power to save even one of them from trouble or pain or injustice. They had, very likely, suffered more because of her.

Her hope that she might find satisfaction here was drowned in the flood of memories. Her acts of defiance now seemed doubly futile. They had gained nothing for her, and they had hurt too many of those she loved.

"If you had stayed here," Lurinda said, "you'd be one of us—meeting secretly at night, helping us make our plans. I've always believed that. After all, you were the first one."

"The first one?

"The first one to defy them. I'll never forget how bright and beautiful you looked that first time you walked out of the meeting-house. Imagine a woman having that much courage. I'll never forget how straight you stood during your trial. And you never recanted, never begged to be taken back even though you were shut off from everything. We often speak of what you did—Tim and I and the others." She paused thoughtfully. "You told me once that you hoped I'd develop some strong convictions and that if I did, I wouldn't be afraid to act on them. I always remembered those words."

I was the first, Ann thought. A warmth, a surge of confidence lifted her heart. Although she had only dimly perceived what kind of satisfaction she had felt this visit might bring, she knew now it had been the hope that she would find that her acts of defiance and years of sacrifice had not been completely without value.

"I suppose you're right," she said. "In a way I *was* the first—the first, at least, to seek independence and justice. And if I had remained and had known of your activities, I surely would have been one of you."

"Of course."

Ann sighed. "It could have been a great colony."

"Yes, it could have been."

At last Ann rose to leave. With a sadness she could not conceal she said, "We will probably never see each other again."

"I'll write. And I'll think of you often."

"You've been almost like a daughter to me."

Putting her baby down, Lurinda gave Ann a quick hug. "You've been more than a mother to me. Much more."

Ann left quickly, before either had time for tears. As she went down the street toward her old home, she saw John Davenport standing in his open doorway.

"Ah, my dear," he said in his rich pastoral voice, "I heard you had arrived in town. I was hoping I might see you."

"Really?" She gave him a polite smile.

"Won't you come in and take a little refreshment with me? Elizabeth is out calling right now, but she should be home soon."

She could hardly refuse. "Well, perhaps for a few moments. How is Elizabeth?"

"Not too well. She is much troubled with the ague and with gripings and fever."

"And you?" He did not look well.

"I have recurring attacks of malaria. Beyond that I am in good health. But we do not need to stand here talking. Please do come in."

"People won't talk?" She could not resist being faintly teasing. He still had the same old pompousness.

"When we're such old friends? Of course not."

Inside, he pulled out a chair for her. Was it the one in which Theophilus used to sit? Night after night? After he had brought her some Madeira, he sat down opposite her. She noticed that as he lifted his cup, his hand trembled.

"To old times," he said.

Something unpleasant stirred within her. "To which old times? To all the evenings you kept Theophilus over here, or to all the days when you hounded me to give up my independence?"

"You exaggerate," he said mildly. "Besides, that was long ago. Our troubles in those days were no more than a ripple in a puddle compared to the serious troubles that beset us today. All this horrible pressure for union with Connecticut."

"But isn't there strength in unity?"

"My dear woman, do you realize that if we unite with Connecticut all orderly property owners will be eligible to vote and to hold office whether or not they are members of the church?" His lower lip trembled. "I cannot bear the thought of the purity of our church being marred."

"What if you refuse to honor the charter?"

"We have refused. But who are we—Governor Leete and I—whom do we represent?"

"New Haven Colony, I suppose."

As he shook his head, the soft skin of his once round cheeks quivered. "People from Southold, Guilford, Stamford, and Greenwich have already joined with Connecticut. Milford will surely be next. And the people right here in town—I'm not sure I can count on them. Even Governor Leete is advising capitulation, fearing reprisals from the Crown."

He swallowed audibly. His eyes looked watery. With a quaver

in his voice he said, "The Lord Jesus Christ has turned his back on New Haven Colony. I cannot understand it. It is the only independent state in America whose sole purpose has been to glorify Him. This was all we worked for. Theophilus and I. Your husband and I. For His glorification." His voice broke. "I gave nearly thirty years of my life for this. All for nothing." He bowed his head. "I feel I have wasted my life."

The rheumy eyes, the desolate voice, the air of defeat gave her a strange feeling. Where were the power, the arrogance, the certitude of rightness, the sure knowledge that he could defeat any opposition? Staring at him, at the despairing bend of his neck, she saw that he was nothing but an old man, an impotent old man. She wanted to tell him that he had brought on his failure by his own actions. But it was too late, too late for recriminations, too late for hatred, too late for anything but pity.

Finally she said, "Perhaps Jesus Christ as He went to the cross felt the same way—a wasted thirty years."

"He gave His life to save mankind."

"And may well have felt that mankind cared little for His sacrifice."

Slowly he lifted his head. "You are an intelligent woman. We might have profited by listening to you more often."

At one time such words would have filled her with elation. Why did she feel nothing now but sadness, and regret, and that overwhelming pity? Speaking quietly but without malice, she said, "Should have listened to me more often? Why, you never listened to me at all."

"Ah, we did. We listened. But you were too dangerous. You would have turned too many of them away from the church, from our designated way of life. You were too important an example. It was necessary to chastise you, to silence you." Hitching his chair a little closer to hers, he said, "You are still a beautiful woman."

"Am I?"

"You will probably remarry."

"I might. Some day."

He sighed. "When are you planning to leave."

"Probably the day after tomorrow."

"But that is Friday, my dear. It is never good to make a new beginning on a Friday. You'd best delay your departure."

She shrugged; he did not pursue the point, but suddenly he

reached out—reached out with both hands as if one hand had not the strength to communicate his feelings—and took her hand.

"I wish you weren't leaving," he said. "There are so few of us left, so few who knew each other really well in London. If you stayed . . ." He looked at her earnestly, letting the words hang in the air like a bridge that needs a place on the opposite bank where it can rest its timbers.

If she stayed, what would he not offer her? Perhaps even her old seat in the meetinghouse. But even as she savored the moment, this, his reaching out to her, she gently drew her hand from his.

"If I stayed," she said, "you might find I am still a dangerous woman, even more difficult to silence, perhaps impossible now to chastise."

Comprehension came quickly to his intelligent eyes. "Then it is well that you are leaving."

She rose. "Please convey my greetings to Elizabeth."

"I shall."

"And I hope that in the end your dealings with Connecticut will bring you some satisfaction."

With dignity he replied, "I tell myself that no matter what happens, it is God's will." He gave her a long look. "I'll pray for you on your journey."

"Thank you. I'll pray for you, too."

ANN EATON/OCTOBER 1662

As the shallop slipped away from the wharf, Elihu moved close to her and slipped his hand into hers.

"After we leave Boston, how long will it take to sail to England?" he asked.

"It will depend on the weather. When we came over, it took two months."

"Two months?" She heard the dismay in his voice. "What if things don't go well when we get there? Uncle William says this new King was raised in a French court. He doesn't know what it is to be really English. Look at how he has hounded the regicides. What if he mistreats us?"

"He won't. I'm sure we have nothing to fear."

"I wish Grandfather were alive and could go with us," Elihu said.

She smiled down at him and then lifted her eyes again. In the distance the red rocks rose warm and majestic. She remembered the night in Boston when Theophilus had described his first view of those red rocks and of the fine harbor, and how later he had held her in his arms as he talked of his dream.

"He never would have left," she said. "He had a dream about this place and he never would have stopped trying to make it come true."

Wind swelled the sails; a gull circled silently overhead.

"Are you sorry to be leaving?" Elihu asked.

For a moment she was silent; then she began speaking softly. "I knew an Indian once, Elihu. I didn't really *know* him, but when he was to be executed for killing a white man, he drew himself up with the dignity of a man who feels he is being treated justly and he said, 'It is *weregin.*' "

"*Weregin?*"

"It is *weregin,*" she said.

The outlines of the red rocks were blurring.

"You're crying, Grandmother."

"No, no."

Goodbye. Goodbye, Theophilus. The Lord bless you and keep you.

EPILOGUE

New Haven continued to resist the merger with Connecticut until late in 1664. The settlers refused to submit unless assured that the terms of the fundamental agreement would remain in force for people within their jurisdiction and unless Connecticut reversed its acceptance of the defecting citizens from towns within New Haven Colony. They also wished to have their magistrates, rather than juries, decide on court cases.

Attempts to negotiate these points suddenly ceased when, late in the summer of 1664, two English warships entered Boston harbor. It quickly became known that Charles II had bestowed all former Dutch-claimed lands on his brother, the Duke of York, a Roman Catholic. Fearful of being absorbed by him, New Haven yielded to Connecticut without getting any of the originally hoped-for concessions.

After this failure John Davenport began negotiating to take over the First Church in Boston and secured this post in 1668. About half the congregation, objecting to what they felt were Davenport's narrow views about the halfway covenant, walked out at the time of his appointment and founded the Second Church.

At the time of leaving the New Haven church, Davenport had withheld some of the letters his parishioners had written, in order to make it appear that all were willing to let him go. In 1670 a scandal related to these letters broke. Davenport died shortly thereafter, an embittered man who felt the Lord had deserted him.

Ezekial Cheever, after teaching in Ipswich and then in Charleston, moved in 1670 to Boston where he became a master at the

Boston Latin School. He lived to be ninety-four years old and was a schoolmaster for over seventy years.

Elihu Yale, Ann Eaton's grandson, eventually became Governor of Madras where he amassed a huge fortune. When, after its beginnings in Saybrook, a collegiate school was moved to New Haven, Governor Yale was solicited for a gift. He sent a gift of books. In optimistic but unfounded anticipation of much larger gifts to come, school officials named the college after him.

SELECTED SOURCES

Atwater, Edward E. *History of the Colony of New Haven to its Absorption into Connecticut*. New Haven: Printed for the Author, 1881.

Bacon, Leonard. *Historical Discourses on the Completion of 200 Years from the Beginning of the First Church in New Haven*. New Haven: Durrie & Peck, 1839.

Barber, John Warner. *Connecticut Historical Collections*. New Haven: John W. Barber, 1836.

Boorstin, Daniel. *The Americans*. New York: Vintage Books by Random House, 1958.

Decrow, W. E. *Yale and the City of Elms*. Boston: W. E. Decrow, 1885.

Deforest, John W. *History of the Indians of Connecticut from the Earliest Known Period to 1850*. Hartford: Wm. Jas. Hamersley, 1851.

Dexter, Franklin Bowditch, editor. *Ancient Town Records Vol. 1: New Haven Town Records 1649–1662*. New Haven: Printed for the New Haven Colony Historical Society, 1917.

Earle, Alice Morse. *Costume of Colonial Times*. New York: Charles Scribner's Sons, 1911.

Earle, Alice Morse. *Home Life in Colonial Days*. New York: Grosset & Dunlap, 1898.

Hoadly, Charles J. *Records of the Colony and Plantation of New Haven from 1638 to 1649*. Hartford: Case, Tiffany & Company. 1857.

Hoadly, Charles J., editor and transcriber. *Records of the Colony of Jurisdiction of New Haven. Vol. 2*. Hartford: Case, Lockwood & Company, 1858.

Kelly, J. Frederick. *Early Domestic Architecture of Connecticut*. New York: Dover Publications, Inc. 1963.

Lambert, Edward R. *History of the Colony of New Haven*. New Haven: Hitchcock & Stafford, 1838.

Leighton, Ann. *Early American Gardens*. Boston: Houghton Mifflin Company, 1970.

Mather, Cotton. *Magnalia Christi Americana or the Ecclesiastical History of New England*. Hartford: Silas Andrus & Son, 1853.

Osterweis, Rollin G. *Three Centuries of New Haven, 1638–1938*. New Haven: Yale University Press, 1953.

Perry, Charles Edward. *Founders and Leaders of Connecticut 1633–1783*. Boston: D. C. Heath & Company, 1934.

Trumbull, Benjamin. *A Complete History of Connecticut, Civil and Ecclesiastical*. Hartford: Hudson & Goodwin, 1797.

Trumbull, J. Hammond, transcriber. *The Public Records of the Colony of Connecticut Prior to the Union with New Haven Colony, May 1665*. Hartford: Brown & Parsons, 1850.

Woodward, Sarah Day. *Early New Haven*. New Haven: The Edward P. Judd Company, 1929.

Publications of the Colonial Society of Massachusetts, Vol. 25. Boston: Published by the Society, 1924. (For accurate genealogy of Ann Eaton.)

Collections of the Connecticut Historical Society. Vol. I. Hartford. Published for the Society, 1960. (For "The Trial of Ezekial Cheever.")

Papers of the New Haven Colony Historical Society. Vol. II. New Haven: Published by the Society, 1877. (For "The Life & Writings of John Davenport.")

Papers of the New Haven Colony Historical Society. Vol. V. New Haven: 1894. (For "Mrs. Eaton's Trial.")

Papers of the New Haven Colony Historical Society. Vol. VII. New Haven: 1907. (For "Theophilus Eaton, First Governor of the Colony of New Haven.")

The Geneva Bible, a facsimile of the 1560 edition. Madison: The University of Wisconsin Press, 1969.